the BISHOP'S DAUGHTER

Daughters of Lancaster County 3

WANDA & BRUNSTETTER

BARBOUR BOOKS

An Imprint of Barbour Publishing, Inc.

© 2006 by Wanda E. Brunstetter

Print ISBN 978-1-63409-218-0

eBook Editions:
Adobe Digital Edition (.epub) 978-1-60742-570-0
Kindle and MobiPocket Edition (.prc) 978-1-60742-571-7

All scripture quotations are taken from the King James Version of the Bible.

All Pennsylvania Dutch words are taken from the *Revised Pennsylvania German Dictionary* found in Lancaster County, Pennsylvania.

This book is a work of fiction. Names, characters, places, and incidents are either products of the author's imagination or used fictitiously. Any similarity to actual people, organizations, and/or events is purely coincidental.

Cover design: Müllerhaus Publishing Arts, Inc.
www.mullerhaus.net

Published by Barbour Books, an imprint of Barbour Publishing, Inc., P.O. Box 719, Uhrichsville, Ohio 44683, www.barbourbooks.com

Our mission is to publish and distribute inspirational products offering exceptional value and biblical encouragement to the masses.

Member of the
Evangelical Christian
Publishers Association

Printed in the United States of America.

To Arie, Sue, Betty, and Ada Nancy—
four special women who have taught Amish children.

*Suffer little children to come unto me, and forbid
them not: for of such is the kingdom of God.*

LUKE 18:16 KJV

Prologue

I want you to promise me something."

Jim cringed when he thought of all the times he had reneged on a promise he'd made to his wife. "What do you want me to promise, Linda?"

"Would you see that. . . ." Her voice faltered. "I. . .I want to be sure Jimmy continues to go to church—after I'm gone. Will you take him?"

A knot formed in the pit of Jim's stomach, and he nodded.

"I'm glad we adopted Jimmy. He's brought such joy into my life." Linda fingered the edge of the Amish quilt tucked around her frail form. "I. . .I know we agreed not to tell him that he's adopted while he's too young to understand." She paused. "But I want you to tell him about the adoption when he's older. He needs to know the truth. It. . .it wouldn't be right to keep it from him."

"Yeah, I know."

"And you won't tell him until he's old enough to handle it?"

"I promise I won't." Jim gritted his teeth. *Should I tell her the details of Jimmy's adoption? Would it be wrong to let Linda die without revealing the truth?* He buried his head in his hands. *It would be cruel to tell her what I did when I know she's dying. The news in itself might kill her, and it would certainly add to her agony. And for what purpose? Just to ease my guilty conscience? I did what I did because I loved her and wanted to give her a child, so I can't let her die with the truth of my betrayal on her mind.*

"What is it, Jim? Are you all right?"

He lifted his head and reached for her hand. "I will tell Jimmy about his adoption when I think he's old enough."

"Thank you." Tears matted Linda's lashes, speckling her pale cheeks. "I love you and Jimmy so much, and . . .and I pray you'll find comfort in knowing that I'm going home soon. . .to be with my Lord."

Jim gave a brief nod. The motion was all he could manage. He knew Linda believed in God and thought she would go to heaven, but he'd never been sure about all that religious mumbo jumbo. He only went to church when he felt forced to go—whenever Jimmy was in some special program. Even then, he always felt uncomfortable. Linda had said many times that she thought God had an answer for everything. But where was God when Linda had been diagnosed with breast cancer five years ago? And where was God when the cancer came back and spread quickly throughout her body?

Linda drew in a raspy breath. "Will you and Jimmy be able to manage on your own. . .after I'm gone?"

Jim groaned. He didn't need these reminders that she was dying or that their son would be left with only one parent. "We'll get along. I'll raise him the best I can."

"I know you will."

He leaned over and kissed her cheek. *If it were within my power, I would move heaven and earth to keep you from dying.*

Chapter 1

Tears welled in Leona Weaver's eyes as she glanced around the one-room schoolhouse where she'd been teaching the last four years. Her days of teaching would have been over in two weeks, when the school year ended. The school board would have then selected a new teacher to take Leona's place in the fall, due to her plans to marry.

"But that won't be happening now," she murmured. "I'll be teaching in the fall again—not getting married."

Leona closed her eyes as she relived the shocking moment when she had been told that Ezra Yoder, the man she was supposed to marry, had been kicked in the head while shoeing a horse and had died.

⚭

"Uh—Leona, I've got something to tell you."

"What's that, Papa?"

"The thing is—"

"You seem kind of naerfich. *Is there something wrong to make you so nervous?"*

Papa pulled in a deep breath as he motioned for Leona to take a seat on the sofa. "There's been an accident, daughter. Ezra is—"

"Ezra? Has Ezra been hurt?"

He nodded soberly. "I'm sorry to be the one havin' to tell you this, but Ezra is dead."

Dead. Ezra is dead. *Leona sank to the sofa as her* daed's *words echoed in her mind.*

Papa took a seat beside her, and Mom, who'd just come into the room, did the same.

"How did it happen, Jacob?" Mom asked, reaching over to take Leona's hand.

"Ezra was shoeing a skittish horse and got kicked in the head. His brother Mose saw it happen."

The tightness in Leona's chest interfered with her ability to breathe. "Ezra can't be dead. I just spoke to him last night. We were making plans for our wedding, and. . ." *Her voice trailed off, and she gulped on a sob.*

Papa kept his head down, obviously unable to meet her gaze. " 'The Lord giveth, and the Lord taketh away.' It must have been Ezra's time to go."

Her daed*'s last words resounded in Leona's head.* " 'The Lord hath taken away.' It must have been Ezra's time to go." *She gripped the edge of the sofa and squeezed her eyes shut.* No, no, it can't be! I love Ezra. Ezra loves me. We are going to be married in the fall!

When Leona opened her eyes, she saw a look of pity in her mamm*'s eyes.*

"You'll get through this, daughter. With the help of your family and friends, God will see you through."

As the reality of the situation began to fully register, Leona's body trembled. " 'The Lord gave, and the Lord hath taken away,' " *she murmured.* "Never again will I allow myself to fall in love with another man."

∞

Bringing her thoughts back to the present, Leona pushed her chair away from her desk and stood. She saw no point in grieving over what couldn't be changed. Ezra had been gone for almost three months, and he wouldn't be coming back. Leona would never become a wife or mother. She must now accept a new calling, a new purpose for living, a new sense of mission. She would give all her efforts to being the best schoolteacher she could be.

"Maybe a few minutes in the fresh spring air might clear my head before it's time to call the scholars into the schoolhouse from their morning recess," she murmured. "Maybe I'll even join their game of baseball."

As a young girl, Leona had always enjoyed playing ball. Even now, with her twenty-fourth birthday just a few months away, she could still outrun most of her pupils and catch a fly ball with little effort.

She opened the door, stepped onto the porch, and hurried across the lawn. She stepped up to home plate just as Silas, Matthew Fisher's ten-year-old boy, dropped his bat and darted for first base. Sprinting like a buggy horse given the signal to trot, Silas's feet skimmed the base, and he kept on running. His teammates cheered, and the opposing team booed as the boy made his way around the bases.

When Naomi Hoffmeir's eleven-year-old son, Josh, nearly tagged Silas with the ball, the exuberant child ducked and slid into third base. Sweat rolled down the boy's forehead as he huffed and puffed, but his smile stretched ear to ear.

"It's my turn," Leona called to Emanuel Lapp, the pitcher. She grabbed the bat, bent her knees slightly, and planted both feet with toes pointing outward. "Get ready, Silas, 'cause I'm bringing you home!"

"And she can do it, too," Leona's niece Fern shouted from the sidelines.

Leona glanced at Fern, her older brother's eleven-year-old daughter. Several wisps of the girl's golden blond hair had come loose from her white *kapp*, and it curled around her ears. *She reminds me so much of her daed,* Leona thought. *Ever since Arthur started working for Papa, he's always said exactly what he thinks. Truth be told, Arthur probably can't wait for Papa to retire from painting so he can take over the business.*

Fern lifted her hand in a wave, and Leona waved

back. *She's so sweet. I'd hoped to have a child like her someday.*

Her thoughts went to Ezra again. *But there will be no kinner for me. Ezra's gone, and I'll never know what our children would have looked like. I'll never. . . ."*

Forcing her thoughts back to the game, Leona gripped the bat and readied herself for Emanuel's first pitch. She knew the twelve-year-old had a steady hand and could throw straight as an arrow. He was also known to pitch a good curve ball, which she would have to watch out for. If the Amish schoolteacher got anything less than a good hit, she would never live it down. *Keep your eye on the ball,* she reminded herself. *Don't give Emanuel an edge, and don't think about anything except playing this game.*

The pitch came fast and hard, but it was too far to the right. Leona didn't swing.

"Ball one!" Harley Fisher hollered from the place where he crouched behind her, ready to catch the ball.

She shifted uneasily as her metal-framed glasses slipped to the middle of her nose. She mostly needed them for reading or close-up work and should have left them on her desk. But it was too late to worry about that. She had a ball to hit.

Leona took one hand off the bat and pushed her glasses back in place. *Whish!* The ball came quickly, catching her off guard.

"Strike one!" Harley shouted.

Leona pursed her lips in concentration. *If I hadn't tried to right my glasses, I could have hit that one. Might have planted it clear out in left field.*

Setting her jaw as firmly as her determination, she gripped the bat tighter, resolved to smack the next one over the fielders' heads and bring Silas home.

Emanuel pulled his arm way back, and a sly smile spread across his face.

"Teacher, Mary's bein' mean to me!"

Leona's gaze darted quickly to the left. When she saw it was only a skirmish over the swings, she turned back. But before she could react, the oncoming sphere of white hit her full in the face, sending her glasses flying and causing her vision to blur. She swallowed as a metallic taste filled her mouth. When she cupped her hand over her throbbing nose, warm blood oozed between her fingers. The ground swayed beneath her feet, and the last thing Leona remembered was someone calling her name.

∽∽∽

"How come you wanted to go out for lunch instead of dinner tonight?" Jimmy Scott asked his dad. They had taken seats in front of the window at a restaurant overlooking Commencement Bay and given the waitress their orders.

"I thought it would be easier to get a table with a view of the water when they aren't so busy." Jimmy's dad ran his fingers through his dark hair, which over the last couple of years had become sprinkled with gray. "Maybe after lunch we can take a ride to Point Defiance Park, or would you rather do something else to celebrate your birthday?"

Jimmy chuckled. "I won't turn twenty-one until Sunday, Dad. I had hoped the two of us could attend church together and then maybe play a round of golf in the afternoon."

His dad's dark eyebrows furrowed, causing the wrinkles in his forehead to become more pronounced. "I planned it so we could take today off, figuring you'd want to spend Sunday with your friend Allen or some of the other young people from your church."

Jimmy stared out the window as disappointment

rose in his chest. Dad had never gone to church that often, not even when Mom was alive. Since her death nine years ago, all his dad had ever done was drop Jimmy off at church, and he'd even stopped attending the special holiday programs. What would it take to make the stubborn man see his need for Christ, and why hadn't Mom been able to get through to him? She'd tried plenty of times; Jimmy had heard her almost beg Dad to accept the Lord as his Savior. But Dad always said he didn't need church or anything God had to offer.

Jimmy studied a passing sailboat, which glided through the bay with ease and perfect rhythm. *If only life could be as serene and easy to handle as a boat skimming along the water on a calm spring day.* He thought about his mother's untimely death and how sad he had been when the ravages of cancer had taken her from them. *Still, it was because of Mom that I found a personal relationship with Christ. She set a Christian example, saw that I went to church every Sunday, and read me Bible stories when I was a boy.* He reached for his glass of water and took a drink. *At least Mom was set free of her pain, and I'm sure I'll see her in heaven someday.*

"So, have you made any plans with Allen for Sunday?"

Dad's question drove Jimmy out of his musings. "Uh. . .no, not really. I guess if you want to celebrate my birthday today and don't plan to go to church with me on Sunday I'll do something with Allen and his family."

"That's a good idea. I've got a lot of paperwork to do, and it'll take me most of the weekend to get it finished."

Sure, Dad, if this weekend is like so many others, you'll probably be camped out in some bar instead of at home doing paperwork. "Yeah, okay. I understand," Jimmy mumbled.

Dad reached across the table and handed Jimmy

a small box wrapped in white tissue paper. "Happy birthday, son."

Jimmy took the gift and tore off the wrapping paper. When he opened the lid, he discovered an expensive-looking gold watch.

"So you're always on time for work," his dad said with a grin.

"Thanks. Even though I already own a watch, it'll be nice to have a new one I can wear when I'm not working and won't be running the risk of getting paint all over it." Jimmy had started working part-time for his dad when he was a teenager, and he'd continued painting after he'd graduated from high school. The only time he hadn't worked for his dad was when he'd taken a couple of classes at the community college in Tacoma.

"The watch belonged to my father, and I thought you might like to have it," Dad said.

Jimmy studied the heirloom. If it had been Grandpa Scott's, then he felt proud to own it, even though he'd barely known his dad's father. Mom's parents came to visit often, and Jimmy's folks had driven to Boise to see them several times over the years. But Grandma and Grandpa Scott lived in Ohio, and the only times Jimmy remembered going there was when Grandpa had been in the hospital having open-heart surgery and again five years ago when Grandpa died. Jimmy's grandparents had come to Washington a few times for short visits, but after Grandpa's health began to fail, their trips to the West Coast stopped; he hadn't seen Grandma since Grandpa's funeral.

"Do you like the watch?" Dad asked, breaking into Jimmy's thoughts.

"Sure. It's a beauty. I'll take good care of it."

Their waitress approached, bringing champagne for Dad and lemonade for Jimmy.

"To your health and to many more birthdays," Dad

said, lifting his glass in a toast.

Jimmy cringed as their glasses clinked, leaving him with a sick feeling in the pit of his stomach. "I wish you wouldn't use my birthday as a reason to drink."

"Can't think of a better reason." His dad gulped down the whole drink and smacked his lips. "That wasn't the best champagne I've ever tasted, but it's good for what ails you."

Jimmy turned his gaze to the window again. There would have been harsh words on both their parts if he had reminded Dad that he drank too much or mentioned that if Mom were still alive, she would have gotten on him about ordering champagne in the middle of the day. When Jimmy was a boy, he'd known that his dad drank some, but after Mom died, it had gotten much worse. Jimmy thought his dad might be using her death as an excuse to drown his sorrows or bury the past, but he also knew the way to deal with one's pain wasn't found in a bottle. Dad needed the Lord.

"Oh, I almost forgot," Dad said, halting Jimmy's thoughts. "This came in the mail for you this morning. It has a Boise postmark on it, and I'm guessing it's a birthday card from your grandparents."

Jimmy reached across the table and took the envelope, stuffing it inside his jacket pocket.

"Aren't you going to open it?"

"Naw. I think I'll wait until Sunday, so I have something to open on my actual birthday."

∞

Abraham Fisher had just entered the barn when he heard a horse and buggy pull into the yard. He glanced through the open doorway and smiled when he recognized his friend Jacob Weaver.

"Wie geht's?" Abraham asked, extending his hand when Jacob joined him inside the barn.

Jacob exchanged a strong handshake and grinned, causing crinkles to appear around his hazel-colored eyes. "I can't complain. How are you this warm April afternoon?"

Abraham nodded toward the bales of straw piled along one side of the barn. "I was about to clean the horses' stalls and spread some of that on the floor."

"By yourself? Where are those able-bodied *buwe* of yours?"

"Norman, Jake, and Samuel went home to their families for the day, and I sent the twins inside to wash up." Abraham shook his head. "Titus pulled one of his pranks, and he and Timothy ended up with manure all over their clothes."

"*Phew!* Sure am glad I missed seeing those two." Jacob removed his straw hat and fanned his face with the brim. "Can we sit and talk a spell, or would ya rather work while we gab?"

Abraham gave his nearly gray beard a quick pull. "Me and the buwe worked hard in the fields all morning, so I think I deserve a little break." He motioned to a couple of wooden barrels. "Let's have a seat."

Jacob sat down and groaned. "You oughta get some padding for these if you're gonna keep using 'em for chairs."

Abraham snickered. "*Jah*, well, if I got too comfortable out here in the barn, I might not appreciate my old rockin' chair in the house."

"You've got a point."

"How come you're not working on some paint job this afternoon, and what brings you out our way?" Abraham asked.

"I'm headed to Bird-in-Hand to bid on a paint job for the bank there, and I thought I'd drop by to see you first." Jacob's fingers traced the side of his prominent nose. "I know today is Zach's twenty-first birthday, and I figured you might be feeling kind of down."

Abraham leaned his head against the wooden planks behind him. It always amazed him how Jacob seemed to know when he needed to talk, and his friend's memory for dates was even more astonishing. Ever since Abraham had known Jacob Weaver, he'd been impressed by the man's wisdom and ability to offer godly counsel. When Jacob had been chosen as their new bishop some fourteen years ago, he'd become even more knowledgeable and helpful during times of need. Everyone in the community seemed to admire, respect, and appreciate the way Bishop Jacob Weaver led his flock.

"You're right," Abraham admitted. "I did feel a pang of regret when I got up this morning and looked at the calendar." He drew in a deep breath and sighed. "For many years, I prayed that my son would be returned to us, but after a time, I came to accept the fact that Zach's not comin' home. Even though I don't talk about him much anymore, I've never forgotten my boy or quit praying that God would protect Zach and use his life for good."

Jacob reached over and touched Abraham's arm. "I've prayed for your missing son all these many years, too."

"Jah, I know." Abraham cleared his throat. "Truth is even if Zach were to come home now, he wouldn't know us, and we wouldn't know him. We'd be like strangers." He gave his beard another good tug. "Just wish I knew how he was gettin' along out there in the English world. It would have helped if we'd have gotten more than one message in *The Budget* from the man who stole Zach—something that would have let us know he was still doin' all right."

"You must remember that God's ways are not our

ways. He has His hand on Zach," Jacob reminded.

"I realize that, and rather than dwelling on what can't be changed, some time ago I made up my mind to get on with the business of livin' and enjoy the family I have right now."

"That's good thinking." Jacob thumped Abraham on the back and stood. "Guess I should be on my way."

Abraham walked his friend out to his buggy, and Jacob was about to climb in when another horse and buggy rolled into the yard. Abraham's grandson Harley was the driver, and as soon as the horse came to a stop, he jumped down from the buggy and dashed over to the men.

"What are you doin' out of school?" Abraham asked, placing his hand on the boy's shoulder.

Rivulets of sweat trickled off Harley's forehead and onto his flushed cheeks. "I went by Jacob's place, but nobody was at home, so I decided to come over here, hopin' you might know where Jacob was."

"And so you found me," Jacob said. "What can I do for you, Harley?"

"It—it's Leona," the boy panted. "She got hit with a baseball and has been taken to the hospital."

Chapter 2

Miss Weaver, can you hear me? Try to open your eyes if you can."

Leona forced one eye open and blinked against the invading light that threatened to blind her. The other eye wouldn't cooperate. It felt as though it were glued shut. She tried to sit up, but the blurry-looking, middle-aged English woman dressed in a white uniform laid a gentle hand on Leona's shoulder.

"Wh–where am I?" Leona rasped in a nasal tone. Her nose seemed to be plugged, and she needed to open her mouth to breathe.

"You're in Lancaster General Hospital. You were brought here a few hours ago."

Leona pushed against the pillow as memories rose to the surface. She'd gone outside during afternoon recess, hoping to clear her mind of the painful memories concerning Ezra's death, and had planned to play ball with her students. She remembered Silas standing on third base, and it had been her intention to hit a good ball and bring him on home. Someone had called her name, and she had looked away. Then. . .

"How. . .how bad am I hurt?"

"Your nose is broken, one eye is swollen shut, and you have a slight concussion," the nurse replied. "You were unconscious when the ambulance brought you to the hospital, and you were moved to this room after your injuries were diagnosed and treated. The doctor wants to keep you overnight for observation."

Leona squinted her one good eye and tried to focus. "My glasses. Wh–where are my glasses?"

"I've not seen any glasses," the nurse replied. "I

suspect they were broken when the ball hit your face."

Leona groaned. "I need them in order to teach. I don't see well enough to read without them."

"You probably won't be able to return to work for a few weeks, and I'm sure you'll be able to get a new pair by then."

"But. . .but school will be out for the summer soon." Leona fought against the tears clogging her throat. "I. . . I must be able to teach my students."

"I'm sure you will in due time. You'll just need to be patient." The nurse patted Leona's hand. "Your folks are in the visitors' lounge waiting to see you. Should I show them in?"

"Please."

The nurse left the room, and a few minutes later, Papa's bearded face stared down at Leona. "Ona, what's happened to you?"

"I. . .I got hit in the face with a ball I should have seen coming. That's what I get for thinking I'm still a young girl." Despite her discomfort, Leona managed a weak smile. She always felt better whenever she and Papa were together.

Papa reached out to stroke the uninjured side of her face. "No matter how old you get to be, you'll always be my little *maedel*."

Tears sprang to Leona's eyes. "Oh, Papa, your little girl has gone and broken her glasses, and I can't possibly teach school without 'em."

"One of your students found them in the dirt, but they were busted up pretty bad," Leona's mother said as she stepped up to the bed.

"I knew it." Leona sniffed, then winced as a sharp pain shot through her nose. "There's only a few weeks till summer break, and—"

"A substitute teacher will be taking your place," Papa interrupted.

Leona shook her head, ignoring the pain radiating from her forehead all the way down to her chin. "I'll be all right in a few days. I'll need new glasses, though."

Papa clicked his tongue. "If you could see how swollen your nose and left eye are right now, you'd realize you're not gonna be wearin' your glasses for some time yet." He reached for her hand and gently squeezed her fingers. "The best thing you can do is rest and allow your body to heal. The school board will find someone to fill in for the rest of the year."

Leona shook her head again, but a jolt of pain shot through her nose, and she winced. "I must teach, Papa. It's all I have left now that Ezra's gone."

"Oh, Leona, don't say that." Mom patted Leona's arm. "One of these days, the pain of losin' Ezra will lessen, and then—"

Leona shook her head again, this time more slowly. "*Nee.* I just want to teach my students. They are all I have now."

∞

This has not been a good day. Not a good day at all, Naomi Hoffmeir thought as she stood in front of her propane cookstove, preparing to cook her family's supper. First thing this morning, Kevin, her youngest, had spilled syrup all over his clean trousers. Then Millie fussed and fretted because she wanted to accompany her parents and older sisters to the store rather than stay with Grandma Hoffmeir for the day. Next, a tour bus unloaded a bunch of Englishers in front of their general store, and Naomi, Caleb, and their two oldest girls had been bombarded with a whole lot of questions. Even Naomi's sister-in-law, Abby, who ran the quilt shop next door, had been busy all morning with the curious tourists. Around one o'clock when Naomi had finally taken the time to eat lunch, she'd glanced at the calendar and realized that today was Zach's twenty-first birthday. For twenty years, her little brother had been missing, and her heart still ached whenever she thought of him.

Hardly a day's gone by that I haven't said a prayer for my missing bruder, she thought ruefully. *Is he happy and doing well among the English? Does he have a job? A girlfriend? Could he even be married by now?* Of one thing Naomi felt sure: If God had seen fit to return Zach to them, He would have already done so. Papa and all Zach's siblings had moved on with their lives, and she was sure Zach didn't know any of them even existed. How could he? He'd only been a year old when a stranger snatched him from their yard. And it wasn't likely that the kidnapper had told Zach about them.

"Mama, guess what happened at school today?"

"Jah. You'll never believe it."

Naomi turned from the stove to greet her two sons, who had just rushed into the kitchen, faces flushed and eyes wide open. It appeared as if they had run all the way home from school. "Have a seat and tell me what happened," she said.

"Teacher got hit in the face with a ball," nine-year-old Nate announced.

"That's right," his older brother, Josh, agreed. "Emanuel Lapp was pitchin', and he smacked her right in the *naas*."

"You should've seen it, Mama," Nate said, his dark eyes looking ever so serious. "Never knew a person's naas could bleed so much."

Naomi sat down across from the boys. "I'm sorry to hear about Leona. I hope she wasn't hurt too bad."

Josh's blond head bobbed up and down. "Teacher passed out. One of the Englishers who lives near the school called 911, and Leona had to be taken to the hospital in an ambulance."

Naomi gasped. "How *baremlich*."

Nate nodded in response. "Mama, it will be terrible for *all* of us if Teacher isn't in school tomorrow."

"From the sounds of it, she's not likely to be there, but we'll have to wait and see. In the meantime, we need to pray for her."

The boys agreed, their faces somber.

"Can we have some cookies and milk?" Josh asked abruptly. "I'm starvin'!"

"Sure. You can get the milk from the refrigerator while Nate brings some glasses from the cupboard." Naomi stood. "I'll run upstairs and get Kevin and Millie. I'm sure they'd like a snack, too."

"I hope you don't mind if I'm not here for dinner tonight," Jimmy said as he and Jim entered the house through the garage entrance. "Allen called earlier and asked if I'd like to go bowling. We'll probably grab a hot dog or something at the snack bar there."

Jim shrugged. "Not a problem. I'm still full from that huge platter of oysters and shrimp I wolfed down during lunch."

"Yeah, I can relate. I ate more than my share of fish and chips." Jimmy hung his jacket on the coat tree in the hallway. "Sure am glad I didn't grow up anywhere but here in the Pacific Northwest. Everyone I know says we've got the best fish around."

"Yeah, nothing better than our fresh-from-the-sea food."

"I guess I'll head upstairs and take a shower," Jimmy said. "I told Allen I'd meet him at six."

"Sure, go ahead." Jim was glad he would be home alone all evening. It would give him time to think things over and decide whether he should broach the subject of Jimmy's adoption, as he'd promised Linda he would do when Jimmy was old enough.

An hour later, with a bowl of clam chowder and a stack of saltine crackers piled on a tray, Jim settled himself on the couch in the living room, prepared to watch TV while he ate. When Linda was alive, she would have pitched a fit if he'd wanted to eat in the living room, but she wasn't here to tell him what to do. And since Jimmy had left to go bowling a short time ago, Jim didn't have to answer to anyone.

"I still miss you, Linda," he mumbled. "Even though we had our share of problems, I always loved you."

Jim thought about the day of Linda's funeral and how his folks had flown in from Ohio and Linda's parents and sister had driven to Puyallup from their homes in Idaho. Both sets of parents had suggested that Jim move closer to them, saying it would be good for Jimmy to be near his grandparents. But Jim had refused their offers. Linda's mother was a control freak, and he knew she would have tried to take over raising Jimmy. Besides, he had his painting business to consider. Jim had worked hard to establish a good relationship with the general contractors in the area, not to mention the jobs he got from individual homeowners. If he were to sell his business and move to Idaho or Ohio, it would mean having to start over, and he had no desire to do that.

A curl of steam lifted from the bowl of chowder, letting Jim know it was probably still too hot to eat. He grabbed the TV remote and pushed the ON button. *Jimmy and I have done all right by ourselves since Linda died. If she could see our son now, she'd be real proud. Jimmy's a good kid, and he's a dependable worker. One of these days when I'm ready to retire, I hope to turn my painting business over to him.*

Jim clicked through several channels, hoping to find something interesting to watch, but it was no use. All he could think about was Jimmy and the promise he'd made to Linda to tell their son the truth about his adoption.

His gaze came to rest on the photo album lying on the coffee table, and he leaned over and picked it up. Turning to the first page, he saw pictures of Jimmy during his first year with them, surrounded by little sayings and drawings Linda had made. *Jimmy takes his first step. Jimmy cuts a tooth. Jimmy turns two.*

He flipped a couple more pages. *Jimmy's first Christmas. Jimmy playing in the mud. Jimmy eating chocolate ice cream.*

There were pictures of Jimmy on his first day at school, learning to ride a bike, helping Jim rake leaves in the backyard, running through the sprinkler, and so many others depicting the boy's life over the twenty years he'd been with them. He'd been a happy child, always eager to please and ready to help out. For the first several years, Jimmy had been a mama's boy, but Linda had finally let go and allowed their son the freedom to find himself.

"I guess she found herself, too," Jim murmured. "At least she said she had after she started going to church with Beth Walters." He set the photo album aside. Beth's husband, Eric, had tried to befriend Jim after Linda died, but Jim didn't want any part of a holier-than-thou religious fanatic. He had let Jimmy continue to go to church because he'd promised Linda that he would, and for a while, Jim had gone to Jimmy's church programs, but he didn't care to go any further with religion.

He reached for his bottle of beer and took a long drink, hoping it would help him relax.

When he'd finished the beer, he leaned against the sofa, no longer in the mood for the chowder, which had grown cold. A wave of heaviness settled on his shoulders. *Maybe when we finish the paint job we're doing on the new grocery store across town, I'll sit Jimmy down and tell him he's adopted. I need all my workers for that job, and I won't take the risk of Jimmy getting upset and walking out on me before it's done.*

Chapter 3

Leona eased onto the front-porch swing and tried to relax. It had been almost a week since she'd been hit in the face, and still her nose and one eye were swollen. She had no glasses to wear, either. A new pair had been ordered, but they hadn't come in. Even if they had, she knew she would never be able to put them on. Her nose was too sore, and there was so much inflammation.

Cinnamon, the Irish setter Leona had been given for her twelfth birthday, moved closer to the swing and laid her head in Leona's lap. It was as if the dog knew she needed sympathy, and Leona had always found comfort in being able to tell Cinnamon her troubles. Sometimes Mom accused her of caring more for the dog than she did for people, but Leona simply liked being able to bare her soul to one who wouldn't sit in judgment or tell her what to do.

"You know whenever I need a listening ear, don't you, girl?" Leona patted Cinnamon's head and situated herself against the pillow she'd positioned in one corner of the wooden swing. She missed her students—missed teaching them and preparing for the last day of school when they would have a picnic on the lawn. Leona's friend Mary Ann Fisher had been hired to take Leona's place for the remaining weeks of the school year. That had worked out well for Mary Ann, since Anna Beechy had passed away three weeks ago, leaving Mary Ann without her job as Anna's maid.

A warm breeze eased its way under the eaves of the porch, and Leona sighed.

"Mail's here," Mom said, waving a stack of envelopes

as she stepped onto the porch.

Cinnamon wagged her tail and let out a *woof.*

"Anything interesting today?" Leona asked.

"Looks like more letters from your pupils." Mom smiled and took a seat beside Leona. "Seems they're really missin' you, jah?"

Leona nodded and blinked back stinging tears that threatened to spill over. She'd been weepy ever since Ezra's death. "Will you read the letters to me?" she asked, knowing she couldn't see well enough to read them without her glasses.

"Of course." Mom opened the first one and announced that it was from Emanuel Lapp.

> *Dear Teacher Leona,*
> *I'm sorry about the ball hitting you in the*
> *face. Maybe my brother will bring me by to see*
> *how you're doin' on Sunday since it's an off-week*
> *and there won't be any preaching.*

"It wasn't Emanuel's fault I didn't have enough sense to keep my eye on the ball. I should have called the kinner in from recess instead of trying to join their baseball game."

"Accidents have a way of happening when we least expect them. We can't stop living for fear that something bad will happen." Mom reached over and patted Leona's arm.

Cinnamon added her agreement by placing one huge, red paw in Leona's lap.

Leona groaned. "My accident was one that could have been avoided if I hadn't been so eager to join the game."

A horse and open buggy rolled into the yard just then, interrupting their conversation and causing Cinnamon to bark. The driver pulled up beside the barn, jumped down, and secured his horse to the hitching post. Then he sprinted for the house.

Even without clear vision, Leona could see that it was Abner Lapp, Emanuel's older brother. Abner worked at a furniture shop in Strasburg and had been overseeing his young sibling ever since their daed had been killed in a buggy accident last winter.

"Wie geht's, Leona?" Abner's heavy black boots clunked noisily over the wooden planks as he stepped onto the porch. "I was on my way home from work and decided to stop and see how you're doing. I'd meant to do it sooner, but I've been workin' a lot of overtime lately."

Cinnamon released a throaty growl, and Leona laid a firm hand on the dog's head to let her know everything was okay. "I'm feeling a little better, although I still don't have my glasses and my nose is pretty swollen yet."

"Sorry to hear that." Abner shied away from Cinnamon and took a seat in the chair beside Leona. He studied her so intently that she felt like a horse being inspected on auction day. "You're right about your naas being swollen. Looks awful painful to me."

Leona nodded, and when Cinnamon let out another little *woof*, she leaned down to pat the dog's silky head. "It's okay, girl."

Abner glanced over at Leona's mamm, and when he smiled, the corner of his mouth lifted in a slight slant. "How're things with you, Lydia?"

"Can't complain." She stood and smoothed the wrinkles in her dark green dress. "I think I'll take this mail inside and get something cold to drink. Would either of you like a glass of iced tea?"

"That sounds good to me," Abner was quick to respond. "It's a warm day, and somethin' cold would feel mighty good on my parched tongue."

"All right then." The screen door squeaked as Mom stepped into the house. Cinnamon flopped onto the porch beneath Leona's feet.

Abner removed his straw hat and placed it over one knee. Then he lifted his hand to run long fingers through the back of his thick brown hair. "I feel real bad about my brother hittin' you in the naas. Was he foolin' around with the ball? 'Cause if he was, I'll see that he's punished."

"Nee. He wasn't fooling around. I just wasn't paying close enough attention, that's all."

"That's good to hear. I mean, the part about Emanuel not foolin' around." Abner's clear blue eyes clouded over as he slowly shook his head. "Ever since Pop died, Emanuel's sure been a handful."

Leona nodded. "His grades were down for a while, too, but he's been doing better lately."

"I'm glad of that."

They sat in silence, Leona rocking back and forth in the swing, and Abner fanning his face with the brim of his hat and tapping his boot in rhythm with each forward motion of the swing. "You. . .uh. . .think you'll be goin' back to teaching soon?" he finally asked.

Leona touched the bridge of her nose and cringed when her fingers made contact with the tender, bruised flesh. "Well, I'm hoping. . . ." She let her words trail when her mamm stepped onto the porch with two glasses of iced tea.

"Here you go." Leona's mamm handed one to Abner and one to Leona then turned back toward the house.

Leona wished Mom would stay on the porch. Being alone with Abner or any other single man made her feel about as comfortable as a hen setting on a pile of rocks. She hoped he would gulp down his tea and head for home soon.

❦

"You done messing with pictures?" Jim asked when Jimmy entered the living room.

"Yeah. For now, anyway."

Jim yawned. They'd gotten off work early this afternoon, thanks to an unexpected rainstorm that had wreaked havoc with the outside paint job they'd been doing on the Save-U-More grocery store. He and Jimmy had eaten a late lunch, and while Jim spent the rest of the afternoon reclining on the couch with a bag of pretzels and a couple of beers, Jimmy had hidden out in his darkroom downstairs. It made no sense that the kid would want to mess around with an antiquated camera and a bunch of chemicals to develop pictures when he could snap some decent-looking shots with a digital camera and print them off on his computer.

Jimmy took a seat in the rocking chair across from Jim. It had been Linda's favorite chair, and Jim remembered all the nights she had rocked Jimmy to sleep when he was little.

His heart twisted as he thought about the lullabies she used to sing to their son. When he closed his eyes, he could almost smell her rose-scented perfume and feel the softness of her long blond hair between his fingers. *I should have been a better husband. Should have spent more time with her and Jimmy.*

In the nine years since Linda had been gone, Jim had only gone out with a couple of women, and those had just been casual dates. His mother had mentioned once that she thought Jimmy needed a mother, but Jim didn't see it that way. It would have been stupid to get married again just so Jimmy could have a new mom. No one could ever love the boy the way Linda had.

"You drifting off to sleep, Dad?"

Jim's eyes snapped open. "Nope. Just doing a bit of reminiscing."

"Thinking about Mom?"

"Yeah."

"It's hard to believe she's been gone nine years, isn't it?"

"Yep. Nine long years." Jim sat up and reached for a freshly opened bottle of beer and took a long swig.

At the same time, Jimmy reached for the newspaper lying on the coffee table between them. "Wonder if there's anything good playing at the movies this week," he said. "Allen wants me to go on a double date with him and Sandy on Friday night."

"Speaking of Allen, what'd the two of you do on Sunday to celebrate your birthday?"

"Nothing spectacular. After church, I went over to his house, and his mom fixed my favorite meal—stuffed cabbage rolls and mashed potatoes. And of course Beth had baked me a birthday cake."

Jim grimaced. "Ugh. I hate cabbage rolls." He took another swallow of beer. "Doesn't sound like a very exciting day to me."

"It was quiet but nice. I always enjoy spending time with Allen's family."

"Your mom liked to hang around those religious fanatics, too."

"Dad, they're not—"

"So what was in that birthday card your grandparents sent? Did they give you a hundred dollars like last year?"

"Oh man!" Jimmy jumped up and dashed over to the coat tree near the front door. "I put that envelope you gave me in my jacket pocket when we had lunch last Friday, and I forgot all about it."

Once Jimmy was seated in the rocker again, he ripped the envelope open. It was a birthday card all right—with a sailboat on the front and a check for a hundred dollars. There was also a smaller envelope tucked inside, and Grandma had scribbled a note to Jimmy on the bottom of the card, explaining that the note had been written by his mother and that she'd asked Grandma to see that Jimmy got it on his twenty-first birthday.

"How much money did you get?" Dad asked, his words slurring a bit.

"Same as last year, only Grandma included a letter Mom wrote before she died." Jimmy squinted as he silently read the note.

> Dear Jimmy,
>
> I'm sure by now your father has told you the truth about your adoption, but he isn't always good about sharing details, so I wanted to be sure you knew and understood the whole story.
>
> First, I want you to know that the reason we didn't tell you from the beginning that you were adopted was because we wanted to be sure you were old enough to understand.

The words on the page blurred as Jimmy reread the first two lines. Could it be true that he was adopted? He'd never suspected it, and neither Mom nor Dad had ever let on. He blinked a couple of times and forced his eyes to focus, determined to finish reading the letter.

> Your dad and I were unable to have children of our own, and when we decided to adopt, it was because we both wanted a child and knew we could offer that child a good home with all the love he or she would need. So when Max Brenner, our attorney here in Puyallup, told us that a lawyer friend of his in Bel Air, Maryland, had contact with a single mother who couldn't care for her one-year-old son, we jumped at the chance to adopt you. After Max set the wheels in motion on this end, we drove to the East Coast to pick up our baby.
>
> As it turned out, I ended up with one of my sick headaches and had to stay behind in the

hotel while your dad went to Carl Stevens's office in Bel Air.

Oh, Jimmy, I can't tell you how excited I was when I held you for the first time. It was as though you had always been mine. Raising you has been such a joy and a privilege. I couldn't love you more had you been my own flesh-and-blood son.

Your dad loves you, too, although I know he has an odd way of showing it sometimes. He may come across as harsh and indifferent, but I think he covers up his true feelings with his brashness. I believe the reason he sometimes drinks is because he can't deal with certain things.

I thank God for leading me to church, and I'm grateful you've found a personal relationship with the Lord, too. Even though I've never been able to convince your dad that he has a need for Christ, I've continued to pray that he will someday come to know Him as we do. Maybe you will be the one to show him the way, so please continue to pray for your dad.

Always remember that I love you, Jimmy, and I have ever since that amazing day when I first held you in my arms.

All my love,
Mom

With tears clogging the back of his throat, Jimmy lifted the piece of paper. "Mom told me the whole story in this letter."

"The whole story? What whole story is that?" Dad plunked the beer bottle on the coffee table and clambered off the couch.

"About me being adopted. She thought you would have told me by now. Why haven't you, Dad?"

"I was going to, Jimmy." Dad's face had turned red, and a trickle of sweat rolled off his forehead and onto his cheek.

"Mom said the two of you drove back East to get me and that you went to the lawyer's office alone."

"Yeah, that's right. Your mother had one of her migraines that morning." Dad leaned over Jimmy's shoulder and stared at the letter. After a few minutes, he straightened, and his face seemed to relax. "She's right, Jimmy. We both loved you, and the only reason we didn't tell you about your adoption sooner was because—"

Jimmy waved the letter in front of his face. "I know all that. What I don't understand is why you didn't tell me yourself. Why'd I have to find out like this?"

"I'm sorry about that, but I. . .I just kept putting it off." Dad shrugged. "I would've gotten around to it sooner or later."

"Really? I'm not so sure."

"So I'm not perfect. You know about the adoption, and you know we both loved you. Now let's get on with our lives, okay?"

Jimmy sprang to his feet, and Dad staggered backward. "Get on with our lives? I just found out I'm adopted, and now you want me to get on with my life like nothing's any different than it's always been?"

"I said I love you, and I loved your mother, too. Loved her enough to—" Dad sank to the couch, and with shaky fingers, he reached for his beer.

"Yeah, that's right, Dad. The answer to everything is in that bottle, isn't it?" Jimmy rarely spoke to his dad like this, but he was getting tired of covering for him when he didn't show up at work and tired of putting up with his drunkenness and hearing all his lame excuses for why he drank. Learning that he'd been adopted and realizing his dad was supposed to have told him made

Jimmy feel things he'd never felt before and say things he'd always wanted to say but had kept bottled up inside.

Dad gulped down some more beer and wiped his mouth with the back of his hand. "I. . .I need something to take the edge off. You know, to help me calm down."

"Yeah, right. Whatever." Every muscle in Jimmy's body tensed, and his head swam with so many unanswered questions: things he wanted to know, things he needed to understand. But now wasn't the time for more questions. He had to be alone. He was afraid that if he stayed he might explode.

Driven by a force he didn't question, Jimmy sprinted across the room and rushed out the front door.

Chapter 4

Leona remained on the swing with Cinnamon's head in her lap as she watched Abner head for his buggy. He seemed like a lonely person, and she wondered why he didn't have a girlfriend by now. Maybe he'd been hurt by someone and had decided to remain single. Or maybe he stayed single so he could better care for his mamm and little bruder. His only other siblings were two married sisters who each had families of their own to care for.

"I sure miss my students," she murmured, thinking about Emanuel and the other children she'd come to care about. "I wish I was at the schoolhouse cleaning the blackboard right now, not sitting here like a lazy lump of clay."

Cinnamon whimpered and nudged Leona's hand with her cold, wet nose. "And too bad I can't see well enough to read without my glasses," she added.

Leona stared at the lawn, and as she watched the tall blades of grass shimmer in the breeze, she thought about the letters from her students that had come in today's mail. Mom had taken them inside when Abner showed up.

She reached for her glass of tea, which she had set on the wide porch rail, and stood. "Guess I'll go inside and see if Mom has the time to finishing reading me the mail."

Cinnamon followed Leona to the door, but Leona didn't allow the dog to go inside. Papa had never been keen on pets in the house, and Cinnamon was no exception.

The sizzle of strong-smelling onions and the hiss

of their propane stove greeted Leona when she stepped into the kitchen a few seconds later. She spotted Mom in front of the sink, peeling potatoes.

"I didn't realize you were starting supper already. You should have called me," Leona said, moving quickly across the room.

Mom lifted the potato peeler. "Thought I'd get an early start, and I didn't want to interrupt your conversation with Abner." She smiled. "He seems to be a right-nice young fellow."

"Jah. Abner's a good bruder, too. He's concerned because Emanuel has been rather unruly since their daed died last spring, and he was worried the boy might have been fooling around when the ball hit me in the face."

"Did you set him straight on that?"

"I did. Accidents happen, and I'm sure Emanuel was only trying to strike me out, not break my naas." Leona got out a paring knife. "Want me to cut up the potatoes for you?"

"Without your glasses? You might end up cutting yourself."

"I mostly need them for reading, Mom, but if it would make you feel better, I'll peel, and you can cut."

"That's fine by me."

For the next few minutes, they worked in silence as Mom cut potatoes and checked on the cooking onions while Leona peeled potatoes and thought about her students' letters. When the last potato was peeled, cut, and placed in the frying pan to cook with the onions, Leona turned to her mamm and said, "Since Papa won't be home for a while, would you have time to read me the other letters that came from my students today?"

"Jah, sure. I can do that right now." Mom pulled out a chair at the table, and Leona did the same. As her mamm read letters from Josh and Nate Hoffmeir, Elmer and John Fisher, and Leona's youngest student, Selma

Stauffer, Leona sat with her eyes closed, basking in the pleasure of hearing what her students had to say and picturing each of their precious faces.

When the last letter had been read, Leona yawned. "Sorry about that, but I feel kind of sleepy all of a sudden."

"Why don't you go upstairs and lie down awhile? I'll call you when it's time to get the rest of supper going."

With a deep sense of appreciation, Leona gave her mamm a hug. "*Danki*."

"You're welcome."

∞

As Naomi guided her horse and buggy up the Weavers' driveway, Leona's dog rushed out to greet her, barking her usual friendly greeting.

Naomi halted the buggy in front of the hitching post near the barn, climbed down, and bent to pet the dog. "Hey, Cinnamon, how are you doin' this afternoon?"

Cinnamon responded with two quick barks and lots of tail wagging.

"That good, huh?" Naomi reached into the buggy and withdrew a wicker basket that contained the shoofly pie she'd baked last night. The dog sniffed the cloth draped over the top of the pie and released a pathetic whine.

Naomi shook her finger. "I baked the treat for Teacher Leona, not for you, girl." She started toward the house, and the dog slunk toward the barn with her tail drooping.

Naomi hurried around the back side of the house. When she stepped onto the porch, it creaked beneath her feet. *Guess our bishop's got so much to do these days that he can't keep up with things around here.*

She knocked on the edge of the screen door, and a

few seconds later, Lydia made an appearance, bidding her to enter.

"How nice of you to stop by. What have you got there in the basket?" the older woman asked with a mischievous twinkle in her blue eyes.

Naomi smiled. Lydia had always been one to get right to the point, but that's just who she was. Everyone knew it. "I brought over a shoofly pie for Leona. It's a gift from my two oldest boys, who of course had nothing to do with the baking of it."

Lydia laughed and motioned to the kitchen counter. "You can put it over there. If you're not in a hurry, maybe you'd like a glass of iced tea or some lemonade."

Naomi set the basket down, lifted the pie, and placed it on the counter. "I was hoping for the chance to visit with Leona, and I'd very much appreciate a glass of cold tea. It's way too warm for the end of May."

"Leona's upstairs resting right now, and I hate to disturb her. So if you don't mind my company, maybe the two of us can visit awhile."

"Sounds good to me." Naomi took a seat, while Lydia prepared tall glasses of iced tea.

"How's Leona doing?" Naomi asked. "Is there any chance of her going back to teach before the school year is out?"

Lydia shrugged. "Her new glasses aren't ready yet, and without those, she can't see well enough to read. So she can't return to teaching till they come in. The bridge of her nose is still real sore, so even if she did have her glasses, I doubt she could wear 'em for long."

Naomi swallowed the cool liquid in her mouth, savoring the delicate flavor of Lydia's homemade mint tea. "Sure was a shame about the ball hitting her in the face and breaking her naas. Josh said Emanuel blamed himself for the whole thing, but it sounded like it wasn't really the boy's fault."

"Leona says she was in the wrong for not paying closer attention."

Naomi shook her head. "Seems like most folks have a way of blaming themselves when things don't go right. I guess it helps make some sense out of the tragedies in life if we've got someone to blame." She sucked in her bottom lip. "It's been twenty years since my little bruder was taken from us, and sometimes I still find myself going over the details of that day and putting the blame on my shoulders again. Then I'm reminded of how God forgives our sins and doesn't want us to beat ourselves over the head because of our mistakes. It's the lessons we learn that matter most, and you can be sure I learned a powerful lesson the day Zach was kidnapped."

Lydia reached across the table and touched Naomi's arm. The tender look on the woman's face made Naomi realize how much she sympathized with her pain.

"Last week was Zach's twenty-first birthday, and I had to wonder if Papa wasn't hurting that day as much as I was. Of course, he never said anything about it to me."

"I don't believe any parent ever gets over the loss of a child," Lydia said in a near whisper. "Whether it's from a kidnapping or having them taken in death."

Naomi recalled hearing that Lydia had lost a baby boy due to crib death a few years before Leona was born. She figured there were probably times when Lydia still mourned her loss.

"I'm thankful Papa had a friend like Jacob to help him through the rough days after Zach was taken," she commented. "Your husband's a good man, and we're fortunate to have him as our bishop."

"Jacob would say, 'That's what friends are for,' and I'm sure Abraham would do the same for my husband if he had such a need." Lydia smiled. "What God doeth is well done."

Naomi nodded. "Absolutely."

⸎

As Jim began painting the back of the store he and his crew had been working on, he gripped the paintbrush so hard his fingers ached. It was difficult to keep his mind on the job when he knew Jimmy was upset with him.

Last night, after Jimmy left the house, Jim had stayed up late, waiting, hoping for his son's return. He needed the chance to explain things better and make his son realize why he hadn't told him about the adoption before. But Jimmy hadn't returned home all night, or this morning, either.

He gritted his teeth. *How can we clear things up if Jimmy doesn't come home so we can talk about all this?*

This morning, Beth Walters had phoned, saying Jimmy had slept at their place last night but that he'd left soon after breakfast. She'd also mentioned that Jimmy seemed upset about something and asked if Jim knew what it could be. Jim assured Beth that it was nothing to worry about. The last thing he needed was for that religious fanatic to stick her nose in where it didn't belong, the way she had done countless times when Linda was alive.

Jim yawned loudly. He'd spent most of last night pacing the floor, sulking over the mistakes he'd made during the last twenty years, and drinking one beer after the other until he'd finally fallen asleep in a stupor. When he'd awakened on the couch this morning, he had such a pounding headache he didn't know if he'd be able to make it to work or not. But after two cups of coffee, a couple of aspirin, and a warm shower, he'd managed to pull himself together.

I wish Linda hadn't written Jimmy that letter. It should have been me telling him that he was adopted, not her, he told himself. *Maybe she didn't trust me to keep my promise.*

Jim dipped the paintbrush into the bucket sitting near his feet and tried to concentrate on the job at hand. It was no use. All he could think about was the look of confusion on Jimmy's face when he'd read his mother's letter. *The kid must hate me now, and I guess I can't blame him. If Jimmy would just come home so I could explain things better, everything would be all right.*

"What's wrong, Boss? You look upset, and you're dripping on the sidewalk—not to mention all over those new work boots you're wearin'."

Jim glanced down. Ed was right. A puddle of white paint had collected on the sidewalk, and a long streak dripped across the toe of one boot. "I—I didn't sleep well last night," he mumbled. "I've got a splitting headache, and I'm having trouble staying focused this morning."

"You can say that again." Ed shook his head. "A couple of the guys said they'd tried to ask you some questions earlier, and you never did answer any of them."

"I've got a lot on my mind." Jim frowned. "Besides, you're the foreman. Why didn't they ask you?"

"They did ask. After they got no response from you. Is there a problem?"

Jim dipped his brush into the paint again but made no comment. He shouldn't have to answer to anyone. He owned this business, could do whatever he wanted, and had the right to speak or not to speak whenever he felt like it. If Ed couldn't handle things, then he could—

"Where's Jimmy this morning?" Ed asked suddenly.

Jim shrugged. "Beats me."

"I hope he shows up soon. We need every available painter if we're gonna get this store done before the weekend."

"I doubt we'll see Jimmy today," Jim muttered, refusing to make eye contact with his foreman.

"How come? Is the kid sick or something?"

Jim fought the urge to rail at his faithful employee, but he knew none of this mess with Jimmy was Ed's fault. "He's not sick, and we'll manage fine without him today."

Ed squinted, tugged on his mustache, and walked away. Jim had a sinking feeling that this was going to be a long, grueling day.

∞

"It's so good to finally have my new glasses," Leona said to her mother as the two of them sat next to each other in the backseat of Vera Griffin's station wagon. Vera, their English driver, had taken them to the optical shop in Lancaster in the morning, and after they'd picked up Leona's glasses, they had stopped at a fast-food restaurant for a quick lunch. Then they'd done a bit of shopping until Mom insisted it was time to go home because Leona looked tired. Leona had protested that she felt fine, but truthfully she was happy to be heading for home. Today was the first day she'd been away from the house since her accident, and her nose was beginning to throb.

"How do the new glasses feel?" Mom asked. "Are they too heavy for the bridge of your naas?"

"They felt okay when the optician adjusted the earpieces and put them on my face, but they've been hurting a little ever since." Leona shrugged. "Maybe he didn't get them fitted just right."

"And maybe your naas is still too tender to wear the glasses for long," Mom said with a shake of her head. "It may take another week or so till you can wear them all day. You'll need to be patient."

Leona was tired of being patient and tired of staying home when she should be at school. She removed her glasses and gingerly rubbed the bridge of her nose. "I have no more time for patience."

Her mamm's pale eyebrows drew together, and her lips formed a frown. "What's that supposed to mean?"

"Friday's the last day of school, and I need to be there."

"Why would you need to be there for the last day of school?"

"Because we always have a picnic that day, and I want to spend some time with my pupils and say good-bye for the summer."

"I see."

Leona thought about Emanuel Lapp and how his brother had brought him by the house to see her last Sunday afternoon. He'd said several times how sorry he was for hitting her in the face with the ball.

Leona smiled as she pictured the sincere expression on Emanuel's youthful face when he and his older brother presented her with a birdhouse that Abner said he had made. Abner seemed pleased when Leona thanked them and said she would enjoy watching to see if any birds made a nest in it.

"I really think you should stay home and take it easy for the rest of the week," Mom said, breaking into Leona's thoughts. "You look awful tired right now, and I doubt you'd be able to make it through the whole day at school."

Leona felt her defenses begin to rise. "Mary Ann will be there to help. Besides, we'll be having a picnic, and school will get out early, so there won't be much work for me to do." She clenched and unclenched her fingers. *Why is Mom so overprotective? Sometimes she treats me as if I'm still a little girl. We would get along much better if she saw me as a grown woman, the way Papa does.*

Leona could tell by the determined set of her

mamm's jaw that she was tempted to argue further, but they had just pulled into their yard and Daed was waiting for them on the front porch, so the discussion ended.

Cinnamon was there, too, lying on the porch beside Daed's favorite wicker chair. While Mom paid Vera for their ride, Leona hurried over to greet Papa and Cinnamon.

"How'd your appointment go at the optical shop?" Papa asked as soon as she stepped onto the porch.

"I got my new glasses." Leona bent over to pat Cinnamon's head, and the dog responded with a muffled grunt.

"Are they *aagenehm*?"

"I'm sure the glasses will be comfortable enough once the soreness leaves my nose." Before her daed could respond, she added, "I'm going back to school on Friday; I want to be there for the last day."

His forehead wrinkled slightly. "You think you're ready for that?"

"Jah."

He nodded slowly. "I'll drive you then."

"Danki, Papa." Leona was glad he hadn't tried to talk her out of going and that he'd agreed to take her to school. *At least Papa doesn't try to smother me as Mom often does. If I had half as much wisdom dealing with people as my daed does, I'd be the best schoolteacher in all of Lancaster County.*

Chapter 5

As Jimmy steered his small truck toward Point Defiance Park, all he could think about was the letter he'd read from Mom yesterday evening. It had been a shock to discover he was adopted. He found the news all that much harder to accept after learning that his dad was supposed to have told him about his adoption long ago but hadn't. After Jimmy had left the house, he'd gone over to Allen's to spend the night but, unable to talk about his adoption, he had merely said that he'd had a disagreement with his dad and needed some time away.

Beth and Eric Walters were good people, and they'd raised three of the nicest boys Jimmy had ever known. He knew they wouldn't think any less of him if he told them he'd been adopted, but he needed more time to think about all this before he discussed it with anyone.

His hazy mind swept over the events of last night one more time, and he gritted his teeth in an attempt to control his swirling emotions. Maybe some time at the beach would make him feel better. Ever since he'd gotten his driver's license, he had often gone to Owen Beach or someplace along the waterfront to think and pray, and he'd always felt closer to God whenever he was near the water.

A short time later, Jimmy drove into the park and headed through the stretch of road known as Five Mile Drive. He let his pickup coast down the hill leading to the beach. When he found a parking place not far from the water, he parked, turned off the engine, and stepped out of the truck.

As the salty, fresh air teased Jimmy's senses, he drew

in a deep, cleansing breath. For one brief moment, he felt as if things could be right in his world again. But then he thought about Mom's letter, and his confusion resurfaced.

He hopped across a couple of logs and jogged up the rocky beach, hoping to work off his frustrations. The brackish air blew against his face and felt invigorating, yet it was almost painful. "If only Mom and Dad had told me I was adopted from the very beginning."

On and on, Jimmy ran, trying to block out the pain and focus his thoughts on something other than his adoption. Finally, in a state of emotional and physical exhaustion, Jimmy halted below the pier. Eager fishermen leaned against the railing with their fishing poles hung over the sides. He drew in a breath and bent over at the waist, trying to calm his racing heart.

His stomach growled as the smell of deep-fried fish and steamed butter clams tickled his nose. He glanced at the deck outside Anthony's Restaurant. People sat around tables, eating with friends and admiring the view of Commencement Bay. Jimmy realized then that he hadn't had anything to eat since breakfast. He was tempted to grab a bite at the restaurant but decided against it.

"I doubt I could keep anything down," he mumbled. "What I need more than food is some answers." He turned and started back up the beach. "It's time to go home. It's time for a serious talk with Dad."

∽

As Jim passed the health food store near the entrance of the Tacoma Mall, his thoughts turned to Linda. In conjunction with chemotherapy, radiation, and several surgeries, she had tried various kinds of vitamins, herbs, and homeopathic remedies during her bout with cancer. While nothing had cured her disease, she had found some relief from her pain, and he figured the vitamins she'd taken might have helped strengthen her immune system, which had given her a bit more time.

He glanced at the stack of bodybuilding nutrients displayed in the store window. *Maybe I should go inside and see if they have anything to help calm my nerves.* He'd thought about stopping somewhere after work for a couple of drinks, but in case Jimmy decided to come home this evening, Jim wanted to be sure he was sober and able to carry on an intelligent conversation.

"Yeah, right. Like anything I've ever done was intelligent," he mumbled.

"May I help you, sir?"

Jim studied the woman who had been stocking shelves near the front door. Her skin was smooth, with barely a wrinkle, and her short blond hair was shiny and thick. If she was as healthy as she looked and it was due to the products sold here, then he figured he had come to the right place. "I. . .uh. . .do you have anything that might help a person relax?" he asked.

"I sell several herbal preparations that seem to work pretty well." She smiled, and her pale blue eyes appeared to scrutinize him. "Say, you look familiar. Aren't you Jimmy Scott's dad?"

Jim nodded. "How do you know my son?"

"We go to the same church, and I believe I've seen you there for some of the programs Jimmy's been in." She extended her hand. "I'm Holly Simmons, the owner of this store."

Another religious fanatic, no doubt. He forced a smile and shook her hand. "My name's Jim."

Holly motioned to the back of the store. "The herbal and homeopathic remedies are right this way."

∞

"Did Leona go inside?" Lydia asked her husband when she stepped onto the front porch.

"We visited a few minutes, and then she said she was going to get supper started."

"Did she show her new glasses to you?"

"Jah, the optical shop sure took their time gettin' them done, wouldn't ya say?"

Lydia shrugged. "It's just as well if you ask me. If our daughter had gotten her glasses any sooner, she'd have insisted on going back to teach at the schoolhouse."

He nodded. "I think you're right about that."

"Did she tell you she's planning to go there on Friday?"

"Jah."

"I hope you told her it wasn't a good idea."

"Now why would I say that?"

"Because her naas still hurts, and I'm sure she can't last the whole day with those glasses on her face," Lydia said with a click of her tongue.

"Maybe she won't have to wear 'em all day."

"What do you mean?"

"There's to be a picnic on Friday, so she won't be expected to teach the whole day. If her naas starts hurtin', she can take the glasses off. Besides, I'll be drivin' her to and from school, so she won't have to worry about that, either."

Lydia pursed her lips and shook her head. "I think Leona pushes herself too hard. She uses her teaching to cover up the pain of losing Ezra, too."

"It's good for her to keep busy, and she needs a purpose, Lydia." Jacob bent over and scratched Leona's dog behind its ears.

"I suppose you're right. I just hope she works through her grief soon." Lydia trudged across the porch, gave the screen door handle a sharp pull, and went inside.

∞

Jimmy entered the house through the back door, figuring his dad would be in the kitchen eating dinner by now. He was right. Jim sat at the kitchen table with a bowl of soup in front of him. A couple of store-bought rolls were wedged on a plate, and a glass of milk sat to the right of it. At least it wasn't a bottle of beer this time.

As soon as the door clicked shut, his dad turned around. "I'm glad you're home. We need to talk."

"Yeah. That's why I'm here." Jimmy struggled with the desire to rush downstairs and hide out in his darkroom, but there were too many questions he needed to have answered. He strode across the room, pulled out a chair, and took a seat at the table.

"I was worried about you last night when you didn't come home," Dad said. "I wish you would have called."

"I spent the night at Allen's."

"So I heard."

Jimmy didn't bother to ask who had told. He figured Allen's mother had probably phoned to let Jim know where he was. That's how Beth was—always thinking of others. She'd been a real help to Mom, especially during her illness.

"Did you tell the Walters about being adopted?"

Jimmy shook his head. "I haven't told anyone yet."

"I'm sorry about the way you found out, Jimmy. I should have kept my promise to your mother and told you sooner." Dad lifted the glass of milk to his lips and took a drink. "You were probably old enough to hear the truth by the time you were sixteen."

"Sixteen? Why didn't you just tell me the truth as soon as I was old enough to understand the concept of adoption? What'd you think I was going to do—run away from home?"

Dad shrugged. "I. . .I don't know. We were just afraid you wouldn't understand or might think we didn't love you as much because—"

"Because I wasn't your flesh-and-blood son?"

"Yeah."

"I've always known you and Mom loved me." Jimmy shifted on his chair and inhaled slowly. "I've thought about this a lot in the last twenty-four hours, and I need some answers, Dad. I need to know who my birth mother was."

"She lived in Maryland, just like your mother's letter said." A muscle in Dad's cheek quivered, and Jimmy realized he wasn't the only one struggling with a bundle of emotions.

"I think I'd like to try and find her, and see if I can learn who my real dad is, too."

Jim's forehead wrinkled as his eyebrows pulled together in a frown. "I hope you're not planning to go looking for them. That would be a huge mistake, Jimmy."

"Why would it be a mistake?"

"Think about it. If they gave you up, then it's pretty obvious that they didn't want any contact with you."

"They didn't love me? Is that what you're saying?"

"I'm not saying that at all." Dad pushed away from the table and headed over to the refrigerator. He removed a can of beer and flipped open the lid.

Jimmy's fist came down on the table. "Can't we have this conversation without you having to get liquored up?"

Dad sank to a chair and took a swig from the can. "I'm not *liquored* up. This is the first beer I've had all day."

They sat there for several minutes, both staring at the table, and the silence that permeated the room felt like a heavy fog creeping across the waters of Puget Sound. Wasn't Dad going to tell him anything? Didn't he want him to know any of the details of his adoption?

"I don't know what I'm going to do," Jimmy said, "but if I decide to search for my roots, I'll need to have as much information as you can give me."

Dad's next words came out slowly, almost as though he had rehearsed them. "I don't know the name of your biological parents. The lawyer said your mother was a single parent and couldn't provide for you."

"What about my father? What'd he say about him?"

"Nothing much—just that your birth mother had severed ties with him and that he'd married someone else and was living in another state. Oh, and that he had signed away all parental rights to their baby."

Jimmy swallowed and slowly released his breath. He couldn't imagine anyone giving up their paternal rights, but then he'd never been put in the position his biological parents had been in, either. "Maybe I ought to call your lawyer here and see what he can tell me."

"Max moved several years ago, and I'm not even sure he's still alive." Dad placed his fingertips against his forehead, moving them up and down, then back and forth in a circular motion.

"Then maybe I should call the lawyer in Maryland. Do you have his phone number?"

"I. . .uh. . .it might be in the safe with your adoption papers."

"Can you get it for me?"

Dad dropped his hands to the table, clenching and unclenching his fingers. "Uh. . .well. . ."

"I need some answers, Dad."

"Yeah, yeah, I know you do." Dad stood and grabbed up his dishes, hauling them over to the sink.

"Are you going to help me with this or not?" Jimmy asked, feeling more frustrated with each passing moment.

"I'll see what I can do."

"You'll let me look through the safe for those adoption papers?"

"No!"

"Why not?"

Dad moved back to the table. "How about this—I'll look for the lawyer's phone number, and then I'll give him a call and see what I can find out for you. How's that sound?"

Jimmy shrugged. "I suppose that would be okay. It's a start, anyway."

Dad nodded then took a long drink of beer. Jimmy cringed. *If he doesn't keep this promise, then I'm going to take matters into my own hands.*

Chapter 6

Leona was nearly finished helping Mom with the breakfast dishes when a knock sounded at the back door. She dried her hands and went to answer it.

"Guder mariye," Abner said when she opened the door.

"Good morning," she responded. "What brings you by here so early?"

"Emanuel and I came to give you a ride over to the schoolhouse."

Leona wondered how Abner knew she had planned to go to school this morning but didn't bother to raise the question. "I appreciate the offer, but my daed will be taking me."

Abner shook his head. "I ran into him on my way home from work last night, and he asked if I could come by and get you—said he had to be in the town of Blue Ball early this morning to bid on a paint job."

She stared at him, dumbfounded. "Papa never mentioned anything to me about leaving early today, and I'm sure he would have said something if he hadn't been able to drive me to school."

"Jah, well, he must have gotten busy and forgot to tell you." Abner lifted his straw hat from his head and shifted his weight from one foot to the other. "Maybe he figured you'd find out from me."

Leona leaned against the doorjamb as she tried to piece everything together. It wasn't like Papa to be so forgetful or promise to do something and then not follow through. She was about to say that she would need to speak with her daed about this, when she remembered that he had left the house right after breakfast. She figured he'd gone out to the barn to do a few chores, but maybe Richard Jamison, his English employee, had come by in his van. He and Papa could be halfway to Blue Ball by now.

Abner nodded toward his open buggy, parked alongside the house, and she noticed Emanuel sitting in the back. "Are you about ready to go then?"

Leona wished she could drive herself to school today, but she knew neither one of her folks would condone that idea. Not with the headaches that snuck up on her when she least expected them. "I'll need to speak to my mamm first and see if she knows whether Papa's left for work or not," she said.

He nodded. "Okay. I'll be waitin' in the buggy with my brother then."

∞

Jim removed a five-gallon bucket of paint from the back of his van and glanced over his shoulder. Jimmy and two of his employees stood on scaffolding as they sprayed one side of the grocery store they had been painting this week. He'd felt a sense of relief when Jimmy said he would be here today, but he cringed when he thought about the promise he'd made to his son about calling the lawyer in Maryland. *I'll wait a couple days, and then I'll tell him I called the lawyer but that he had no information to give. Maybe then Jimmy will stop asking questions and give up on the idea of trying to find his biological parents. He needs to let it drop, that's for sure. And I'll need to make sure that he does.*

Jim had fought to get to sleep again last night but finally found some relief when he took the herbal tablets he'd bought at Holly Simmons's health food store. A shot of whiskey would have done the trick just as well, but he was already pushing his luck with Jimmy and couldn't risk angering him by getting caught guzzling a drink.

"Where do you want this paint to go?" Jim's foreman asked.

"You can take it to the guys working on the other side of the building," he mumbled.

"Sure thing, Boss." Ed started to walk away but turned back around. "It's good to see Jimmy at work this morning."

Jim nodded.

"The kid's been acting kind of quiet, though. Do you know if there's something wrong?"

Yeah, plenty, Jim thought while shaking his head to indicate the opposite. "Everything's fine, Ed." He clenched his fists. "Never been better."

∞

"I hope you won't be late for work because you took the time to drive me to the schoolhouse," Leona said, glancing over at Abner in the driver's seat of his open buggy.

"He took the day off so he could come to the picnic with me," Emanuel chimed in from his seat in the back.

"Yeah, and if you should get tired and need to leave early, I'll be there to take you home," Abner added.

Leona clung to the edge of her seat as they jostled down the driveway heading to the main road. "That's kind of you, but I'm sure I'll be fine."

"Maybe so. Maybe not."

Irritation welled up within her. It was bad enough that the humidity this morning was stifling. Now her emotions were getting the best of her, too. Abner had no reason to be worried about her. She was tempted to tell him to turn around and take her back home, but that would mean she would miss seeing her students today.

"There's sure been a lot of corn goin' into the ground this past week," Abner said as they passed a neighboring farm where an Amish man and his son worked side by side in the field.

Leona nodded. She wasn't in the mood for small talk. *Why did Papa have to leave early this morning? And why did he ask Abner to drive me to school? He should have at least told me about it.*

"Oats, hay, and wheat are growin' nicely now," Abner droned on. "It won't be long 'til the womenfolk in our community can start cannin' peas and strawberries."

Emanuel smacked his lips. "I sure can't wait for our mamm's strawberry pie. She makes the best in all of Lancaster County, ain't that right, Abner?"

"Jah, she sure does," his brother agreed. "And strawberries should be getting ripe by the middle of June."

Leona's head had started to throb, and her nose quickly followed suit. The pain couldn't be blamed on her glasses, because she wasn't wearing them. *I wish we would hurry up and get there. It's times like this when I'd like to be riding in a car.*

Half an hour later, they pulled into the school yard. Several children milled about, some on the swings and others playing on the set of teeter-totters. The sight brought tears to Leona's eyes. Oh how she had missed her pupils these past few weeks!

Hannah Fisher bounded up to the buggy as soon as Abner stopped the horse. "Teacher Leona, it's so good to have you back!"

"That's for sure," Emanuel chimed in.

"It's good to be here." Leona climbed down from the buggy. "Danki for the ride, Abner."

He nodded. "I have a couple of errands to run in town, so I'll take care of those now, but I'll be back in time for the picnic."

"My mamm's comin' to the picnic, too," Hannah said, bouncing up and down.

Leona nodded at Hannah and then Emanuel. "Shall we go inside now?"

"Jah," they said in unison.

∞

At noontime Jimmy decided to take his lunch to the park, which wasn't far from the store they had been painting. It would be a welcome relief to get off by himself for a while, rather than sitting around with the guys trying to make idle conversation. The morning had gone by quickly, and for that he was glad. He'd made an effort to keep busy and had tried not to think about anything other than the job they were doing. He still hadn't made up his mind about what to do concerning his search for his birth family once his dad contacted the lawyer.

Jimmy had just grabbed his lunch pail from the back of his pickup and closed the tailgate when his dad showed up. "Where are you going, son?"

"I thought I'd walk over to the park to eat my lunch."

"Want some company?" Brad, one of the new painters, called out.

"I'd. . .uh. . .rather be alone. Maybe some other time." Jimmy hurried down the sidewalk, and a short time later, he entered the park and took a seat on a bench. He flipped open his lunch pail and stared at the contents—a tuna sandwich he'd made this morning and a couple of store-bought cookies. Neither appealed, so he grabbed his thermos of milk and poured some into the lid. When he took a drink, the cool liquid felt good on his parched throat. However, it did little to relieve the tension that seemed to be working its way through every muscle and nerve in his body.

Jimmy stared across the playground at the swings and spiral slide. It made him think of the park close to home—the one he and Mom had visited many times when he was a boy. He'd met Allen there, and it hadn't taken long for the two of them to become friends. Mom and Allen's mother had hit it off, too, and soon after that, they'd started going to the same church the Walters family attended.

"Those were happy times," Jimmy murmured. "Wish I could slip back to those days and stay there."

A horn honked, and his gaze went to the parking lot where a black sports car had pulled in. "What are you doing here?" he called as Allen exited the car.

As his friend sauntered up to him, a lock of dark brown hair fell across his forehead. "I didn't have to work at the lumber mill today, so I stopped by the grocery store where your dad's paint crew has been working."

"How come?"

"I was looking for you, and your dad told me you had come to the park to eat your lunch."

Jimmy nodded. "I needed to be alone for a while."

Allen took a seat on the bench beside him. "I know something's bothering you, Jimmy. You wouldn't have stayed overnight at my house on a weeknight if not. And you wouldn't have been acting like your best friend had just died, either."

Jimmy smiled despite his dour mood. "You're my best friend, and I'm thankful you're still very much alive."

Allen pointed to the lunch Jimmy hadn't touched. "Just one more proof that something must be eating you."

Jimmy groaned. "You're right, there is. And it's a *big* something."

"Want to talk about it?"

"No. Yes. Well, I guess maybe I should."

"If it's something you don't want repeated, you can count on me to keep my mouth shut."

"I know. You've never blabbed anything I've told you in confidence."

Allen snickered. "Yeah, like you've ever told me anything exciting enough to want to blab."

Jimmy shivered despite the sun's warming rays. "What I have to say wouldn't be considered exciting. It was a pretty big shock, though."

His friend leaned closer and squinted his blue eyes. "You'd better spill it then, 'cause I can't stand the suspense."

Chapter 7

It was all Leona could do to help her mother fix supper that night. Not only was she exhausted from her long day at school, but her nose hurt something awful, as well. She removed her glasses and set them on the window ledge, then went to the refrigerator to get out the ingredients she would need for a tossed salad. It would go well with slices of cold ham, leftover baked beans, and potato salad. The day had turned out to be quite warm, so they'd decided not to heat up the kitchen any further by cooking a hot meal this evening.

"How'd the school picnic go?" Mom asked as she set the ham on the cupboard and began to slice it.

"It went fine. Everyone seemed to have a good time."

"And you, daughter? How'd you get along today?"

"I did all right." Leona placed the salad ingredients on the table, pulled out a chair, and sat down. If she were being completely honest, she would have to admit that things hadn't gone nearly as well as she'd hoped they would. She'd suffered with a headache most of the day, even though she hadn't been wearing her glasses. She didn't want her mamm to know that, though. Mom would only have reminded Leona that she'd returned to school too soon, and then there would have been tension between them.

Things will go better next term, when the scholars go back to school in late August, Leona thought. *Then again, though my nose will feel better by then, I'm not sure my broken heart will ever mend.*

Leona had just finished making the salad when Papa showed up. He looked tired, yet despite the slump

61

of his shoulders and his slow-moving gait, he wore a smile on his suntanned face. "How'd your day go, Lydia?" he asked, setting his metal lunchbox on one end of the counter.

Mom held a piece of ham out to him. "It went well enough."

"*Danki*," Papa said, eagerly accepting it. He wandered over to the table and took a seat beside Leona. "How was your day? Were the kinner happy to see you at school?"

She nodded and placed the finished salad on the table.

"I see you're not wearin' your glasses. Is your naas hurtin' again?"

"A little." She shrugged. "Besides, I don't need them for salad making."

"Is there something bothering you? You seem awfully sullen this evening."

A few uncomfortable seconds passed between them before Leona wiped her hands on the dish towel lying in her lap and said, "If you must know, I'm a little upset because you arranged for Abner to pick me up this morning without telling me about it."

Papa's bushy eyebrows drew together. "I had to leave for work early, and I thought I was doin' you a favor by asking Abner. I ran into him yesterday on my way home from work, so he seemed like the likely one to ask."

"You weren't trying to play matchmaker, were you, Jacob?" Mom chimed in from across the room.

Leona clasped her hands tightly around the towel as she looked at her daed. "Is that what you were doin', Papa?"

He gave his earlobe a quick tug. "Well, I—"

"Papa, Abner seems nice enough, but I'm not looking for another man, because I won't be thinking of marriage ever again."

"Oh, Leona, you don't mean that," her mamm said. "You're still hurting from losing Ezra, and it's too soon for you to think of anyone else courting you, that's all."

"I enjoy teaching school, and that's enough for me," Leona said. "I don't need love or marriage."

Papa grunted. "That's just plain *lecherich*. Teaching's a fine vocation, but you should concentrate on finding a suitable husband so you can begin a life of your own as a *fraa* and *mudder*."

So now her father thought she was being ridiculous? Tears welled up in Leona's eyes, and she struggled to keep them from spilling over. She had wanted to be a wife and mother when she'd thought she was going to marry Ezra. But those plans had dissolved the day Ezra died, and she couldn't think of loving another man or risk losing him.

"Our daughter will find someone when her heart has had time to heal," Mom said, touching Papa's arm.

He pushed his chair aside and stood. "I'm sure she will, but closing her mind off to love and marriage isn't a good thing."

Leona gritted her teeth. Her folks were talking about her as if she wasn't even in the room. And Papa seemed determined that she forget about Ezra and find someone else to marry. *Well, at least Mom stood up for me this time*, she thought. *Guess that's something to be grateful for. I just hope Papa has no more plans of trying to get Abner and me together.*

⚬⚬⚬

Jimmy was glad his dad was out on the deck soaking in the hot tub. It gave him a chance to be alone. After supper, he'd decided to look through a couple of old photo albums in the living room.

He settled himself on the couch and opened the

first album. It was full of pictures that had been taken of him from the time he was one-year-old up until his first day of school. Jimmy grinned when he spotted a picture of himself holding one end of the garden hose. Water squirted out of the hose, just missing his face, and a puddle of mud lay beneath his feet. His light blue overalls were wet clear up to the waist, but he wore a smile, nonetheless.

The next picture that caught Jimmy's eye was one of him bent over a branch on their Christmas tree, trying to blow out the twinkle lights. Several pictures were from his second birthday, with blue balloons and matching crepe paper decorating the dining room. Two-year-old Jimmy sat in his high chair, staring wide-eyed at a clown cake and clapping his chubby hands.

He turned the page, and his gaze came to rest on a picture of himself sitting in the middle of his parents' bed, on top of Mom's colorful Amish quilt. A pang of regret surged through him, and he snapped the album shut. *I miss her so much, and I wish she'd been able to tell me about my adoption in person so we could have discussed the details face-to-face. Well, at least I was able to talk about my feelings with Allen this afternoon.*

Jimmy leaned against the back of the couch and closed his eyes as he reflected on the information he'd shared with his best friend while they were at the park. . . .

∞

"I'm not who you think I am," Jimmy said in a near whisper.

"What are you talking about? You're Jimmy Scott, a great photographer and the truest friend I've ever had." Allen squeezed Jimmy's shoulder.

"I'm not Jim and Linda Scott's son. I was born to someone else."

Allen's forehead wrinkled. "Oh, you mean you were adopted?"

Jimmy nodded.

"Well, that's no big deal. Lots of kids are adopted."

"I know, but I've only known the truth for a few days."

"You mean your dad just told you? Is that why you spent the night at our place?"

"Yeah, and I found out about the adoption only because of a letter Mom wrote me before she died." Jimmy paused and pinched the bridge of his nose to ease the strain he felt between his eyes. "The letter came in a birthday card from my grandparents. I guess Mom asked her mother to see that I got the letter on my twenty-first birthday."

Allen's mouth hung slightly open. "That must have been a real shock, learning it that way."

Jimmy nodded. "I guess Dad was supposed to tell me, but he conveniently never got around to it."

"Do you think he kept it from you on purpose?"

"Maybe."

"Could be that he was worried you might not understand, or maybe he thought you'd think he and Linda didn't love you as much as your real parents might have."

"Mom loved me, I'm sure of that, and I guess, in Dad's own way, he loves me, too."

Allen nodded. "I don't think he always knows how to express himself, but I've never doubted his love for you." He gave Jimmy's shoulder another squeeze. "What now? Are you going to try and find out who your real parents are?"

"I want to, and Dad's promised to call the lawyer who set up the adoption for them and see what information he can get."

"Isn't there some kind of client confidentiality that would keep a lawyer from divulging that information?"

Jimmy shrugged. "Maybe, but it's the best place I can think of to start looking."

"I'll be praying that you find the answers you're seeking," Allen said.

Jimmy clenched his hands so tightly that his fingers dug into his palms. "While you're at it, you'd better pray that my dad won't renege on this promise."

❧

The irritating buzz of a lawn mower as it zipped across the yard next door brought Jimmy's thoughts back to the present. He opened his eyes and looked around. This had been his home for as long as he could remember. He'd watched television in this living room, played games, put puzzles together, listened as Mom read him Bible stories, and wrestled around on the floor with his dad. In his wildest dreams, he'd never imagined that they weren't his biological parents.

Jimmy swallowed around the lump clogging his throat. *Mom was worried about me being old enough to deal with the truth about my adoption; yet here I am twenty-one years old, and I'm still not dealing with it well.*

Jimmy exhaled and closed his eyes, knowing he needed to pray. *Dear Lord, even after all these years, I still miss Mom so much. She was the only mother I've ever known, and I'll always love her. If only she were here now to tell me what to do. What should I do, Lord? What should I do?*

❧

When Jim entered the living room after changing from his swimsuit into his sweatpants, he spotted Jimmy sitting on the couch, his head bowed and eyes closed. *The kid's just like his mom,* he thought as irritation welled up in his chest. *Every time he turns around, he's praying about something.*

Jim cleared his throat, and Jimmy opened his eyes.

"I'm glad you've come inside because I need to

ask you something, Dad."

Jim took a seat in the rocking chair across from Jimmy. "What's up?"

"I was wondering if you were able to call that lawyer in Maryland today."

Jim groaned inwardly. "Nope. I was too busy. I'll do it later in the week."

"Are you sure?" Jimmy's expression was as stoic as a statue.

"Of course I'm sure. And don't start pressuring me. You know how busy we've been at work." He stood and moved toward the door leading to the hallway.

"Where are you going?" Jimmy called after him.

"Out to the kitchen to get a beer so I can unwind."

"I thought that was why you had gone in the hot tub."

Jim whirled around. "It was, but it wasn't enough to make me relax."

Jimmy grimaced. "You shouldn't have to drink in order to relax, Dad. I don't think you realize how much you're drinking these days. I'm worried that you'll lose your business if you don't get some help. Maybe you should consider going to AA."

"Alcoholics Anonymous?"

Jimmy nodded.

"You've got to be kidding!"

"I'm serious, Dad. There's a lady from church who's a recovered alcoholic, and she says she's gotten a lot of help from AA. She spoke to our young adult Sunday school class last week and told us that, even though she's been dry for years, she still goes to those meetings as often as she can."

"If she's recovered, why would she need to keep going?"

"Partly to remind herself that she is and always will be an alcoholic. But I think the main reason she goes is to help others who are new to the group and need some support."

"Each to his own, I guess."

Jim had almost made it to the hallway door when Jimmy called out, "Would you like me to see when and where the next meeting is going to be held?"

"No!"

"How about going to church with me this Sunday? I can introduce you to—"

Jim squinted as he looked over his shoulder at Jimmy. "What part of no don't you understand?"

"If it weren't for me and Ed covering your back at work much of the time, you might have lost your business by now. Have you considered that?"

Jim whirled around. "I'm not an alcoholic—and with or without Ed's and your help, I would not have lost my business!"

∞

As Leona prepared for bed that night, her head pounded like a herd of stampeding horses. *I should have listened to Mom when she suggested I not go to school today. It was good to see the kinner again, but I'm not sure it was worth this headache.* She moved across the room to stand in front of her bedroom window. *If I had stayed home, Papa wouldn't have felt the need to ask Abner to give me a ride, either.*

She leaned wearily against the window frame. *I can't believe he actually thought I might be interested in courting someone when it's only been a few months since Ezra died.*

Woof! Woof! Woof!

Leona glanced into the yard below. There sat Cinnamon, staring up at her as if begging to be let in. Leona opened the window and leaned her head out. "You know you can't come inside the house. You'd better go out to the barn or find a comfortable spot on the porch to sleep."

Woof! Woof!

"Hush up, Cinnamon. You'll wake Papa and Mom with all that barking."

Woof!

"Okay, okay, you win. I'll be right down." Leona smiled as the dog wagged its tail and swaggered toward the porch as though she'd won a prize.

Grabbing her cotton robe from a wall peg, Leona slipped quietly out of her room, tiptoed down the stairs, and hurried out the back door.

A chilly wind met her as she stepped outside. She shivered, wrapping her arms around her chest. It might be plenty warm during the day, but nighttime was another matter.

Cinnamon pranced up to Leona, licking her hand as she bent to pet the dog. "I can't stay out here long, but we can sit awhile and listen to the crickets sing if you promise to be real quiet."

The dog answered with a soft whine then flopped down beside Leona when she took a seat on the top porch step. Without an invitation, Cinnamon laid her head in Leona's lap.

"Did you miss me today, girl?" Leona asked, scratching behind Cinnamon's left ear.

The dog gave a quiet grunt.

"I missed you, too." Leona closed her eyes and reflected on her childhood when Cinnamon had been her constant companion.

With her sisters and brother being several years older than she, Leona had little in common with them. Sometimes Leona had felt like an only child, especially after both sisters had gotten married and moved to Kentucky. Arthur always seemed to be busy helping Papa with the painting business. Truth was, even if he had been around home more before he married Doris, Leona was sure he wouldn't have wanted his little sister tagging after him all the time.

So from the time Papa gave her Cinnamon, Leona and the dog had been best friends. Leona rather liked it that way. A dog wasn't likely to place demands on you the way people sometimes did. And a faithful dog loved unconditionally, which was more than could be expected from a lot of folks.

As Cinnamon's heavy breathing turned to soft snores, Leona opened her eyes and stared at the sky. The silver pinpoints overhead reminded her of the Lone Star quilt on her bed. She sat for several minutes watching the stars twinkle, talking to God, and wondering what her future might hold.

Chapter 8

Sure is nice that you and your family could join us for supper tonight," Abraham said, thumping his friend on the back as they followed Lydia and Leona toward the house.

"I'd never pass up a free meal." Jacob chuckled. "Especially not when one of Fannie's delicious turkey potpies is involved."

"We're having banana cake for dessert," Abraham announced. "So be sure you don't eat too much supper."

Lydia glanced over her shoulder and smirked at him. "Oh, you can be sure my husband will eat more than his share this evening." She laughed, along with the others.

When they entered the house, Abraham noticed that Fannie and Mary Ann were scurrying around the kitchen like a couple of excited chickens.

"What can I do to help?" Leona asked.

Abraham's youngest daughter, Mary Ann, smiled and motioned to the table. "The glasses need to be filled with water."

"Okay."

"And what would you like me to do?" Lydia questioned.

"How about cutting some radishes? They're fresh from the garden," Fannie replied.

"Sure, I can do that."

Abraham leaned close to his wife. "Call us when supper's ready."

"Jah, we sure will," she said with a nod.

Abraham brushed Jacob's shoulder as he pointed to the living room. "Make yourself comfortable, and I'll go round up my youngest sons."

A short time later, Abraham sat at the head of the table with Jacob at the other end. The women took their seats on Abraham's left, and his twin sons, who would turn fifteen in the fall, found their way to the bench on the other side of the table. All heads bowed for silent prayer. When Abraham finished his prayer, he cleared his throat and said, "Now, let's eat ourselves full!"

"I know I'll eat my share," Titus announced. At least Abraham thought it was Titus. Sometimes, when the boys were in a teasing mood, they would pretend to be the other twin, wearing each other's clothes and answering to the other brother's name.

He leaned to the left, hoping to get a good look at his son's eyes. Titus had one eye a little bigger than the other.

The boy turned his head before Abraham could get a good look and confirm which twin was speaking. "Say, Bishop Weaver, I've been wonderin' about something."

Jacob forked a couple of Fannie's homemade bread-and-butter pickles onto his plate. "What do you want to know, Timothy? It is Timothy, right?"

"Nope. I'm Titus."

"All right then. What do you want to know, Titus?"

Timothy snickered, and Titus jabbed him in the ribs. "Knock it off!"

Fannie gave both boys a warning glance, and Abraham did the same. "You two had better quit fooling around and eat," he said sternly.

"I was eating till my *mutwillich bruder* decided to stick his bony elbow in my ribs."

"Jah, well, it hasn't only been your brother who's been playful—you've been pretty rambunctious yourself all day, and I've had enough of it." Abraham passed the platter of radishes over to Titus. "Why don't you have a couple of these? They ought to cool ya down some."

"No thanks. I'm sure they're too hot for me."

Jacob chuckled behind his napkin. "Now what was that question you had for me, Titus?"

"I was wonderin' if you're too poor to put a front window glass in your buggy?"

"Don't be rude, son," Abraham said with a shake of his finger. "You surely know that a missing front window is one of the things that distinguish a bishop's buggy from others in this community."

"Are ya *dumm*?" Timothy asked, giving his twin a sidelong glance.

"I ain't dumb," Titus shot back.

Timothy looked over at Jacob and said, "Say, I've got a question of my own."

"What's that?"

"I was wonderin' if anyone's ever fallen asleep during one of your long sermons."

Jacob slid his finger down the side of his nose and squinted. "Hmm. . . Well, there was this one time when Harley King dozed off. Deacon Paul sat near me, so I leaned over and whispered in his ear, 'Would ya please wake up the brother who's fallen asleep?' "

Timothy plunked his elbows on the table and leaned slightly forward. "What happened then?"

Jacob grunted. "The helpful deacon looked me right in the eye and said, 'It was you who put him to sleep, so you're the one who oughta wake him up.' "

A round of laughter filled the room.

"I'd like to know something else," Titus piped up.

"That'll be enough with the questions." Abraham stared hard at his son, for this time he had a clear view of the boy's eyes. Neither one looked any bigger than the other did, so he knew it must be Timothy sitting closest to him, not Titus. "Say, are you two tryin' to pull a fast one?"

"What do you mean, Papa?" Timothy asked, rather sheepishly.

"I know which of you is which, so you can quit trying to fool everyone. And since you've been actin' silly all day, you can both clear the table and wash the dishes after we're done eating."

Titus opened his mouth to protest, but another jab to the ribs from his brother kept the boy quiet.

Abraham stuck his spoon in his potpie and popped a piece of turkey into his mouth. There were times, like now, when he wanted to throttle his youngest sons. Even so, he was glad the good Lord had given him and Fannie such a miracle when the twins were born. They hadn't taken Zach's place, but they'd sure filled a big hole in his heart, and he loved them dearly.

During the drive home from the Fishers', Leona reflected on the pleasant evening they'd had. Other than the twins acting like a couple of silly kinner, there had been amiable conversation around the table during supper, and for most of the evening, she'd been able to think about something other than how much she still missed Ezra.

When the meal was over, the women had gathered on the front porch to chat, while the men retired to the living room for a game of checkers. Titus and Timothy had spent the remainder of their evening in the kitchen but didn't finish with the dishes until it was time for dessert.

Leona smiled to herself, thinking what it was like when she'd had the twins in her classroom. On more than one occasion, they had both tried to pass themselves off for the other brother. Sometimes they'd managed to fool the entire class—including their teacher. The boys liked to pull a few pranks now and then, too, but they'd never done anything harmful.

As soon as the Weavers pulled into their yard, Leona realized another buggy was parked near the barn.

"Looks like Abner Lapp's rig," Papa commented.

Leona held onto her skirt and climbed down from the buggy without saying a word. *I hope Papa didn't set this up.*

Abner waved and stepped off the front porch, where he'd obviously been waiting. "Came by half an hour ago," he said, heading toward them with his usual bowlegged walk. "Figured since it was gettin' dark, you'd be home most anytime."

Papa headed quickly for the barn, leading the horse, and Mom glanced over at Leona with raised eyebrows. Leona started for the house, mumbling a quick hello to Abner as she approached the spot where he stood. "Papa's gone to the barn."

Abner smiled. "It's you I came to see, Leona, not your daed."

Leona looked at her mamm, who had just caught up to her. She hoped Mom might come to her rescue, but she only smiled, shrugged, and went inside the house.

Not wishing to hurt Abner's feelings, Leona seated herself on the porch swing. Abner followed suit. "I came by to see if you knew about the wood-stacking bee that's to be held next Saturday at my grandpa Lapp's place," he said.

She kept her gaze on the sky, colored a pale yellow flushed with pink on the rim of the horizon. "I heard something about it."

"Were you planning to go?"

"I'll have to wait and see." Leona scanned the front yard, wondering if Cinnamon might show up. She didn't think Abner cared much for the dog. If Cinnamon made an appearance, maybe Abner would make a hasty exit.

Abner leaned toward her, but just then, Leona's mamm opened the screen door. "I hate to interrupt,

Leona, but I need your help with something."

Leona stood, sighing with relief. "You'll have to excuse me, Abner. Maybe we can visit some other time."

"Jah, sure. Guess I'll head out to the barn and say hello to your daed." He stood, shuffled his feet a few times, and mumbled, "Hope to see you on Saturday."

Leona gave a quick nod then scurried into the house.

∞

As soon as his dad left the room, Jimmy reached for the cordless phone, which had been lying on the small table near the end of the couch. He punched in Allen's number and headed to the basement while he waited for one of the Walters to answer his call.

He had just entered his darkroom when Allen's voice came over the phone. "Hello?"

"Hi, it's me."

"Hey, buddy, it's good to hear from you. How's it going?"

"Not so great. My dad still hasn't phoned that lawyer, and we nearly got into an argument when he said he was going to the kitchen for some beer."

"Has he been staying sober lately?"

"Yeah, but he has to have a drink or two almost every night."

"Did you talk to him about going to AA or ask if he'd see our pastor for some counseling?" Allen asked.

Jimmy sank to the stool in front of the desk where he kept all his negatives. "He won't even admit he's got a drinking problem, much less agree to get any help."

"Sorry to hear that. Guess there's not much you can do except to pray for him."

"I'm afraid he's going to lose his business if he doesn't get his life straightened out soon."

"Some people have to hit rock bottom before they'll admit they have a problem and get help."

"I know." Jimmy moaned. "He uses every excuse in the book to drink, and I'm not sure how much longer I can keep covering for him at work."

"You shouldn't have to cover for him. He's a grown man and needs to be responsible for his own actions." After a brief pause, Allen added, "Remember when Holly spoke to our Sunday school class?"

"Yeah."

"She mentioned that those who live with alcoholics are often enablers and that they have to practice tough love."

"I remember."

"So that's what you need to do, Jimmy. You've got to quit covering for your dad and allow him to sink or swim."

"Yeah, maybe so." Jimmy paused. "Well, I'd better go. I want to get a few pictures developed, and then I'm going to bed. We're still working on that big grocery store, and I'm sure Dad will want to get an early start tomorrow morning."

"Okay. Keep looking up. And remember, I'll be praying for you and your dad."

"Thanks, I appreciate that." Jimmy hung up the phone and closed his eyes. "Oh, Lord, give me the courage to do whatever I need to do concerning my dad—and show me what to do about finding my birth parents."

Chapter 9

I'm heading to Tacoma to run some errands. I told Ed if he has any questions, he can ask you."

Jimmy set his paint roller over the top of the bucket at his feet and turned to look at his dad. "Won't you have your cell phone on?"

"Yeah, sure, but I don't want to be bothered with twenty questions."

"How long will you be gone?"

"I don't know. All depends on how long it takes me to get everything done."

"Will you be back by noon?"

"Probably. See you later, Jimmy."

"Oh, hey, wait a minute."

"What? I'm in a hurry." Dad started walking and didn't even look back.

Jimmy rushed to his dad's side. "I was wondering if you called the lawyer in Maryland this morning."

"Not yet. I haven't had time. I'll do it later."

"East Coast time is three hours ahead of us," Jimmy reminded. "So you'd better make the call before—"

Dad screeched to a halt and glared at Jimmy. "I'm not stupid! I know how to tell time."

"I never said you didn't. I just wanted to be sure you—"

"I said I would call, so get off my back!" Dad climbed into his van and slammed the door.

"Whew! He's sure testy today, isn't he?" Ed stepped up beside Jimmy as his dad peeled out of the parking lot. "Or maybe I should say he's testier than usual."

Jimmy nodded and mumbled, "He needs help."

"What was that?"

"Oh, nothing. I'd better get back to work. This store won't paint itself."

∞

"Guder mariye," Leona said as she and her friend Mary Ann walked up the path leading to Herman and Bertha Lapp's home, where there was to be an all-day wood-stacking bee.

"Good morning." Mary Ann smiled, her evenly matched dimples looking more pronounced than usual. "I'm doin' all right. How 'bout you?"

"Okay, I guess."

"Are you still having those headaches?"

"Jah, but they've gotten some better since I started seeing Mom's chiropractor. He thinks my neck went out of alignment when that ball hit my face."

"Guess that makes sense." Mary Ann leaned closer. "Are you dealin' with Ezra's death any better yet?"

Leona winced as though she'd been slapped. "How could I? I doubt my heart will ever mend."

Mary Ann turned her palms upward and shrugged. "Of course it will. Once an open wound has turned to a scar, it's not so hard to deal with."

Leona kept on walking. Mary Ann didn't know what it felt like to lose the man she loved. She'd never gotten serious enough about any of the men who had courted her to want to get married. Some said she was too particular, but Leona figured Mary Ann was either holding out for the right man or she just preferred to remain *en alt maede* at twenty-five years of age. On one hand, the thought of being an old maid at such an age seemed absurd, but most Amish women were married by then. *Of course*, Leona reminded herself, *I'm not so far behind my friend, so I guess we'll both be old maids together.*

Mary Ann gave Leona's arm a gentle squeeze. "Let's

try to have fun today, okay?"

"Jah, sure."

"Oh, I almost forgot to tell you that starting Monday I'll be working in Abby's quilt shop."

"That's good. You've become an expert quilter, so I'm sure you'll do real well there."

"I hope so. Abby says they're so busy that she and her daughter, Stella, can hardly keep up." Mary Ann pivoted toward the Lapps' house, which was connected to the home where their eldest son, William, lived with his wife and six children. "Guess we'd best get into the kitchen and see what needs to be done."

Leona followed Mary Ann up the steps and onto the back porch. She was about to go inside the house when someone called her name.

"Leona. I'm glad to see you made it today."

She turned and saw Abner stroll up the walk, pushing a wheelbarrow filled with split poplar wood. His face was red and sweaty, and streaks of dirt dotted his blue shirt.

"I came to help in the kitchen."

"Figured that's what you were here for."

She dipped her head. "Well, I'd best be getting inside."

"Okay. See you at noon if not before." Abner headed for the growing stack of wood piled alongside the shed.

Leona hurried into the house, anxious to get to work—and as far away from Abner as possible.

∞

As Naomi put the OPEN sign in the store window, she thought about the wood-stacking bee that was probably going full force by now. She'd been hoping to go and help serve food to the men, but tourist season had already begun in Lancaster County, and they'd had an abundance of customers in the past few weeks. It wouldn't be right to leave Caleb alone to run the store, even if she had left the children behind to help out. All hands were needed on the busiest days, and Saturdays, especially during the summer months, were the most hectic of all.

Naomi glanced into the adjoining quilt shop where Abby and Stella were stacking bolts of fabric onto shelves. *I wonder if Abby wishes she could have taken the time to attend the wood-stacking bee. She's been so busy lately that she hardly has time for a lunch break, so it's a good thing my little sister will begin helping her and Stella next week.* She folded her arms and smiled. *I'm glad to have someone as sweet and kind as Abby for a sister-in-law. Poor thing went through a lot when she first came to Pennsylvania to help her mamm, and it's good to see her so happy now.*

Abby was a good wife to Naomi's older brother, and the Lord had blessed them with five special kinner. Naomi knew that if Abby hadn't allowed God to heal her heart after she lost Lester she and Matthew might never have gotten together.

"You gonna stand there all day starin' into the other room with a silly grin on your face, or do ya plan to help me unload those boxes of books that came in yesterday afternoon?" Caleb touched Naomi's arm as he spoke.

She turned to face him and smiled. "I was thinking about the past and how God has taken so many bad things that have happened to our family and turned them into something good."

"That's because God is good and full of blessings."

Naomi nodded. "Jah, no truer words were ever spoken."

❦

Leona pushed a wayward strand of hair away from her face where it had worked its way loose from under her kapp. She and the other six women who'd come to cook for the men had been busy all day. Besides the two stockpots of homemade noodles and a kettle of wieners they had served for lunch, they'd taken turns running back and forth with jugs of water, coffee, and iced tea for the men to drink whenever they needed a break from the woodcutting, hauling, and stacking. For dessert, they'd served store-bought ice cream and some of Bertha Lapp's delicious peanut butter cookies. By three o'clock, most of the wood had been hauled over to the pile, and the remaining pieces were now being stacked by the men while the boys and young women began a game of volleyball.

"Looks like they're havin' fun out there," Mary Ann said, staring wistfully out the kitchen window as she and Leona finished up the last of the dishes needing to be washed and dried.

Bertha stepped between them. "There's no reason the two of you can't join the game. Fannie's still here, so she and I can finish up."

"That's right," Fannie agreed. "You two go have yourselves a little fun in the sun."

"You can play ball if you want to," Leona said to her friend. "I think I'll just watch from a chair on the porch."

Mary Ann tipped her head. "I thought you liked to play volleyball. Always did when we were kinner."

"I do enjoy playing, but I won't chance getting hit in the face with the ball and reinjuring my naas."

"That makes sense." Mary Ann dried her hands on a towel, and she and Leona scooted out the door.

For the next hour, Leona sat in a wicker chair, alternating between watching the game in progress and staring at the sky, which had suddenly grown dark.

"Looks like we might be in for a storm."

Leona jumped at the sound of Abner's deep voice.

"Jah, the wind's picked up considerably in the last few minutes," she said, wrapping her arms around her middle and suppressing a shiver.

Abner tromped up the steps, his knees bowed slightly, and dropped into the chair next to Leona's. He looked over at her with a crooked grin. "Wonder if we'll get some *wedderleech* and *dunner*."

"I hope not. It will be hard enough to drive home in the rain, and if there's lightning and thunder, my horse will become skittish, the way she always does in a storm."

"Guess everyone will have to hang out here till the storm passes."

"How come you're not out there playing ball with the others?" she asked.

He shrugged and ran his fingers through the sides of his dark hair. "Aw, I'd probably just make a fool of myself."

A clap of thunder cut off Leona's reply. Suddenly, a burst of wind came up, lifting the trampoline that was used by the Lapps' grandchildren high into the air. She watched in horror as it sailed over the wood-shed, making two holes in the roof and landing upside down on the ground several feet away. Everyone who'd been playing ball rushed toward the house, and the men who'd been stacking wood made a mad dash for the barn.

"That was unbelievable!" Abner shouted, rising to his feet. "I've never seen anything like it before. Have you?"

Leona shook her head.

"Guess we'd better wait awhile before we head for home," Mary Ann said as she stepped onto the porch.

Leona stood. "Think I'll go in the house and see if my help is needed. Bertha might have some refreshments she wants to serve." She hurried away, leaving Abner to stand beside Mary Ann.

∞

As Jimmy pulled his pickup into the driveway, he frowned. Dad's van was parked at an odd angle. He'd either been in a hurry when he got home or he was drunk. Jimmy suspected the latter, because his dad hadn't returned to the job site today, nor had he answered any of Jimmy's phone calls. It was his usual pattern whenever he decided to go on a bender; only sometimes Dad didn't come home until the next morning, and then he would be out of sorts and worthless for days.

Jimmy gritted his teeth. "He'd better not be drunk, because if he is, I'm going to—" What was he going to do? Go to work tomorrow morning and cover for his dad, the way he'd done countless other times? Tiptoe around the house, sidestepping Dad and cleaning up the mess he always made when he drank himself sick?

"I'm getting tired of this," Jimmy mumbled as he exited his truck. From what he could remember, when Mom was alive, his dad's drinking hadn't been so bad. Dad had always been one to have a few too many beers now and then, but he never used to come home drunk or allow his work to become affected by his drinking. Dad's drinking binges had become more frequent in recent years, and it had fallen on Jimmy's shoulders to hold everything together at home, as well as on the job.

Maybe this time will be different, he thought. *Dad may have forgotten to turn his cell phone on, and he may have had more errands to run than he first thought. He could be in the house right now, starting supper.* He let himself in through the back door and soon discovered that the kitchen was empty. There was no sign of his dad's lunch box where he usually left it. "Dad, I'm home!" Jimmy called, stepping into the hallway.

All he heard was the steady *tick-tock, tick-tock* of the

grandfather clock.

"Where are you, Dad?" Jimmy stepped into the living room and halted. There lay his dad on the living room floor with five empty beer bottles on the coffee table and another one in the curled fingers of his hand.

Jimmy groaned and dropped to his knees beside his dad. *Well, at least he's still breathing.* He shook the man's shoulders. "Wake up, Dad. You need to get off the floor. Come on, I'll help you get upstairs to bed."

His dad's head lulled to one side, and he moaned. "I did it for you, Linda. You wanted a baby. . .so I gave you one. . .the only way I knew how."

Even though the words were slurred, Jimmy knew what his dad had said. He'd obviously been using the fact that Jimmy knew about his adoption as an excuse to get drunk. *Dad must feel guilty because he couldn't give Mom any children of his own.*

"Come on, Dad. You've got to get up."

No response except for a loud hiccup.

"You can't stay on the floor all night." Jimmy shook his dad's shoulder again, but the only reply he got was a plea for more beer. "I'm not getting you anything more to drink. You need to sleep this off, but not here on the living-room floor."

Dad closed his eyes, and his heavy breathing turned to loud snores.

Sometimes family members can be enablers. You need to practice tough love. His friend's recent admonition echoed in Jimmy's ears. "I know Allen's right, but it's a lot easier said than done," Jimmy mumbled. He squeezed his eyes shut and opened them again. Rising to his feet, he grabbed the lightweight throw from the couch, threw it across his dad's chest, and left the room. It was time for Dad to sink or swim. It was time for Jimmy to make a decision.

Chapter 10

Jim's eyelids felt heavy as he struggled to sit up. He blinked against the invading light streaming in through the window and glanced around the living room. *What am I doing here, and what's that horrible smell?* As his eyes began to focus and reality set in, he realized that he was wearing the same white shirt and painter's pants he'd had on yesterday, and the putrid smell was his own body odor, combined with the pile of vomit not far from where he lay.

Where's Jimmy? Why didn't he put me to bed like he always does whenever I can't make it there on my own?

Jim moaned as he stood on shaky legs. There seemed to be no way to hold his head that didn't hurt. *I need some coffee and a couple of aspirin. I need—*

He glanced at the mess he'd made on the carpet and grimaced. *I need Jimmy—where's Jimmy?*

He stumbled out to the kitchen, figuring Jimmy might be there making coffee, even though his nose told him otherwise. Maybe Jimmy was still in bed or had left for work already, figuring Jim would be too hung over to make it today.

When Jim realized Jimmy wasn't in the kitchen, he staggered over to the coffeemaker and was about to reach for the pot when he saw an envelope lying on the counter with his name on it. *Jimmy must have left me a note so I'd know he's gone to work without me.*

He got the coffee going, took a seat at the table, and ripped open the envelope.

Dad,
   I think I know what triggered this recent

bender, but it's still no excuse. I've got a feeling the reason you still haven't called that lawyer in Maryland is because you're afraid if I find my real parents that I won't love you anymore or might not come home.

Jim moistened his lips and squinted at the page. *Come home? Has Jimmy gone somewhere?*

He read on.

Last night after I found you passed out on the living room floor, I made a decision. Since I'm the one who was adopted, it's really my job to search for information about my biological parents, not yours. So I left for Maryland early this morning. I'll let you know as soon as I find out anything.

Take care, Dad. I'll be in touch.

Love,
Jimmy

Jim let the note slip to the floor as he dropped his head to the table. "Oh, Jimmy, what have you done?"

❦

On Monday afternoon, Leona entered the schoolhouse and glanced around the room. She'd come to see what all needed to be done before the school year began in August. As soon as she had lit a kerosene lamp, she pulled out the chair at her desk, took a seat, and opened the top drawer, withdrawing a tablet and pen. She wrote the following list:

1. *Outside and inside of building need to be painted.*
2. *Roof leaks and needs to be patched.*

3. *Need a new blackboard—one of those white ones that use an erasable marking pen rather than chalk.*

4. *Floors and desks need to be cleaned and polished.*

Leona's list making came to a halt when a horse and buggy trotted into the school yard. The horse's hooves clip-clopped against the gravel, and the animal neighed as it came to a stop. Leona went to the door, pleased to discover Mary Ann climbing down from her buggy.

"Wie geht's?" Leona called.

"I'm doing good, danki."

"What brings you out here in the middle of the day?" Leona asked when her friend joined her on the porch. "I figured you'd be working at the quilt shop all afternoon."

"Actually, I am working today. I'm on my way over to Margaret Byler's place to pick up some quilts she has ready to sell."

Leona opened the door and led the way into the schoolhouse. "How come Margaret didn't bring them to the store herself?"

"Yesterday at church, her granddaughter mentioned that Margaret had come down with the flu and was home in bed."

"That's a shame." Leona clucked her tongue. "I hope you won't be exposed to the bug by going over to the Bylers' house."

"I won't be there long, and someone in the family will probably have the quilts ready when I arrive." Mary Ann smiled. "I was wondering if you're planning to go to the singing this Sunday night. It's to be held in my daed's barn, you know."

Before Leona could formulate a response, Mary Ann added, "You've missed the last couple of young people's gatherings, and I think it would be good for you to get out and do something fun for a change."

"I'll probably be busy that night."

Mary Ann squinted. "Want to know what I think?"

"What's that?"

"You work too hard and need to socialize more."

Leona took a seat at her desk and motioned to the tablet lying before her. "Busy schoolteachers always have something to do."

"But it's summer, and you shouldn't be working here now."

"I'm making a list of the things that need to be done before school starts, and there's also some cleaning and organizing I want to do yet."

Mary Ann placed one hand on the desk. "But you won't be working on Sunday, and when it's time to get the schoolhouse ready, the students' parents will help with the repairs and cleaning. So there's no excuse for you not to come to the singing or any other social event that might be held this summer."

"I don't feel much like socializing these days, but I'll think about it."

"Jah, okay." Mary Ann turned toward the door. "Guess I'd best be on my way or Abby will wonder what's taking me so long."

Leona lifted her hand in a wave. "See you later then."

∞

Jim left the house around noon after phoning Ed to say he would be late. Then he headed for the Tacoma Mall, hoping to stop at the health food store again to see what else they might have for his nerves. He'd tried to call Jimmy several times but had only gotten his voice mail. He needed to talk to Jimmy before he got to Maryland.

A short time later, he pulled his van into the mall parking lot and turned off the engine. When he entered the health food store, he discovered Holly was waiting on a customer. Not wishing to interrupt, he wandered up and down the aisles looking at various vitamins and herbal preparations.

"It's nice to see you again, Jim. May I help you with something?" Holly asked as she stepped up to him a few minutes later.

He smiled, feeling rather self-conscious yet pleased that she had remembered his name. "I'm. . .uh. . .feeling kind of shaky today, and I was hoping you might have something else I could try for my nerves."

"Didn't that homeopathic remedy you bought help any?"

"It did at first, but I'm still having a hard time sleeping, and. . .well, I'm kind of going through a rough time right now, so I really could use—"

"I know all about the problem of not sleeping," she said. "Plus I've dealt with a host of other things that affected my health for some time."

Jim studied the woman a few seconds. Her pale-blue eyes and blond hair, worn short and fringed around her cheeks, looked even healthier than he had remembered. He couldn't imagine that she'd ever had any kind of health problems.

"I'm a recovered alcoholic," Holly said. "I'm not proud of my past, but with God's help and the support of Alcoholics Anonymous, I've remained sober for the past ten years."

Jim's mouth dropped open. He never would have guessed that this pretty, pleasant woman had ever had a drinking problem. *I wonder what got her started? Could she have had a troubled marriage or been dealing with guilt from her past, like me? Could Holly be the recovering alcoholic Jimmy had mentioned not long ago?*

"You seem surprised by my confession." Her lips curved into a smile. "Just because I go to church every

Sunday doesn't mean I've lived my life on Easy Street. Accepting Christ as my Savior was the first step to my recovery, but I had to do many other things to help myself, too."

Jim thought about his own problem with alcohol, but it was nothing he couldn't control; he wasn't about to tell someone he barely knew that he had awakened on the living-room floor this morning because he'd had a few too many beers last night.

Holly pointed to the shelf in front of her. "I've got several things here that might help you sleep, but of course none of them will be as strong as what a doctor might prescribe."

"That's okay. I don't need any more drugs," he mumbled.

"What was that?"

"Nothing. Just give me some herbs to help me relax, and I'm sure I'll be good to go."

∞

Jimmy loosened his grip on the steering wheel and tried to relax. He'd never made a trip this far alone. For that matter, he and his folks had never driven any farther than to one of the ocean beaches or down to Boise to see his mom's parents.

"They've never really been my grandparents," he muttered, squinting against the glint of the morning sun on his truck's window. "And neither were Grandma and Grandpa Scott." He clicked on the radio, hoping to diffuse his thoughts with some mellow music. The only stations he could pick up either played repetitious country songs or broadcast the local news. Remembering that he'd brought along some of his favorite Christian CDs, he finally popped one into the CD player. "Ah, that's better."

Jimmy hummed along with the music for a while, keeping his focus on the road and his thoughts off his unknown future. If he were to find his birth mother, then what? He couldn't just march up to her and announce, "Hi, my name's Jimmy Scott, and I'm the son you gave up for adoption twenty years ago." He'd never been in a situation like this before, and he had no idea what he would say or do if he were to meet either his biological mother or father face-to-face.

Jimmy drew in a deep breath and tried to relax. There was no point thinking about any of this until he had something to go on. "I need to trust God to give me the right words—if and when the time comes for me to meet my real parents."

Chapter 11

W hat are you doing home in the middle of the day?" Lydia asked when her husband stepped into the kitchen around three o'clock.

Jacob grinned and hung his straw hat on a wall peg near the door. "My crew's paintin' Daniel King's barn, and since it's not so far from here, I thought I'd run home and give my fraa a great big hug." He took a few steps toward her, and Lydia went willingly into his arms.

"I've always known you were a fine painter, Jacob Weaver," she said, closing her eyes and leaning against his chest. "And ever since the day you were chosen by lots to be our new bishop, I was sure you would be a good one." She gave him a squeeze. "But to my way of thinking, the thing you're the best at is being a loving, *schmaert* husband and father."

He leaned down and kissed her gently on the mouth. Then Lydia opened her eyes and reached up to stroke his long, full beard, which seemed to have more gray than brown in it these days. She felt blessed to be married to such a caring, considerate man. He had not only looked out for her needs these nearly thirty-six years they'd been together—and for their children's needs, as well—but he guided, comforted, and befriended his entire flock.

"So, then, have ya got anything cold to drink for your smart husband?" Jacob asked. "It's sure a hot, sticky day out there. Can't believe how warm it's gotten already this year."

Lydia eased out of his embrace and tipped her head to one side. "Ah, so that's the reason you came by the house. I'll bet you were hoping to have a few cookies to go with that cold drink, jah?"

His hazel eyes twinkled, and he chuckled, which made his beard jiggle up and down. "Some cookies and a cool drink would be good, but that's not the only reason I dropped by to see you, my love."

Lydia clucked her tongue as she headed to the refrigerator. "We aren't a couple of young sweethearts anymore, so you don't have to say things like that to get me to pour you a glass of iced tea." She glanced over her shoulder. "Or would you rather have some cold goat's milk?"

Jacob ambled across the room and pulled out a chair. "Milk and cookies would be fine and dandy."

A few minutes later, they were both seated at the table with tall glasses of milk and a plate piled high with molasses cookies.

"Umm... These cookies are sure tasty," he said, smacking his lips and lifting his eyebrows until they nearly disappeared into his hairline.

"Danki. I'm glad you like 'em."

"What's our youngest daughter up to today?" Jacob asked. "I figured she might be out workin' in the garden this afternoon, but I didn't see any sign of her when I pulled into the yard."

"She went over to the schoolhouse soon after lunch. Said she wanted to do some cleaning and make a list of things that need to be done before school starts."

He nodded. "It won't be long till the kinner's summer break is over. I'm thinkin' the outside of the school will need to be painted before then. That will no doubt be on her list."

"Jah, I'm sure you're right about that."

"You think our daughter's gonna be okay, Lydia?" Jacob asked as he rubbed the bridge of his nose.

"Well, I know she's still havin' some headaches, but I believe after a few more visits with the chiropractor, she'll be good as new."

He shook his head. "I wasn't talkin' about her physical condition. I was referrin' to her broken heart. She's not really been the same since Ezra died."

A knock sounded at the back door. Lydia stood. "I'd best see who's come a-calling."

When she opened the door, she was surprised to see Abner Lapp standing on the front porch. "Is Leona here?" he asked.

"She's not at home just now."

His dark eyebrows lifted under his straw hat as he frowned. "She ain't, huh?"

"Sorry, no."

"Mind if I ask when she might be home?"

"She's gone over to the schoolhouse to get some work done, and I doubt she'll be here much before supper."

Abner nodded. "Guess I'll drive on over there, 'cause I need to talk to her about Emanuel."

Lydia pursed her lips. "Your little bruder isn't still blamin' himself for Leona's accident, is he?"

Abner shrugged. "I'm not sure, but all of a sudden, he's sayin' he doesn't want to go back to school when it starts up again in August, and I'm hopin' Leona might have some idea what I can do to persuade him. Short of me takin' a board to the seat of his pants, that is."

Before Lydia could respond, Jacob joined them at the door. "Maybe I should have a talk with the boy. I was always able to get through to my kinner—even Arthur, my headstrong one—without having to resort to physical punishment."

Abner smiled. "That'd be much appreciated. Since I'm only Emanuel's big bruder and not his daed, it's hard on our relationship when I have to discipline too much."

"I'll drive on over to your place sometime this week and have a little heart-to-heart with Emanuel then,"

Jacob said with a nod.

"Danki." Abner turned and started down the porch steps. "Tell Leona I'm sorry I missed her," he called over his shoulder.

Lydia watched Abner climb into his buggy and drive away, and then she turned to Jacob and said, "*Er is en erschtaunlicher mann*—he's an astonishing man. He seems a bit shy, but he's sure devoted to his family, and in my estimation, that says a whole lot." She sighed. "I know it's probably too soon for Leona to think about courting, but maybe in the days ahead, she and Abner will get together."

Jacob grinned and reached for her hand. "That's what I've been thinkin', too."

∞

When Leona opened the schoolhouse door, about to empty the bucket of water she'd used to clean the floor, she was surprised to see Abner Lapp climb down from his buggy. She had been so busy scrubbing that she hadn't heard him drive up.

"I stopped by your house to see you," he called, "but your mamm said you were over here."

She set the bucket on the porch. "Jah, I'm doing a bit of cleaning."

He stepped onto the porch and removed his straw hat. "I thought a group of parents would be doin' that."

She nodded. "Several are planning to come by in the next week or so to help with some other cleaning and repairs, but I thought as long as I was here I'd do a few things on my own."

"I see." Abner shuffled his boots a couple of times and stared down at the porch. "Wanted to tell you that Emanuel's been sayin' he doesn't want to attend school next term." He leaned against the porch railing and folded his arms. "But your daed said he'd have a talk with him, so that might be enough. I sure don't want to have to force the boy to go, but I will if it becomes necessary."

If you think Papa speaking to Emanuel will be enough, then what are you doing here? Leona wondered as a sense of irritation rose in her chest. *Did Papa send Abner out to the schoolhouse in the hopes of getting the two of us together?*

Before Leona could comment, Abner spoke again. "I wasn't going to bother you with this, since your daed made his offer to help, but I wanted you to know what's going on, too."

She pursed her lips. Emanuel had given her a few problems after his daed died, and though she knew the boy didn't like to study, she'd had no idea he disliked school so much that he didn't want to come back for the next term. "Maybe it's me Emanuel doesn't like."

"Now why would you be sayin' that?"

"I was thinking—if he got in trouble with either you or your mamm because of the ball that hit me in the face, maybe he's blaming me for whatever punishment he received." Leona's pupils were all she had now that she was destined to be an old maid, and the thought of any of them not liking her sent shivers up her spine.

Abner shook his head. "I never really punished the boy, except to give him a lecture on being careful where his aim was whenever he acted as pitcher. Besides, he felt really bad about your naas gettin' broke, and if he didn't like you, I doubt he would have kept askin' me to drive him over to your place so's he could see you."

A sense of relief came over Leona as she thought it all through. Emanuel had seemed genuinely sorry for throwing the ball, and he'd never given her any reason to believe he didn't like her.

"Guess I should be gettin' on home," Abner said.

"Danki for takin' the time to talk to me, Leona."

"I'll try to think of some ways to convince Emanuel that he needs to come back to school—just in case my daed doesn't get through to him," she said.

Abner smiled, and his cheeks turned a light shade of pink. "Wish I'd had a teacher as nice as you when I attended school."

Unsure of what to say to that comment, Leona merely nodded and mumbled, "See you at preaching service on Sunday, Abner."

❦

As Jimmy drove into the town of Bel Air, his stomach tumbled like a cement mixer. He'd gone online and done a search for the lawyer's address and phone number before he'd left home, and then he had called and made an appointment for four o'clock this afternoon.

What if he refuses to give me any information? What if he doesn't know where my real mother is? Jimmy's head swam with unanswered questions, and as he pulled into the parking lot in front of Carl Stevens's office, he knew he had to pray.

"Dear Lord, please slow my racing heart. Put the right words on my tongue. Let me leave here with enough information to begin my search for the woman who gave birth to me. Amen."

Jimmy climbed out of the truck and entered the building feeling a little less anxious than he had before his prayer.

"May I help you?" a middle-aged, redheaded woman asked when Jimmy stepped up to the reception desk.

He nodded and wiped his sweaty palms along the sides of his jeans. "I'm Jimmy Scott, and I have a four o'clock appointment with Mr. Stevens."

She glanced at her computer screen and said, "Mr.

Stevens is running a little behind this afternoon, but he'll be with you shortly." She motioned to a group of chairs sitting against the far wall. "You can wait over there."

"Okay, thanks." Jimmy took a seat and picked up a magazine from the nearby table. He thumbed through a couple of pages and glanced at his watch—the one his dad had given him for his birthday. *I hope Dad understands why I haven't answered any of the messages he's left on my voice mail. I can't deal with talking to him right now. He'd only try to convince me to come home.* Jimmy grimaced. *If Dad had called Mr. Stevens like he said he was going to, I might not have felt the need to come here on my own.*

"Mr. Scott?"

Jimmy's thoughts came to a halt when the receptionist called his name. He stood.

"Mr. Stevens isn't ready to see you yet, but I was wondering if you would like a cup of coffee or something cold to drink?"

"Uh, yeah, I guess so."

"Which would you like?"

"Something cold would be great."

"We have several kinds of soda. Do you have a favorite?"

When Jimmy said any kind of soda would be fine, the receptionist opened a small refrigerator behind her desk and handed him a bottle of grape soda. "Would you like a glass?"

"No, thanks. This is fine." Jimmy opened the bottle and took a big gulp.

He'd just finished the last of the soda when the receptionist said, "Mr. Stevens will see you now." She opened the door to her left and motioned Jimmy inside.

A young man with dark hair and metal-framed glasses greeted Jimmy when he stepped into the office.

"I have an appointment with Carl Stevens," Jimmy said, glancing around the room. If Dad had met Mr. Stevens twenty years ago, then he knew the man standing before him couldn't be the same lawyer.

"I'm Carl Stevens."

"But. . .but, I was expecting a much older man," Jimmy stammered.

The young man smiled, and his blue eyes twinkled. "Did you think you'd made an appointment with Carl Stevens Sr.?"

"I guess so."

"That would be my father. He's retired now. I'm Carl Stevens Jr., and I took over Dad's practice five years ago."

Jimmy felt as if the wind had been knocked out of him. If this wasn't the lawyer who had initiated his adoption proceedings, then he had probably made the trip for nothing.

Carl nodded to the straight-backed chair in front of his desk. "Have a seat, and you can tell me why you're here."

Jimmy sank to the chair, and Carl seated himself in the leather chair behind a mammoth oak desk. "I. . . uh. . .I'm not sure you can help me, but my dad—my adoptive dad—came here twenty years ago to get me." He felt moisture on his forehead and reached up to swipe it away. "Your dad—Carl Stevens Sr.—was the lawyer handling the adoption case."

Carl Jr. nodded. "I see."

Jimmy squirmed restlessly, trying to find a comfortable position and wishing he knew what to say.

"So what is it you want from me?"

"Actually, it was your dad I wanted information from, but since he's no longer practicing law, maybe you might—would you still have the adoption records that took place twenty years ago?"

"I'm sure we would, but you should know up front that a lawyer is bound by client confidentiality, so even if I were to find those records, I wouldn't be able to tell you the name of your birth parents."

Jimmy's heart felt as if it had dropped clear to his toes. Had he driven all this way for nothing? "Isn't there anything you could tell me? Maybe what hospital I was born in, or—"

"I'll tell you what," Carl interrupted. "Let me go in the back room and check through some old filing cabinets, and I'll see if I can come up with anything helpful for you."

"Thanks, I'd appreciate it."

Carl grabbed a pen and a tablet from his desk. "What are your adoptive parents' names, and when was the date of the adoption?"

"Jim and Linda Scott, and it took place twenty years ago. It was sometime in June, but I'm not sure of the exact date. I was one year old at the time."

"Okay. Be right back." Carl stood and exited the room.

While Jimmy waited, he reached into his jeans and pulled out his pocket change; determined to keep his mind busy and his hands from shaking, he began to count the coins. Once he'd counted the fistful of money, he glanced at his watch, wondering how long it might take Carl to find the information he'd gone looking for.

When he'd confirmed the amount of loose change in his pockets at least ten times and the lawyer still wasn't back, he stood and began to pace between the window and the watercooler. Traffic was steady on the street out front, and he wondered if it would take him long to find the hotel where he'd made reservations to spend the night.

He stopped in front of the watercooler and was thinking about getting a drink when the door opened.

Carl stepped back into the room with a nod. "Sorry to keep you waiting."

"That's okay." Jimmy took a seat again, and the lawyer did the same.

"I'm afraid I've got bad news," Carl said. "I did find a Jim and Linda Scott in our database, but the adoption my dad had begun on their behalf fell through when the birth mother changed her mind and decided to keep her baby."

Jimmy's mouth dropped open, and once more his lungs felt breathless. "But that can't be. My mom—my adoptive mom—wrote me a letter before she died. She said my dad had come here alone to pick me up because she'd had a headache that day. She told me how excited she'd been when Dad came back to the hotel with me in his arms." He stared at the lawyer. "How could that have happened if there'd been no adoption?"

Carl shrugged. "I have no idea, but if there was an adoption, it didn't take place in this office." He tapped his pen along the edge of the desk. "Even if there were another adoption, then it couldn't have happened the same day your dad came here. It would have taken some time for him to find another lawyer and begin new adoption proceedings."

Too numb to move, too confused to respond, Jimmy sat silently. *If I'm not the baby Dad came to pick up that day, then who am I, and where did he get me?*

Chapter 12

Leona reclined on an old quilt by the pond near their home. With Cinnamon lying contently by her side, she stared at the sky, noting the pale blue graduating to a deeper color. She relished the peace and quiet after her private picnic lunch.

A cool breeze tickled her nose, and she breathed in the fresh scent of the wildflowers growing nearby. She reached over and patted Cinnamon's head. The Irish setter responded with a grunt and rolled onto her back. "You want your belly rubbed, don't ya, girl?"

Cinnamon's head lulled to one side as Leona massaged the animal's soft stomach. While she continued the rhythmic motion, she thought about Abner Lapp's visit to the schoolhouse yesterday afternoon and wondered when Papa would visit with Emanuel. She hoped things would go well and that he'd be able to convince Emanuel that school was a good place to be. She knew the boy would be forced to attend, regardless of whether he wanted to or not, but it would be easier on both teacher and student if Emanuel wanted to be there.

She moved her hands up to Cinnamon's ears, stroking them both at the same time. "Teaching is all I have left, and I want to be the best teacher I can be." She closed her eyes, enjoying the gentle warmth of the sun's healing rays. For the last couple of days, the weather had been mild and not the least bit muggy. She wished every day of summer could be this way.

An approaching buggy crunched against the hard-packed dirt and halted Leona's thoughts. She opened her eyes and saw Naomi Hoffmeir and her youngest daughter, Millie, climb down from their buggy. "What brings you two out here today?" she asked as they neared.

"We were on our way home from a dental appointment and decided to stop at the pond to see if there were many mosquitoes," Naomi explained. "Our family hopes to have a picnic supper later this evening. That is, if there aren't too many nasty bugs here to bite us."

Leona shook her head. "I haven't noticed any mosquitoes at all."

"That's good to hear."

Leona smiled at Millie. "I'm looking forward to having you in my class when school starts up in August," she said in their Pennsylvania Dutch language, knowing Millie wouldn't learn English well until she started the first grade.

Millie nodded and gave her soon-to-be teacher a shy grin. Then she flopped down beside Cinnamon. When the dog licked the child's hand, Millie giggled and patted the animal's head.

"How much longer do you think you'll teach?" Naomi asked, taking a seat on the edge of the quilt.

"For a long time, I hope," Leona replied.

"Maybe you'll be Kevin's teacher when he starts school in two years."

"I should be."

"He's content to stay with his grandma Hoffmeir while Caleb and I are at the store every day, but I'm sure he will enjoy going to school once he's old enough." Naomi smoothed her long green dress over her knees and wrapped her hands around them. "Abner Lapp's mamm came into the store the other day, and she said something about Abner having been over to your house to see you a few times."

Leona nodded.

"So, if Abner's courting you, maybe you won't be

teaching as long as you think."

Leona sat up straight, her back rigid. "I don't know where you got the idea that Abner and I are courting, but it's not true. He dropped by the house a couple of times to see how I was doing after my nose got broke, and then he came once to talk about his brother."

"Guess I was wrong then." Naomi plucked a blade of grass from a patch growing nearby and twirled it around her fingers.

Leona glanced at her dog. The critter nuzzled Millie's hand, and the young girl seemed to be eating it up.

"Looks like my Millie has made herself a new friend," Naomi commented.

Leona stroked the dog's floppy red paw. "Jah, and the feeling seems to be mutual."

Naomi smiled. "Dogs make *wunderbaar* pets, but they can't take the place of a loving, caring husband."

"That may be true for some," Leona said with a shrug.

❦

Jim's alarm clock blared in his ear. He rolled over with a groan, wishing he could sleep a few more minutes. The hangover headache he'd had most of yesterday had finally abated, but he'd stayed up until late last night trying to call Jimmy. "That kid must have shut off his cell phone," he mumbled into his pillow.

Just then, the telephone on the table beside his bed rang, and Jim quickly reached for it. "Scott residence. Jim here."

"Hi, Dad, it's me."

"Jimmy! Where are you? Why haven't you been answering your phone? Did you get the messages I left?" Jim sat up and swung his legs over the side of the bed.

"Slow down, Dad. I can only answer one question at a time."

"Well, you can start by telling me where you are."

"I'm in Bel Air, Maryland, and I just checked out of my hotel."

"You—you drove all the way to Maryland by yourself?"

"I'm not a little kid, Dad, and I told you I was coming here in the note I left on the kitchen counter. You did get my note, didn't you?"

Jim stretched one arm over his head and yawned. "Yeah, I got it, and I was pretty upset when I discovered you were gone."

"Sorry about that, but you were passed out on the floor in the living room when I left, so—"

"Don't remind me," Jim said with a groan. He still couldn't get over the fact that his son had left him there. It wasn't like Jimmy to take off on a trip by himself— not to mention that he'd left in the middle of a big paint job, which had affected Jim's entire paint crew.

"I went to see Carl Stevens yesterday," Jimmy said.

"You—you did?"

"Yeah, only it wasn't the Carl Stevens you had dealings with. It was his son, Carl Jr., who took over his dad's practice five years ago."

Jim breathed a sigh of relief. If Jimmy had only met the lawyer's son, then maybe he was still in the clear. It wasn't likely that the son would know anything about what had gone on in his dad's office twenty years ago. Still, there might have been some records kept on the prospective adoption. "Wh–what'd the lawyer say?"

"He looked your name up in his database and dis-covered that the birth mother of the baby you'd gone there to adopt had changed her mind and decided to keep the child." After a brief pause, Jimmy asked, "Is that true, Dad? Did you leave Carl Stevens's office without a baby?"

Jim stood and ambled across the room. He pulled back the curtain and stared out the window.

"Dad, did you hear what I said?"

Jim leaned against the window casing and closed his eyes. "Yeah, I heard your question."

"So what's the answer?"

"I. . .uh. . .no, I didn't leave there with a baby." Jim's eyes snapped open as the truth hit him full in the face. He was caught in his own web of deceit, and there didn't seem to be a way out, short of telling Jimmy what had really happened that day. But could he risk losing his son forever by revealing the truth?

"If you didn't leave the lawyer's office with a baby, then how could you have shown up with me at the hotel where Mom was waiting?"

Jim glanced around the room as a feeling of panic threatened to overtake him. He needed a drink—needed something to give him courage and calm his nerves. His gaze came to rest on the bottle of herbal tablets he'd bought at the health food store yesterday. They'd helped him get to sleep last night, but it had taken almost an hour for them to take effect. He didn't have that kind of time now. He needed something that would work fast.

"Dad, are you still there?"

"I'm here. Just thinking is all."

"Thinking about what—the next lie you're going to tell me?" Jimmy's tone was sarcastic, and Jim knew he'd better come up with something good if he was going to keep Jimmy from knowing the truth. But what could he say—that he'd gone to some other lawyer's office and adopted another baby? He swallowed around the lump lodged in his throat. "The. . .the truth is we did get another baby—"

"The same day?" Jimmy's voice had raised a notch, and Jim could tell his son was feeling as much frustration as he was. "How about the truth, Dad? Think you could handle that?"

"Well, I—"

"The truth is always better than a lie."

"This truth might not be."

"What are you talking about?"

"Are you sitting down, Jimmy?"

"Yeah, I'm in my truck."

"Good, because what I'm about to tell you is gonna be a real shock." Jim stumbled back to the bed on shaky legs and flopped down. "I hardly know where to begin."

"Why not start at the beginning?"

"Yeah, okay. I guess it's time you knew the truth about your real family."

"You mean my birth parents—the ones you adopted me from?"

"No. There was no adoption."

"Huh? I don't get it. If there was no adoption, then how—"

"Stay with me, Jimmy." Jim drew in a deep breath, hoping it would give him added courage. "The day I went to pick up our adopted son at the lawyer's office in Bel Air, I was told that the birth mother had changed her mind and decided to keep her one-year-old boy. I was pretty upset and didn't know what I was going to tell your mother when I got back to the hotel."

"So if you didn't get the baby you'd gone there to adopt, then how did I—"

"I'm getting to that." Jim shifted on the bed as he tried to form his next words. "When I drove out of Maryland, I was in a state of panic, and by the time I got back to Pennsylvania, I could barely function. I drove up and down some backcountry roads for a while. There were a lot of Amish farms there, and when I spotted a sign advertising homemade root beer, I pulled into the driveway." He paused and swiped his tongue across his chapped lips. "A young Amish woman came out of the house holding a baby, whom she said had recently turned one." Another pause. "That baby was you, Jimmy. You were born in Lancaster County, Pennsylvania. Your real family is Amish."

∽∽∽

Lancaster County, Pennsylvania? Amish? Jimmy let his dad's words sink in. His brain felt numb, like he might be dreaming. He couldn't be Amish. He'd grown up in Puyallup, Washington, and his parents were Jim and Linda Scott. But then, he'd recently learned that he was adopted, so they weren't really his parents.

"After I asked the young woman for some cold root beer, she left you on the picnic table and went back inside to get it," his dad continued. "I expected her to return right away, but she didn't. Then you started getting restless, and I picked you up because I was afraid you might fall off the table. And then I ran to the car and drove off."

"Dad, have you been drinking this morning?"

"No, of course not. I haven't had a drop to drink since the night before last."

"Then why are you making up this crazy story? Do you really expect me to believe that you kidnapped some Amish baby and that the kid you took was me?"

"Yeah, that's right. I did it without thinking. But then as I drove away, everything started to make sense."

"How could kidnapping a child make any sense?" Jimmy didn't actually believe his dad's wild story, but if he was going to make him admit he was lying, then he needed to ask the right questions.

"I guess it didn't really make sense, but it's the truth, Jimmy. As odd as it might sound, I believed finding you was a twist of fate and that it was meant to be."

Jimmy's face felt like he'd been out in the sun too

long. Could the person on the other end of the phone—the man he'd called Dad for the last twenty years—really be a baby snatcher? He shook his head. *No, it's not possible. Dad has to be making this story up to discourage me from searching for my birth family.*

"The young Amish woman told me there were eight kids in the family and that her mother was dead," Dad continued. "I figured I might have done them a favor by giving them one less mouth to feed."

Jimmy set the phone down on the seat and leaned forward, resting his head on the steering wheel. A spot on the side of his head began to throb as his thoughts ran wild. After several seconds, he sat up again and picked up the phone. "I've got to go now, Dad. I'll call you later, once you've sobered up and are ready to tell me the truth." He clicked off the phone before his dad could respond.

Chapter 13

Leona stepped into the kitchen the following morning and found her mamm cutting thick slices of ham. Mom looked at her and smiled. "Did your daed tell you he stopped by the Lapps' place last night and had a little talk with Emanuel?"

"No, he never mentioned it."

"He was awful tired last night. Maybe that's why he forgot to say anything."

"So how did it go?" Leona asked as she moved over to the cupboard and removed three plates.

"Guess it went well. Emanuel said the reason he didn't want to go to school this fall was because he thought he should get a job and help support his mamm."

Leona shook her head. "That's ridiculous. The boy's too young to be going to work yet, and besides, Abner's taking care of his mamm and little bruder just fine with what he makes at the furniture shop in Strasburg."

"That may be true, but apparently, Emanuel feels he should be helping out, too."

"So what'd Papa tell him?"

"Said he needed to learn all he could while he's young so he knows more when he's older and can do a better job of whatever type of work he chooses."

Leona smiled. "Papa's just like Solomon in the Bible—full of good wisdom."

Mom nodded. "Jah, my Jacob's been blessed with a special gift, all right."

"I'm going to see the chiropractor this afternoon," Leona said. "So if you have any errands you'd like me to run, I'll be happy to do them for you."

111

"I do have a quilt finished that I'd like to have dropped off at Abby's shop. Will you be going near there?"

"It won't be a problem. I'll go by the quilt shop on my way home after seeing Dr. Bowers."

"Are his treatments helping any?" Concern showed on her mamm's face.

"My neck's feeling better, but the headaches are still there. That ball must have done more damage than I realized."

"Or maybe the headaches are from tension. You're still grieving over Ezra, and I know—"

"I'm not grieving, Mom," Leona said a bit too sharply, and she winced at her own snappish words. "Sorry, I didn't mean to sound so testy. It's just that I'm getting tired of being reminded that Ezra's dead. How am I ever going to get over him if everyone keeps bringing him up?"

"Your heart will heal in time, daughter, regardless of how many times you hear Ezra's name." Mom moved away from the cupboard and drew Leona into her arms. "Sooner or later, some other man will come along and win your heart, and then you'll look forward to getting married again."

Leona leaned her head on Mom's shoulder and let the tears flow. If she lived one hundred years, she didn't think she would ever stop loving Ezra, and she wasn't about to open her heart to love again.

∞

As soon as Jimmy clicked off his cell phone, he put the truck in gear. His dad's kidnapping story was the most ridiculous thing he'd ever heard, but just to prove his dad was lying, he would drive over to Lancaster County and check things out. If an Amish child had been kidnapped twenty years ago, someone in the area should know about it. And if the trip turned up nothing, then he would call Dad again and demand to know the truth about how he came to live with them.

Two hours later, as Jimmy headed down Route 30 in Lancaster, he spotted an Amish buggy. It looked similar to the ones he'd seen in Ohio during one of the few trips he and his folks had made to see Grandpa and Grandma Scott, only this buggy was gray instead of black. Traffic was a lot heavier than he'd thought it would be, and he noticed a multitude of shopping malls, restaurants, and tourist attractions on almost every block.

I wonder how the Amish manage with their horses and buggies in all this congestion, he thought as he turned into the parking lot of a visitors' center.

Inside the building, Jimmy found a rack near the front door full of brochures advertising Pennsylvania Dutch restaurants, authentic buggy rides, Amish country tours, hotels, and many local attractions.

"Guess I'd better start by finding a place to stay," he muttered.

"How long will you be in the area, and would you like a couple of recommendations?" the young, dark-haired woman behind the information desk asked.

Jimmy scratched his head. "I'm not sure how long I'll be staying, but I'd appreciate any ideas you can give me."

She pulled out a brochure from the stack on her desk and handed it to him. "There's a nice bed-and-breakfast in Strasburg that has fairly reasonable rates. It's run by a Mennonite couple and comes highly recommended."

Jimmy studied the information, noting the picture of the tall, stately looking white house. It was surrounded by farmland, and an Amish buggy was shown heading up the road in front of the bed-and-breakfast.

"Thanks. I should be able to find the place with

these directions," he said as he studied the map on the back of the brochure.

"Can I help you with anything else?" the woman asked.

Jimmy leaned on the counter. "Well, I'm. . .uh . . .looking for a place that sells homemade root beer. Would you know of any in the area?"

"There's lots of homemade root beer sold around here. You might find some at the farmer's market in Bird-in-Hand."

He shook his head. "The place I'm looking for is an Amish farm. I was told they had a sign out front by the road advertising root beer."

"Many Amish families have begun supplementing their income by selling produce and various other items from roadside stands or shops built near their homes. I think I've seen a couple of places selling root beer near Strasburg, so you might ask the folks at the B and B."

Jimmy started to turn away but hesitated. "I don't suppose you'd know about any Amish babies being kidnapped in the area?"

The woman's forehead wrinkled. "How long ago?"

"About twenty years."

"Sorry, but I wasn't living in Lancaster back then. You'll have to ask someone who's lived in the area that long."

"Okay. Thanks for your time." Jimmy put the brochure in his shirt pocket, along with a few others he'd plucked off the stand. He would head over to the bed-and-breakfast and see about getting a room. He'd then spend the rest of the day taking pictures of whatever he saw that interested him while searching for an Amish farm selling homemade root beer, which he felt sure was a complete waste of time.

∞

"I'll be taking off early today," Jim told his foreman. "You and the rest of the crew can keep working if you want, or you can quit at noon, like I plan to do."

"I thought you wanted to get this job done by Monday."

"I did, but after starting it yesterday, I've come to realize that there's too much work involved for us to be able to finish today. We may as well quit for the weekend and get an early start on this old, peeling house come Monday morning." The house really would take longer to paint than Jim had figured, but the real reason he wanted to quit work early was so he could spend the rest of the day at his favorite tavern, drowning his sorrows and trying not to think about the confession he'd made to Jimmy earlier today.

"I don't think we should quit working for the day just because we can't get the job done until next week, and I can't believe how much work you've missed lately." Ed squinted at Jim. "I hope you're not hitting the bottle again."

"What I do on my own time is my business!"

"Okay, okay, don't get so testy." Ed lifted his hands. "You can take off whenever you want, and since you're the boss and this is your business, I'll just look the other way when your business folds." He started to walk away but turned back around. "Of course, that will mean I'll be out of a job, so I'd like to suggest something."

"What's that?"

"I have a brother-in-law who's a recovered alcoholic, and he's gotten a lot of help from AA."

Not the AA thing again. Jim gritted his teeth. *Is everyone out to see me reformed?* "I'm not an alcoholic, Ed, so get off my back."

"Whatever you say." Ed studied Jim intently. "Mind if I ask you something else?"

"What now?"

"I'm curious to know why Jimmy hasn't been at work all week, and I'm wondering why you've been late almost every day."

"Not that it's any of your business," Jim said gruffly, "but Jimmy's back East."

Ed's bushy eyebrows lifted on his forehead. "Back East? What's he doing there when we need him here?"

"He's on a quest."

"What kind of quest?"

"To find his biological parents."

Ed's mouth dropped open. "Huh?"

Jim glared at his foreman. "Well, as you know, we got Jimmy from back East twenty years ago."

"Yeah, and you asked me not to mention Jimmy's adoption to anyone because you wanted to tell him when he was old enough and you didn't want him finding out some other way."

"Right."

"So now he knows?"

"Yeah, and he's determined to find his birth mother." *Which, of course, he won't be able to do because she was Amish, and his sister said their mother was dead.* Jim grimaced. *If Ed knew what really happened, I wonder if he'd blow the whistle on me.*

"Do you know when Jimmy might be coming back?"

Jim rubbed the side of his face, wishing he and Ed weren't having this conversation. "I'm not sure. Guess it all depends."

Ed shrugged. "Guess we'll just have to get along without him until he gets back then."

Jim cringed. *Yeah, if he ever does come back.*

∞

"Maybe I should take one of those buggy rides I saw in a brochure I picked up on Saturday," Jimmy said to himself as he snapped on the radio. He had checked into the bed-and-breakfast and had driven around Strasburg and the outlying area, but so far he'd seen no Amish farms selling root beer. He'd talked to a couple of people and asked if they knew about an Amish baby who'd been kidnapped twenty years ago, but no one had any helpful information to give him.

A short time later, Jimmy parked his truck near Aaron and Jessica's Buggy Rides, outside the town of Bird-in-Hand, and waited on a bench with several other tourists for the next buggy. When his turn finally came, he climbed into the front of a closed-in buggy, taking a seat beside the gray-haired driver with a long, gray beard. The man said he wasn't Amish but belonged to some other Plain group living in the area. The couple who had been waiting with Jimmy took the backseat, situating their little boy between them.

Jimmy removed his camera from its case.

"No pictures allowed on this trip," the driver announced. "We'll be stopping by several Amish farms and meeting some of the people who live there. It goes against their religious beliefs to have their pictures taken, so we ask that you respect those wishes."

"I read an article in the newspaper that said their opposition to having their pictures taken has something to do with the scripture about not making any graven images," the woman sitting behind them said.

The elderly man nodded and picked up the reins, urging the horse to move forward. Jimmy slipped his camera back into its case.

Once they'd left the parking lot, they traveled at a fairly good pace down a narrow country road. The wind whipped at Jimmy's body through the open windows, and the rhythmic *clip-clop, clip-clop* of the horse's hooves echoed against the pavement.

Soon they pulled onto a driveway leading to a well-kept farmhouse. An Amish woman and a little girl stepped out of the house and approached the buggy, each holding a tray filled with cookies and homemade bread.

"This is Mary and her daughter, Selma," their driver explained. "They make extra money for their family by selling bakery items to the tourists I bring along my buggy route."

Jimmy reached into his pocket and pulled out his wallet. "I'd like to buy a loaf of bread and six cookies, please."

Just before the horse started moving again, Jimmy leaned out the window and said to Mary, "Would you happen to sell any root beer here?"

She shook her head. "Just baked goods, that's all."

Jimmy slouched against the seat. He should have known it wouldn't be so easy to find an Amish farm selling root beer—if there even was such a place. *I'm sure Dad made this whole kidnapping thing up just to throw me off course. He's been a control freak for as long as I can remember, and I'm almost sure there's more to my adoption than he's willing to tell.* He studied the tall barn behind the Amish house as they pulled out of the yard. *Maybe I ought to see about getting a job in case I decide to stay in the area awhile. It will give me a chance to ask around some more before I call Dad again.*

After the buggy ride was over, Jimmy spent the next few hours driving along the back roads, taking pictures of barns, Amish men and boys working in the fields with their draft mules, and children playing in their yards.

By late afternoon, he was tired, thirsty, and thoroughly discouraged, so he pulled into the parking lot of a place called Hoffmeirs' General Store, hoping he might find something cold there to drink.

Naomi was busy dusting empty shelves near the back of the store when she heard the bell above the front door jingle. Knowing that Caleb and the children had gone out to run an errand, she went to see who had come into the store. A young English man with light-brown hair stood near the counter. "Can I help you?"

He nodded. "I was wondering if you sell anything cold to drink in this store."

She shook her head. "Except for some candy, we don't sell any food or drink items. I do have a few bottles of soda in the cooler I keep in the back room, though."

He moistened his lips with the tip of his tongue. "Would you be willing to sell me some of that? It's awfully hot and humid today, and I could sure use something cold to drink."

"I'd be happy to give you some soda. I'll be right back." Naomi hurried off, and returned with a bottle of orange soda, which she handed to him.

"Thanks. What do I owe you?"

"Nothing. Nothing at all." She studied the man, thinking he looked kind of familiar and wondering if she had met him before. "Mind if I ask where you're from?"

"I grew up in Puyallup, Washington." He took a drink and a dribble of orange liquid ran down his chin. He swiped it away with the back of his hand. "This is sure good."

"So, you're from out West then?"

He nodded and took another drink.

Naomi's thoughts went to her days of living in Oregon, and she reflected on how much she had missed her home and family during that stressful time. "Are you here on vacation?" she asked.

"Kind of." He finished the last of the soda and handed her the empty bottle. "Are you sure I can't pay for this?"

She shook her head. "No payment's necessary. Is there anything else I can help you with?"

He ran his fingers through the back of his wavy hair and shuffled his feet a couple of times. It reminded her of the way Matthew acted whenever he was mulling things over.

"I've been looking for a place that sells root beer, but I haven't had any luck so far."

Naomi opened her mouth to tell him that the ice-cream shop down the street sold several kinds of soda and made root beer floats, but she was interrupted when Leona Weaver entered the store with a dahlia-pattern quilt draped over her arm.

Chapter 14

As Leona stepped into the Hoffmeirs' store, she almost bumped into a young English man who stood near the front counter. He smiled. She returned the smile but then glanced quickly at Naomi, who stood nearby. "I came by to drop off a quilt my mamm finished for Abby. I also wanted to see if you'd gotten those rubber stamps in that you ordered for me awhile back. I'm planning to do some art projects with my students when we start back to school in August, and I thought I'd let them use the stamps."

"I'm expecting the order any day." Naomi motioned toward the back of the store. "I've got a couple of empty shelves dusted and all ready for them."

Leona skirted around the Englisher and moved toward the connecting quilt shop. "Guess I'll stop by another time to check on the stamps. Right now I need to give this quilt to Abby."

"Abby's not there, but you can leave it on her desk; when I see her tomorrow, I'll let her know it's from your mamm."

"Where is Abby?"

"She closed the shop for the rest of the day."

Leona halted. "How come?"

"She had to take all five of her kinner to the dentist for checkups."

"What about Mary Ann? Isn't she working today?"

"I talked with Fannie earlier. Seems my little sister's come down with the flu and is home in bed."

"I'm sorry to hear she's *grank*. I'll either stop by your folks' place and check on her or drop by here again later in the week."

The Englisher cleared his throat, and both women turned around. "I didn't realize you were still here," Naomi said. "Did you need something else?"

He shuffled his leather sandals across the wooden floor. "I wanted to say thanks again for the pop—I mean, soda. It was real refreshing."

"You're welcome."

He started for the door but turned back around. "Say, I was wondering if you would know of anyone in the area who might be looking for a painter."

Leona stepped forward. "Have you had any experience?"

He nodded. "My dad owns his own painting business in the state of Washington, and I've been working part-time for him since I turned sixteen. When I graduated from high school, I painted during the summer when I wasn't taking classes at our local community college."

Leona took a few minutes to deliberate as she sized up the English man. He looked nice, dressed in a pair of blue jeans and a light blue, short-sleeved shirt. There was something about his serious brown eyes and the way he smiled that made her believe he was trustworthy. "My daed—I mean, dad—owns his own business, too," she said. "He mentioned the other day that he has a lot of work right now and might need to hire another painter."

The young man smiled. "Would you mind giving me the name of your dad's business or tell me where I might meet him to talk about the possibility of a job?"

"It's called Weaver's Painting, and I think Papa's got his crew working on the outside of a restaurant down the street. So if you head over there now, you might catch him."

"What's the name of the restaurant?"

"Meyers' Home Cooking. Just ask for Jacob

Weaver—that's my dad."

"Thanks. I'll go there right away."

⁂

As Jimmy headed down the sidewalk toward the restaurant that the young Amish woman had mentioned, he was plagued with nagging doubts. How long would he stick around Lancaster County? Did he really need a job, or could he manage on the money he'd brought along? Was there even any point to him being here? Since he was here, and since he didn't want to return to Washington without some definite answers, he may as well stay awhile and get to know the area. Besides, he found the Amish culture kind of interesting.

Jimmy cleared his throat as he approached a middle-aged Amish man who knelt in front of a can of paint, stirring it with a flat stick. "Excuse me, but do you know where I might find Jacob Weaver?"

The man squinted and tipped his head to one side. "I'm Jacob Weaver. Do I know you from somewhere?"

Jimmy shook his head. "My name's Jimmy Scott, and I'm looking for a job."

"As a painter?"

"That's right. I spoke to your daughter over at Hoffmeirs' General Store, and she said you might be looking to hire someone."

Jacob placed the paint stick on the edge of the bucket and stood. "Have you had any experience?"

Jimmy nodded. "My dad owns a paint contracting business out in Washington."

Jacob pursed his lips and stared at Jimmy. "So you're not from around here, then?"

"No, I came to Lancaster County to—"

"Jacob, can you come here a minute?" A young Amish painter who was working nearby motioned to Jacob. "I'm having some problems getting this new paint to cover."

"Excuse me a minute." Jacob nodded at Jimmy. "I'll be right back."

Curious to see what the problem with the paint might be, Jimmy followed Jacob around the side of the building, where a couple of other Amish men stood painting with brushes.

"It might go on better if you used a roller rather than the brushes," he suggested.

"What makes you think so?" one of the fellows asked.

"You can cover a larger area quicker using a roller instead of a brush."

Before the young Amish man could reply, Jacob stepped forward, placed one hand on Jimmy's shoulder, and said, "Son, you're hired."

∞

Jim's cell phone rang. He pulled it from his belt clip and frowned. "Now what?" he mumbled with irritation. "If this phone keeps ringing, I'll never get to the tavern. And it had better not be another disgruntled customer wondering why we haven't started working on their house yet." All morning, he'd had complaints, and he was tired of the interruptions. He hadn't even left the job site yet because he kept getting phone calls.

He checked the caller's number showing in the screen on his phone. When he realized it was Jimmy, he answered right away. "Hi, Jimmy. I'm so glad you called. After our last conversation, I was afraid you might—"

"I'm in Lancaster County, Dad," Jimmy interrupted. "I've spent all day driving around looking for Amish farms selling root beer, but as you may have guessed, I haven't found one."

"Jimmy, I—"

"You made that kidnapping story up, didn't you?"

"No, no, it's the truth." Jim leaned against the side of his van. "It took every ounce of courage for me to tell you the truth, Jimmy, and now that the story's out, I'm really scared."

"Scared of what?"

A trickle of sweat rolled down Jim's forehead and dribbled onto his cheek. "If you find your Amish family and tell them who you are, they might press charges against me. I could end up in jail."

"Come on now, Dad."

"No, really. Why do you think I kept this story a secret all these years?"

"Because you were afraid of going to jail?"

"That's right, and if your mother were still alive and knew about this, she'd be scared to death that if this leaks out I might be charged with kidnapping."

"What are you saying—that Mom didn't know the adoption had fallen through or that you'd snatched an Amish baby out of his own backyard?" Jimmy's tone was mocking, and Jim's frustration escalated.

"I couldn't tell her. It would have broken her heart."

"So you just let her believe I was the one-year-old kid you had planned to adopt?"

A muscle in Jim's cheek quivered. "Right. I did it because I loved her and wanted to give her the child she'd been wanting for so long. And if you could have seen the expression on your mother's face when I returned to the hotel with you in my arms, you'd know why I did it. She was ecstatic."

There was a long pause, and Jim wondered if Jimmy had hung up. "Jimmy? You still there?"

"Yeah, Dad. I'm just trying to piece this all together. If you really did take me from an Amish farm, then I need to know exactly where it was."

"I. . .uh. . .I'm not sure where it was." Jim opened

the door to the van and climbed in. If Jimmy stayed in Amish country long enough, there was a good chance he might find his Amish family. And if that happened, Jim felt sure he would be arrested. Worse than that, Jimmy might never return to Washington. Jim had already lost his wife, and the thought of losing his son was almost unbearable. "When are you coming home, Jimmy?" he ventured to ask.

"Look, Dad, I'm really not convinced that you're telling me the truth, but I think I'll stick around here awhile anyway."

"Do you need me to send you some money?"

"No, I found a job today—working for an Amish painter."

Jim grimaced. "Why would you need a job? I just told you, I'll send money if you need it."

"Working for Jacob Weaver will not only provide me with a paycheck, but it'll give me the chance to get to know some of the Amish people. Maybe I'll learn something that might lead me to my real family—if you're telling the truth about that."

Jim massaged his throbbing temple. "How many times do I need to say it, Jimmy? I'm not lying—I kidnapped you from your Amish family, just like I told you yesterday." He paused. "Uh, Jimmy—have you told anyone the reason you're there?"

"Not yet. It wouldn't make much sense for me to walk up to some Amish man and blurt out, 'Oh, and by the way, Jimmy Scott's not my real name. I'm actually the kidnapped child of an Amish family who live somewhere in Lancaster County.' "

"You're right, it wouldn't. Besides, they might not like you prying into their personal business. They may even think you're a reporter trying to get a story on them or something, and I'm sure that wouldn't be appreciated."

"I doubt they would think that. It isn't likely that a reporter would take a job working as a painter, Dad."

Jim shifted the phone to his other ear. "What if you do find your real family and they have me arrested, Jimmy? What if I have to spend the rest of my life in jail?"

"Listen, Dad, I've got to go. The battery on my phone is running low, and I need to get back to the B and B and get it charged."

"Okay, but listen, Jimmy—"

The phone went dead, and Jim moaned as he leaned against his seat. A part of him wanted Jimmy to find his real family because it might relieve his guilt. But another part wished he could turn back the hands of time—back to the way things had been when Jimmy was a boy and knew nothing about his past.

Chapter 15

Jimmy had been working for Jacob Weaver a little over a week, and already he felt accepted by his easygoing boss. Jimmy was impressed with how well Jacob got along with all his employees—Amish and English alike.

This morning Jimmy had been asked to work with Eli Raber, one of Jacob's young Amish painters. They were scheduled to begin painting a one-room schoolhouse in the area. Jacob said he was pleased to have another English painter working for him who owned a truck. That would make it even easier when he had equipment that needed to be hauled to the job sites.

As the two young men headed down a narrow road, jostling up and down in Jimmy's small pickup, Jimmy took the opportunity to get to know Eli better.

"Have you been working for Jacob Weaver long?" he asked.

"Started a year ago. How long have you been in Lancaster County?"

"A little over a week. Got here a few days before Jacob hired me." Jimmy turned on the air conditioning, noting that the cab of his truck had become stuffy on this warm, summer morning.

"You just passin' through, or are ya plannin' to stick around?"

Jimmy shrugged. "It all depends on how things go."

"You mean with your job?"

"That and a few other things."

"Where you stayin'?"

"At a bed-and-breakfast in Strasburg. But I'll need to make other arrangements, since it looks like I might be here awhile."

"My folks have a trailer out behind our place that they've decided to rent. If you're interested, you can come by after work and take a look."

Jimmy nodded. "That sounds good to me."

"I think you'll enjoy workin' for Jacob," Eli said.

"He seems like a nice man who is respected by his employees."

Eli nodded, and his blond hair bobbed up and down. "He's highly thought of—not only as a paint contractor but also as the bishop of our community."

Jimmy's mouth dropped open. "Jacob's a bishop?"

"Jah. Has been for a good many years."

"I didn't realize Amish bishops worked as tradesmen."

"Some do. Others farm for a living."

"So they don't get paid for their position in the church?"

"Oh no. When they're not fulfilling their preachin' duties, they work, same as the rest of us Amish men do."

Jimmy pursed his lips. "Guess there's a lot I don't know about the Amish way of life. Would you be willing to teach me?"

Eli smiled and nodded enthusiastically. "Jah, sure. I'll tell ya anything you wanna know."

❧

When Leona heard a vehicle pull into the school yard, she glanced out the window. A small red truck was parked in the graveled lot, and two men were climbing out. She hurried to the other side of the schoolhouse and opened the door. She recognized one of the men as Eli Raber, who worked for her daed. Eli wore a pair of blue jeans and a white short-sleeved shirt, which was typical work attire for an Amish man who hadn't yet joined the church. The other man was an Englisher, also dressed in blue jeans and a white shirt, but he wore a painter's cap on his head. When the two men came up the walk, she realized that the Englisher was the same man she'd met at Caleb and Naomi's store a week ago. Apparently, he'd taken her suggestion and asked her daed about a job. From the looks of the equipment she saw piled in the back of his pickup, he'd obviously been hired.

"Wie geht's, Leona?" Eli asked, stepping onto the porch.

"I'm fine. How are you?"

"Feelin' hot and sticky, but that's to be expected for this time of the year." He turned to the English man at his side. "This is Jimmy Scott. Your daed recently hired him, and we've come to paint the outside of the schoolhouse."

Leona nodded. "If Papa didn't own his business, the schoolhouse would be painted by my students' parents. But he figured his men could get the job done much quicker."

Jimmy smiled and reached out his hand to her. "We met at the general store in Paradise last week, remember?"

"I do remember, and it's nice to see you again," she said, shaking his hand.

"Thanks for suggesting I speak to your dad about a job. He hired me right away, and I really appreciate it."

Leona was about to comment when Eli said, "How come you're at the schoolhouse today? I didn't figure anyone would be around the place."

"I came to do some cleaning and organizing inside, so I won't be in the way of your painting the outside of the building."

"Will the inside walls need to be painted, too?" Jimmy asked.

She nodded. "Probably so. It's been a few years since they've had a new coat of paint."

"By the time we're done, this old schoolhouse will look as good as new." Jimmy grinned at Leona.

"Well, I'd best be gettin' back to work," she said, feeling kind of flustered. "Give a holler if either of you should need anything."

"Danki," Eli said.

Leona stepped inside the schoolhouse and quickly shut the door. Leaning her full weight against it, she moaned quietly. *I can't figure out why I feel so jittery all of a sudden. Maybe it's the heat, or maybe I had too much coffee this morning. Jah, that must be it.*

❧

As Jimmy's paintbrush connected with each wooden board, he thought about the Amish world here in Lancaster County and wondered if he'd really been kidnapped when he was a baby. As far-fetched as Dad's story seemed, Jimmy couldn't help but wonder if he had been born Amish what he might be doing at this very moment. Would he have become a farmer like some Amish men in the area, or might he have learned a trade the way Eli and the others who worked for Jacob had done?

I can't believe I'm even considering this, he thought with a shake of his head. *But if there's any possibility that my dad's crazy story about me being Amish is true, then maybe I need to keep looking for answers. I wonder if Eli would know anything about an Amish baby being kidnapped in Lancaster County twenty years ago.*

Jimmy squinted against the hot sun and pulled the bill of his painter's cap over his forehead. *Probably not, since he would have been a baby himself back then. And the Amish schoolteacher doesn't look much older than Eli or me, so she probably wouldn't know anything, either. But if I start asking questions and discover there really was a*

131

kidnapping, then Dad might go to jail. He gripped the paintbrush a little tighter. *Mom wouldn't want that—I know she wouldn't.*

Forcing his thoughts back to the job at hand, Jimmy decided that the best thing to do was get better acquainted with the Amish, learn more of their ways, and ask questions only when he felt the time was right.

∽∾

Abraham was about to leave Naomi and Caleb's store when he bumped into his best friend, who was heading inside. "*Gut daag*, Jacob. How are things with you?"

"Good day to you, too, friend. Everything is fine and dandy as far as I'm concerned," Jacob said with a grin. "I hired me a new painter last week, and things are workin' out real good."

"Does that mean you've got lots of work these days?"

"Jah, and I'm gettin' more jobs all the time. Counting myself and Arthur, I've got a crew of seven men now, and two of 'em are English."

Abraham stepped to one side. "Guess you've got to have some Englishers so they can haul your equipment around in their rigs."

Jacob nodded. "That's right. We've been using Richard Jamison's van for a good many years, ever since he began working for me. Jimmy Scott, the new fellow I hired, drives a small pickup, so that will also come in handy."

Abraham was about to comment when Naomi called out to him. "Papa, Edna Yoder's daughter is on the phone. She has a message for Fannie. I figured it would be best if you spoke to her since you're about to head for home and will see Fannie sooner than I will."

"Excuse me, Jacob," Abraham said, giving his friend a quick nod.

"Go right ahead," Jacob replied. "I'm gonna get what I came for and head out to the schoolhouse to see how things are goin' with the paint job."

Abraham went around the other side of the counter and picked up the telephone. "Abraham Fisher here."

He listened for several seconds to the distraught voice on the other end. "I'm sorry to hear that. I'll be sure to let Fannie know. I'm certain you'll be hearing from her soon."

Abraham hung up the phone and turned to face Naomi, who wore a worried expression. "I don't know how I'm gonna tell my dear wife this distressing news, but her cousin Edna passed away this morning, apparently from a heart attack."

Naomi's eyes filled with tears. "Oh, how sad. Edna was such a fun-loving person. She will surely be missed."

He nodded. "I'd best be on my way. I know Fannie will fall apart when she hears about Edna, and she'll no doubt need a shoulder to cry on." Abraham hurried out the door, whispering a prayer for all of Edna Yoder's family.

∞

"Hello, Papa," Leona said, when her daed entered the schoolhouse shortly before four o'clock. "Did you come to check on the painters?"

He nodded solemnly. "I'll be going by the Fishers' place when I'm done here."

"How come? Do they need some painting done?"

He shook his head. "When I dropped by Hoffmeirs' General Store a bit ago, I learned that Fannie's cousin Edna died this morning."

Leona gasped. "I'm sorry to hear that."

"I wonder how Gerald and Rachel are taking the news. First they lose their son, and now Gerald's mamm."

A vision of Ezra flashed across Leona's mind, and she winced. *If he were still alive, he'd be at his grandma's funeral service, and I'd be there to offer him support and comfort.*

"Fannie and her cousin Edna were so close," Papa went on to say. "So I'm sure Fannie will take this pretty hard."

"You're probably right." A stab of remorse shot through Leona as she thought about Ezra's funeral. It had taken all her willpower not to break down in front of everyone. Ezra's mamm had been so distraught, and Leona had kept her emotions in check that day to keep from causing Rachel further pain.

"Abraham was at the store, and he was planning on telling Fannie right away," Papa continued. He combed his fingers through the ends of his long beard as he slowly shook his head. "I'll need to go by and see her as well as those in Edna's immediate family. So whenever you decide to go home, would you mind tellin' your mamm what's up?"

"Sure, Papa. Should we hold supper for you?"

He shook his head. "Tell your mamm to keep something warm, but the two of you should go ahead and eat without me. I don't know how long I'll be."

"Okay." Leona pondered the idea of volunteering to go along with her daed, but the thought of trying to offer comfort to the Yoders was too much to bear. It would probably bring back a flood of painful memories for her, and even though she knew she would have to work through it on the day of Edna's funeral, she just couldn't deal with that today.

Papa's eyes narrowed as he studied the room. "Looks like these walls are gonna need a good coat of paint after the outside gets done."

"I've been thinking that, too." Leona's gaze went to the front window, where she caught a glimpse of Jimmy taking two cans of paint from the back of his pickup. "Will the same painters you have doing the outside work do the inside, as well, or should we let some of my students' parents do that painting?"

"I'll probably ask Jimmy and Eli to do it, and the parents can do some of the cleaning and repairs you still need to have done." He grinned. "I'm real happy with that new English fellow. He says his daed owns his own painting business out in Washington. Evidently, Jimmy started workin' for his father when he was a teenager. 'Course, the young fellow ain't much more than that now."

"He does look young," Leona agreed, "but he seems to know a lot about painting."

"That's what I thought, too."

"What else do you know about Jimmy Scott?" she questioned. "I mean—other than he comes from the state of Washington."

Papa shrugged and leaned against one of her pupil's desks. "That's about all."

Leona glanced out the window again, but Jimmy was out of view.

"Guess I'd best be going." Papa leaned over and kissed Leona's forehead. "See you later this evening."

She nodded. "And don't worry about your chores. I'll see that all the animals are fed and watered if you're not back in time."

"Danki, Leona. You're a real good *dochder*." He headed for the door, calling over his shoulder, "And you're gonna make some lucky fellow a mighty good wife some day."

Leona's gaze went to the ceiling. *I'm glad he thinks I'm a good daughter, but I sure hope he gives up soon on that idea of me being any kind of a wife—good or otherwise.*

∽

Sweat beaded on Jimmy's forehead and trickled onto his cheeks. This hot, sticky weather was a lot harder to deal with than the milder climate he was used to on the West Coast. Even during the warmest days of summer, they never had to endure humidity and heat such as this. He wondered if the people who lived here ever got used to this kind of weather.

He reached into his back pocket and pulled out a rag. He wiped his damp face with it and groaned. "Guess I'd better head for that water pump out behind the schoolhouse," he told Eli, who kept right on painting. Apparently, the man didn't mind the heat at all. "I drank my last bottle of water when I ate lunch. Sure wish I'd thought to bring a few more along."

"The water from the pump will have to do then," Eli said, moving past Jimmy to grab another bucket of paint. "I can't believe we're on our second coat already. These old boards sure have soaked up the paint."

Jimmy was about to head around back when Leona showed up carrying a thermos, two paper cups, and a few cookies. "You two have been working hard all day, and I thought you might want to take a break," she said.

Jimmy nodded appreciatively, noticing the way her green eyes sparkled when she smiled. Apparently, she didn't mind the heat, either. "Thanks."

"Danki, Leona," Eli said with a nod.

"You're welcome." She took a seat on the top porch step, opened the thermos, and poured them each a cup of cold tea. Then she removed the plastic wrap from the cookies and offered those to the men. "If I'd known anyone was coming to paint the schoolhouse today, I'd have brought more treats. These cookies were supposed to be my snack, but I've had all I can eat."

Jimmy took two cookies and popped one into his mouth. "Umm. . . they're really good. Peanut butter is my favorite kind." He took a seat beside Leona, but Eli remained standing as he gulped down his iced tea.

"This tea is real *gut*," the Amish man said.

"The word *gut* means 'good,' right?" Jimmy asked.

"Yes, it does," Leona replied.

"I took a year of German in high school, so I know a few words." Jimmy grinned. "Of course, I'm not very fluent in the German language, and I don't understand most of the Pennsylvania Dutch that you Amish speak."

"I think it's best learned by listening," Eli said. "Hang around me awhile, and by the end of summer, you'll have learned a lot more of our *Deitsch*."

Chapter 16

When Abraham entered the house, he found Fannie and the twins sitting at the kitchen table eating pieces of apple crumb pie with tall glasses of milk. It was a happy scene. He hated to interrupt, but the news he had to share couldn't wait.

He cleared his throat twice, and Fannie glanced over her shoulder. "I didn't expect you'd be back so soon, Abraham. Figured you and Naomi might get to gabbing or that you'd want to spend a little time with those *kinskinner* of yours."

Abraham moved over to the table and pulled out a chair. "Sarah and Susan were helping their mamm in the store, but I don't know where Naomi's other four kinner were today."

"Nate and Josh were probably out behind the store playing," Titus spoke up. "They like to hang out there and pretend like they're carin' for the buggy horse they keep in the small corral."

"That's so they don't have to do any work in the store," Timothy put in. "I'd like to see those two follow us around in the fields all day. A couple of hours out there in the hot sun, and they'd understand what hard work's all about."

"Josh is only eleven, and Nate just turned nine," Fannie said with a shake of her head. "They should be allowed to play once in a while. Besides, their daed owns the general store. He doesn't farm for a living."

"Looks like you two are pretty good at finding ways to take a break." Abraham leaned over and poked Titus on the back. "For a couple of strong teenagers, you can sure figure out ways to get out of doin' a full day's work."

"Ah, Papa, we ain't sloughing off," Timothy said with a grunt. "We got hot out there in the fields and decided to come up to the house to get somethin' cold to drink."

"Jah, and when Mama saw us standin' out back at the pump, she invited us inside for pie and milk," his twin brother added.

Abraham smiled despite the sad news he had to share. "I think you've had enough of a break for now. If you eat more of your mamm's pie, you won't want supper."

"I'll be able to eat again by supper time," Timothy announced.

"Even so, I want you to get back to work, because there's a lot to be done in the fields yet today."

Titus slid his chair back and stood. "You comin', Papa?"

Abraham shook his head. "I've got something I need to say to your mamm first."

The boys gave him a questioning look, but neither one said a word. They gulped down the last of their milk, grabbed their straw hats from the pegs by the back door, and rushed out of the house.

Fannie turned to Abraham and smiled. "What'd you need to speak to me about?"

Abraham took hold of her hand. "I'm afraid I've got bad news."

Fannie's face registered alarm. "What is it, Husband?"

"While I was at the store, I received word that Edna had passed away this morning. They think she had a heart attack."

Fannie covered her mouth and gasped. "*Nee, nee,* she can't be dead. I saw Edna last week at a quilting bee, and she looked just fine."

Abraham waited for his news to register fully. He

realized that Fannie would need time to process this distressing news.

After a few minutes, Fannie spoke. "Ever since I moved to Pennsylvania, Edna and I have been best friends. How can I go on without my dear cousin?" Her chin trembled as tears gathered in the corners of her eyes.

Abraham quickly wrapped his arms around her. "You've been through worse in years past, and you'll get through this, too. With God's help, we can survive any of life's tragedies."

∞

"Given that your mamm's coming down with a cold, I sure appreciate you goin' to the Fishers' place with me," Leona's daed said as the two of them headed down the road in his buggy the following day.

Papa glanced over at her and smiled. "I know I've said this before, but you're gonna make some man a real good wife someday."

Leona's face heated, and she quickly changed the subject. "When you went over to see Fannie yesterday, did you feel that she had accepted her cousin's death?"

"Afraid not," Papa said with a shake of his head. "Fannie was so distraught, and nothing either Abraham or I said seemed to offer much comfort, so I thought I'd try again today. We need to get her feeling as if she can cope better before Edna's funeral service."

"Now that she's had a few days to mourn, maybe she's calmed down some."

He nodded. "I'm eager to know if that's the case."

"How are Ezra's folks coping with Edna's death?" she asked.

"As well as can be expected. I spoke with Gerald's sister, Gretchen, too, and she's holding up pretty well."

They pulled into the Fishers' yard, and Papa parked

the buggy near the barn. Leona reached behind the seat and retrieved the wicker basket she'd brought. Then she climbed down from the passenger's side. As soon as Papa had the horse tied to the hitching rail, they strode toward the house, arm in arm.

Mary Ann greeted them at the back door. "I'm glad you've come," she whispered, glancing over her shoulder. "Mama Fannie's not been herself since she heard about Edna, and I'm worried about her."

"Where is she now, and where's Abraham?" Leona's daed asked.

"Papa's out in the fields with my brothers. Mama Fannie's in there huddled on the sofa." Mary Ann motioned to the door that led to the living room. "I found her that way when I got home from the quilt shop awhile ago."

"Maybe she's tired and needed a nap," Leona suggested.

Mary Ann shook her head. "She's heartsick over losing Edna."

"I'll have a word with her." Papa turned to Leona. "Why don't you stay in the kitchen with Mary Ann? You two can visit while I speak to Fannie."

"That might be best." Mary Ann pulled out a chair at the table. "I'll pour us some lemonade."

Papa left the room, and Leona took a seat. "How are things at the quilt shop?"

"Busy as usual for this time of the year. Abby says she's glad she hired me to help out because there's just too much work for her and Stella to do by themselves. Besides, once the school year begins, Stella will be back in school and won't be able to help Abby at all." Mary Ann took out a pitcher of lemonade from the refrigerator and placed it on the table. Bringing two glasses with her, she sat in the chair across from Leona. "I'm sorry you haven't made it to any of the young people's functions so far this summer. I think it would be good for you and help take your mind off—"

"Edna's funeral will be hard for many to get through," Leona interrupted. She didn't want to talk about her going to any young people's functions.

Mary Ann reached over and patted Leona's hand. "It's bound to bring back memories of Ezra's funeral, but you'll get through it, Leona."

"Let's talk about something else, okay?"

"Jah, sure. So how's the painting on the schoolhouse comin' along?"

"Good. The outside's done, and Jimmy and Eli will be starting on the inside tomorrow or the next day."

Mary Ann filled the glasses with lemonade and handed one to Leona. "Isn't Jimmy that English fellow your daed hired?"

Leona nodded and took a sip of her cool, tangy drink.

"I wasn't working at the quilt shop the day he came into the general store, but Naomi told me later that he reminded her of someone."

"Really? Who?"

"She didn't say. Just thought he looked kind of familiar."

"I don't see how he could be anyone she knows," Leona said. "He's from Washington."

"I've heard it said that everyone has a double somewhere." Mary Ann glanced at the door leading to the living room. "Sure hope your daed can get Mama Fannie calmed down."

"If anyone can, it will be him." Leona knew it was wrong to be full of *hochmut*, yet she couldn't help but feel a little pride in her daed's abilities to minister in such a gentle, caring way.

~~~~~

"I need to run over to Naomi's place," Abraham told his twin boys after they had quit work in the fields for the day. "Would one of you let your mamm know I'll be a few minutes late for supper?"

"Sure, Papa," Titus said with a nod.

"How come you're goin' over to our big sister's?" Timothy questioned. "Won't ya be seein' her at the funeral in a few days?"

"Jah, but I'm needing something from Naomi right now." Abraham headed for the stable to get one of their buggies. He hoped his oldest daughter had a homeopathic remedy that might help Fannie get through the funeral service. He figured it was best not to mention it to the boys. No point getting them all worried about their mamm.

Half an hour later, Abraham guided his horse and buggy up to Caleb's barn. He entered the house through the back door, and seeing no one in the kitchen, he cupped his hands around his mouth and called, "Are ya at home, Naomi?"

"Mama and Papa aren't back from the store yet; I'm upstairs, and so are the two younger ones."

Abraham recognized Susan's voice. "You comin' down, or should I come up there?"

"Come on up," she hollered.

Abraham found Susan in Naomi and Caleb's room, stripping sheets off the bed.

"What's goin' on?" He grimaced as the sour smell of *kotz* greeted him.

"Kevin and Millie both came down with the flu and have been throwing up all morning," she replied. "So I stayed home to care for them, and Sarah, Josh, and Nate went in with the folks today. Grandma Hoffmeir usually watches the younger ones, but she's got the flu, too."

"Sorry to hear they're sick. I take it the kinner must have been sleeping in this room."

Susan nodded and pushed a strand of ash-blond hair away from her face where it had worked its way from under her kapp.

"How come they weren't in their own beds?" he questioned.

"They were, but they both missed the bucket and ended up vomiting on their sheets. While I was changing their beds, I put them in Mama and Papa's room." She frowned. "By the time I was done and had their beds made up again, they'd thrown up in here, too."

Abraham shook his head, remembering the days of raising his own kinner. "I dropped by to see if your mamm has a homeopathic remedy that might help Fannie get through Edna's funeral without falling apart," he said. "Do you know where she keeps that kind of thing?"

Susan nodded toward the bathroom across the hall. "It could be either in the medicine chest or on the top shelf of the linen closet."

"Danki. I'll take a look." Abraham rushed out of the bedroom, anxious for some fresh air. The disagreeable odor of kotz had always made his stomach churn.

The bathroom didn't smell much better, giving proof that the children had probably gotten sick in there, as well. He searched quickly through the medicine chest but found no homeopathic remedies.

Frustrated, Abraham hurried into the hall and opened the linen closet. He discovered a stack of towels on the bottom shelf. There were a few bottles of aspirin and a jar of petroleum jelly on the top shelf, but he didn't see any remedies there, either. He was about to give up when he noticed a colorful piece of cloth sticking out of a box, also on the top shelf. Curious, he pulled it out, and his breath caught in his throat. *Why, this was Zach's quilt! I haven't seen it since the night before he was kidnapped, when I tucked him into bed, but I would recognize this anywhere.*

"Papa, what are you doing?"

Abraham whirled around and faced Naomi. He hadn't heard her come up the stairs. "I was looking for a homeopathic remedy that might calm Fannie's nerves." He thrust the quilt out to her. "Is—is this Zach's?"

∞

Naomi nodded as tears clouded her vision. She reached out a trembling hand and touched the edge of her brother's quilt. "Jah, Papa, it's his."

His steely blue eyes seemed to bore right through her. "How'd you get this, and how long have you had it?" he demanded.

A sense of guilt mixed with deep regret pricked Naomi's heart. "Abby gave it to me when she returned from her trip to Montana several years ago. She said Elizabeth, the woman she'd stayed with there, had found it in a thrift store somewhere in the state of Washington."

"But Abby came back to Pennsylvania fourteen years ago. If you've had Zach's quilt that long, why have you been keeping it from me?" Papa's hand trembled as he held the quilt against his chest.

"I was afraid of getting your hopes up."

"Why would I get my hopes up?" He grimaced, and a shadow passed across his face. "My son's been missing for twenty years, Naomi. Don't ya think I had the right to know the quilt had been found?"

"Jah. You had the right. I was wrong." Tears streamed down her cheeks, and she hung her head, unable to meet his piercing gaze. At the time Naomi had decided to keep the quilt hidden from her daed, she had felt that she was doing the right thing. She'd planned to put the quilt in her baby's room but had changed her mind and stuck it in the linen closet instead. She'd almost forgotten about it until now. "I should have shown it to you right away. It would have saved us both this awkward, painful moment," she murmured, lifting her head.

Her daed blinked a couple of times as though he was struggling not to cry. His protruding Adam's apple bobbed up and down. "Do you suppose this means Zach is dead?"

She gasped. "Oh no, Papa! Surely, it doesn't mean that. Abby told me once that she thought the man who took Zach must have sold the quilt to the thrift shop—probably to get rid of any evidence that he'd taken an Amish baby."

"Maybe so. Maybe not." Papa buried his face in the folds of the quilt and sniffed deeply. "All these years I've prayed for Zach, asking the Lord to watch over my boy and bring him safely back home." His shoulders trembled, and his voice cracked. "I. . .I guess God's answer was no. Otherwise, your little bruder would have returned to us by now."

Naomi didn't know how to respond. Maybe Papa was right. God's answer to their prayers for Zach's safe return must have been no.

"The time for talking about my missing son must end right now." Papa stared hard at Naomi, and his eyes glazed over. "Zach's gone for good, and it only hurts to keep bringing him up. It's over and done with, and I'm not going to discuss him with you or anyone else ever again." He threw the quilt on the floor, whirled around, and hurried down the stairs.

Naomi released a sob as she bent over to retrieve the small covering. "I'm so sorry, Papa. Sorry for all the grief I've brought to this family."

Chapter 17

Leona scurried about the kitchen, helping Edna's daughter, Gretchen, and several other women serve the funeral dinner. She noticed that Fannie, wearing a placid expression, kept busy filling platters and plates for the younger women to carry outside to the tables. During the funeral service, which had been held in the barn, and again at the graveside committal, Fannie had appeared to be in control of her emotions.

It must be due to Papa's visit with her the other day, Leona thought. Her daed seemed to have a calming effect on everyone—herself included. She certainly needed some calming today after spending time with Ezra's family and, despite her determination not to do so, reliving the day of Ezra's funeral in her mind.

Leona's thoughts halted when she glanced across the room and noticed Naomi sitting at the kitchen table and staring at a bowl of salad greens as if in a daze. Surely, Naomi couldn't be taking Edna's death harder than Fannie was. Edna wasn't a blood relative of Naomi's, and as far as Leona knew, Naomi had never been that close to her stepmother's cousin.

Leona wiped her hands on a dish towel and moved across the room. She stopped behind Naomi's chair and placed one hand on the woman's trembling shoulder. "You doin' okay?"

Naomi gave a quick shake of her head.

"Would you like to go outside for a while? The fresh air might do you some good."

"I'm not sure the air's so fresh out there, but I guess it must be less stuffy than it is in here," Abby interjected as she passed by the table. "I think the men have all been served their meal now, so why don't the three of us find a place to eat our lunch where we can visit?"

Naomi made no move to get up. "I'm really not hungry."

"Oh, but you've got to eat," Leona insisted. "Once you walk up to that table and see all the good food that's been provided for this meal, I'm sure you'll find something that will appeal."

"Jah, okay." Naomi sighed and followed Abby and Leona outside.

The other women had already gathered at the tables that had been set up in the yard, so Leona filled her plate and found them an empty table under the shade of a leafy maple tree. Abby sat beside Naomi, and Leona took the bench across from them.

"Your mamm seems to be doing well today," Leona said to Abby.

Abby nodded. "Abraham gave her some kind of a natural remedy he got from the health food store. Between that and whatever your daed said to her when he stopped by their place yesterday afternoon, Mom's been able to get through the day pretty well."

Leona glanced at Naomi, wishing she knew what was troubling her. *Should I come right out and ask?*

"Abraham said he stopped by your place the other day," Abby said, turning to Naomi. "He mentioned that Millie and Kevin had come down with the flu."

"Jah."

"Are they still sick?" Leona asked.

"They're doing some better, but Sarah stayed home with the sick ones so that Susan, Josh, and Nate could come to the funeral with Caleb and me," Naomi replied.

Abby's wrinkled forehead revealed her obvious concern. "I hope no one else in your family comes down with the flu. You've got enough to keep you busy this summer without having to care for sick kinner."

Naomi stared at her plate full of food but made no effort to take a bite, and she gave no reply to Abby's comment.

Something is troubling her, and I've got a hunch it's more than sorrow over Edna Yoder's passing. Leona could hardly stand to see the gloomy expression on Naomi's face. She was about to express her concerns when Naomi scooted off the bench and stood. "I think I'll take a walk down to the creek." She hurried off before either Leona or Abby could say a word.

Naomi trembled as she knelt on the grass near the edge of the water. *Papa will hardly look at me today. I was wrong to keep the truth from him about Zach's quilt. I should have told him as soon as Abby gave it to me. Will I ever learn?* Tears stung the back of her eyes, and she gulped on a sob. *If I could change the past, I surely would—starting with that horrible day I left Zach sitting on the picnic table.*

Naomi felt the pressure of someone's hand on her shoulder, and she turned her head. Leona and Abby stood behind her, both wearing looks of concern.

"What's wrong, Naomi? Why'd you run off like that?" Leona questioned. "Why are you crying?"

"I've wronged my daed, and now he's upset with me," she said with a moan.

Abby knelt beside her, and Leona did the same. "What did you do? Or would you rather not say?" Abby asked.

Naomi swallowed hard and fought for control. "Papa dropped by our house yesterday, and he discovered Zach's quilt."

Abby's mouth dropped open. "How did that happen? I thought you had decided not to show it to him."

"I put it in a box in the linen closet some time ago,

never thinking Papa would have any reason to look there."

Leona toyed with the strings on her kapp as she stared at the ground in front of her. "Maybe I should go. This sounds like something I'm not supposed to hear."

Naomi shook her head. "You don't have to go. The secret's out now, so I suppose it doesn't matter who knows."

Abby reached for Naomi's hand and gave it a gentle squeeze. "I'm sure once your daed thinks things through he will realize why you didn't tell him that I'd given you the baby quilt."

"How'd you end up with Naomi's little brother's quilt?" Leona asked, giving Abby a curious look.

Abby quickly relayed how she had acquired the quilt, and then Naomi explained that she hadn't wanted Papa to know about it because she was afraid seeing the quilt and not knowing where Zach was would have opened old wounds. "And now Papa wants everyone to stop talking about Zach. He thinks it's time to lay the past to rest once and for all."

"I understand that reasoning." Leona put her arm around Naomi and gave her a hug. "Things will work out between you and your daed. I'll be praying that they will." She stood and brushed a chunk of grass off her skirt. "I think I'll head on back to the house. I need to speak with Ezra's folks again before my family heads for home."

"Danki for your concern," Naomi said with a nod. It came as no surprise to her that the bishop's daughter would have such compassion and understanding.

∞

When Jimmy finished work for the day, he decided to drive down a few of the roads he hadn't been on yet so he could take more pictures and continue his search for an Amish farm that sold root beer.

He stopped at a covered bridge near Highway 222 and took several shots. Then, seeing nothing else that interested him, he headed up Highway 23. He'd only gone a short distance when he spotted a sign nailed to a tree near the end of a driveway that advertised root beer. He turned in, and his pickup bounced along the narrow, graveled road until he came to a makeshift stand several feet from the house. Jimmy turned off the engine and got out of his truck. *Was Dad telling me the truth? Could this be the place he told me about?*

He walked up to the stand and, seeing no one in sight, gave the bell on the wooden counter a good shake.

A few minutes later, a freckle-faced Amish boy came out of the house and slipped behind the counter. "Are ya wantin' a jug of root beer?" he asked with a friendly grin.

"Do you sell it by the glass?"

The boy nodded. "Got some paper cups right here. You want a small one or large?"

"Uh. . .large, I guess." Jimmy paid the boy, and while he waited for his root beer to be served, his gaze roamed over the spacious farmyard where cows grazed in the pasture and chickens ran about clucking and pecking at one another. *Could this have been my home? Is it possible that I was stolen from this yard?*

"Here ya go."

Jimmy snapped his attention back to the boy. He reached for the paper cup and took a drink. "This is real tasty root beer."

"My daed makes it."

Could your daed be my daed? Jimmy shifted his weight and took another swallow of the mellow, tasty beverage. "I. . .uh. . .need information."

"Are ya lost?" the boy asked with a tilt of his head. "Some folks who stop by here needin' information are on the wrong road and don't know how to get to where they're goin'."

"No, I'm not lost."

"Then what do ya need to know?"

"I was wondering if—has anyone here ever lost a baby?"

The boy blinked a couple of times and then gave a quick nod.

Jimmy set the paper cup on the wooden counter and wiped his sweaty palms along the sides of his jeans. "Really? How long ago?"

" 'Bout a year, I'd say. Lost my baby goat when its mamm wouldn't feed it. The poor thing up and died."

At first Jimmy felt irritation. Then he realized the boy must have misunderstood his question. "I wasn't talking about an animal. I was referring to a baby boy—about a year old."

The child's auburn-colored eyebrows lifted so high they nearly disappeared under the brim of his tattered straw hat. "Is somebody missin' a baby?"

"Not now. It was about twenty years ago. A man supposedly went to a root beer stand and kidnapped an Amish baby."

The boy looked at Jimmy like he'd taken leave of his senses. "You sure you got the right place? Ain't no baby been taken from here. If there was, my folks sure woulda said somethin' about it."

"I guess I must have the wrong place." Jimmy turned and started toward his truck as a feeling of frustration threatened to knock him to the ground. Was all this hunting for an Amish farm selling root beer a waste of his time? Was there any point in continuing to look?

"Don't ya want the rest of your root beer?" the boy called after him.

"No thanks. I'm not thirsty anymore." *Maybe what I'd better do is call Dad again. If he really did kidnap me, then he's got to give me some better answers. And if he's made the whole story up, then he'd better tell me the truth.*

Chapter 18

Jimmy climbed into his truck and pushed his painter's hat down on his head as he waited for Eli to come out of the house. A lot had changed for him in the last few weeks. Thanks to Eli's parents, Jimmy now rented a small trailer at the back of their property. And because of his new friend's patient teaching, he had learned a few words of Pennsylvania Dutch and was beginning to feel more comfortable with his surroundings here in Amish country. He and Eli had finished up the job on the schoolhouse a few weeks ago, and then, with the other men in Jacob's crew, they had painted a couple of houses and the outside of a gift store in Lititz. Today they would begin work on Mark Stauffer's barn.

Jimmy had learned from Eli that Mark was married to Nancy, one of Naomi Hoffmeir's sisters. He'd been told that the couple had three children and lived next door to Mark's folks, Elmer and Mandy. It seemed like everyone in this community was related somehow.

"Guder mariye," Eli said, climbing into Jimmy's pickup.

"Guder mariye to you, too." Jimmy grinned. "Did I say 'good morning' right?"

Eli nodded. "You're catchin' on real good to the Deitsch."

Feeling rather pleased with himself, Jimmy turned on the engine and steered his vehicle down the driveway. A short time later, they arrived at the Stauffers' place.

Jimmy noticed right away that the barn had already been scraped and primed. With a crew of five painters working on the building, including the bishop, it should take them only a few days to complete the job.

Jacob gave everyone instructions, telling the men to begin work on the shaded side of the barn. He asked his son, Arthur, to work with Jimmy on the back side, while Eli and Richard painted the doors and trim around the windows.

"I'll climb the forty-foot ladder and do the high spots," Jacob announced. "That way, I can look down and see how things are goin'."

"Why don't you let me or one of the younger men do that, Pop?" Arthur suggested. "You're gettin' too old to be up on a tall ladder."

Jacob leveled his son with a most determined look and shook his head. "I ain't old, and since I'm the boss, I'll decide who gets to do what."

Jimmy bit back a chuckle and looked the other way. He got a kick out of the bishop's spunky attitude. *I'll bet my dad will be that way when he gets to be Jacob's age. He has always liked to be the one in control.*

Thinking about Dad caused Jimmy to worry a bit. He'd tried several times in the last few days to reach his dad by phone, and all he ever got was the answering machine at home or voice mail on his cell. *I hope he's not on another drinking bender. If he is. . . Oh, man, I wish I'd thought to bring Ed's number with me. Maybe I'll give Allen a call when I get off work today and ask him to check up on Dad.*

∞

Jim rolled over in bed, grabbed the extra pillow beside his head, and covered his ears. Even so, his alarm clock continued to blare in his ear. He knew it was 6:00 a.m., and he also knew he was supposed to leave for work in one hour. But he didn't know how he would make it. He'd been drinking steadily for nearly a week—sometimes not even bothering to come home at night.

Last night, he'd finally sobered up enough to realize he needed a bath and a good night's sleep, so he'd left his van parked at The Gold Fish Tavern and called a cab to take him home.

I've missed a week's worth of work, too, he thought ruefully. *But then I'm sure Ed's been keeping our jobs going.* He moaned and swung one leg, then the other, over the side of the bed. "Oh, my head's killing me."

Jim rubbed his blurry eyes, and as his vision began to focus, his gaze came to rest on the picture sitting on the dresser across the room. It was the last picture of Jim, Linda, and Jimmy together, taken a year before Linda died.

He grimaced, remembering how he'd put up a fuss when Linda told him about the appointment she'd made with the portrait studio across town. He'd said he was too busy to go but had finally relented when Linda reminded him that she might not have much longer to live. "I was such a lousy husband. Never could do anything right, and I guess I still can't."

He thought of all the times Linda had tried to get him to go to church, and how her friends, Beth and Eric Walters, had attempted to be his friends after she'd died. But he'd continued to reject all forms of religion, and he sure didn't need any Bible-thumping friends of Linda's to hold his hand.

A feeling of sadness and deep regret swept over him like a heavy fog as he thought about Jimmy and how he had failed him, too. *If I hadn't kidnapped the boy when he was a baby, he wouldn't be on a quest to find his rightful heritage now, and I wouldn't have to worry about the possibility of going to jail.*

Jim stood on rubbery legs and ambled across the room toward his closet. *I don't care whether he believes me about the kidnapping or not. Maybe if he thinks I made up the whole story, he'll stop searching for his real parents and come home.*

Feeling the need for some kind of comfort, he halted when he reached his dresser and grabbed the half-empty bottle of beer he'd left sitting there the night before. "At least I've got one friend I can count on," he mumbled as he lifted the bottle to his parched lips.

⌒⌒⌒

As Leona drove her horse and buggy down Harristown Road toward Nancy and Mark Stauffer's place, the sounds of summer engulfed her. The *buzz* of insects, the *click-click-click* of sprinklers, and the continual chirp of birds overhead—all brought a sense of peace she hadn't experienced in many days.

She thought about the conversation she'd had with Naomi when she stopped by Hoffmeirs' General Store yesterday afternoon. Naomi had mentioned that things were still strained between her and her daed, and she said she was sure that, even though many years ago Abraham had said he'd forgiven her for leaving Zach alone, he'd never truly let it go.

"So much pain and distress some people must endure." She inhaled deeply, savoring the pleasant aroma of freshly cut hay. Then she glanced across the road to see where the smell came from. A newly mowed field bordered the Stauffers' place, and in the distance, she could see their stately white house with the faded red barn sitting behind it.

As Leona drew closer, she caught sight of Papa's crew painting on one side of the barn. She directed the horse onto the graveled driveway and stopped near the house where there would be less chance of getting paint on the buggy.

Jimmy waved to her, and she lifted her hand in response. Then she climbed down from the buggy, secured the horse to a maple tree, and headed for the barn.

"What brings you over here today?" Jimmy asked as she drew near.

"I brought my daed's lunch. He left it on the kitchen counter when he went to work this morning."

"Pop must have been in a hurry to get over here and begin work on Mark's barn," Arthur interjected as he came around the corner, carrying a bucket of paint.

"I think so," Leona said with a nod. "Where is our daed, anyhow?"

Arthur turned and pointed to a ladder leaning against one side of the barn. "Up there."

Leona shielded her eyes from the glare of the sun and tipped her head to get a better look. There stood Papa on the third-to-the-last rung of the ladder with his paintbrush zipping back and forth faster than she could blink. She sucked in her breath. "*Ach*, my! He shouldn't be on that tall ladder."

"He insisted on doing the high painting," Arthur said, shaking his head. "I tried to talk him out of it, but he reminded me, like always, that he's the boss."

Leona knew how stubborn her daed could be when it came to anyone telling him how to run his business—including his only son.

"Jacob's doing fine so far." Jimmy's long legs filled the space between them. "I'm sure he would have let one of the younger men do the high painting if he didn't think he was capable of doing it himself."

Leona looked over at Jimmy and was about to comment when her daed hollered down, "Can someone run up to the house and see if Nancy's got some *weschp* spray? There's a wasp's nest up here, and some of them critters have been buzzin' me real good." The ladder wobbled as he lifted his straw hat from his head and waved it in the air. "Get away from me, you crazy weschp!"

"Be careful, Papa, the ladder is—" Leona gasped

as the ladder lurched and her daed lost his grip, falling straight to the ground.

Every man dropped his brush and rushed to their boss's side, but Leona just stood there, too numb to move.

"Pop! Can ya hear me?" Arthur looked at Leona with a pained expression. "He's out cold, and there's blood coming out of his ears. Someone with a cell phone had better call 911!"

Chapter 19

"Dear Lord, why did You allow such a terrible thing to happen? How will we ever get through this?" Leona lamented as she stood in front of her bedroom window and stared out at the gray skies. It had been raining steadily since yesterday evening. Leona was exhausted, and her eyes burned from lack of sleep. The dismal, dark clouds that hid the sun matched her melancholy mood to a T. She leaned against the window casing, tears coursing down her cheeks as she thought about that fateful morning two weeks ago when their lives had been changed in one split second—the moment Papa took his hand off the ladder to swat at a buzzing wasp. Jimmy Scott had been the one to call for help, using his cell phone. Then he'd covered her daed with a blanket and instructed everyone not to move him. After the ambulance took Papa away, Jimmy had given Leona, her mother, and her brother a ride to the hospital. The rest of the day had been spent waiting and praying for some word on Papa's condition. Leona's two older sisters, who lived in Kentucky, had been notified and said they would come as soon as they were able to secure transportation. Jimmy had remained at Leona's side the entire day, although she barely remembered anything he'd said to her.

Leona closed her eyes as she relived that day in the hospital, after all the tests had been done and the doctor had taken the family aside to give them his prognosis. . . .

❦

"Jacob has had a severe trauma to the brain, and there's a good deal of swelling," Dr. Collins told the family as they stood just inside the door of Papa's room. "Amazingly enough, he has no broken bones—just scrapes and bruises on his arms and legs, but the blow to his head seems to have caused an acute memory lapse that has taken him all the way back to his childhood."

"Will my husband ever be the same?" Mom asked as she clutched the doctor's arm. "Please say he will recover from this."

Dr. Collins's gaze went to Papa lying in the bed with his eyes closed. Then he looked back at Leona's mamm. "There's no way of knowing at this point, Mrs. Weaver. Once the swelling goes down, Jacob could regain all or part of his memory. Or he might remain this way for the rest of his life."

"We need to pray for a miracle," Arthur interjected. "Jah, that's what we surely need."

Mom nodded as tears matted her lashes and trickled onto her cheeks. "God is able to do all things, and if it's His will, then He'll make my husband whole again."

Leona leaned against the wall with her arms folded and her lips pressed together, her eyes closed. God, You could have prevented this from happening. Why didn't You? Don't You care about Papa? Doesn't it matter that he is Your servant and so many people depend on him?

"Jacob will need to go through some therapy here at the hospital before he's released," Dr. Collins continued. "And of course, there are things you can do at home to help him adjust."

Mom nodded once more. "We'll do all we can."

Leona clenched her fists so tightly that her nails dug

into her palms. Adjust? How can my daed adjust to anything when he thinks he's a little boy?

⚯

Leona shuddered and moved away from the window, allowing her thoughts to return to the present. She was thankful Papa was alive. However, the thought of him spending the rest of his days as a child in a man's body was unthinkable. How could he run his painting business or do the chores he normally did around their place? And what of his position as bishop? He could hardly preach or minister to the people if he thought like a child. Poor, confused Papa didn't know he'd ever been their bishop or that he owned a successful painting business. He thought his wife was his mamm, and he believed Leona and her brother were his siblings. He hadn't known his oldest daughters, Peggy or Rebecca, at all when they'd come to visit soon after the accident.

Leona held her arms rigid at her side. Resentment welled up in her soul like a cancer. She fought the churning sensation in her stomach. *Unless God provides a miracle, Papa might never know any of us again.* She stumbled across the room, flopped onto her bed, and covered her mouth in an effort to stop the tears. *It isn't fair. This terrible tragedy never should have happened!*

⚯

Jimmy had just stepped out of his truck and placed a bucket of paint on the porch of Norman Fisher's house when his cell phone rang. He removed it from the clip on his belt and lifted it to his ear. "Hello."

"Hi, Jimmy, it's Dad. I—I haven't heard from you in a while, and I was getting worried."

"You were worried? Do you know how many times

I've tried to call you? And all I ever got was the answering machine at home or your voice mail on the cell."

"Sorry, but I wasn't up to taking any calls."

"Have you been sick?"

"Yeah—well, sort of."

Jimmy groaned. "You've been on another drinking spree, haven't you, Dad?"

"So what if I have? It's my life, and I don't need you or Ed telling me what to do."

Jimmy knew Dad's foreman was aware of his drinking problem, and he figured Ed had probably given Dad a lecture about how he might lose his business if he didn't straighten up. *Guess there's not much point in me doing the same, because it's obvious that he isn't going to listen. Maybe Allen was right when he said Dad might have to hit rock bottom before he ever admits he has a problem or is willing to seek help.*

"Are you still there, Jimmy?"

"I'm here."

"How are things going? Have you found your Amish family yet?"

"No, but I did find an Amish farm selling root beer, and the kid looked at me like I was nuts when I asked about a stolen baby."

"You must have been at the wrong place."

"Yeah, well, what's the *right* place, Dad?"

"I don't know. I told you before that I was almost in a daze that day, and I don't remember what road I was on, or even what part of Lancaster County I was in."

"Are you sure you're not making this story up to confuse me?"

"Why would I do that? I put my neck in the noose when I admitted that I'd kidnapped you." There was a pause, and he added, "I. . .I've been keeping this secret for twenty years, Jimmy, and it's taken a toll on me."

"On you? What about the family you took me

from?" Jimmy's own words echoed in his head as he allowed the truth to sink in. *Dad really did kidnap me. He wouldn't be so worried about going to jail if he hadn't committed the crime, and he wouldn't be going on long drinking benders if he wasn't dealing with guilt and fear.*

"It's true, isn't it?" he squeaked. "You stole me from an Amish farm twenty years ago."

"That's what I've been trying to tell you. I did it for your mom. I did it because I thought it was meant to be."

"How could stealing a child ever be right or 'meant to be'?" Jimmy's voice shook with unbridled emotion as he struggled with the anger he felt toward the man he'd thought was his dad.

"Wh—what are you going to. . .to do, Jimmy?" Dad's tone sounded desperate, and his words were shaky.

"I'm going to stick around Lancaster County awhile longer."

"To look for your family?"

"That and to help the Weaver family."

"Who is this Weaver family, and why do they need your help?"

Jimmy quickly shared the story of Jacob's accident. "Jacob's home from the hospital now," he ended by saying. "And since his son wants me to keep painting for them, I'll be around to help the Weaver family deal with Jacob's injury." Jimmy pulled a rag from his back pocket and wiped the perspiration from his forehead.

"So this is the Amish fella who hired you to paint for him?"

"Right. The doctor told Jacob's family that, short of a miracle, he might never fully recover."

"That's too bad, Jimmy. You're a good kid for wanting to help."

"I'm not a kid anymore. I just turned twenty-one, remember?" A sudden, sinking feeling hit Jimmy with such force he thought he might topple over. "You don't even really know how old I am or when I was born, do you, Dad?"

"I. . .I don't know the exact day you were born, but your Amish sister said you had recently turned one, so when I had your phony birth certificate made up, I asked my friend to give you an April birthday."

Phony birth certificate? A made-up April birthday? Jimmy sank to the grass. This whole kidnapping thing was getting thicker and sicker. He gave his forehead another swipe with the rag. "Listen, I. . .uh. . .need to get back to work."

"Okay. I'll talk to you again soon, son."

Jimmy clicked off the phone without even saying good-bye.

∽∽

"I don't see why we had to tag along with you this morning," Titus complained from his seat at the back of Abraham's buggy. "Shouldn't we be helpin' our older brothers work in the fields today?"

"Yeah," his twin brother agreed. "I feel funny around Jacob Weaver since he fell on his head and turned into a kid. It's hard to know how we should act around him."

Abraham glanced over at Timothy, who sat beside him. "Don't you be talkin' that way. Jacob can't help that he's lost his memory. Since he's not able to do many of the things he used to do, his family needs all the help they can get. Just act like yourselves and help me with some chores that need doin'." Abraham thought of all the times Jacob had helped him in the past. He'd offered his friendship and spiritual counsel when it was needed the most, so now Abraham wasn't about to let his friend down in his hour of need. He would help the

Weaver family as long as it was required.

"Can't the bishop's son help him?" Timothy questioned.

"I'm sure Arthur's helping as much as he can, but he has his daed's business to run now, which is a full-time job."

Titus leaned over the seat and tapped his father on the shoulder. "What about Leona and her mamm? Aren't they gonna be helpin' out?"

Abraham groaned. "Of course they are, but they have their own chores to do; there are some tasks only a man can manage."

Timothy snorted. "Jacob might be thinkin' like a little kid now, but he's still got the body of a man. I'm sure he could handle most of the chores if he was told what to do." He folded his arms and looked straight ahead. "Me and Titus have been doin' our share of chores ever since we could walk."

"Yeah, that's right," his twin agreed. "I've been haulin' wood in our old wheelbarrow since before I can remember."

Abraham clenched his teeth. It was bad enough that things between him and Naomi were strained. He didn't need two complaining teenagers to deal with this morning. "I'm sure there will be certain chores that Jacob's capable of doing, but the doctor wants him to take it easy and give his body a chance to recover from that nasty fall." He looked at Timothy, then over his shoulder at Titus. "I don't want to hear another word about your not wantin' to help. Is that clear?"

"Jah," the twins said in unison.

A short time later, Abraham guided his horse and buggy onto Jacob's property and pulled back on the reins, halting the horse in front of the rail near the barn. *Oh, Lord,* he silently prayed. *Please give my good friend his memory back.*

Chapter 20

Leona glanced at the other side of the barn where the men sat on backless, wooden benches during their Sunday preaching service. This week's service was being held at Jake Fisher's place. She spotted Papa sitting beside Arthur. On the other side of him sat Abraham Fisher. Abraham was a kind yet determined man, who had gone through many trials over the years, and Leona knew he cared about her family. He had proven that by all he'd done since her daed's accident—coming over to do some of the more difficult chores, bringing dishes of food Fannie had prepared, and letting Mom know that he and his family had been praying. Others in the community had been kind and offered their assistance and prayers, as well.

Leona stared at the veins protruding from her clenched hands as her thoughts continued to drift. Jimmy Scott had also been a big help since her daed's mishap. He often dropped by the house, offering to do chores and spending many hours with Papa. They talked, went for walks, and even played with the animals in the barn. Papa seemed to enjoy being around the barn animals, and he'd even made a pet out of one of the baby goats.

It's nice that Jimmy wants to be with Papa, but I don't know what they would have to talk about, she thought. *With Papa thinking he's a little boy, it's not likely that he'd have much in common with Jimmy or any other grown man, Amish or English, and yet he carries on as though he's known Jimmy all his life. Maybe Jimmy reminds Papa of one of his childhood friends. Jah, that's probably it.*

Leona remembered how distressing it had been the

first day her daed came home from the hospital and saw his face in Mom's hand mirror. He'd clutched Mom's hand and begged her to take away that old man with the beard who stared back at him. No matter how much explaining Mom did, Papa couldn't seem to grasp the concept that he was a grown man with a family, even though he had seen himself in the mirror several times since then.

Leona heard a scuffle on the other side of the room and glanced over to see what was going on. She was shocked to discover her daed standing in the aisle with his hands on his hips, staring at Leona's brother. "I need a drink of water. I told ya three times already—I'm thirsty," he said, his voice a little too loud.

Arthur's face turned cherry red, and he reached out and grabbed hold of Papa's hand. "Sit back down, please."

Papa jerked his hand away and took a step backward. "Mama said I could have some water whenever I feel thirsty!"

Leona quickly scanned the room. Everyone seemed to be watching Papa instead of Matthew Fisher, the song leader for the day. She knew if her daed were really a little boy, and not their bishop who'd lost his memory, he would have been taken outside for a good tongue-lashing or maybe even a sound *bletsching*. Amish children were taught at an early age to sit quietly during church, and no parent would allow an outburst such as this. Although her daed couldn't lose his title as bishop, he wouldn't be required to do any of his previous duties right now. Even so, he should be expected to sit still during the three-hour service, like all the kinner who were present.

Papa gave Arthur's hand another tug, and finally, Arthur grunted, stood, and led their daed out of the room.

Leona breathed a sigh of relief and forced her gaze back to the songbook resting on her knees. *"The innermost life of the true Christian shineth, tho' outwardly darkened by trials on hand."* The words on the page blurred, and she closed her eyes.

∞

The following morning, Leona awoke with a headache. She hadn't slept well, and the weather had turned hot and muggy after a heavy rainfall, which didn't help her mood any. Her stomach growled, yet she didn't feel hungry. It was as though her body and mind waged a war on one another these days.

Despite the pounding in her temples, Leona knew she must wash up and get dressed because Mom would need help making breakfast. She lifted herself off the bed and started across the room, but every move took courage and stamina she didn't seem to have.

Sometime later, she descended the steps and was on her way to the kitchen when the back door flew open and a baby goat trotted into the house. Papa followed, his face all red and sweaty.

"You'd better get that animal out of here before Mom sees him. And you're tracking mud into the house with your wet feet." Leona crossed her arms and glared at him. It seemed odd to be speaking to her daed in such a way, but if he was going to act like a child, he needed to be treated like one.

"I ain't got wet feet. I'm wearing my *gammschtiwwel.*"

Before Leona could scold him about wearing his rubber boots inside, the goat darted into the living room, circled the rocking chair a couple of times, and then leaped onto the sofa. Papa laughed as he chased after it, angering Leona further. "This isn't funny, Papa. The living room is no place for a goat!" She could hardly believe the same man who had been so adamant about no pets in the house all these years could now be entertaining a goat—and right here in the living room, of all places!

"I'll take him upstairs to my bedroom." Papa grabbed hold of the goat's underbelly, lifted the squirming animal into his arms, and started across the room.

Leona positioned herself in front of the staircase. "That animal belongs outside in his pen, so please take him there now."

He glared at her defiantly. "You're not my boss, Sister."

"I'm not your sister, but if you don't do as I say, I'm going to call Mom."

Papa's lower lip jutted out, and his forehead wrinkled. "Everything is out of kilter for me."

"I know," she said, her anger abating.

Papa hugged the struggling goat tighter and sauntered over to the front door. "Want me to make the door shut?"

"Jah, please."

Just as his hand touched the knob, he called over his shoulder, "Ya know what? You're not much fun, Ona!"

His words stung, but Leona kept quiet.

The door closed behind Papa, and as his final word registered in her brain, Leona stood there, too numb to move. He'd called her "Ona"—the nickname he had given her when she was a little girl. Did her daed know who she was now?

She rushed out the door after him. "Papa, wait up!"

He halted at the bottom of the steps, glanced around the yard, and then turned to face her. "Where's Papa? I don't see him nowhere. How come our daed's never around anymore?"

A weary sigh escaped Leona's lips. If Papa had momentarily remembered her, his memory had already vanished. "Papa's gone away," she said with a moan. "Papa's gone away and might never come back."

Her daed squinted and stared at her. Then unexpectedly, his face broke into a wide smile. "Ah, you're just kiddin' with me, ain't ya, Mary?"

He thinks I'm his sister again. Leona gulped in a deep breath and released it quickly. "Jah. I'm just kidding." With her shoulders slumped and a heart full of regrets, she turned toward the house. *I'm a schoolteacher, and I should be accustomed to children's silly ways. But dealing with the mind of a child inside a man's body is an entirely different matter.*

≪≫

"Would ya mind stoppin' by Hoffmeirs' General Store on our way to the next job site?" Eli asked as he and Jimmy drove into the town of Paradise. "I'm needing a new lunch pail, and Caleb usually keeps a pretty good supply on hand."

Jimmy shrugged. "Sure, I guess we have time to stop." A few minutes later, he pulled his truck into the parking lot next to the store and turned off the engine.

When the two men entered the store, Eli headed straight for the shelves where the lunch pails were kept. Jimmy glanced around the room and was surprised to see Jacob standing in front of the candy counter with a look of longing on his bearded face.

"How are you doing today?" Jimmy asked, stepping up beside the bishop.

"I'd be better if I had some candy." He looked over at Jimmy and blinked a couple of times. "Licorice is my favorite kind."

Jimmy reached into his pocket and withdrew a dollar. "Pick out a few hunks, and I'll buy them for you."

"Really?"

Jimmy nodded.

Jacob glanced around, kind of nervous-like. "You think my mamm will care?"

"Maybe we should ask. Where is she?"

Jacob pointed toward the adjoining quilt shop. "She and Mary went in there."

Jimmy knew the confused man was referring to Leona, since the other day she'd told him that her dad still thought she was his sister."

"Why don't you wait here? I'll go speak to Lydia about the candy."

Jacob's eyebrows furrowed. "Who?"

He patted the bishop's arm. "I'll speak to your mamm."

"Jah, okay. Hurry back."

Jimmy found Leona and her mother talking to Abby Fisher, who sat at a table working on a quilt. The vivid blue colors and unusual star-shaped pattern reminded him of the quilt that had been on his parents' bed during his childhood. After Mom passed away, Dad had put the quilt in a closet, saying it brought back too many painful memories. At the time, Jimmy thought he meant the covering reminded him of Mom. But since he'd been told about his kidnapping and had now accepted the story as truth, he wondered if the fact that the quilt had been Amish-made was what really had bothered Dad.

Jimmy thought about last Saturday and how he'd driven all over the area around New Providence looking for a place that sold root beer. It had been a waste of time, just like all the other places he'd already looked. Even though Jimmy felt discouraged and realized that he might never locate his real family, he'd begun to wonder if God might have brought him to Lancaster County to help the Weavers, not to find his Amish roots. In fact, that was all that seemed important to

Jimmy right now.

"Can I help you with something?" Abby asked.

Jimmy blinked and pushed his musings aside. "I. . . uh. . .was wondering if Lydia would mind if I bought Jacob some licorice."

Lydia smiled. "I have no problem with it. He is a grown man, after all."

Jimmy nodded, then glanced over at Leona, but she seemed preoccupied as she fiddled with the spool of thread she held in her hands. He looked back at Lydia. "How are things going this week? Is Jacob showing any signs of improvement?"

Lydia shook her head, and even though a look of sadness swept over her face, he sensed her determination to look on the brighter side of things. "I haven't lost faith," she murmured. "If it's God's will for Jacob's memory to return, then it surely will."

Leona moved over to stand by the window. Jimmy was tempted to follow and offer some words of encouragement, but he decided against it. The last time he'd stopped by the Weavers' place and mentioned the idea of putting Jacob to work on some of the schoolhouse repairs, Leona had stared at him in obvious disbelief and said, "You can't be serious. My daed would never be able to help with repairs. He may look like he's capable of a man's work, but he thinks like a child, so he can't be expected to do anything more than a boy would do." The decided edge to her voice and the look of defeat he'd seen on her face let Jimmy know Leona still wasn't dealing well with her father's accident. His heart went out to her—and to everyone else in Jacob's family.

A short time later, as Eli and Jimmy were about to climb into his truck, he overheard Lydia, who stood near her closed-in buggy, ordering Jacob to get in. Leona sat in the driver's seat, and her deep frown conveyed her frustration. Jimmy knew he couldn't drive off without offering to help.

"Is there a problem?" he asked, stepping between Lydia and her husband.

She nodded, and a tear trickled down her cheek. "Jacob refuses to get into the buggy."

"Is that true?" Jimmy asked. He looked at the bishop, who stood with his arms folded in an unyielding pose.

"Mama won't let me have more candy."

"I bought you some licorice. Did you eat it all?"

"Jah, it's gone." Jacob patted his stomach and gave Jimmy a sheepish-looking grin.

"It will soon be time for lunch," Jimmy said, taking hold of the man's arm. "You don't want to spoil your appetite by eating too much candy, do you?"

Jacob lowered his eyebrows and stared at the ground. "My eatin' went away."

Jimmy glanced over at Lydia and shrugged. He had no idea what the man was talking about.

"I think he means that his appetite has left him."

"And no wonder, what with him eating candy so close to lunch," Leona chimed in from her seat in the front of the buggy.

"Would you like me to stop by your house later tonight? We can play with your goat if you like," Jimmy said, hoping to get Jacob's mind on something else.

"That'd be nice."

Jimmy nodded at the buggy. "Then climb inside, and I'll see you later on."

Without a word of argument, Jacob climbed into the back, smiling like a happy child.

"Thank you, Jimmy." Lydia took a seat beside her daughter and lifted her hand in a wave.

"I'll see you later this evening," Jimmy called as the buggy pulled out of the parking lot.

Eli, who had been standing beside Jimmy's truck during the whole ordeal, shook his head. "That was sure somethin' the way you handled things with our bishop. You've got a way with him that no one else seems to have, that's for certain sure."

Jimmy opened the truck door. "I only wish I could do more."

Chapter 21

J immy had just placed his breakfast dishes in the sink when his cell phone rang. He glanced at the clock on the wall and wondered who would be calling him so early. When he pulled the phone from his belt clip to check the incoming number, he was relieved to see that it wasn't his dad. "Hey, Allen," he said. "Why are you calling so early? It's seven o'clock here, which means it's only four on the West Coast."

"I know it's early, but I'm going with some of the young people to the Oregon coast today, and we want to get an early start," Allen explained.

"Sounds like fun. Wish I was going with you."

"Yeah, me, too." There was a brief pause, then, "Hey, it's sure good to hear your voice. It's been awhile."

"I know. I've been really busy."

"Are you still painting for that Amish bishop you told me about?"

"Yeah, but since Jacob's memory hasn't returned, he's no longer able to run his business. And since he doesn't remember hiring me, it's really his son, Arthur, I'm working for now."

"It's too bad about him falling off the ladder. I've still got our church's prayer chain praying for him."

"Thanks. Jacob and the rest of his family need all the prayers they can get."

"Oh, by the way, I wanted you to know that I did try to get ahold of your dad," Allen said. "He hasn't answered the door or his phone whenever I've dropped by the house or called. Have you heard anything from him since the last time we talked?"

"I spoke to him the other day, and as much as I hate

to say this, I've decided that he's telling the truth about kidnapping me."

"Seriously?"

"Yep."

"You think he really took you from an Amish farm?"

"That's what he says, and he's scared to death that if I find my real family he'll end up in jail."

"The information I got off the Internet said the Amish don't sue. So I doubt they would press any kind of criminal charges against your dad," Allen said.

"Jim. His name is Jim. He's not my dad—not even my adopted dad," Jimmy muttered as he moved across the room and grabbed his lunch pail off the table.

"I know your dad's not a Christian and he can be kind of hard to deal with sometimes, but I can't picture him walking onto an Amish farm, snatching you away, and then passing you off to your mom as the baby they'd gone to Maryland to adopt."

Jimmy groaned. "It was hard for me to accept at first, too, but now that I've had a chance to think things over and have talked with Da—Jim again, I'm beginning to understand why he drinks so much and didn't want to go to church with me or Mom."

"He's probably been eaten up with guilt all these years. I'll bet he's feeling convicted, which means there's still hope that he will—"

"Look, Allen, I've got to go. I'm going to work for Arthur part of the day, and then I'll be stopping over at the Weavers' place to see Jacob."

"Oh, okay. I need to head out, too."

"I'll call you soon." Jimmy grabbed his painter's hat off the wall peg near the back door of his rented trailer and started to leave the kitchen.

"One more thing," Allen said before Jimmy clicked off his cell phone.

"What's that?"

"I sensed some anger in your voice when you were talking about your dad."

"As I said before, he's not my dad."

"He might not be your flesh-and-blood father or your adopted father, but he is the man who raised you."

"Mom had more to do with raising me than he did." The feelings of bitterness Jimmy felt since his last conversation with Jim mounted higher, and he swallowed against the taste of bile rising in his throat.

"You've got to find a way to deal with this, Jimmy. If you don't, it will eat you alive."

"I'm not sure I'll ever come to grips with what that man did to me, Mom, and my real Amish family." He clenched his teeth so hard that his jaw ached, as he jerked open the door. "Can you imagine how my sister must have felt when she returned to the yard with a jug of root beer and discovered I was gone? It gives me the chills just thinking about it."

"I'll bet even after all these years they're still missing you."

Jimmy said nothing as he walked across the yard and opened the door to his truck.

"Are you going to look for your real family?"

"I started looking for them—even before I fully believed Jim's story."

"So what else will you do to try and find them?"

"I'm not sure. Guess I'll have to rely on the Lord to help me."

"You don't really think God's going to help you find your real family as long as you continue to harbor anger and hatred toward Jim, do you?"

Jimmy halted. "I. . .I don't know."

"I'm sure you don't need to be reminded what the Bible says about forgiveness. The only way you'll ever have any peace is if you forgive your dad."

Jimmy grimaced. He knew Allen was right, but he

wasn't sure he could forgive. "I'd better go. Talk to you later, Allen."

"Bye, Jimmy. I'll be praying for you."

❧

Since school would be starting in a few weeks, Leona spent most of her free time at the schoolhouse getting things ready. At least that was her excuse for being here. Truth be told, she'd begun to look for ways to get away from her daed and his childish antics. Her faith in God, which had once been strong, was faltering in the midst of all her disappointments.

It helped some whenever Jimmy came over and kept Papa occupied. The young English man seemed to be Papa's best friend these days, which Leona felt sure her daed needed. However, she had a hunch Papa's friendship with Jimmy had hurt Abraham's feelings. Papa had not only forgotten who Abraham was, but he didn't perk up whenever Abraham came around the way he did with Jimmy. Leona had noticed the last couple of times Papa's old friend had dropped by, her daed acted kind of strange. She figured Papa's friendship with Jimmy might be the reason.

Leona glanced around the schoolhouse, wondering what she should do today. The walls had been painted. With the help of several parents, the desks had been cleaned and polished and a new blackboard had been put up—the kind Leona had requested.

"Maybe I should clean and organize my desk," she said, turning in that direction. "Anything to keep my hands and thoughts occupied."

Leona had been working only a few minutes when she heard a vehicle rumble into the school yard. She hurried to the front door and saw Jimmy and Papa climb out of Jimmy's truck. *I wonder what they want.*

I hope they're not planning to stay long. I don't need this interruption.

"Hi, Mary," Papa said with a cheery wave. "We come to give you some wood."

Leona glanced at Jimmy, who grinned at her and said, "I figured you'd be needing some firewood cut and stacked before school starts."

"Actually, my students' parents usually take turns bringing wood over during the school year."

"That's okay. This is something your dad can do, so I guess you'll have some extra wood this school term."

Papa shuffled his feet a few times and looked at Jimmy as if he'd taken leave of his senses. "I ain't Mary's daed. I'm her bruder."

Jimmy shrugged, and Leona looked away. They had tried several times to explain things to Papa about his accident. Sometimes he seemed to grasp the fact that he had lost his memory, but other times he would only give them a blank stare. Even though Papa had called her "Ona" on a few occasions, he was still insistent that he was her little bruder, not her daed.

"Where would you like us to stack the wood once we get it cut?" Jimmy asked, halting Leona's thoughts.

She motioned to the side of the building. "Are you sure it's safe for him to be handling an ax? I mean, if he doesn't remember how to use it. . ."

"I'll do the cutting, and he can haul the wood over to the building and stack it."

"I guess that would be okay." Leona turned toward the door. "I'll be inside if you need me for anything."

When she returned to her desk, she noticed that her hands were shaking, and she clasped them tightly together. *If stacking wood would bring my daed back to me, I'd ask for a ton of wood and let him stack all day.*

Lydia sank into a chair on the front porch as a feeling of relief swept over her. For the first time in several days, she had some time alone. Ever since Jacob had come home from the hospital, she'd felt as if she were playing the role of babysitter rather than that of a wife who'd been married almost thirty-seven years. She released a sigh and reached for the glass of iced tea sitting on the small table beside her. *I probably should be out working in the garden or doing some cleaning, but it's awfully nice to sit here and relax awhile.*

Lydia closed her eyes and leaned her full weight against the wicker chair. It was peaceful this afternoon, with the birds chirping in the nearby trees and an occasional grunt coming from Leona's dog, which lay on the porch a few feet away. For the first time in many days, Lydia felt God's presence. Maybe she'd been too busy these past weeks to realize He'd been there all along, helping her cope with Jacob's handicap. *Will my husband always be this way, Lord? Is there more we can do to help his memory return?*

The *clip-clop* of a horse's hooves and the rumble of buggy wheels brought Lydia's prayer to a halt. She opened her eyes and saw Fannie Fisher climb down from her buggy.

"Wie geht's?" Fannie called with a wave.

"I'm fair to middlin'. How about you?"

"Still missin' Edna, but otherwise doin' okay." Fannie strolled across the yard and stepped onto the porch. "I was on my way home from town and thought I'd drop by and see how you're getting along."

Lydia motioned to the empty chair beside her. "I'm taking some time off from my chores, so have a seat, and we can visit awhile." She started to get up. "Can I get you something cold to drink?"

Fannie waved a hand. "I'm fine. I had a bottle of cold root beer out of the vending machine down the street from my daughter's quilt shop not long ago."

Lydia smiled, remembering how delicious the root beer was that Abraham used to make. "Don't suppose that husband of yours has made any of his own root beer lately?"

"In all the years we've been married, Abraham's only made it a couple of times." Fannie slowly shook her head. "I think every time he's made root beer it's reminded him of the day his little boy was stolen, although he never speaks of it anymore."

Lydia clicked her tongue. "Sometimes when I'm feeling sorry for myself because of Jacob's accident, I think about all you and Abraham have been through, and I have to stop and count my blessings."

"Abraham, Naomi, and my daughter Abby, they're the ones who've really had their faith put to the test." Fannie reached over and patted Lydia's arm. "Keep trusting God; He will see you through."

Lydia nodded as tears clouded her vision. It was easy enough to say God was in control, but when one's faith was put to the test, it was another matter.

"Is Jacob getting any better?" Fannie asked.

"Not really. Some days he's hard to deal with because of his silly antics. Other days he seems calmer and more cooperative." Lydia drew in a breath and released it with a huff. "He's called Leona by her nickname a couple of times, which gave me some hope that he might remember she's his daughter. But then he goes right back to calling her Mary again. Leona gets set down pretty hard whenever her daed doesn't respond to things the way she would like."

"It has to be *hatt* for you, Leona, and Arthur to see Jacob like that and know there's nothing you can do but pray and try to be there for him."

"Jah, it's difficult, to be sure. Our other daughters, Peggy and Rebecca, are concerned, too. But with them both living in Kentucky, they only know what I write them and don't get to see it firsthand." Lydia forced a smile. "Jacob's birthday is this Saturday; he'll turn fifty-nine."

"Are you planning a party for him?"

"I hadn't given it much thought, but maybe I should. Might do him some good to have his family and close friends gathered together." Lydia shrugged. "Who knows, it may even be helpful in bringing back his memory."

"I think it's a fine idea."

"You, Abraham, and your whole family are invited, of course," Lydia said, feeling a surge of excitement she hadn't felt in a long time. "Maybe we can have a barbecue with cake and homemade ice cream for dessert."

Fannie licked her lips. "Sounds good to me. Just tell me what time the party will begin and what I can bring."

Chapter 22

Jimmy whistled as he drove down the road toward the Weavers' place. He seemed to be fitting in more all the time and was pleased that Lydia had invited him to attend the barbecue in honor of her husband's birthday. It would give him a chance to get to know some of the others he hadn't become well acquainted with yet.

Abraham Fisher was one of those he had met on a few occasions but didn't know so well. Abraham always kept his distance, and Jimmy wondered if the man might be prejudiced against him because he was English. Or maybe Abraham felt threatened by Jimmy's friendship with the bishop. Leona had mentioned once that her dad and Abraham used to be good friends before Jacob's accident. Now that he'd lost his memory and didn't know who Abraham was, they had little to talk about. Of course, Jacob didn't remember meeting Jimmy before the accident, either. But for some reason, he seemed taken with Jimmy and had quickly become his friend.

When Jimmy pulled into the Weavers' yard a short time later, he noticed several Amish buggies lined up beside the barn with their shafts resting on the ground. The horses had been unhitched, and he could see them moving around the corral.

"I hope I'm not late. I thought Lydia said six o'clock, and it's only two minutes after that now," he mumbled, glancing at his watch—the one his dad had given him for his birthday. He flinched, realizing once more that he still hadn't come to grips with the anger he felt over Jim's deceit. The only way he'd been able to keep from thinking about it was to stay busy and concentrate on helping Jacob. That had become his primary focus. Looking for his family had taken a backseat. *Of course,* he reasoned, *part of me is afraid to find my family, because I know that if Jim went to jail for kidnapping, I would feel disloyal to the only mother I've ever known.*

The pungent aroma of meat cooking on the grill drew Jimmy's thoughts aside, and when he stepped out of the truck carrying a paper sack with the gift inside that he'd bought for Jacob, his stomach rumbled. He hadn't eaten anything since breakfast, figuring he would make up for it tonight.

Jimmy hurried around to the back side of the house and discovered several people, including Leona and her parents, seated at two oversized picnic tables. They were already eating, and he glanced at his watch again. The time was the same as it had been a few minutes ago, and he realized then that his watch had stopped.

"Sorry I'm late," he said, stepping up to the table where Lydia and Jacob sat. "Guess the battery in my watch is dead."

Jacob grinned up at him. "Hi, Jimmy. Glad ya could make it to my party."

Lydia smiled and nodded. "You're not so late."

"We just started eating a few minutes ago," Arthur put in from across the table. "Grab yourself a burger from the grill and have a seat."

Jimmy handed Jacob the paper sack. "This is for you. Happy birthday."

Jacob's smile widened. "What is it?"

"Open the sack and take a look."

Jacob pulled it open and peered inside. "Umm. . . licorice." He smacked his lips. "That's my favorite candy."

Jimmy nodded. "There's something else in there, too."

Jacob stuck his hand into the sack again and withdrew a paintbrush. He gave Jimmy a quizzical look then turned to Lydia and swished the brush against the tip of her nose. "Does that tickle, Mama?"

She chuckled and looked over at Jimmy.

"I thought it might help spark a memory for him," he said.

She nodded. "Maybe so."

Jimmy glanced around, wondering where would be the best place to sit.

"There's a vacant spot next to Mary," Jacob said, pointing to the bench where Leona sat.

Jimmy smiled, and Leona offered him a brief smile in return. "You're welcome to sit here if you like," she said.

Jimmy didn't have to be asked twice. He enjoyed Leona's company and thought if he was Amish or she was English, he might even be interested in dating her. *I'm almost Amish,* he reminded himself. *After all, I was born to an Amish couple.* He forked a juicy burger onto his plate and took a seat, hoping to focus his thoughts on something other than his past—a past he'd thought he had known all about until he'd learned the truth concerning his so-called adoption.

"I'm glad you were able to come to the party," Leona said as she passed him a package of buns. "Would you like some ketchup or mustard to put on your meat?"

"I'd like both, please."

"How about lettuce, tomatoes, or onions?"

"Yeah, all three." He wiggled his eyebrows, and Leona giggled. It was good to see her in better spirits. She had been sullen ever since he'd met her, and even more so since her dad's accident. She hadn't actually said so, but the way she acted whenever she was around her dad made Jimmy think she was embarrassed by her father's juvenile actions. The other day at the schoolhouse, Jacob had dropped a hunk of licorice Jimmy had given him, and he'd bent down, picked it up, and popped it into his mouth. Leona looked mortified, gave him a lecture about the ground being full of germs, and barely said more than two words to her dad after that.

"Would you like some potato salad?" Leona asked, touching Jimmy's elbow with her hand.

He felt a strange tingling sensation, and he gave his arm a quick once-over to see if some bug might have landed there. Relieved when he didn't see anything, he bit into his burger and mumbled, "Sure, I'd love some."

∞

Abraham folded his arms and leaned back in the wooden chair where he'd taken a seat on the Weavers' front porch. A game of croquet was being played in the yard, and most of the young people were involved in it—everyone except Jacob's youngest daughter, that is. Leona and that young English painter who Jacob had hired awhile back left the yard a few minutes ago.

Abraham's gaze went to the driveway where Leona walked between Jimmy and Jacob. *Not only is my good friend taken in by that young Englisher, but his daughter seems to be, as well. I need to nip this in the bud, because I'm sure Jacob's not going to do anything about it. Most of the time, he doesn't even realize Leona is his daughter, much less show any concern for her welfare.*

He reached under the brim of his straw hat and scratched his forehead. *Just who is this Jimmy Scott, and why's he been hanging around Jacob so much? No one seems to know a lot about him other than the fact that he paints and comes from the state of Washington.*

"You ready for some ice cream?"

"Huh?" Abraham looked up at his wife. She held

a heaping bowl of vanilla ice cream in her hand. "Jah. Danki, Fannie."

"How come you're sitting here by yourself?" she questioned.

"I figured you'd be visiting with the birthday boy."

Abraham took the bowl from her and groaned. "That's exactly what Jacob is, too. He might be fifty-nine years old on the outside, but inside he's just a kid." He pointed to the game in progress. "Did you see him out there earlier, snappin' that ball around and hollering like he don't have a lick of sense? Now he's walking down the driveway with Leona and that Englisher like they're the best of friends."

"You need to calm yourself down, Husband," Fannie said, easing into the chair beside him. "It's not Jacob's fault he can't remember how old he is. Maybe if you talked to him more about the things you used to do together, it might help jog his memory."

Abraham spooned some ice cream into his mouth, savoring the rich, creamy taste and mulling over what his wife had said. Finally, he swallowed and cleared his throat. "I have tried talking to him some, but so far nothin' I've said has made any difference."

"Try to be patient and remember to keep praying."

"I have been praying." His gaze went to the driveway again. Jimmy, Leona, and Jacob had disappeared. No doubt they'd decided to walk up the road apiece.

"What are you looking at?" she questioned.

"Nothin'," he mumbled. "Just thinkin' about what I might do to make things better for my good friend."

"Maybe you should concentrate on trying to make things better between you and Naomi." Fannie shook her head. "I know you're still angry with her for hiding Zach's quilt, but giving her the cold shoulder whenever she's around isn't the way to handle it. It's not God's way, either."

"I know, but what she did was wrong."

"That may be, but is your trying to punish her the right thing to do?"

"I'm not trying to punish Naomi," he said, furrowing his brows. "I just can't trust her anymore, plain and simple."

∞

As Jim approached the Tacoma Mall on his way back from picking up some paint and other supplies, he decided to drop by the health food store. Holly Simmons had mentioned during his last visit there that she was a recovered alcoholic. Maybe he could talk to her about the way he felt.

This is probably a dumb idea, he told himself as he climbed out of the van and headed across the parking lot. *She'll probably think I'm a hypochondriac who keeps coming back to her store to look for something to help calm his nerves.*

Despite his doubts, Jim kept on walking. Once he was inside the mall, he hurried to the health food store before he changed his mind. As soon as he walked in, he spotted Holly behind the counter and was relieved to see that there were no other customers.

Holly noticed him right away and stepped out from behind the counter with a friendly smile. "How's your son doing, Jim? I heard from someone at church that he'd taken a trip to the East Coast and might be gone awhile."

Jim nodded with a grimace.

"You look upset. Is everything all right?"

He started to nod again but shook his head instead.

"Are you still having trouble sleeping?"

"Yeah, that—and a few other things."

"Is there something in particular I can help you with?"

He shifted from one foot to the other, trying to work

up the nerve to say what was on his mind. "I. . .I was wondering if you— Well, if you haven't had your lunch break yet, would you be interested in going somewhere with me to eat?"

"Kim and Megan, my helpers, should be back from their break soon," Holly said. "So if you have the time to wait, we could go to one of the restaurants in the mall as soon as they get back."

He nodded. "That would be great."

A short time later, Jim and Holly sat across from each other at a table inside a restaurant not far from her store.

"So what did you want to talk about?" Holly asked after they'd placed their orders.

Jim cleared his throat a couple of times, searching for the right words. "Well, uh. . .the last time I came into your store, you mentioned that you. . .uh. . .used to have a drinking problem."

She nodded. "I'm a recovered alcoholic. I haven't had a drink in ten years."

He reached for his glass of water and took a sip. "So. . .uh. . . how did you get on top of your drinking problem?"

"AA helped a lot. So did the support I got from my pastor and friends at church."

Jim frowned. There was that *church* word again. First Linda, then Jimmy, and now the health food store owner. It seemed like he could never get away from religious fanatics.

"Is there a reason you're looking at me with such a glum expression?" Holly asked.

Jim drew in a breath and blew it out quickly. "Jimmy thinks I have a drinking problem."

She leaned her elbows on the table and studied him intently. "Do you?"

"I do have a few drinks now and then—whenever

I'm feeling uptight and need to relax."

"Do you ever get drunk?"

Unable to meet her probing gaze, he stared at the table. "Yeah, sometimes."

"Has your drinking affected any of your personal relationships?"

"I. . .guess it has."

"What about your job? Have you ever lost time from work because you were drunk or hungover?"

He lifted his gaze to meet hers. "Maybe a couple of times, but I have a great foreman, and he's always taken over when I'm not there."

She pursed her lips. "You mean he *covers* for you?"

"I wouldn't put it that way," Jim said, feeling his defenses begin to rise. *This was a mistake. I shouldn't have come here. I'll bet Holly thinks I'm a worthless drunk who shrugs his responsibilities and then drops the ball in someone else's lap. She probably thinks I'm a lousy father, too. She might even believe Jimmy took off for Pennsylvania to get away from me.* He reached for his glass of water and took another drink. *If she only knew. . .*

"Have you ever considered attending an AA meeting?"

He gave a quick shake of his head.

"If you'd like to see what one of the meetings is like, I'd be happy to go with you."

The idea of spending more time with this attractive woman was kind of appealing, but the thought of going to an AA meeting and listening to a bunch of strangers talk about their drinking problems scared Jim to death. "I appreciate the offer," he mumbled, "but I'm not an alcoholic, and I can quit drinking anytime I want."

Chapter 23

As Jimmy turned onto Oak Hill Drive and headed toward the job he would be doing all week, he thought about Eli, who wouldn't be working with him today because he'd had all four of his wisdom teeth pulled yesterday. Eli would not only miss a few days of work, but he was worried that he might not be able to see his girlfriend on Saturday. Lettie Byler was an Amish schoolteacher who lived near Strasburg. Eli had told Jimmy that he and Lettie had been courting for the last six months.

Thinking about Eli and his girlfriend led Jimmy to mull over the way he felt about Leona. He reflected on Saturday night and the fun he'd had with her during Jacob's birthday party. He'd enjoyed visiting with many of the people—but none as much as the bishop's daughter.

During the walk they'd taken with Jacob after their meal, it had been obvious by the way Leona had responded to some of her dad's comments that she felt uncomfortable whenever he said or did something childish. While Jacob chased fireflies, Leona had told Jimmy about her fiancé dying and how her faith had been badly shaken then—and that it had weakened even further after her dad's accident.

Jimmy could understand why her faith had been shaken. His faith had been strong until he'd learned about his kidnapping. Yet despite his own problems, he still felt concern for Leona. The sadness he'd seen in her eyes had tugged at his heartstrings. He'd also seen a look of determination on Lydia's face and noticed the confusion Jacob experienced whenever he was asked to do a task that might be expected of a man. Such things made him even more determined to stick around Lancaster County and offer his help. The Weavers didn't deserve this kind of pain—no one did.

Jimmy's mind drove him unwillingly back to the day he'd learned of his mother's cancer diagnosis. He had been afraid of losing her then. And a few years later, when he was told that she was going to die, he felt as if his world had been turned upside down. But with God's help and the encouragement of his pastor and friends, Jimmy had made it through the darkest days.

Too bad Jim didn't do as well, he thought ruefully. *Drinking until he's too numb to care seems to be the only way that man can deal with anything. It's amazing that he hasn't lost his business by now, and if he keeps up the way he's going, he might lose it yet.*

Jimmy shook his head. *I can't worry about that anymore. I did all I could to get him to go to church, and he flatly refused. I covered for him whenever he couldn't go to work because he was on a drinking binge or suffering from a hangover. Now it's time for him to sink or swim.*

A fast-moving semitruck whipped around Jimmy, and he had to steer his pickup toward the shoulder of the road to avoid being sideswiped. "Slow down! You shouldn't be going so fast," he grumbled. "Don't you know there could be an Amish carriage on this road?"

Since Jimmy's arrival in Lancaster County nearly two months ago, he'd read several accounts of buggy accidents in the newspaper. One had caused a tragic fatality, and another had left an Amish man paralyzed.

"People need to relax and not be in such a hurry," he continued to fume. "Drive slower, share the road, and more accidents will be prevented."

When Jimmy rounded the next bend, he caught sight of a team of horses pulling an empty wagon and running down a driveway at full speed. As soon as his truck came to the entrance of the drive, he put on the brakes, blocking the horses from gaining access to the road. Two men he recognized as Jake and Norman Fisher ran behind the wagon, and their red-faced father wasn't far behind. *This must be the Fishers' place.* Jimmy had never had a reason to come here, so he hadn't been sure where they lived.

By the time Jimmy got out of his truck, Norman and Jake had grabbed hold of the horses' bridles. "Danki," Norman called. "If these critters had managed to pull the wagon out on the road, there's no telling what might have happened."

"How'd they get away from you?" Jimmy questioned.

Jake opened his mouth to reply, but Abraham spoke first. "My two youngest boys were supposed to be keeping an eye on the team while Jake, Norman, and I got the sickle-bar mower ready to cut hay. Instead of doing as I asked, Titus and Timothy were foolin' around with those dumb yo-yos they bought the last time we stopped by the general store."

Jimmy glanced up the driveway and noticed Abraham's twin boys heading for the barn with their heads down and shoulders slumped. "I'm glad I happened along when I did," he said.

Abraham made no reply. Instead, he nodded at his older boys and said, "Why don't you fellows get the horses and wagon turned around and back into the field?"

"Sure, we can do that," Norman replied.

"What about you, Papa?" Jake asked. "Aren't you comin'?"

"I'll be along soon." Abraham looked back at Jimmy. "I need to have a few words with this young man first."

A trickle of sweat rolled down Jimmy's forehead, and he swiped it away with the back of his hand. Abraham's furrowed brows and tightly compressed lips made Jimmy wonder if the man might be perturbed. "I need to get to work," he said, taking a step toward his truck. "We're starting a new paint job today, and—"

Abraham clasped Jimmy's shoulder. "I won't keep ya long."

"Well, okay." Jimmy leaned against the side of his truck and folded his arms, hoping he looked calmer than he felt. There was something about the tall, slightly overweight Amish man that made him feel nervous.

Abraham cleared his throat. "I know you're working for the son of my friend, Jacob Weaver, but I'm wondering why you've been hangin' around their place so much."

"I care about Jacob and want to help him in any way I can."

Abraham moved closer. He was so close that Jimmy could actually feel the man's hot breath. "And what about Jacob's daughter?"

"Leona?"

"Jah."

"What about her?"

"I'm wondering exactly what your relationship is to her."

"Leona's a good friend, and I'm concerned about her as well as Jacob's wife and son. They've all been under a burden since Jacob lost his memory, and they need help from all their friends."

Abraham's steely blue eyes seemed to bore right through Jimmy as he stared at him with pursed lips. "I'm wonderin' if you might not care more for Leona than you ought to. I've seen the way you eyeball her whenever you think no one's lookin'."

Jimmy couldn't deny that he had feelings for the bishop's daughter. He just wasn't sure how deep those feelings went—or what he should do about them.

"When I was going through rough times some years

ago, Jacob was always there for me," Abraham continued. "He's the best friend I've ever had, and I won't stand by and watch you make his life more complicated than it already is."

Jimmy dropped his arms to his sides and clenched his fists. He didn't think he had done anything to deserve this lecture, and he told Abraham so.

"Jah, well, I needed to be sure you knew how things were. You're not Amish, ya know, and Leona ain't English. So, for the good of everyone, it would be better if you backed off and didn't hang around their place so much."

Jimmy was tempted to tell Abraham the reason he'd come to Pennsylvania, but he held his tongue. Even though he was still angry with Jim for his dishonesty, he felt some sense of loyalty to the man who'd raised him. And if there was a chance that Jim would go to jail if the truth were revealed, Jimmy wasn't sure he wanted to be responsible for that. Besides, Abraham might not believe his story. In all likelihood, the irksome man would think Jimmy had made it up in order to get close to Leona.

Turning toward the truck and grasping the door handle, Jimmy mumbled, "You don't have to worry. I'd never do anything to hurt Jacob or anyone in his family."

∞

For the first time in many days, Leona had felt a sense of excitement when she'd gotten out of bed. Today was the first day of school, and she looked forward to teaching her pupils again. Besides, it gave her a good excuse to be away from the house.

As she finished up the dishes, she glanced over at Mom, who sat at the table helping Papa read a book. *He should be in school. But then, I guess that wouldn't be good, since the kinner would probably make fun of a grown man coming to school for learning.*

She dried her hands, grabbed her black bonnet from the wall peg, and placed it over her smaller white covering. "I'm heading out now, Mom."

"All right, Leona. Have a good day."

"Jah, Ona. Have a good day," Papa added.

Ona one day, Mary the next. Will Papa's memory ever return? Leona opened the back door and stepped onto the porch, gulping in a breath of air. She could feel the first hints of fall as crisp, clean air filled her lungs. It made her appreciate being outdoors. She felt so confined whenever she was in the house, especially if her daed was in the same room asking ridiculous questions or acting like a silly child.

Leona leaned against the porch railing and squeezed her eyes shut. *What's wrong with me, Lord? Why can't I accept everything that has happened to my family and me these past months and go on with the business of living?*

As usual, there seemed to be no answers from the heavenly Father. It was as if God had stepped away—or maybe it was the other way around. Leona knew she was guilty of not spending much time in prayer, and she'd all but given up on reading the scriptures.

Pushing the despairing thoughts aside, Leona entered the barn to fetch a buggy horse. Filling her lungs with the sweet smell of hay, she bent over to pet Cinnamon, who'd been sleeping in a patch of straw. The dog responded with a flick of one ear and a lazy whimper.

"You be good today, you hear? No chasing chickens. And you'd better stay away from Papa's silly goat!"

❧

Jim moaned as he tripped over his shoe and kicked it across the room. He'd been out drinking the night before, and now, even after a couple of aspirin and two cups of coffee, his head felt like it was the size of a basketball.

"There's no way I'm going to be able to work today," he muttered as he stumbled back to bed. He glanced at the clock on the nightstand. It was still early, so he could set the alarm, sleep a few hours, and call Ed right before he started work. *Or maybe I should call him now so he has enough time to set out everything he'll need for the day.*

Jim reached for the phone and, in so doing, knocked over a picture of Jimmy that had been taken during his senior year of high school. He'd kept it near his bed ever since Jimmy left, but instead of offering comfort, it only reminded him of the mess he'd made of his life and Jimmy's.

He bent over and retrieved the picture, thankful the glass wasn't broken. "Oh, Jimmy, don't hate me for what I did," he blubbered. "I'd do most anything if I could make things right between us."

He gulped in a deep breath and flopped onto his pillow. "Dear God, if you're as real as Linda always said You were, then bring my son home to me."

Chapter 24

Leona leaned wearily against the front of her desk as the students filed out of the schoolhouse. For the most part, this had been a good day. The majority of her scholars had been eager to learn, but she was exhausted.

"See you tomorrow, Teacher," Norman Fisher's son, John, said as he sauntered past her desk.

"Have a good evening," she replied.

"Are ya coming over to our place for supper on Friday night with Grandma and Grandpa?" Arthur's daughter Jolene questioned.

"I'm hoping to." Leona smiled at her six-year-old niece. She was the one child who had been the most attentive today. Not like Millie Hoffmeir, who hadn't shown a bit of interest in learning to read or write.

Maybe it's because this was her first day of school, Leona thought. *I'm sure once Millie gets used to being here, she'll become more attentive.* She glanced at her niece, who was actually skipping out the door. *This was Jolene's first day of school, too, and she showed a lot more interest in learning than Naomi's daughter did.*

When the last child left the building, Leona headed over to the blackboard to erase the day's assignments as she pondered the situation with Millie. *If things don't go better by the end of the week, I'll have a talk with Millie's folks.*

A few minutes later, she heard the front door open and click shut. Thinking one of her pupils had forgotten something, she kept on cleaning.

"How'd the first day of school go?"

Leona whirled around at the sound of Abner Lapp's

deep voice. "Oh, it's you. I thought maybe one of the kinner had come back."

Abner removed his straw hat and grinned. "Just came by to pick up my bruder." He scanned the room. "Looks like I got here too late, though."

She nodded. "The scholars left several minutes ago. If Emanuel didn't cut through the Zooks' cornfield, you might catch him along the road on your way home."

Abner shuffled his feet a couple of times, which brought him closer to where Leona stood. "Sure was plenty warm today, jah?"

"Hot and humid," she agreed.

"How's your daed doin'? Any of his memory comin' back yet?"

"Not really. There are times when he says or does something that makes us believe he might remember some things from his adult life, but then he starts acting like a boy again."

Abner twisted the brim of his hat. "Sure is a shame to see him like that."

Leona gave a quick nod. She didn't feel like discussing Papa's condition. All she wanted to do was go home and relax on the front porch with a glass of iced tea and her best friend, Cinnamon.

"It seems odd to go to church and not hear our own bishop preachin'," Abner continued. "He used to be such a fine man."

Leona bristled. "He still is a fine man. He's just lost in the past, that's all." She didn't know why she felt the need to defend her daed—especially since she, too, had been having such miserable thoughts about him.

Abner took another step toward her. "I meant no disrespect. And I sure didn't mean for you to get all riled."

"I'm not riled." As the words slipped off Leona's tongue, she knew they weren't true. She was riled. In fact, talking about Papa's predicament made her feel edgy and depressed. As time went on and they continued to see little or no improvement, she became more convinced that her daed would never remember he was Bishop Jacob Weaver and not a little boy.

Abner touched Leona's arm, and she jumped. "Sorry. Didn't mean to startle ya. You just look so sad, and I was wonderin' if there's anything I can do to help."

She shook her head. "There's not much anyone can do except God, and He seems to be looking the other way these days."

Abner's forehead wrinkled. "I can't believe I'm hearin' that kind of talk from the bishop's daughter."

Leona stared at the floor. She didn't feel close enough to Abner to bare her soul, and she didn't want him feeling sorry for her.

"I. . .uh. . .should be getting home," she mumbled.

"Jah, me, too." Abner plopped his hat back on his head and pivoted toward the door.

When she heard the door click shut, she released a sigh. Did everyone in the community think like Abner did—that she wasn't a good bishop's daughter because she couldn't accept her daed's accident and had lost faith in God?

"Well, they can think whatever they want," she mumbled as tears pushed against her eyelids. "No one understands all that I'm going through right now."

❧

"Are you sure you don't mind me leaving the store a little early today?" Naomi asked Caleb as she set her black bonnet in place over her white kapp.

He shook his head. "I know you're anxious to hear how the kinner did in school, and since Sarah and Susan are here to help, we'll get along fine."

She smiled, feeling grateful to be married to such a good man. "If I leave right now, I may be able to catch them before they get to your folks' place."

Caleb chuckled. "Knowing Josh and Nate, they're probably halfway there by now."

Naomi's smile turned upside down. "They'd better not have left Millie to walk alone."

"I'm sure they wouldn't do that." Caleb opened the back door and leaned down to kiss Naomi on the cheek. "See you at supper time."

"I'll make sure it's ready on time." Naomi hurried down the steps and out to the corral where they kept their horse and buggy. She was soon on her way. A short time later, she turned onto the road where the one-room schoolhouse was located. It was the same school she'd attended when she was a girl.

So much has occurred in my life since then, Naomi mused. *If I had known all that would happen once I became a woman, I might not have been in such a hurry to grow up.* She clucked to the horse to get him moving faster, determined not to dwell on the past. But then she thought about her daed and how he still acted cool toward her. *I've asked his forgiveness for hiding Zach's quilt. What more can I do?*

Naomi noticed several children walking along the shoulder of the road, but there was no sign of her three. She'd just reached the entrance to the school yard when she spotted Leona's buggy pulling out, so she tugged on the reins and guided her horse to the side of the road.

"If you came to pick up your kinner, they've already headed for home," Leona called as she drew near.

"I figured as much, but I thought I might catch 'em walking along the way."

"That's probably the case."

"How'd the first day of school go? Did my three behave themselves?"

Leona nodded. "No problems with discipline, although Millie didn't seem very interested in learning."

Naomi frowned. "What do you mean?"

"When I tried to get her to write the letters of the alphabet, she got several of them mixed up and acted as if she didn't want to try."

"Maybe she was too nervous to concentrate. During breakfast this morning, she expressed some concern about her first day of school."

"That's probably all it was," Leona agreed. "I'm sure in a couple of days she'll be fine."

Naomi opened her mouth to reply, but a noisy truck pulled alongside her rig. Jimmy Scott, wearing a straw hat like the Amish men wore this time of the year, leaned out the window and offered them a friendly wave.

If Jimmy had a different haircut and wore suspenders, he would almost look Amish, Naomi noted. *I wonder if he's wearing that hat to keep the sun out of his eyes, or if he's trying to fit in with the fellows he works with.*

"Are you on your way home or heading to a job?" Leona asked, nodding at Jimmy through his open window.

"I'm basically done for the day, but Arthur asked me to drop by your folks' place and see about painting their kitchen."

"I thought Arthur was planning to do the painting for us."

"He was, but he's been busy with other jobs and doesn't think he'll get around to it for several weeks, so I told him I'd be happy to do it."

Naomi couldn't help but notice the eager smile Jimmy offered Leona—or the one that Leona gave Jimmy in return. It made her wonder if her daed had been right when he'd mentioned to Caleb recently that he thought the Englisher was too interested in Jacob's daughter. *Of course,* she reasoned, *Papa might be jealous because Jacob seems to enjoy Jimmy's company these days more than he does Papa's.*

"I'm heading home now, Jimmy," Leona said. "So if you'd like to meet me there, I can show you what needs to be done."

"That would be great." He gave the steering wheel a couple of taps. "If you want to go ahead of me, I'll drive slow and follow you."

"All right then. See you at the house." Leona got her horse moving and turned onto the main road. Jimmy pulled out behind her.

Naomi clucked her tongue. *I've not seen Leona smile at any fellow that way since Ezra died. Maybe Papa's right. Maybe there is cause for concern.*

∞

Traffic was sparse on this sunny stretch of road, and through the undercarriage of Leona's buggy, Jimmy could see the horse's feet clopping briskly along. As he drove slowly behind Leona, he thought about how much he enjoyed being with her. Leona was pretty in a plain sort of way, and even though she wore glasses some of the time, it didn't detract from her natural beauty. *It's good to see her smiling today,* he thought. *She's been so sad since her dad's accident.*

Jimmy's cell phone rang, and he grabbed it off the seat. "Hello."

"Hi, son. How are you?"

"I'm a little bit sunburned and kind of thirsty right now, but other than that, I'm doing okay," he said with little enthusiasm.

I wish he would quit calling. It only adds to my frustration.

"I. . .uh. . .had lunch with a friend of yours the other day."

"Oh? Who was that?"

"Holly Simmons, the lady who goes to your church. You know—the one who owns the health food store at the mall."

A ray of hope flickered in Jimmy's soul. If his dad was getting friendly with Holly, maybe he would see the light and start going to church, which was exactly where he needed to be if he was ever going to see his need for Christ.

"Jimmy, are you still there?"

"Yeah."

"Holly invited me to attend an AA meeting with her."

"What'd you tell her?"

"I said I wasn't an alcoholic and could quit drinking any time I wanted."

"You really believe that?"

"Well, I—"

Jimmy tapped the brake pedal a few times, realizing that he was getting too close to the back of Leona's buggy. "If you can quit drinking on your own, then why don't you?" he asked, feeling his irritation mount further.

"I will—when I'm ready." There was a long pause, and then Jim asked, "So, what's new with you? Any luck finding your Amish family?"

"No. I've struck out at every place I've looked, and I'm beginning to wonder if I should forget about trying to find them and concentrate only on helping the Weavers."

Jim grunted. "Maybe you should come home and forget about trying to rescue that family."

Jimmy tensed as his face grew hotter, and he knew it wasn't from the sunburn he'd gotten earlier today. He needed to get off the phone before he said something he might regret.

"I miss you, son, and it's awful lonely here without you."

It's not my fault you're alone or can't deal with your guilt. I didn't ask to be kidnapped, and I shouldn't have to pay for your trickery or lack of self-control where your drinking's concerned. "I've got to hang up now. Bye."

Jimmy followed Leona up her driveway, feeling a sense of relief to be off the phone. Maybe now he could concentrate on something more positive.

He turned off the ignition and hopped out of the truck the minute her horse stopped in front of the barn. "Want me to put him away for you?" he called to Leona.

"You wouldn't mind?"

"Not a bit. Eli's been teaching me how to handle his horse, and I've even driven his buggy a couple of times."

She smiled and nodded toward the house. "I'll go inside and fix us a glass of iced tea. Then, as soon as you get the horse put away, we can cool down with our drinks before you look at the kitchen to see what needs to be done."

"Sounds good to me."

∞

The sun beat upon Leona's back, causing rivulets of sweat to trickle down her spine. She hurried for the house, anxious to get out of the intense heat.

Entering the kitchen, she found it empty. By the time Jimmy came in, she had two glasses of cold tea and a plate of peanut butter cookies waiting on the table.

He removed his straw hat, placing it on the nearest wall peg.

"I got a little too much sun today, so a cold drink will hit the spot."

Leona studied his face and realized that it was quite red. "Let me get something to put on that burn," she said, heading for the refrigerator.

"You keep sunburn medicine in there?"

"It's aloe vera, and it feels better going on if it's cold."

"Ah, I see." Jimmy took a seat at the table and gulped down half of his iced tea before she returned with the leaf from an aloe plant that had been sliced open.

"Would you like me to put it on for you?" Leona asked. "Or would you rather do it yourself?"

"You can see better where I need it the most, so if you don't mind, I'd be much obliged." Jimmy leaned his head back and closed his eyes as Leona gently slathered the gel on his face.

When her fingers made contact with his warm skin, it sent unexpected shivers all the way up her arm. *What's wrong with me? Why should being close to this man make me feel so giddy?* For an unguarded moment, she let herself imagine what it would be like to be courted by Jimmy.

Drawing in a deep breath, she ordered her runaway heart to be still. *I'm just attracted to him because he's been so kind and helpful since Papa's accident.*

"That feels better already. Danki," he said, pulling her thoughts aside.

She pulled her hand back and stared at him. "You said 'thank you' in Pennsylvania Dutch."

He grinned up at her. "Eli's been teaching me that, too."

"It's good," she said.

"Jah, is gut."

She nodded. "Yes, it's good."

Feeling the need to put some distance between them, Leona moved aside. She sat in the chair across from Jimmy and took a drink of her iced tea. It was hard to make sensible conversation or think straight with him looking at her in such a peculiar way. The only sound to break the silence was the steady *tick-tock* of the battery-operated clock on the wall and the persistent hum of the propane-operated refrigerator.

After Jimmy had eaten a few cookies and finished his tea, he stood. "Thanks for the refreshments and the sunburn remedy."

"You're welcome."

"Guess I'd better see what needs to be painted in here."

"I didn't realize you'd come home already," Mom said, stepping into the room. "Your daed's taking a nap, and I was resting on the sofa. Must have dozed off and didn't hear you come in."

The whites of Mom's eyes were red, and the skin around them was kind of puffy, making Leona wonder if things hadn't gone well with Papa today. She was about to voice her concerns when Mom squeezed Leona's arm and said, "I'm so sorry to be tellin' you this, daughter, but Cinnamon is dead."

Chapter 25

Leona sat there several seconds as she let her mamm's words sink in. *My dog can't be dead. Cinnamon was alive this morning when I went to the barn to get the buggy horse. She hasn't even been sick.*

"I'm awful sorry," Mom said, shaking her head. "It was an accident, plain and simple."

"Wh–what happened?" Leona rasped.

"Your dog ran into the road and was hit by a car."

Leona's spine went rigid, and tears gathered in her eyes, wetting her lashes and threatening to spill over. "Cinnamon never goes into the road. I've trained her to stay on our property."

Mom pulled out the chair beside Leona and sat down. "Your daed was outside playing with his goat, and then Cinnamon came along and got in on the act. The goat chased the poor dog around the barn so many times I feared they would both get dizzy." She paused and drew in a quick breath. "I kept calling to the dog, and your daed chased after the goat. But the two of them ignored us and ran down the driveway and into the road. Then a car came whizzing past, and Cinnamon—"

Leona held her hands tightly against her ears, hoping to drown out her mother's next words.

"Cinnamon was killed instantly, and the goat ran into the cornfield with your daed right behind him."

Leona clenched her fists and tightened her features as she screamed, "This was Papa's fault!"

"I don't think you should put the blame on your dad's shoulders," Jimmy spoke up.

She looked at him, but tears clouded her vision.

In the pain of hearing about Cinnamon's death, she'd almost forgotten Jimmy was in the room. "If Papa had been at work, the way he used to be, this would not have happened."

"Leona, please be reasonable," Mom said. "It's not your daed's fault he had an accident and lost his memory. And he's not to blame for the car hitting your dog, either."

Leona trembled as she fought for control. Mom didn't understand the way she felt. She never had. "Where is she? Where's Cinnamon now?"

"Your daed wanted to bury the poor dog, but I knew you'd want to see her first. So after he captured the goat, I had him move Cinnamon's body to the barn."

Leona stood, and with a convulsing sob, she rushed out the door.

∞

Jimmy started after her, but Lydia reached out a hand to stop him. "I think it's best to let her go. She needs time to be alone and think things through."

"I can't believe she would blame Jacob for this. Doesn't she realize it wasn't his fault that the animals ran into the road?"

Lydia shrugged as a swirl of emotions spun around in her head. "Leona's been moody and depressed ever since her boyfriend died, and then, after Jacob's accident—well, I think she blames God for allowing it all to happen. I'm afraid if her daed's memory never returns, she might spend the rest of her life angry at God and leery of establishing any close relationships for fear of losing the one she loves."

Jimmy slowly shook his head, and Lydia wondered what he might be thinking, but before she could ask, the sound of heavy footsteps clomping outside the kitchen turned her attention to the door leading to the hallway. A few seconds later, Jacob entered the room with his arms stretched above his head. When he spotted Jimmy, he rushed over to the table and pulled out a chair. "I didn't know you was comin' here today. Did ya want to go fishin'? I'll bet Mama would fix us a picnic supper to take along."

"I can't go fishing this evening, Jacob," Jimmy said. "I came by to look at the kitchen."

"Mama's got a good kitchen. She makes wunderbaar peanut butter cookies in this kitchen." Jacob tapped Jimmy on the arm. "You hungry? I sure am." He looked over at Lydia and smiled. "Can me and Jimmy have some cookies and milk?"

She nodded and headed over to the ceramic cookie jar sitting on the cupboard. *If only Jacob would remember that I'm his wife and not his mother. I can understand why Leona gets so upset with him. Some days it's all I can do to keep a smile on my face.* She piled several peanut butter cookies onto a plate. *For Jacob's sake, I'll keep trying to have a positive attitude, and I can't give up hope that he will recover someday.*

"I've already eaten my share," Jimmy said when Lydia placed the cookies in front of him. "I need to see if the cupboards in here need to be painted as well as the ceiling and walls. Then I'll be on my way."

"You can't go now," Jacob mumbled, grabbing a cookie and popping the whole thing into his mouth. "I ain't seen ya yet today."

"My husband enjoys your company," Lydia said to Jimmy. "So if you have a few more minutes, maybe you could sit and visit awhile." She glanced toward the back door and frowned. "I think my daughter's had enough time alone, so I'm going to check on her now."

"I'll have a couple more cookies; then Jacob can help me look the kitchen over, and we'll see what all needs to be done," Jimmy said.

In Jacob's present condition, Lydia didn't see how he could be any help in deciding what part of the kitchen needed painting, but if it gave him something to do, then she had no problem with it. "There's a jug of milk in the refrigerator," she called on her way out the door.

∞

"I think Mama's mad at me," Jacob said, leaning his elbows on the table. "She don't like my pet goat. I saw her kick at him once when she was hangin' clothes on the line and he kept trying to steal 'em from the basket."

"Maybe it would be best if you kept the goat locked in the pen with the other goats."

Jacob frowned. "That's what Ona says all the time."

Jimmy was pleased that Jacob had referred to Leona as Ona and not Mary. He'd either begun to remember that she was his daughter, or he'd simply come to accept the idea because his family had told him it was so. He'd obviously not figured out that Lydia was his wife, though, and that had to be hard on the poor woman.

Jacob scooted his chair back and ambled over to the refrigerator. He removed a gallon of milk and placed it on the table. Then he marched across the room and grabbed a glass from the cupboard. "You want some milk, Jimmy? It's plenty cold."

"No thanks." Jimmy pointed to his empty glass. "Leona and I had some iced tea awhile ago."

"Ona's gonna be real upset 'cause her dog is dead. Got hit by a car, she did."

"Yes, I heard about it from Lydia."

Jacob's face sobered. "Bad things happen to people, too. Mama keeps tellin' me that I fell and hit my head, but I don't remember fallin'." He gave his beard a couple of pulls. "Last thing I remember is walkin' home from school with my bruder, Dan. We stopped and picked some cherries that were growin' in the field along the way." He wrinkled his nose. "Guess they wasn't ripe yet 'cause they sure was sour. Dan took one bite and spit it right out. You never seen a person make such an ugly face."

Jimmy thought back to the time when his mother had made a cherry pie and hadn't put enough sugar in. She had cried when she realized that she'd ruined the pie.

Thinking about Mom made Jimmy feel sad, and he stared across the room at nothing in particular, fighting a wave of despair that gripped him as suddenly as a summer storm. Not only had the only mother he'd ever known been taken from him, but he'd also never had the opportunity to know his real mother or any of his Amish family. Life could be unfair, and it was hard to understand why God allowed so many tragedies. Then he glanced up at Jacob and reminded himself that the man who sat across from him couldn't remember anything past the first grade. It made his problems seem small by comparison.

Jacob tapped Jimmy on the arm. "How come you're lookin' so down in the mouth? Are you sad about Ona's dog dyin', or is there somethin' funny up?"

Something funny up? Jimmy smiled. *That must be Jacob's way of asking if there's something amiss.* "I do feel bad about Leona's dog dying," he said with a nod, "but I was thinking about other things that make me feel sad."

Jacob leaned closer. "What makes ya sad? Did your dog die, too?"

"No. I never had a dog when I was growing up."

"How about a cat? Ever have one of them?"

Jimmy shook his head.

"Then why are ya sad?"

"You really want to know?"

"Jah."

"Well, for one thing, I recently learned that I was stolen when I was a baby."

"Really?"

Jimmy didn't know what had made him blurt that out, but now that he had, he felt like sharing more. He was sure the bishop wouldn't think he was making up the story or question his motives, and it might feel good to finally tell someone the reason he'd come to Pennsylvania.

"My real family is Amish," Jimmy said. "And I believe they live somewhere in Lancaster County."

Jacob's bushy eyebrows drew together, and he stared at Jimmy. "Ya don't look Amish to me. Your hair's not cut right, and ya ain't wearin' no suspenders."

"I'm not Amish now. The man who kidnapped me is English." Jimmy picked up his glass and rolled the remaining chunks of ice around, letting them *clink* against each other. "Until recently, I didn't know I'd been born Amish. That's why I'm here in Pennsylvania—to look for the family I lost."

Jacob brushed some cookie crumbs off the table. "I lost a kitten once. Somebody must have stole it 'cause it never came back."

Jimmy inwardly groaned. *I shouldn't have expected him to show much interest in my story.*

"You gonna look for your mamm and daed?" Jacob asked, taking another gulp of milk.

"I think my real mother is dead. At least that's what my dad—I mean, the man who took me—said."

"Dead, like Ona's dog?"

Jimmy nodded and drank the liquid from the melted ice in his glass. "I don't suppose you might know of anyone in these parts who sells homemade root beer or had a child taken from their yard?"

"Don't know nothin' about no baby bein' snatched

away, but Mama bought me a bottle of root beer the other day. It came out of a machine in front of a store in town."

Jimmy blew out his breath and stood. This conversation was going nowhere, and it was time to do what he'd come here for. "Say, Jacob, how would you like to help me paint this kitchen next week?"

The bishop blinked a couple of times, clapped his hands together, and his deep laughter bounced off the kitchen walls. "I'd like that. Jah, I'd like that a lot!"

Chapter 26

The next few weeks were difficult as Leona mourned the loss of her dog and tried to stay away from Papa as much as possible. She still blamed him for Cinnamon's death, and rather than saying things she would regret later on, she'd decided it was best to keep some distance between them. She knew it wasn't right to hold a grudge, but her daed still did things to embarrass her, which only fueled her frustration.

During the last preaching service, Papa had stood up in the middle of one of the minister's sermons and quoted a Bible verse. Some said it was a sign that he was improving, but Leona thought it had been a childish thing to do, even if Papa had cited Luke 18:16 by memory. "But Jesus called them unto him, and said, Suffer little children to come unto me, and forbid them not: for of such is the kingdom of God."

Shrugging her thoughts aside, Leona moved to the window so she could watch her pupils playing in the school yard during recess. She'd sent her helper, Betty Zook, to oversee things while she looked over the afternoon reading assignment. *Maybe I should be the one outside with my students. Being in the fresh air and joining the kinner in a few games might do me some good. It would be better than standing here thinking about how mixed up my life has become.* She sighed. *If things could only be the same as they were when I was a girl. Papa and I aren't close like we once were, and things between Mom and me feel more strained than ever.*

"Papa is some better, though," she murmured, turning away from the window. Last Saturday, her daed had helped Jimmy work in their kitchen. Of course, Papa had only done some of the easier things like covering the floor with a drop cloth, stirring the can of paint, and sanding some of the cupboards before Jimmy painted them. At least it had kept him occupied, which had given Leona and her mother a chance to get something done without having to check up on him.

When the kitchen was finished, Jimmy had told Leona that he wanted to give her daed the chance to do more meaningful things, and he'd said he was planning to ask Arthur if they could find some chores for Papa to do on some of their paint jobs.

Leona appreciated the time Jimmy spent with her daed, but having the Englisher around so much made her feel rather unsettled. She'd been fighting a growing attraction to Jimmy, and that upset her almost as much as dealing with Papa's memory loss. It wasn't right that she should feel drawn to someone outside of her faith. It wasn't good for her to think so much about the Englisher, even daydreaming about what it would be like if they were married. Was this weakness in her spirit a product of her declining faith? *Maybe I'd better speak with someone about it. Maybe. . .*

A shrill scream halted Leona's thoughts, and she drew her attention back to the school yard. She noticed a group of children gathered in a circle, and thinking one of them might have been injured, she dashed out the front door.

"What happened?" she asked Emanuel Lapp, who came bounding up the steps as she was descending them.

"Some of the younger ones were playin', and Millie Hoffmeir fell," he said breathlessly. "Betty sent me to get you."

Leona rushed across the school yard and over to the group of children. Millie lay on the ground in the middle of the circle whimpering and holding her right arm. "What happened, Millie?"

The child looked up at Leona with tears in her eyes. "I fell off the teeter-totter. My arm hurts, Teacher."

"Can you wiggle your fingers?"

Millie nodded as she opened and closed them a few times.

"Are you able to move your arm?"

The child winced as she tried to lift her arm. It might only be a bad sprain, but Leona knew X-rays were needed to determine if it was broken. She decided to take the girl to the Hoffmeirs' store so her folks could get her to the doctor. She put a makeshift sling around the child's arm. Then, after instructing her helper to take charge of the class, she led Millie over to the buggy and carefully helped her climb in. As soon as Millie's older brother had the horse hitched up, Leona situated herself in the driver's seat, gathered up the reins, and headed out of the school yard.

∽∾

"Here's a basket of fruit and some cookies," Fannie said to Abraham as he stashed two fishing poles into the back of his buggy. "There's also a thermos full of cold milk."

He smiled gratefully and took the wicker basket from her, placing it on the front seat of the buggy. "Danki. It's much appreciated."

"I think it will do both you and Jacob some good to spend a few hours together," she said.

"I hope you're right about that. Me and the boys have been so busy in the fields lately that I haven't had much time for socializing." Abraham leaned down to kiss his wife on the cheek. "I've been lookin' for an opportunity to be alone with Jacob, and I'm hoping during our time together he might remember something about the good times we used to have."

She nodded. "It would be wunderbaar if he did."

"That young English fellow from out West has been takin' up way too much of Jacob's time." Abraham frowned. "I probably shouldn't be sayin' this, but I don't trust Jimmy Scott any farther than I can toss a bale of hay. Maybe not even that far."

"He seems like a nice man to me." Fannie gave Abraham's arm a gentle squeeze. "Maybe you should get to know him better."

Abraham climbed into his buggy. "Not sure I want to get to know him." He grabbed up the reins and gave them a quick snap. The horse moved forward, and he turned to offer Fannie a wave. "I'll be home before supper."

By the time Abraham had picked up Jacob and headed his horse and buggy in the direction of the pond, the afternoon sun had reached its hottest point. He didn't care, for he knew they could find solace under the shade of a maple tree near the water. Besides, it would be good to spend time with his old friend again, and the heat of summer seemed like a small thing.

He glanced over at Jacob, who'd been leaning out the window and making remarks about the things he saw along the way. *Dear Lord,* Abraham prayed, *let me say or do something today that will stir some memories in my good friend's jumbled head.*

A short time later, Abraham lounged beside Jacob on the grassy banks near the water's edge, both of them holding a fishing pole.

"I like to fish," Jacob said with an eager expression, "and I'm hopin' to get me a couple today."

Abraham smiled. "Maybe you will."

Jacob gripped his pole and stared at Abraham. "Mama says you're my good friend."

"That's true. We've been friends since your folks moved to this area when you were twelve years old."

Jacob's forehead wrinkled, and he squinted as

though he was trying to recall. "Sometimes my head hurts when I try to think about things I can't remember."

"That's all right." Abraham pointed to the water. "Let's just fish and enjoy our time together."

"Jah, okay."

They sat in companionable silence for the next half hour. Then, suddenly, Jacob leaned over to Abraham and said, "Jimmy's my friend, too, did ya know that?"

Abraham gave a brief nod. The last person he wanted to talk about was Jimmy Scott. He didn't think Jacob needed to discuss the Englisher, either.

"Jimmy let me help him paint Mama's kitchen. That was fun."

Abraham clenched his teeth.

"Jimmy's sad 'cause someone stole his kitten and he don't know where to find it."

"I didn't know Jimmy had a kitten."

"Jah. Some man came along and snatched it away, so Jimmy came here to find it. I had a kitten stolen once, but now I've got me a pet goat named Billy."

Abraham groaned. All this talk about missing kittens and pet goats didn't give him much hope that Jacob's memory would ever return. He needed to find something they could talk about that might trigger some recent recollections.

"Ona don't like my goat," Jacob continued. "She thinks it's my fault her dog got killed 'cause the goat chased it into the street." He sniffed. "I don't like havin' her mad at me. I think she wishes it had been Billy who died 'stead of Cinnamon."

The dejected look on Jacob's face made Abraham's heart clench. For the first time since his friend's accident, Abraham found himself caring less about the man's memory returning and more about finding some way to offer comfort to one who was obviously hurting.

He pulled the wicker basket Fannie had given him

between them and flipped open the lid. "How about some cookies and milk?"

Jacob nodded eagerly and smacked his lips. "Are they oatmeal cookies? Those are my favorite."

Abraham was glad Jacob's mood had improved so quickly. That was something to be grateful for, since they still hadn't caught any fish. "I think my wife made both chocolate chip and oatmeal cookies," he said with a smile.

∞

As Leona drove home from Paradise later that day, she reflected on all that had happened since Millie's accident. When she'd taken the little girl to her folks' store and told them what happened, Naomi had been short with her, asking why she hadn't been outside with her students during recess and accusing her of not watching them closely enough. Leona had tried to explain that her helper had been with the kinner, but Naomi was too upset to listen.

When Caleb and Naomi took Millie to a nearby clinic, Leona waited to find out the extent of the child's injury and to help Naomi's two oldest girls, who had been left to run the store by themselves. Upon the Hoffmeirs' return, Leona was distressed to learn that Millie's arm was broken and she would miss school until she got used to her cast and the pain had lessened. With the problem she was having in learning to read and write, missing any time from school was not a good thing.

Before Leona left the store, she'd mentioned the trouble Millie was still having in school and suggested that she give the girl some extra lessons. Naomi had taken offense at that, and Leona left the store berating herself for being an incompetent teacher.

"If only there was a way to make things better," she murmured. "Ezra's dead, Papa's got amnesia, my dog is gone, and I can't do right by my students anymore. Maybe it would be best if I quit teaching. Maybe I should get away for a while—go off someplace where I can be alone to think things through." Leona tensed and tightened her grip on the reins. "But where would I go, and what good would it do?" She remembered before Papa's amnesia, when he used to say that it didn't pay to run away from your problems. During the time when he'd actively been their bishop, he'd reminded the people to trust God in all things.

Blinking against stinging tears, she whispered a prayer for the first time in many weeks. "Lord, I need help. Please help me to believe again and to put my trust in You."

Chapter 27

While Jim waited for Holly, he stared out the window at a curious seagull that had landed on the deck railing outside the restaurant. Holly had agreed to meet him at noon, and though it was twelve fifteen, she still hadn't arrived. Could she have gotten caught up in heavy traffic or had trouble with her car?

He wrapped his fingers around the glass of iced tea the waitress had brought him. *Maybe Holly's not coming. Maybe she thinks I'm a lost cause because I won't go to church or AA meetings.* He took a drink and let the cool liquid trickle down his throat, wishing it were a bottle of beer. But he knew if Holly showed up and saw him with an alcoholic drink in his hand, she probably wouldn't agree to help him.

The young waitress with curly red hair approached the table a second time. "Would you like to order now, sir?"

"Uh. . .no, I'm waiting for someone." Jim glanced at his watch. It was now twelve thirty.

"I'll check back with you in a few minutes." The waitress smiled and moved away.

Jim tapped the edge of the table with his knuckles. *Why hasn't she called? Maybe I should call her.* He pulled his cell phone from the clip on his belt and punched in the cell number she'd given him when they'd agreed to meet for lunch. After several rings, he got her voice mail and hung up. He dialed the number at the health food store, and one of the employees answered. "This is Jim Scott. Is Holly there?"

"No, Mr. Scott. She's supposed to be having lunch with you."

"Well, she's not here, and I'm beginning to worry." Jim glanced out the window again. The seagull was gone, and so was Jim's appetite. He took another swallow of iced tea and tried to calm himself. *I'm not going to sit here all day waiting for that woman. If she's not here in the next five minutes, I'm leaving.*

When Jim heard footsteps approach, he mumbled, "Sorry, I'm still not ready to order."

"You may not be, but I am."

He looked up, and the sight of Holly standing in front of the table brought relief and a strange sense of excitement. She was wearing a jean skirt and a plain pink blouse, but he thought she looked like an angel. "I . . .I was worried that you wouldn't show," he said.

She smiled, and her matching dimples seemed to be winking at him. "Sorry I'm late, but I had to stop at a gas station because my oil light kept coming on. It was fine after I added a quart of oil. I was going to call, but I left my cell phone at home this morning."

Jim nodded. "I can't tell you how many times I've forgotten my phone." He stood and pulled out a chair for her.

Holly sat down and took a sip of water. "I hope you didn't think I'd stood you up."

Heat flooded his cheeks. "The thought had crossed my mind."

"I would never do something like that, Jim. If I couldn't make it or had changed my mind, I would have let you know."

"I appreciate that." He toyed with his napkin. *Should I tell her what's on my mind, or would it be better to wait until after we've eaten?*

"Have you heard anything from Jimmy lately?" Holly asked.

"Talked to him a few days ago." Jim was glad for the change of subject. He guessed he wasn't ready to put his feelings on the line or risk possible rejection by her saying no.

"How's he doing?"

He shrugged. "He's doesn't call much, but I guess he's okay."

"Do you have relatives living in Pennsylvania, or is Jimmy taking an extended vacation?"

He grimaced. *If I told her the truth, she'd be gone in a flash.*

"He. . .uh. . .recently found out he was adopted, and he's gone on a quest to find his real family."

"Oh, I see."

"I'm worried he may like it in Pennsylvania and decide to stay."

"I think all parents wish their grown kids would stick close to home." Holly compressed her lips and stared out the window. "But since it doesn't always work out that way, it's best if parents allow their kids to make their own decisions about where they will live." Her voice had a soft quality about it, yet she spoke with assurance.

The waitress showed up then, and Jim ordered a french dip sandwich and fries. Holly asked for a shrimp salad and a cup of clam chowder. As soon as the waitress left, he looked over at Holly. "You're probably wondering why I invited you to lunch today, so I might as well get straight to the point."

She picked up her glass of water and took a drink. "Did you have an ulterior motive?"

"Well, I was hoping you might help me with something."

She leaned slightly forward, an expectant look on her face. "What do you need my help with?"

"I'm. . .uh. . ." He groaned. "I've been really uptight lately, and the only way I can unwind or forget about my problems is to have a few drinks."

"A few drinks, or are you getting drunk?"

He flinched. "Well, I. . .sometimes."

"Drinking yourself into oblivion is not the answer, and I speak from experience." She stared at her placemat with furrowed brows. "I grew up in Puyallup. Soon after I graduated from high school, I met Frank Simmons, who was stationed at Fort Lewis."

"An army guy, huh?"

"Right. Frank and I had a whirlwind romance, and two months later, we were married and moved to Fort Polk, Louisiana." She sighed. "Frank really wanted kids, and after we discovered that I wasn't able to conceive, he became hostile toward me, and—" Her voice faltered. When she lifted her gaze to meet Jim's, he noticed tears in her eyes. "Frank died from a drug overdose ten years later, and though I'm not proud to say this, I was actually relieved when he was gone." She stared out the window. "The remorse I felt for feeling that way, coupled with the guilt I felt for not being able to give Frank any children was the excuse I used for drinking."

Jim swallowed around the lump in his throat. "People do unexpected things when they feel guilty."

"I wasn't a Christian back then, and I didn't have the support of family or friends. What started out as social drinking soon became a crutch." She smiled. "I'm grateful that a friend of mine introduced me to Christ, because soon after I confessed my sins and became a Christian, my life began to change."

He grimaced. *Oh no, here it comes—the "you need to go to church" lecture.*

"I thought you mentioned before that you got help for your drinking at AA."

"I did. But help came in the form of my pastor and friends from church, too."

Jim stared at the table. "Would you be willing to help me?"

She reached across the table and touched his outstretched arm. "I'll do whatever I can, but you must be willing to cooperate—and that includes attending AA meetings."

He nodded, and the heavy weight that had rested on his shoulders for many years seemed to lift a little.

∞

Jimmy opened his window as he headed down the road in the direction of the Weavers' place. The cool air ushered in by the coming of fall hit him full in the face. The longer he stayed in Lancaster County, the more he liked it. And the more he liked it, the more confused he became. He enjoyed the Amish people he'd come to know and was impressed with their gentle spirits and the way they helped others whenever there was a need—even those outside their faith. He was inspired by their plain lifestyle and enjoyed their simple, tasty food.

At times he felt as if he truly belonged here. He'd even wondered about the possibility of joining the Amish faith, which would give him the right to court Leona Weaver. *But could I give up all the modern conveniences? And what if I told them what little I know about my Amish heritage? Would it make any difference in how they accept me? Or would they think I'd made up the story in order to win Leona's hand?*

Jimmy groaned. He hadn't seen Leona since last week when he'd given her and Lydia a ride to Lancaster so they could do some shopping at Wal-Mart. After he'd dropped them off at their home and Lydia had gone into the house, he'd been bold enough to invite Leona to go on a picnic with him. At first she seemed to consider it. Then she'd mumbled something about him being English and her not wanting to give anyone the wrong impression. She'd dashed into the house without another word.

"If I were to join the Amish faith, it would mean giving up my photography hobby. I'd have to exchange my truck for a horse and buggy, and adhere to the rules of the *Ordnung*." He gave the steering wheel a sharp rap with his knuckles. *If I hadn't been taken from my rightful family when I was a baby, none of this would even be a consideration. Leona and I might already be dating or even be married by now.*

As Jimmy continued down the road, his thoughts became more jumbled. He tapped the brakes and slowed for a horse and buggy up ahead. *Do I stay through the winter or return to Washington? And if I go back to the only home I've ever known, what's waiting for me there? I'm like a ship without a captain, and no one can help me get where I need to go.* He ground his teeth together. *If I even knew where that was. Jacob's the only person I've told the truth about why I came to Pennsylvania, and he was no help at all. Should I quit worrying about what will happen to Jim if I tell my kidnapping story to someone else?*

∽

Leona sat in a wicker chair on the front porch with a bowl of strawberry ice cream in her lap. Her folks were in the kitchen eating their dessert, but she knew if she'd remained in the house, Papa would have bombarded her with a bunch of ridiculous questions, the way he'd done most of the day. Saturdays were difficult to get through, since Leona was usually at home and couldn't avoid her daed. She held up fairly well during the rest of the week—when she was at school or, on Sundays, when they were either in church or visiting others from their community on the off-weeks.

Leona reached down to rub the top of Cinnamon's

head but stopped herself in time. *Cinnamon's dead, and she's not coming back. Ezra's dead and won't be back. The man I've known as my daed all these years is gone and won't be coming back, either.*

The rumble of a vehicle brought Leona's thoughts to a halt. She glanced up and was surprised to see Jimmy's truck pulling into the yard.

"What brings you by?" she asked when he joined her on the porch a minute later.

"I was out for a drive and thought I'd stop over and see how things are going with your daed." Jimmy grinned as if he was pleased for using one of their Pennsylvania Dutch words.

"Everything's pretty much the same around here," she said with a shake of her head. "No real change in Papa's memory, that's for sure."

Jimmy dropped into the wicker chair beside her. "Sorry to hear there's no change."

She lifted her bowl. "Would you like some strawberry ice cream?"

"Thanks anyway, but I had a huge slice of Esther Raber's apple-crumb pie not long ago." He patted his stomach. "That woman is one good cook, and if I'm not careful, she's gonna make me fat."

"As busy as you keep painting, I doubt you'll ever be fat."

"You could be right. My dad told me once that he's been painting since he was in his early twenties, and he's still fit and trim." He paused. "Of course he's not really my—"

Maa–aa! Maa–aa! Jimmy's words were cut off when Jacob's goat bounded onto the porch, leaped over the railing, and nearly knocked Leona out of her chair as it stuck its nose into her bowl of half-eaten ice cream.

"Get away from me!" she shouted, pushing the animal aside. "You're nothing but a *zwieschpalt*—!"

The goat let out another loud *maa-aa*; then it nosed into her dish again.

Before Leona had time to react, Jimmy jumped out of his chair and scooped the critter into his arms. "Want me to put your so-called troublemaker back in his pen?"

She nodded, inwardly pleased to realize Jimmy understood her rantings in Pennsylvania Dutch. "I'd appreciate it."

Jimmy bounded off the porch and headed to the goat pen, which was behind the barn. Several minutes later, he was back. "Someone must have left the gate open," he said. "I closed the gate and made sure it was secure."

"Danki." Leona set her bowl on the porch. "I have no appetite for this now. Not after that pesky goat stuck his nose full of germs into it."

"Your daed says you don't like his goat much," Jimmy commented as he sat back down.

Leona gripped the arms of her chair. "He's right about that. If it weren't for Billy, Cinnamon would still be alive."

"Jacob thinks you blame him for the goat chasing your dog into the road."

She groaned. "After he made a pet out of the goat, it started getting out of its pen and causing all kinds of havoc around here."

Jimmy stared at his hands, which were folded in his lap. "It's hard to forgive others sometimes, whether you know what they did was wrong or just an accident."

"That's true, and I'm having a hard time forgiving Papa for not keeping that dumb goat penned up." She hung her head as a feeling of anger and frustration threatened to choke her. "My faith was shaken when Ezra died, but this whole thing with Papa's memory loss has made it worse. I'm not sure I'll ever feel the same way about things as I used to."

Jimmy reached over and took her hand as a look of understanding swept over his face.

"I used to believe God was in control and wants the best for us," she murmured. "But after all the losses I've had to endure this past year, I've begun to wonder if God cares what happens to anyone."

"On some level, I think I understand how you feel. I've been hurt, too." Jimmy's dark eyes clouded over, and Leona could see the depth of his pain.

"Do you mind if I ask how you've been hurt?"

"I grew up thinking I was my parents' son—by blood, I mean. Then shortly after my twenty-first birthday, I learned that I'd been adopted."

"Oh, I see."

"After Mom died, I was sure God didn't care about me or my dad. Then, when I realized I'd been adopted, I felt rejected and wondered why my parents hadn't told me sooner." Jimmy winced. "One day, not long ago, I found out that I was—"

A horse and buggy rumbled into the yard, halting Jimmy's words. Leona turned as Abraham and Fannie climbed down from their buggy and started across the lawn toward the house.

"We came to visit your folks," Fannie called with a friendly wave.

Abraham stopped when he got to the porch and glared at Jimmy. "What are you doin' here?"

"I came by to see how Jacob's getting along."

"Then why aren't you in the house talkin' to the bishop instead of sittin' out here with his daughter?"

"I'm sure he'd planned to see Papa," Leona spoke up. "But we got to visiting and then—"

"Jah, I'll bet you did." Abraham continued to stare at Jimmy as though he'd done something wrong.

Jimmy shifted in his chair, and even though his face had turned red, he made no comment. Fannie tugged on her husband's arm, and he glanced over at her. "What?"

"Why don't we go inside, Abraham?"

He nodded and mumbled, "Sure, okay."

"Sorry about that," Leona said once the Fishers had gone into the house. "I don't know why Abraham is acting so ornery tonight."

Jimmy stood. "I'd better go."

"But I thought you wanted to see my daed."

"Some other time—when you don't have company." Jimmy sprinted off the porch without even saying good-bye.

Chapter 28

By the first of December, the thermometer hovered near the freezing point for several days. Rain fell, and the cool air turned it to a thick film of ice. Leona knew it wouldn't be much longer before the young people in their district could enjoy some good ice-skating.

"Do you think this cold weather means we're in for a bad winter?" Leona turned to her mamm, who stood in front of their wood-burning stove one Saturday morning making pancakes.

Mom shrugged and reached for her spatula. "Guess we'll have to wait and see how it goes."

"I may need to have another talk with Naomi about Millie," Leona said as she began setting the table.

"Oh? How come?"

"She's still not doing well in school, and I feel frustrated because nothing I've tried has made much difference."

"Have you brought the problem up at one of your teachers' meetings?" Mom asked. "I'm sure some of the other Amish teachers have dealt with learning problems similar to Millie's. Maybe one of 'em will suggest something you haven't tried yet."

"I'll mention it at next week's meeting."

Mom glanced over at Leona and smiled. "It's good that you're so concerned about your students—just proves what a dedicated teacher you've become."

Leona moved over to the cupboard to get a bottle of maple syrup. She was tempted to mention that if she were able to further her education, she might have more knowledge in dealing with children who had special needs, as Millie obviously had. But she decided to keep her thoughts to herself, knowing that the leaders of their church would never accept the idea of her getting more education.

There were times, such as when Leona encountered a teaching problem she had no answers for, when she wished she hadn't been so hasty to join the Amish church as soon as she'd turned eighteen. If she had more education, she could probably do a better job of teaching, and she might not be having such a difficult time getting through to Millie.

"The pancakes are almost done. Would you mind callin' your daed in from the barn?" Mom's request forced Leona's thoughts to the back of her mind.

With a reluctant sigh, Leona grabbed her heavy shawl off the wall peg and hurried out the back door. She wasn't anxious to spend even a few minutes alone with Papa. Seeing him struggle with his loss of memory was always a reminder of all that she'd lost. She and Papa had been so close in days gone by. Now it was like there was a cavern between them.

When Leona entered the barn, she found her daed bent over a bucket of paint inside one of the horse's stalls, stirring it with a flat wooden stick. "That way and so. That way and so," he mumbled over and over.

"What are you doing, Papa?" She stepped into the stall and closed the door behind her.

He looked up and smiled. "Jimmy says I'm gettin' pretty good at paintin'. He thinks I need more practice. So I'm gonna paint all the horses' stalls today."

"I don't think this is the kind of practice Jimmy had in mind. It's probably not a good idea for you to do any painting when Arthur, Jimmy, or one of the other painters isn't around." Leona touched Papa's shoulder. "Mom sent me out to let you know that breakfast is ready."

He frowned. "I ain't no baby, and you shouldn't be tellin' me what to do. I'm a grown man, and I can paint this stall without anyone showin' me how."

Leona stepped back as a sense of hope lifted her shoulders. Had her daed's memory come back? Maybe God had finally answered her prayers. "Do. . .do you know who I am?"

He nodded. "Sure. You're my sister."

Leona shook her head. Maybe Papa just needed a little reminder. "I'm your daughter."

He blinked a couple of times and stared at her. "You sure about that?"

"Jah. I'm Leona."

Silence draped around them like the shawl covering her trembling shoulders, until Papa finally lifted his eyebrows and said, "Ona?"

"That's right. You made up that nickname when I was a little girl."

His eyes clouded over, but then he gave a quick nod. "Okay."

Leona felt a chill—one that left her feeling colder than the bitter weather outside. Would this nightmare with Papa living in the past one minute, then acting as if he knew something of the present the next minute ever come to an end? Visions of happier times they had spent together in the barn raced through her mind, and her shoulders drooped with a feeling of hopelessness. Those days were gone for good.

Trying to shake off the nagging thoughts, she turned and grasped the handle of the stall door, squeezing it so tightly that her fingers ached. "You'd better come inside for breakfast now. The pancakes Mom has made will be getting cold."

"Okay. Should I make out the lights?"

"Better let me do that."

❦

Jimmy glanced at the cardboard box sitting on the front seat of his truck. "I sure hope she likes her gift. She needs something to get her mind off her troubles."

He felt a compelling need to offer Leona support, and he knew the reason for his concern went beyond his sense of Christian duty. What had begun as curiosity had quickly turned to attraction. His desire to spend time with Leona and shield her from pain had taken him down a road he'd least expected. Jimmy wasn't sure how or when it had happened, but he was well on his way to falling in love with the bishop's daughter. That thought didn't scare him nearly as much as his concern over what he was going to do about it. If he stayed in Lancaster County and joined the Amish faith, he would feel it necessary to reveal his past—despite the fact that he knew so little about it and had not found his real family. He still, for Mom's sake, wanted to keep Jim from going to jail. However, he knew it wouldn't be right to begin a relationship with secrets, so even if he decided to leave Pennsylvania and asked Leona to go with him, he would need to tell her about the kidnapping.

Jimmy reflected on the phone conversation he'd had with Allen a few days ago. Allen had asked Jimmy when he was coming home, and Jimmy had been evasive, saying he wasn't sure what he was going to do. He'd said he was needed here—that Arthur had come to rely on his help with the painting business. He'd also mentioned that he enjoyed spending time with Jacob while he taught him how to paint and do some of the chores he'd done before the accident. He had talked about Leona, too, saying he'd been looking for ways to ease some of the burden she and her folks had been faced with since Jacob's accident. And before he'd hung up the phone, he'd asked Allen to continue praying.

Jimmy's truck jerked, then slid to the right, reminding him that the roads were slippery. He pushed his musings aside, determined to concentrate on his driving. In Puyallup, they didn't get much snow during the winter, but he'd been quick to realize that Lancaster County got more than its share of snow and ice. If he planned to spend the winter here, he would need to drive defensively and be prepared to handle his vehicle in all kinds of adverse conditions.

Soon Jimmy steered his truck up the Weavers' driveway and parked near the barn, where he discovered a horse and buggy tied to the hitching rail. "I hope Leona or her mother isn't planning to go anywhere today," he muttered. The roads were too icy, and even with his studded tires, he had slid in places.

He stepped out of the truck, hoisted the box into his arms, and headed for the back door, where most of the Weavers' friends and family entered whenever they came to visit. Shifting the box to one arm, he rapped his knuckles on the edge of the door. A few seconds later, Lydia answered, wearing a dark blue dress covered with a black apron sprinkled with a dusting of flour.

"I hope I'm not interrupting," he said, "but I was wondering if I could speak to Leona."

"Jah, sure." Lydia smiled. "Ever since we finished breakfast, we've been baking apple pies, so maybe you'd like to come in and try a piece." She held the door open, and that was when Jimmy caught sight of Leona standing in the kitchen holding a rolling pin. She, too, had streaks of flour on her dark apron.

The delicious smell of cinnamon teased Jimmy's senses and caused his stomach to rumble. "A hunk of pie does sound good," he said as he stared at Lydia's daughter. Leona stirred something in him, but he knew that as long as he remained English he could only admire her beauty and strength, never pursue it. *I wonder how it would be to come home to her every night. I wonder how it would feel to kiss—* Jimmy shook his uninvited thoughts aside and stepped forward. He could appreciate Leona's lips, which sometimes turned into a cute little smile, but it would be wrong for him to kiss them.

"I've brought you a gift, Leona," he said, nodding at the box he held. "Consider it an early Christmas present." He pulled out a chair and sat down, balancing the box on his knees.

Leona reached for a dish towel and wiped her hands before coming over to the table to join him. Lydia, obviously curious about what was in the box, also headed toward him.

Jimmy opened the flaps, reached inside, and lifted a very sleepy, very furry red puppy out of the box for Leona's inspection. "What do you think?"

"Such a cute dog," Lydia said excitedly before her daughter could respond. "She looks like Cinnamon when she was a pup. Don't you think so, Leona?"

Leona tilted her head and stared at the puppy in such an odd way that it made Jimmy wonder what she was thinking. "Do you like her?" He extended his arms, hoping she would take the animal from him.

The pup, now fully awake, began to squirm, but Leona sat unmoving.

"She's yours," Jimmy said. He was beginning to think he'd made a mistake in buying the little Irish setter.

"She. . .she's not Cinnamon, and there isn't a dog on earth that could take her place." Leona's chin quivered, and tears glistened behind her glasses.

Jimmy was afraid she might run out of the room, so he put the puppy back in the box. "She needs a good home, and I was hoping you would like her," he mumbled as the little dog whimpered.

Lydia reached into the box and rubbed the pup's

ears. "Sure is a cute one." She glanced over at her daughter, but Leona made no comment.

Lifting the box into his arms, Jimmy stood. "Guess I'd better head back to the pet store and return the puppy." He nodded at Leona. "I'm sorry for upsetting you. I should have realized it might be too soon."

"Jacob's out in the barn trying to paint one of the stalls, and I'm thinking maybe he would like to have that little critter," Lydia said. "He's made friends with nearly every animal on our farm, and I'm sure he'd be glad to have another pet."

Leona jumped up, planting both hands on her hips. "No! Papa's not responsible enough."

Lydia clucked her tongue. "Come now, Leona. Your daed's done real well carin' for the chickens, horses, and his goat."

"If Papa had kept that troublesome goat locked in the pen, he wouldn't have upset my dog and chased her into the street." Leona's voice caught on a sob. "I've said this before, and I'll say it again—Cinnamon would still be alive if it weren't for that goat!"

Lydia wrapped her arms around her daughter's trembling shoulders while Jimmy stood, not knowing what to say or do. What he'd hoped would be a pleasant surprise for Leona had turned into a messy reminder of the dog she'd lost and her anger toward her dad.

Guess I'm no one to talk, he thought ruefully. *I haven't forgiven my dad for what he did, either.*

"I'll put the puppy in my truck and then stop by the barn to see how Jacob's doing." Jimmy offered Leona a quick smile and made a hasty exit. He'd only made it halfway across the yard when Leona called out to him.

"Jimmy, wait!"

He turned and saw her running through the carpet of frozen leaves on the lawn. "You shouldn't be out here with no coat," he admonished. "It's much too cold for that."

"I've changed my mind about the pup. It was nice of you to buy it for me, and I've decided to keep her, after all." Leona opened the flap on the cardboard box, and when she lifted the squirming puppy toward her face, it licked the end of her nose.

Jimmy smiled and took hold of her arm. "Let's get the two of you inside where it's warm, and then I think I would like to sample some of your mamm's apple pie."

She looked up at him, and a shadowy dimple quivered in one cheek. "Danki, Jimmy. Danki for being such a good friend."

Chapter 29

I appreciate your willingness to drive me to town," Leona said, glancing over at Jimmy. His wrinkled forehead let her know that his concentration was on the slippery road.

"Glad I could do it. I didn't think it was safe for you to drive your horse and buggy on these icy roads."

She released a tiny laugh. "I've handled the buggy in all kinds of weather, but it is much nicer to be taxied into town by such a capable driver."

He grunted. "I'm not sure how capable I am. We don't get much snow or ice during the winter in the town where I grew up. When we do, it usually only lasts a few days."

"I appreciate the care with which you're driving. It makes me nervous to travel too fast, whether it be in a car or a horse-pulled carriage."

Jimmy nodded. "You wouldn't care for my dad's driving then. He's one of those 'I don't want anyone ahead of me' kind of drivers."

Leona smiled and relaxed against the seat. "I haven't said much about the time you've spent helping my daed relearn to paint, but I want you to know that both Mom and I appreciate it."

"I'm hoping if Jacob works around the other painters awhile that it might spark some memories for him."

"That would be nice, but I'm not holding my breath."

"I'm sure the Lord has a plan for your daed's life, whether his memory returns or not."

"I wish I had your faith—Papa's, too, for that

matter. He's got all kinds of faith in his ability to paint these days."

"Maybe that's because he thinks like a child. It's much easier for children to have faith than it is for adults, especially when things aren't going so well."

Leona stared out the window. The barren trees hanging over part of the road looked like bony fingers waiting to snatch away anyone's joy if they walked underneath. The truth was, it was easier to have faith and believe in miracles when you weren't the one going through the problem. Jimmy didn't understand everything she was going through right now. It was bad enough that she'd been trying to come to grips with Ezra's death, Papa's childish antics, and her failure as a teacher. Now she had to deal with the swirl of emotions that swept over her whenever she was near Jimmy. Until she'd met him, she'd convinced herself that she would never fall in love again. Now she was afraid she might be falling for the wrong man—an Englisher, no less.

"So, what are you going to name that new pup?" Jimmy asked, breaking into her disconcerting thoughts.

She puckered her lips. "Let's see. . . . The puppy's real soft and fluffy, so I could name her Fluffy."

Jimmy wrinkled his nose. "Not masculine enough."

"It's a girl pup," Leona said with a snicker.

"Oh yeah, that's right."

"She's also quite lively and determined."

"I'll say. I couldn't believe how the little stinker climbed out of that box when we put her in the barn. It was twice as tall as the one I brought her in, but it took a box three times as tall to keep her inside."

"That's how Cinnamon was, too. Always determined to get her own way."

Jimmy smacked the steering wheel with the palm of his hand. "Hey, since your last dog was named after a spice, why not call the pup Ginger or Nutmeg?"

Leona tipped her head as she contemplated his idea. "Ginger. . . I like that. Jah, I'll call her Ginger."

They drove in silence for the next few miles, but as they entered the town of Paradise, Jimmy spoke again. "Mind if I ask you a personal question?"

"What's that?"

"I've been wondering if you think you could be happy if you weren't Amish?"

Leona didn't know what had prompted such a question, but she responded honestly. "I. . .I'm not sure. I've wondered sometimes what it would be like if I were English and could get more education, but it would be hard to leave my folks—especially now, with Papa's condition to consider. It wouldn't be right to leave Mom alone to deal with him, either. Besides, if I were to leave, I would be shunned because I've already been baptized and joined the church."

"I see."

She glanced over at him. "What about you? Could you be happy if you weren't English?"

"I don't know. Maybe, but it would take some getting used to."

They were nearing the Hoffmeirs' store, and Jimmy turned his pickup into the parking lot. "What time would you like me to come back for you?" he asked.

"I should be done in half an hour or so."

"I'll run a few errands of my own and try to be here by noon. Maybe we can stop somewhere for lunch before we head back to your place."

"That'd be nice." Leona climbed out of the truck, wondering if Jimmy enjoyed being with her as much as she enjoyed being with him. Despite her resolve not to become romantically involved with anyone, she had strong feelings for Jimmy. *Is it wrong to have lunch with him? Maybe not.* She'd seen many English drivers having lunch with the Amish people they taxied around.

❦

"You girls can put those books we got in this morning on that empty lower shelf," Naomi instructed her teenage daughters.

Sarah reached into the cardboard box to grab a couple of books. "Okay, Mom. We'll see that it gets done."

"What if there isn't room for all of 'em?" Susan questioned.

"Then we'll find space on some other shelf." Naomi returned to the front counter where a letter she'd received waited to be read. It was from Ginny Nelson, the English friend she'd run away with so many years ago. She hadn't heard from Ginny in over a year. Tearing the envelope open, Naomi silently read the short note.

> *Dear Naomi,*
>
> *Sorry for not writing in such a long time, but Chad and I have been busy trying to remodel the fitness center he bought a few years ago— after we moved from Puyallup to Bellevue.*
>
> *How are things with you? I don't suppose you've had any word on Zach, or you probably would have written and said so. I still think of your little brother whenever I see a boy with wavy brown hair and eyes the color of dark chocolate. Of course, Zach wouldn't be a kid anymore, would he? I guess he'd be about twenty-one years old now.*

Naomi set the letter aside and drew in a cleansing breath. Even now, after all these years, the mention of Zach's name reopened old wounds, making her feel guilty for leaving him on the picnic table. *If only we knew where he was. If we just had some assurance that he was alive and doing okay.*

The bell above the front door jingled to announce the arrival of a customer. Leona Weaver entered the store, and Naomi's husband, Caleb, walked in behind her.

"Thanks for telling me about this, Leona," Caleb said. "It's important that we keep up on how our kinner are doing in school. If we can do anything to help, please let us know."

Naomi was about to ask what Caleb was talking about when Leona turned to her and said, "I came by to speak with you about Millie."

Naomi leaned forward, her elbows on the counter. "What about her?"

"She's still having trouble in school, and I've tried everything I can think of to teach her to read and write, but she doesn't seem to be getting it."

"Maybe we need to work with her more at home," Caleb suggested.

Naomi nodded. She'd planned to do that soon after Leona mentioned Millie was having a hard time, but things had been hectic at the store. Since fall had crept in, nearly everyone in her family had taken turns with the flu, which had kept her busier than ever. Then Millie had broken her arm, and Naomi had allowed her to slack off on everything, including homework. "I'll start reading to her tonight," she promised.

Leona shook her head. "Millie doesn't need to be read to. She needs to learn how to read."

Naomi's defenses rose. She didn't know why she felt so frustrated whenever Leona mentioned the difficulty Millie was having, but talking about it made her feel as if she had failed her daughter. "I'll work with her every night until she knows how to read."

"I was looking through a magazine while I waited in the dentist's office the other day, and I came across an article on learning disabilities." Leona paused and flicked her tongue across her bottom lip. "I think Millie may have dyslexia."

Caleb's forehead wrinkled. "What's that?"

"It involves not being able to read or write correctly," Leona explained. "For some people, the words seem to shake or move. The article said some might even see letters in reverse."

"So what can we do about this problem?" he questioned.

"I'm not sure yet. The article didn't give much information. I'm planning to discuss the problem at our next teachers' meeting and see if anyone has had experience in dealing with dyslexia or knows of anything I might try."

"Let us know what you find out. We'll do everything we can to help." Caleb looked over at Naomi and smiled. "Isn't that right?"

"Uh. . .of course. Danki for coming by, Leona." Naomi turned away. "I guess I'll check on the girls." As much as Naomi wanted Millie to do well in school, she couldn't accept the fact that the child might have a serious problem. And she couldn't help but wonder if she might have caused the problem by not giving Millie enough attention.

∽

Since Leona had finished her business with the Hoffmeirs and knew she had a few minutes before Jimmy would be back, she decided to step into the quilt shop to say hello to Mary Ann. She found her and Abby sitting at the quilting table.

"How's business?" Leona asked, stepping between the two women.

"We're very busy, even with the cooler weather and fewer tourists than we had this summer." Abby smiled then excused herself to wait on a customer who'd entered the store.

Leona glanced at Mary Ann, noticing how her fingers flew in and out of the quilting material like there was no tomorrow. "Sure wish I could sew like that," she said. "Even though Mom taught me all the basic skills when I was a girl, I've never been able to sew as well as some women my age."

"I'm not really an expert at sewing, but I do enjoy making quilts. And I think the more I make, the better I get." Mary Ann grinned up at her. "How are things with you?"

"Not so good." Leona glanced over her shoulder at the door to the adjoining store. "Millie's still having a hard time in school, and when I tried to talk to her mamm about it, she seemed kind of defensive."

"My big sister always has been sensitive about things. When it comes to one of her kinner not doing well in school, I'm guessing she feels as if she's failed as a mudder somehow."

Leona shook her head. "If anyone's failed Millie, it's me."

Mary Ann touched Leona's arm. "How can you say that? You're a good teacher, and from what I hear, all your scholars think you're the *bescht*."

"I don't feel as if I'm the best of anything these days."

"Of course you are. You'll figure out some way to deal with Millie's problem."

Leona was about to comment when Jimmy poked his head into the quilt shop and waved. "Oh, my ride's here, so I guess I'd better go."

Mary Ann nodded. "I'll be praying that God gives you the wisdom you need to help Millie."

"Danki," Leona said and then hurried from the room.

∽

As Leona took a seat across from Jimmy in a booth at the Bird-in-Hand Family Restaurant, she realized how tight her muscles felt. She kept thinking about the response she'd gotten from Millie's parents concerning Millie having dyslexia, and she wondered why Naomi had seemed so defensive.

She scrunched her napkin into a tight little ball. *If I just had more knowledge about things like this, it might not be such a problem.*

"Would you like to choose something from the menu, or would you rather have the lunch buffet?" Jimmy asked.

"Uh. . .it doesn't really matter. I'll have whatever you're having."

He chuckled. "Now that's what I like—a woman who's easy to please."

"Not really. I get frustrated when things don't go as I'd hoped."

Leona studied the geometric design on her placemat, then looked up when she sensed he was staring at her. "You seem to take life as it comes, Jimmy. I mean, look how well you've adjusted to living here. It's almost as if you've been in Lancaster County all your life."

Jimmy's eyes brightened, and he leaned slightly forward. "You really think so?"

"I do. In fact, Arthur mentioned once that whenever you've worn a straw hat while you were working you looked like you could even be Amish."

"Well, maybe that's because—"

Jimmy's words were halted when the waitress came and asked if they were ready to order.

"I think I'll have the buffet. That way I can pick and choose all the things I like best." He smiled at the pretty

English waitress, and she gave him a quick wink.

A pang of jealousy seared through Leona. "I'll have the same." She knew it was silly to feel this way. She had no claim on Jimmy. And never would.

Leona followed Jimmy to the salad bar, determined to shake off the sullen mood she'd been in since they'd left the Hoffmeirs' store.

They returned to the table a few minutes later, and Jimmy suggested they offer a silent prayer.

Leona looked up when she'd finished her prayer. Seeing that Jimmy was done praying, she picked up her salad fork.

"I sure like these pickled-beet eggs," he said, cutting one in half and forking it into his mouth. "I'd never heard of them till I came here."

"Do you miss Washington?" she asked.

"There are some things I miss about it."

"When do you think you'll go back?"

"I don't know. It all depends on how things go."

She tipped her head in question.

"You see, I came here on a mission, but I haven't found what I'm looking for yet."

"What mission?"

Jimmy leaned forward, resting his arms on the table. "I thought I was ready to share some things with you, but until I'm able to make a decision as to whether I should stay, it would probably be best if I don't talk about it."

Leona watched Jimmy fiddle with the end of his spoon, wondering if he had some sort of secret. If so, then why'd he bring up the subject if he wasn't planning to tell her what it was?

Jimmy crossed his arms and stared at her from across the table. She wished he wouldn't do that. It filled her with a strange mixture of longing and fear.

"I shared a few things with your daed not long ago,

but I think I only confused the poor man," he said after a few seconds went by.

Like you're confusing me? Leona's tongue felt as if it was fastened to the roof of her mouth. *Why would Jimmy take Papa into his confidence and not me?*

"There is one thing I'd like to ask you, though."

"What's that?"

"I was wondering what the Amish would do if a person—an Englisher—hurt someone in their family."

Her forehead wrinkled. "I'm not sure what you mean."

"Would they prosecute the guy and send him to jail?"

She shook her head. "That's not the Amish way."

A look of relief spread over Jimmy's face as he leaned against his seat.

"Are you in some kind of trouble? Are you worried about going to jail?"

"Not me," he said in a near whisper. "It's someone I know, and I'm sure he'll be relieved to hear that he won't be prosecuted for what he did."

Leona was tempted to question Jimmy further, but she figured if he wanted her to know he would have shared the details. "I guess I'll go back to the buffet and see what else is there," she said, rising to her feet.

"You go ahead," he said. "I'm going to finish my salad first."

As Leona walked away, feelings of confusion and doubt swirled in her head. What kind of secret was Jimmy keeping from her, and why had she allowed herself to be swept away by a tide of emotions whenever she was with him?

Chapter 30

When Leona answered a knock at the back door one Saturday morning, she was surprised to see Lettie Byler, the Amish schoolteacher Eli Raber had been courting, standing on the porch.

"Guder mariye, Lettie," Leona said. "What brings you by so early this morning?"

"After our last teachers' meeting, when you mentioned the problem one of your scholars was having, I decided to speak to my Mennonite friend, Katherine, who's a nurse. When I told her that you suspected Millie has dyslexia, she gave me this article on children with various learning disabilities." Lettie handed the piece of paper to Leona.

Hope welled up in Leona's soul. "Danki for sharing this with me."

"The article not only lists the symptoms of dyslexia, but it also offers some suggestions you might want to try."

"Jah, I'll surely do that." Leona opened the door wider. "It's too cold for us to be visiting on the porch. Won't you come inside and have a cup of tea with me and my mamm?"

"Maybe some other time," Lettie said sweetly. "I'm on my way to the Rabers' to see Eli. As I'm sure you've probably heard, he fell off a ladder last week while he was painting a supermarket. Thank the Lord he wasn't seriously hurt, but he did sprain his ankle real bad, so he hasn't been down to Strasburg to see me in a while."

The mention of Eli falling from a ladder made Leona shudder as memories of Papa's accident filled her mind with gloom. Even now, she could still see him falling to the ground and landing with a sickening thud.

"You're shivering, and I must let you get back inside where it's warm," Lettie said as she turned to go.

"Danki for coming by. I'll let you know how things go with Millie."

⚭

The following Monday, as Leona opened the door of the woodstove to stoke the fire before her pupils arrived, she thought about the article on dyslexia Lettie had given her. It had been full of helpful suggestions, listing various ideas, such as breaking words and information into smaller chunks and placing colored overlays over the top of the pages the child would be reading. It also mentioned the use of a tape recorder, computer CD, and videotapes, but Leona knew those wouldn't be acceptable tools in her Amish community.

She was, however, determined to try some of the suggestions on Millie today, and she'd even brought a sheet of blue cellophane to experiment with the color-changing idea.

Leona had just closed the door on the woodstove when she heard the sound of heavy footsteps clomping up the front steps. Glancing at the clock on the far wall and realizing it was only seven thirty, she figured the footsteps didn't belong to any of the students since school wouldn't start for another hour.

She smoothed the sides of her dress to be sure there were no wrinkles, checked her head covering to make sure it was properly in place, and went to open the door. She was surprised to discover Abner standing on the porch with a box of firewood at his feet.

"It's my week to furnish wood for the schoolhouse," he said. "So I'm dropping it off now, before I head to work."

She glanced past him into the school yard. "Is Emanuel with you?"

Abner shook his head. "He didn't want to get here early, so he said he'd walk with some of the kinner who live near our place."

"That makes sense." Leona motioned to the box of firewood. "Danki for this, and if you wouldn't mind moving the box to the other end of the porch, it would be much appreciated."

"Sure, I can do that." Abner bent to pick up the box, and he carried it across the porch with little effort. Once he'd set it down, Leona figured he would be on his way. Instead, he shuffled over to where she waited and stood there as though he were waiting for something.

"Is there anything else I can help you with, Abner?"

"Jah, there is." He scuffed his boots against the wooden planks and stared at the porch.

"If it's about Emanuel, you'll be pleased to know that he's done real well here of late. I haven't had a bit of trouble with him misbehaving for many weeks."

"I'm glad to hear that, but it's not my little bruder I want to talk about. I. . .uh. . . wanted to ask you something about a. . .a friend of yours."

"Which friend are you referring to?"

"Mary Ann Fisher."

Leona folded her arms to ward off the cold, wishing she'd had the foresight to grab her jacket before opening the door. "Would you like to come inside where it's warmer?"

"Jah, sure. I guess that would be better than standin' here in this chilly weather." Abner tamped the snow off his boots and followed her into the schoolhouse.

"What did you want to ask me about Mary Ann?" Leona asked, once she'd shut the door and taken a seat behind her desk.

Abner removed his hat and leaned against one of

the desks in the front row. "I. . .I was wonderin' if she's . . .uh. . .bein' courted by anyone."

Leona bit her lip to keep from smiling. Her concern that Abner might be interested in courting her had been put to rest. Apparently, he was interested in Mary Ann and had been too shy to show it. "Why, no, Abner," she replied. "I don't believe Mary Ann's seeing anyone right now."

A look of relief flooded his face, and his cheeks turned pink. "That's good to hear." He stood twisting the end of his hat brim and staring at the floor. Finally, he lifted his gaze and said, "I don't suppose you'd be willing to put in a good word for me."

"You mean with Mary Ann?"

"Jah."

"I guess I could, but don't you think it would be better if you spoke to her on your own?"

"I'd kind of like to find out how she feels about me first. That way I won't be embarrassed if I ask to court her and she says no."

Leona nodded. "I'll speak with Mary Ann when I get a chance, and I'll let you know what she says."

"Danki. I'd appreciate that." Abner plopped his hat on his head, swung around, and headed for the door. "You're a good friend, Leona," he called over his shoulder.

"Seems I'm everyone's friend these days," she mumbled as he shut the door. "Everyone's friend but Papa's."

⁂

Jim glanced at the clock sitting on the small table beside his bed and was shocked to see that it was only 5:00 a.m., yet he felt fully awake, energetic, and ready to meet the day. It was the first time in many weeks that he'd felt so well, and he figured the reason was because he'd attended an AA meeting with Holly on Friday night. On Saturday, they'd gone to dinner so they could get better acquainted and discuss some of the things Jim had learned at the meeting. He'd come to realize during their meal that he was physically attracted to Holly, and he planned to take her on a real date soon.

Jim pondered a couple of things he'd learned at the AA meeting. "*Live and let live. Easy does it. Think, think, think. First things first,*" he quoted from four of the five slogans he'd seen posted on the meeting-room wall. Those all made good sense.

He burrowed into the pillows propped against his headboard, remembering how he'd chosen to ignore the last slogan because it didn't apply to him. "Slogan number five," he muttered. "*But for the grace of God.*"

"Where was God's grace when I learned that I couldn't father a child? Where was God's grace when Linda died from cancer?" Jim groaned. "Where was God's grace when my boy took off for Maryland without telling me he was going and ended up in Pennsylvania searching for his Amish family? And where is God's grace now, when Jimmy won't return any of my phone calls?"

As Jim crawled out of bed and ambled across the room, his initial exuberance melted away with each step. When he reached the window, he pulled the curtain aside and peered out. The predawn darkness greeted him.

He gritted his teeth and crushed the end of the curtain between his fingers. *I'm determined to get my life straightened around, and I don't need God or His grace to do it.*

≈≈

"Good morning, boys and girls."

"Good morning, Teacher."

Leona scanned the room to see if any children were absent, then began the school day by reading James 1:5: " 'If any of you lack wisdom, let him ask of God, that giveth to all men liberally, and upbraideth not; and it shall be given him.' "

I need that verse as much as the scholars do today, Lord, she silently prayed. *Help me to know what to do in order to help Millie learn to read and write.*

When Leona had closed her Bible, the children rose, bowed their heads, and repeated the Lord's Prayer in unison. After the prayer, they filed to the front of the room and stood in their assigned places according to age and size so they could sing a few songs in German and English.

Then the students returned to their seats, and it was time for class to begin. Grades five to eight exchanged arithmetic papers and checked them before handing them to Leona. Grades three and four gave their papers to an older child to check; and grades three to eight began their lesson by doing the assignment Leona had posted on the blackboard before school.

The children in the first and second grades took turns reading by page, but Leona worked individually with Millie, asking her to read out of her primer by sentences. Since the article Lettie had given Leona said that breaking words into smaller chunks had helped some children with dyslexia, she decided to try that approach first. However, after a few tries, she soon realized it wasn't going to work for Millie.

"The letters are shakin', Teacher," the child complained. "And they're movin' around on the page."

Next, Leona tried substituting a rhyming word for another word on the page, to see if Millie was listening, but that didn't work, either.

Finally, she went to her desk and placed the piece of blue cellophane she'd brought over the page Millie was trying to read. "What's this say?" she asked, pointing to the word *dog*.

"D-O-G." Millie smiled up at Leona. "Dog."

With a mounting sense of excitement, Leona pointed to another word.

"C-A-T. Cat."

"That's right." Leona patted the top of Millie's head. "Now keep reading."

Knowing she needed to work with some of the other pupils, Leona put her helper in charge of Millie and moved over to the other side of the room. She'd just reached Emanuel's desk and was about to ask him a question when the front door opened, and Naomi stepped in.

Most parents notified her when they planned to stop by. Once in a while, though, a parent would make a surprise visit. Apparently, that was what Naomi had in mind, for she stepped up to Leona and said, "I came to see how my kinner are doing—especially Millie."

Leona might have felt irritated because of the interruption, but under the circumstances, she thought Naomi's timing couldn't have been more perfect. "Come with me," she said. She couldn't keep the excitement from her voice. "I want to show you how well Millie's doing and explain what I believe is going to help her learn to read and write easier."

As Naomi stood beside the desk watching and listening to Millie read, Leona waited with anticipation to see how she would respond.

"What's the blue piece of cellophane doing on Millie's book?" Naomi asked, turning to Leona with a wrinkled forehead.

"A teacher friend of mine gave me an article on dyslexia," Leona explained. "It lists several things that have helped with the problem." She pointed to the cellophane. "Using a colored overlay has worked well for many children, but since I didn't have any, I decided to try the cellophane. I figured if it worked, I'd order some of the overlays from the company mentioned in the magazine."

Naomi pursed her lips. "I'm not sure I want Millie learning to read and write with fancy things you've read about. What's wrong with her learning the old-fashioned way, like my other kinner have done?"

Before Leona could respond, Millie looked up at her mother and said, "I'm learnin' to read, Mama." She pointed to the page before her and grinned. "See here. . . Dog. Cat. Stop. Go."

"Good, Millie." Naomi squeezed her daughter's arm; then she leaned close to Leona and whispered, "I'll see what Caleb has to say about this; then we'll let you know if we want you to order those fancy overlays or not."

Leona gave a quick nod. As she moved back to Emanuel's desk, she lifted a silent prayer. *Open Naomi's heart to this new idea, Lord. And please, since I can't get more education, fill me with wisdom in knowing the best ways to teach my students.*

Chapter 31

T he walls in the one-room schoolhouse seemed to vibrate with excitement as the children prepared for this evening's Christmas program they were putting on for their parents. Even Leona felt a sense of exhilaration while she scurried about the room, making sure everyone knew their parts and setting all the props in place.

Besides the fact that Christmas was such a happy time of the year, Leona was pleased with how well Millie had been doing these last few weeks. The child's reading and writing skills had improved quite a bit, and she seemed more attentive and willing to learn. After speaking with Caleb and Naomi again, Leona had been given permission to order the colored plastic overlays. It seemed odd that such a simple thing as a change of color could make a difference in the words being read; but it had, and Leona was very pleased. She knew Millie's parents were happy, because Naomi had even thanked her.

Now, if something could only be done to help Papa's memory return, this would be the perfect Christmas. She scanned the room to see who had come to the program. Some of the parents were seated in their children's desks, many sat in chairs placed around the room, and a few stood against the back wall. Leona spotted her folks sitting in chairs beside her brother. Next to Arthur sat his wife, Doris, and their four youngest children, Mavis, Ephraim, Simeon, and Darion. Their other three children, Faith, Ruby, and Jolene, were all students in Leona's class, and they stood near the front of the room with everyone else who had a part in the Christmas play.

She noticed Jimmy sitting in one of the school desks and was glad she'd thought to invite him. Even though she knew they could never have a permanent relationship, it was nice to have Jimmy as a friend. From the looks of his smile, she knew he was glad he'd been invited.

Leona put a finger to her lips to quiet the excited scholars; then she smiled at the audience and stepped forward. "Thank you for coming to share this special evening with your kinner. We'd like to present the story of Jesus' birth and share several recitations and songs." Leona nodded at Josh Hoffmeir, who was dressed as an innkeeper. When he didn't respond, she motioned with her hand.

Josh's face turned crimson, but he quickly took his place behind the cardboard partition in front of Leona's desk. BETHLEHEM INN had been written in bold letters on the front of it. Emanuel Lapp, dressed as Joseph, walked up to the cardboard inn while Leona's niece Faith, who was dressed as Mary, stood off to one side.

Emanuel knocked on the edge of the cardboard, and Josh stepped out from behind the partition. "What can I do for you?"

"My wife and I have come to Bethlehem to pay our taxes, and we need a place to stay."

Josh shook his head. "I have no empty rooms."

"But Mary's due to have a baby soon, and she needs—"

"Sorry. There's nothin' here."

"Please, I implore you."

The innkeeper shook his head.

"She can have my room!" a booming voice shouted from the back of the schoolhouse.

All heads turned, several people snickered, and heat flooded Leona's face. With a look of determination,

Papa shook his finger at Josh. "If Mary's gonna have a baby, it wouldn't be right to turn her away. You're not a nice man!"

Leona glanced at her mother and felt relief when Mom took hold of Papa's hand and whispered something in his ear. Papa hesitated but finally sat down.

Leona was glad her daed had come to see the program, but his childish outburst had been an embarrassment, not to mention another reminder that he wasn't really her daed anymore.

She forced her lips to form a smile and signaled the children to continue with the play. *Why, God? Why did You allow Papa to lose his memory? And why won't You make him well again?*

❦

Jimmy could see by the horrified look on Leona's face that she'd been embarrassed when her dad shouted out his offer to give Mary his room. He wished he could shield Leona from further humiliation, but he knew that, like himself, Leona would have to come to grips with her pain. Besides, as much as he might wish it, she wasn't his girlfriend, so he had no right to try and shield her from anything.

As the play ended and the program continued with songs and recitations, Jimmy's thoughts switched gears. In a few more days, it would be Christmas, and he wondered what Jim would do to celebrate the holidays without him. *Probably get drunk on Christmas and stay that way until the New Year is rung in. Even when I was living at home, he used the holidays as an excuse to celebrate with alcohol, and now that we are at odds with each other, his drinking problem has probably gotten worse.* He stared at his clenched fists resting on his knees and grimaced. *I do feel sorry for him, but I can't reach him. My days of rescuing Jim Scott are over.*

≈

"Are you sure you wouldn't like a hunk of gingerbread to go along with your tea?" Lydia asked Leona as they sat in the living room, drinking the chamomile tea Lydia had fixed soon after her husband had gone upstairs to bed.

"Just the tea is fine for me," Leona replied.

"There was a good turnout at the program tonight."

"Jah."

"It was a joy to watch the kinner act out the Nativity scene, sing Christmas carols, and recite their parts."

Her daughter offered only a deep sigh.

Lydia reached over and touched Leona's hand. "Would it make you feel better if we talked about what happened with your daed during the innkeeper's scene?"

Leona shook her head. "There's not much point in talking about it. What's done is done."

"No harm came from it. . .not really."

Leona set her cup on the end table and turned to face her mother. "Weren't you embarrassed by Papa's outburst? Don't you get tired of him acting like a child?"

Lydia blinked. "Well, I—"

"Everyone was laughing at Papa tonight. Didn't that make you want to hide your face in shame?"

"I did feel bad for my Jacob because he didn't realize it was only a play." Lydia moaned. "My husband can't help what happened to him, and I think it's time you quit thinking of yourself and thank God that your daed is alive."

"I. . .I am glad for that, but—"

"But you think the Lord should heal him because it's what you want—because your daed does and says things that make you feel uncomfortable? You're not the only one who's suffered since your daed's accident. It's been hard on Arthur having to take over the painting business. It's been hard on our church allowing Jacob to hold his position as bishop when he can't fulfill any of his duties." Lydia drew in a deep breath, trying to gain control over her swirling emotions. "And it's been hard on me. When your daed fell off that ladder and suffered a brain injury, I lost my husband and was left with a little boy to raise."

Leona opened her mouth, but Lydia rushed on. "Ever since this horrible tragedy, I've silently grieved— but not because I was embarrassed by my husband's actions. I'm worried about what will happen to him if I die before he does." Her throat constricted, and a tight sob escaped.

Leona turned sideways in her chair and clasped Lydia's hand. "Oh, Mom, I'm so sorry. I've been selfish and should have paid more attention to the way you were feeling. I don't want you to worry about Papa. If something should happen to you, I promise to see that he's cared for."

"You're a good daughter." Lydia squeezed Leona's hand. "I think we should go down on our knees and ask the heavenly Father to give us both more patience and a better understanding of your daed's needs. Faults are thin when love is thick, you know." She lifted herself from the chair and knelt on the floor. Leona did the same. This was one of the few times since her husband's accident that Lydia had felt this close to her daughter, and she thanked God for His goodness and tender mercies.

❧

Abraham stood in front of his bedroom window and stared at the drifting snowflakes. Fannie was already asleep in bed, but he was stewing about his friend. Would Jacob's memory ever return? It had been several months since the accident, and there had been little change in the man's behavior.

A couple of times, Abraham had felt a ray of hope—like the day he'd heard Jacob call his wife by her real name, and another time when he and Jacob had been playing a game of checkers. After winning the game, Jacob had announced that he'd always been able to beat Abraham at checkers.

But then there are other times, he thought regrettably. *Like tonight at the schoolhouse when Jacob didn't realize he was a grown man and shouldn't be speaking out of turn.*

Abraham leaned against the window casing and closed his eyes. *Heavenly Father, please bring comfort to Lydia Weaver and her family during this Christmas season. Let Jacob know You're still with him, and if it's Your will, allow my friend to have his memory back.*

"Abraham, are you coming to bed?"

He whirled around at the sound of his wife's sleepy voice. "Jah, in a minute."

"What are you doing over there by the window?"

"Just thinkin'."

Fannie climbed out of bed and ambled over to his side. "Mind if I ask what you're thinking about?"

"Jacob's been on my mind ever since we got home from the Christmas program. I've been prayin' that God will give my friend his memory back."

"It's good you're concerned about Jacob." She slipped her arm around his waist. "I'm a little concerned about you, though."

"Why's that?"

"Things haven't been right with you and Naomi since you found Zach's quilt in her linen closet, and I'm wondering how much longer you're going to hold a grudge."

He frowned. "I ain't holdin' no grudge."

"Are you sure about that?"

He just moved away from the window and toward the bed.

"Don't you think it's time you put the quilt out of your mind and forgave your daughter? It's kind of hard for our prayers to get through to God when there's bitterness in our hearts," she said, following him across the room.

"Jah, I know."

"In Matthew 6:14, Jesus said, 'For if ye forgive men their trespasses, your heavenly Father will also forgive you.'"

Abraham turned and pulled Fannie into his arms, resting his chin on top of her head. "You're right. I do need to forgive Naomi. I'll clear this up with her soon."

Chapter 32

T he pond not far from Leona's home was frozen solid. So one Saturday in late January, Leona decided to take some of her older students ice-skating, along with a few of her former students.

Several of the girls were in the center of the pond making figure eights. Emanuel Lapp, Josh Hoffmeir, and the Fisher twins had gathered some wood and built a bonfire several feet away. Leona planned to have a hot dog roast after the young people had skated awhile; then she would let them toast marshmallows for dessert. She'd also brought two thermoses full of hot chocolate.

"Leona, come join us on the ice," Stella Fisher called.

"I'll be there as soon as I get my skates on!" Leona dropped to a seat on a fallen log, slipped off her shoes, and placed her feet inside the ice skates she'd received for Christmas a few years ago. This was her first time skating this winter, and it took a few minutes for her to get her balance. By the time she'd made it to the center of the frozen pond, she felt a bit more confident.

Leona had made only two trips around when she spotted Jimmy's truck pull into the area where the horses and buggies had been secured by some trees. She'd told him about her skating plans the other morning when he had stopped by their house to pick up her daed for a paint job, but she'd never expected him to show up here.

Jimmy climbed out of his truck and said a few words to the boys who stood by the fire; then he walked to the edge of the pond. "Looks like a fun way to spend the day!"

Leona glided across the ice and stopped in front of him. Had he come because of her? The thought sent a shiver tingling down her spine. "Would you like to join us?"

"I don't have any ice skates."

She glanced at his brown leather boots. His feet seemed small compared to most men his age. "I think Emanuel's foot is about the same size as yours, and since he seems to be more interested in poking sticks into the fire than skating, maybe he'd be willing to loan you his skates."

Jimmy looked kind of flustered. "I only came to watch. If I tried to take one step on that frozen pond, I'd probably fall on my face."

"No, you wouldn't. Not if you hang on to me." Leona shook her head. *Now, what made me say such a thing? That sounded so bold.*

"All right, you've talked me into it," he said with a chuckle.

Emanuel didn't mind giving up his skates. So once Jimmy had them laced up, Leona took his arm and helped him over to the pond.

"Don't let go," he said. "My legs feel like two sticks of rubber."

"All you have to do is put one foot in front of the other and glide," Leona instructed as she gave his hand a gentle tug.

They made their way slowly around the ice until Jimmy felt more confident. Then she let go of his hand. "Hey, this is fun." He tipped his head back and caught a few snowflakes on the tip of his tongue.

When Leona looked at Jimmy, she thought she saw a reflection of her own longing in his dark eyes, but maybe it was just wishful thinking. *If only we didn't come from two separate worlds. If only I wasn't so afraid. . .*

"Let's go to the middle and try a couple of turns." A

mischievous twinkle danced in Jimmy's dark eyes.

"Are you sure you're ready for that?"

He leaned close to her ear and whispered, "With you by my side, I feel like I can do 'most anything."

"Okay." Leona could barely get the word out; her throat felt so tight. Did Jimmy have any idea how giddy she felt being this close to him?

Stella, Carolyn, and Ada moved aside as Leona and Jimmy stepped into the middle of the frozen pond. "Don't run off on our account," Jimmy said. "I won't knock you over—at least not on purpose."

The girls snickered, and Carolyn motioned toward the glow of the bonfire burning against the frosty air. "We're gettin' cold anyhow, so we'll go stand in front of the fire awhile."

Ada and Stella nodded in agreement, and the girls skated off.

"So how's that puppy of yours doing these days?" Jimmy asked as he and Leona continued to glide around the pond.

"Ginger's doin' great." She smiled. "In fact, I never know what she's going to do. There's not a dull moment around our place since she came to live with us, that's for certain sure."

"What's the little scamp done?"

"Let's see now. . . . Ginger's pretty aggressive, so instead of the goat chasing her the way he did Cinnamon, Ginger keeps him in his place. Then there's her little water-dish trick."

"Water-dish trick? What's that?"

"Whenever I fill Ginger's dish with fresh water, she takes a few drinks, grabs the edge of the dish between her teeth, and tips it over. I think she likes to see me go to the bother of filling it up again."

"I never had a dog when I was growing up, but I always wanted one," Jimmy said in a wistful tone.

"Maybe you should have kept Ginger instead of giving her to me."

He shook his head. "It wouldn't be practical for me to have a dog right now—not with me renting the Rabers' trailer."

"I'm sure they wouldn't mind if you had a pet."

"Maybe not, but since I'm not sure how long I'll be staying in Pennsylvania, it wouldn't be good to settle in with a dog I won't be able to keep if I do go back to Washington."

"Your daed doesn't like animals?"

Jimmy shook his head. "Not unless they're in the zoo behind bars. When I was growing up, I asked for a puppy every year at Christmas, but I never got one."

"Speaking of Christmas," Leona said, "I was surprised you didn't go home for the holiday."

"I feel that I'm needed here right now." Jimmy glanced over at her and smiled, but she saw a deep sadness in his eyes and wondered what he wasn't telling her. "The Rabers invited me to join their family, so it was a good Christmas," he quickly added.

"Ours was nice, too. My sisters and their families came from Kentucky, and our whole family was together on Christmas Day. Except for Papa acting like a kinner, it seemed almost like all the other Christmases we've shared."

"I'm glad." Jimmy skidded to a stop and held his hand out to Leona. "I think I'd be able to stay in better rhythm if I was holding someone's hand."

She hesitated a moment before slipping her hand into his. Immediately, she knew she'd made a mistake. Even through the thickness of their gloves, Leona was sure she could feel the heat of Jimmy's hand. *He's just a friend,* she reminded herself. *A friend who needs my help so he won't fall down.*

Jimmy pushed off quickly, and the wind picked

up, lifting Leona's black bonnet right off her head. She reached up to grab it and had no more than let go of Jimmy's hand when down he went, landing hard on his back. A vision of Leona's daed toppling from the ladder flashed into her mind as she dropped to her knees beside Jimmy with a groan. At that moment, the slanting rays of sun went into hiding, and she closed her eyes, willing the menacing image of Papa's fall to disappear.

∽

"Jimmy, are you okay? Can you hear me?"

Jimmy opened his eyes and blinked a couple of times as Leona's pretty face came into focus. "I think I just had the wind knocked out of me."

"Don't sit up! You may have something broken." The fear Jimmy saw in Leona's eyes and the panic edging her voice made him wonder if she might have strong feelings for him—the way he did for her.

"I'm fine, really." He rolled onto his side with a labored grunt and allowed her to help him to his feet. "Nothing's hurt except my pride."

Leona slipped her arm around his waist, and they made their way off the ice and over to the crackling fire.

Jimmy eased himself onto a log and gratefully accepted the cup of hot chocolate one of the girls offered him. He sniffed the sweet smell of marshmallows and smiled. "Thanks, this is exactly what I need."

"Are you sure you're all right?" Leona dropped down beside him and wrapped the edges of her long dress tightly around her legs. "You took a nasty spill on that ice."

"I'm fine. Just don't know how to ice-skate very well, that's all."

"It takes practice," Harley Fisher said.

Emanuel drew his dark eyebrows together. "Maybe

you fell 'cause my skates were too tight."

Jimmy shook his head. "It wasn't your fault."

"My brother, Abner, likes to go ice fishing," Emanuel said. "That might be somethin' you could try instead."

"I'll give it some thought." Jimmy took a sip of hot chocolate and licked his lips.

"Before his accident, my daed used to go ice fishing with Abraham," Leona said. "Since Papa's not up to something like that right now, maybe you and Abraham could go together."

Jimmy stared at the frozen ground beneath his feet. "I doubt that will ever happen."

"How come?"

He looked up and nodded at the children, who seemed to be hanging on his every word—especially Abraham's twin boys.

"Stella, why don't you and the other girls go to my buggy and get the hot dogs and buns? The boys can look for some roasting sticks," Leona said, motioning with her hand.

The children scampered off, and Leona turned to face Jimmy. "What did you mean when you said going ice fishing with Abraham wasn't likely to happen?"

Jimmy grimaced. "I don't think he likes me."

Leona's forehead wrinkled. "What makes you say that?"

"He said something once about his need to protect you, and—"

"Protect me? Does Abraham think I need protecting from you?" Leona stared at Jimmy with wide eyes.

He nodded. "I think that is what he meant."

"Maybe he's leery of you because you're English."

"He doesn't like the English?"

"I wouldn't say that he doesn't like them." Leona leaned closer to Jimmy, and her voice lowered. "What

I'm about to tell you happened when I was a little girl, so I don't actually remember it. But from what I've heard, an English man came to the Fishers' one day for some—"

"Here's the hot dogs," Stella announced as she and the other girls bounded into the clearing, interrupting Leona's story.

She shrugged. "Guess it's time to eat. Maybe we can finish this discussion some other time."

❧

"I wish we didn't have to work so many Saturdays," Ed complained to Jim as his crew set up the staging on the inside of the new discount store they'd recently been contracted to paint.

"Working on the weekends isn't my idea of fun, either, but this is a big job we need to get done by the end of next week."

Ed reached under his paint hat and scratched his head. "Is everything all right?"

"Sure. Why wouldn't it be?"

"You seem kind of moody today."

"I'm not moody."

Ed grunted. "You were irritable for several weeks after Jimmy headed back East, but after you went on a date with that health nut, you seemed to calm down some."

"Holly's not a health nut." Jim felt his defenses rise. "She runs a health food store and knows a lot about nutrition." He jabbed Ed's paunchy stomach with his finger. "That's something we all could benefit from, don't you think?"

Ed merely shrugged in reply.

Jim wasn't about to admit to Ed that since he'd finally worked up the courage and asked Holly for a date they had gone out several more times. Besides attending AA meetings together, they'd taken in a couple of movies and had gone to dinner twice more. Jim had managed to remain sober during that time, and he gave the credit to Holly, who seemed to be his only support right now. Jimmy sure wasn't there for him anymore. He'd only spoken to him twice in the last few months, and those had been times when Jim had initiated the call. Jimmy always seemed distant and managed to make up some excuse to get off the phone.

I think I've changed in many ways since I met Holly, Jim thought. *But am I ready to tell her that I kidnapped Jimmy? Would she understand the reason I took him, or would she condemn me—the way he has?*

He grabbed a gallon of paint and moved toward the staging that had been set in place. "We haven't got all day, fellows, so let's get to work!"

Chapter 33

I appreciate you bringing in a hot lunch for the scholars today." Leona ushered Naomi and Abby into the schoolhouse. They each carried a cardboard box.

"Since today's Valentine's Day, we thought it would be a nice treat for you and the kinner." Naomi set her box on one end of Leona's desk, and Abby placed hers on the other end. "Besides, I wanted the chance to tell you thanks for helping Millie. She's reading better these days, and it's because you took the time to learn about her problem and work with her."

Leona's cheeks warmed. She didn't need any thanks for what she'd done. It was part of her job as a teacher, and she was glad that, despite her lack of continued education, she'd been able to find a way to reach Millie.

"You looked for solutions even after I refused to accept the fact that my daughter might have a learning disability." Naomi's forehead wrinkled. "When I blamed myself for not taking enough time with Millie, Caleb reminded me that I tend to be too hard on myself, and I guess he's right. Ever since my brother was kidnapped, I've struggled with guilt and tried to do everything perfect, which is why I didn't deal well with Millie's problem. I felt that I had failed her somehow."

"Many parents feel that way when their kinner have any kind of trouble," Abby interjected. "We just need to remember that no one but God is perfect and do the best we can."

"Papa admitted to me the other day that he's not perfect, and he apologized for giving me the cold shoulder after he discovered Zach's quilt in my linen closet," Naomi said.

Abby smiled. "I'm so glad to hear that. I've been concerned because things weren't right between you and Abraham, and so has my mamm."

Leona nodded and squeezed Naomi's hand. Then she motioned to the front door. "I let the kinner go outside for a while, so when they come in, we can serve the hot meal."

"As we were pulling in, I noticed several of them building a snowman," Abby commented. "That brought back memories of when I was a girl growing up in Ohio. One of my favorite things to do during the wintertime was to make a huge snowman."

Naomi shook her head. "Not me. I always preferred to be inside where it was warm and I was safe from the icy snowballs being thrown around the school yard."

Leona leaned on her desk and visited with Naomi and Abby a few more minutes. Then she finally excused herself to ring the school bell. She had just stepped onto the porch when Nate Hoffmeir bounded up the steps. "Teacher, my cousin John couldn't make it to the outhouse in time, and he threw up in the bushes." He pointed across the yard.

Leona felt immediate concern. John had complained of a stomachache earlier that morning, but she hadn't thought much of it because he'd seemed well enough to go outside and play with the others. "Run inside and tell your mamm and Abby to set the lunch out for the others while I see about John," she said to Nate.

The boy raced into the building, and Leona, wishing she'd thought to put on a coat, tromped through the snow to check on the ailing child. She found John hunched over a clump of bushes, groaning and holding his stomach. "I've got a bellyache, and it hurts real bad," he said, looking up at her with tears in his eyes.

Leona patted him on the back "I'm sorry you aren't

feeling well. It's probably the flu. Let's go inside, and I'll ask your aunt Naomi to take you home."

A short time later, they had John loaded into Naomi's buggy, and Abby, who had come in her own rig, agreed to stay and help Leona serve lunch to the children.

The rest of the afternoon passed swiftly, and Leona's pupils headed for home carrying the valentines they'd received, as well as the bag of candy Leona had given each of them.

"I should have thought to send John's candy and valentines with him," Leona said as Abby gathered her children together.

"I'll be going past Norman and Ruth's house on my way home, so I'd be happy to drop John's things off to him." Abby grimaced. "I hope this isn't the beginning of another round of achy-bones flu. My kinner have already been out once with it this winter."

"I hope not, either." Leona closed the door behind Abby and her children. Then she set to work cleaning the sticky spots from spilled punch off the floor. She was nearly finished when she heard the nicker of a horse. She hurried to the window and looked out, wondering if one of the scholars had forgotten something.

As soon as the driver of the buggy stepped down from his rig, Leona realized it was Abner, so she opened the door to see what he wanted.

"I brought a valentine," he said as he started up the steps.

"What? Oh, I see." Gathering her wits about her, Leona motioned him into the schoolhouse.

Abner reached into his jacket pocket and handed her an envelope. She was about to open it when she noticed the words on the front. To: Mary Ann.

"Oh no," Leona moaned.

"What's wrong?" Abner asked with raised brows.

"Did I spell her name wrong?"

She shook her head. "I feel terrible about this, Abner, but I've been so busy I forgot to speak with Mary Ann on your behalf."

His lips drooped as wrinkles appeared on his forehead. "Maybe I'd best take the card back then, since I don't know how Mary Ann will respond."

She contemplated his suggestion for a moment but then came up with one of her own. "How would it be if I delivered the card to Mary Ann? That will open the door for me to speak to her about you."

He nodded, but his frown remained in place. "What if she doesn't accept the valentine? What if she's not interested in me at all?"

Then you'll deal with it—same as I've had to deal with Ezra's untimely death, Leona thought. "It's better to know now, don't you think?"

He gave a hasty shrug.

Feeling the need to offer Abner a ray of hope, Leona quickly added, "Many Amish women Mary Ann's age are already married and starting their families, but I know for a fact that she's been waiting for the right man." She paused, searching for the right words. "I'm surprised Mary Ann hasn't realized you could be that man."

Abner averted his gaze to the floor. "Even though I've admired Mary Ann for some time, I've never had the nerve to say much to her, so there's no way she'd know what kind of man I am. Besides," he added with a grunt, "there ain't nothin' special about me."

"That's not true, Abner. You're kind, considerate, and a good provider for your mamm and little bruder. Those are fine qualities that a woman hoping to get married would look for in a husband."

Abner's ears turned pink as he started back across the room. "Well, guess I'd best be gettin' home. Emanuel's probably there already."

"Jah, the kinner left awhile ago." She followed him to the door. "I'll let you know what Mary Ann has to say about the valentine, and I promise to give it to her right away."

Abner gave Leona a wave and climbed into his buggy. He'd just pulled out of the school yard when Jimmy's truck pulled in.

Reaching up to make sure her covering was properly in place, she stepped forward to greet him. "Come inside. It's awfully cold."

"You can say that again." He offered her a smile so warm she thought it could have melted the snow covering the school yard.

As soon as they stepped into the schoolhouse, Leona motioned Jimmy over to the stove. "There's some treats left from our Valentine's Day party," she said, pointing to some cookies and a jug of punch on the table. "Would you care for something to eat or drink?"

"That'd be nice." Jimmy took a chocolate chip cookie and popped it into his mouth. "Umm. . .This is good." He washed it down with some punch and grinned at her like an eager child. "Did you make these?"

She shook her head. "Naomi Fisher baked 'em."

"Was that one of your students' parents I saw leaving in the buggy?" he asked, glancing toward the front window.

"It was Abner Lapp."

"Came to pick up his little brother, I'll bet."

"Actually, the kinner left some time ago. Abner dropped by to deliver this." She picked up the envelope from her desk. "It's a valentine."

"I see." Jimmy's smile turned to a frown. "Guess you won't be wanting mine then."

Tears welled up in Leona's eyes, and she blinked to keep them from spilling over. "You. . .you brought me a valentine?"

He nodded soberly. "Should have known you

probably had a boyfriend and would be getting one from him. It's just that—well, I'd hoped—" His voice trailed off as he reached into his jacket pocket and pulled out an envelope. "Is it all right if I give it to you, anyway—from one friend to another?"

"Abner's not my boyfriend," she stammered. "The card he brought isn't for me."

"It's not?"

"No. He asked me to deliver it to Mary Ann Fisher. He was afraid to give it to her himself."

Jimmy's contagious smile was back in place, and he quickly handed her the envelope.

With trembling fingers, Leona tore open the flap and removed the card. It read: *In life's garden, friends are the flowers. Thanks for being my friend—Jimmy.*

"Danki. It's a very nice card, and I'm glad you're my friend, too." Her voice was barely above a whisper, and she had to blink several times to keep her tears from spilling over. *Oh, Jimmy, I wish we could be more than friends.*

Jimmy set down his empty cup then took another cookie and stuffed it in his pocket. "I. . .uh. . .need to check on a paint job for Arthur before I head for the Rabers'. I probably should be on my way. Danki for the treat."

"You're welcome." Leona felt a sense of disappointment as she watched him leave the building. If she were willing to open her heart to love again, it would be to someone like Jimmy. But of course that was impossible since she was Amish and he was English. Besides, she was afraid of committing herself to a man, knowing he could be taken from her the way Ezra had been.

As Leona returned to cleaning the room, she sighed. *Life's full of disappointments, and losing a loved one is the worst kind. I've already suffered several injustices, and I'll do whatever I can to protect myself from more.*

Lydia reached for an orange from the fruit bowl on the kitchen counter and was shocked to discover that it wasn't a real orange at all. She turned to face Jacob, who sat at the table drinking a glass of milk. "Have you been playing tricks on me again?"

He grinned like a mischievous boy and bobbed his head up and down. "I wanted to see if you'd take notice."

"Oh, I noticed all right. Almost cut this up to put in the fruit salad I'm making for supper tonight." She held up the plastic orange. "Where'd you get this?"

"Found it in the one of the houses we was paintin' last week. The lady who lived there said I could have it."

Lydia grimaced. *What must that woman have thought when a grown man asked for a plastic orange?*

"What else are we havin' for supper?" Jacob asked.

"Chicken potpie, soft bread sticks, pickled beets, and fruit salad."

"How 'bout dessert?"

"I took a jar of applesauce from the root cellar this afternoon, and we'll probably have cookies if Leona brings some home from the Valentine's Day party she had for the scholars."

"Umm." Jacob smacked his lips. "Know what, Lydia?"

"What's that?"

"You look good in the face."

She smiled. In some ways, her husband hadn't changed so much since he'd lost his memory. He'd always had a sense of humor, and even some of his more boyish pranks seemed to fit with his jovial personality. He'd begun calling her "Lydia" again, but she knew it wasn't because he remembered her as his wife. It was simply a matter of her telling him over and over that she wasn't his mother and her name was Lydia.

"Danki, Jacob," she said. "I'm kind of partial to your face, too."

"Jimmy told a funny joke before he brought me home today," Jacob said.

"Do you want to share it with me?"

"Jah, sure." Jacob drank the last of his milk and wiped his mouth with the back of his hand. Lydia was tempted to say something about his manners but changed her mind. No point in ruining the camaraderie between them over something so small.

"Let's see now," Jacob began. "An Englisher stopped by an Amish man's house one day and said, 'I'm headin' to Blue Ball, so does it make any difference which road I take?'" He paused and rubbed the bridge of his nose. "The Amish man thought for a minute; then he answered, 'Nope. Don't make no difference to me.'"

Lydia chuckled. Thanks to Jimmy, Jacob was able to work half days, and he seemed much happier than he had before.

"Want to hear another joke? Richard told me a couple of good ones today."

"Sure, go ahead."

A knock sounded at the back door before Jacob could begin the next story. "Want me to get it?" he asked.

Lydia reached into the fruit bowl for an apple. "I'd appreciate that."

A rush of cold air whipped into the room when Jacob opened the door. Caleb Hoffmeir stomped his boots on the porch and stepped inside.

"It's good to see you, Caleb," Lydia said. "What brings you out our way on this cold afternoon?"

"Naomi wanted me to let Leona know that our nephew John is in the hospital."

Lydia crinkled her forehead. "I'm sorry to hear that.

What's he there for?"

"He got sick at school today, and since Naomi had gone with Abby to serve the scholars a hot lunch, she volunteered to take him home. By the time they got halfway there, he'd thrown up several times. So Naomi took him to the clinic in town and got word to her brother and his wife, asking them to meet her there."

Jacob ambled across the room and plunked down in the chair. "I don't like doctors. You gotta watch out for 'em 'cause they poke around on you too much and ask a bunch of questions."

Lydia turned to Caleb. "What did the doctor at the clinic say about John?"

"They ran a couple of tests and sent him straightaway to the hospital in Lancaster." Caleb shook his head. "By the time they got him there, his appendix had burst open."

Lydia clucked her tongue. "That can be serious."

Caleb nodded. "They rushed him into surgery, and the last I heard, he's doin' as well as can be expected."

"We should pray for John," Jacob said in a serious tone. "God can heal the boy. I'm sure of it."

Caleb glanced at Lydia with a peculiar expression, and she wondered if his thoughts were the same as hers. Had her husband's comment come from Jacob the bishop, or was he merely repeating something he'd heard at one of their church services?

Before Lydia could voice the question, the back door swung open and Leona entered the kitchen. "Oh, it's you, Caleb," she said, removing her dark bonnet and brushing flakes of snow off the top. "I was wondering whose rig that was outside."

"He dropped by to give you news of John Fisher," Lydia said before Caleb could respond.

Leona nodded. "He got sick at school today, and Naomi took him home. I think he's got the flu."

"He ain't got no flu," Jacob spoke up.

"It's much worse than that," Caleb said. "John's appendix ruptured, and he's in the hospital recovering from surgery."

Leona's face turned chalky white. "All morning the boy complained of a stomachache. I should have realized how sick he was." She paced the length of the kitchen, her hands clasped in front of her as she slowly shook her head. "If he'd gotten to the hospital sooner, they might have caught it before his appendix ruptured."

"Now don't blame yourself," Lydia was quick to say. "You had no way of knowing it was more than a simple flu bug causing him to feel sick."

"Your mamm's right," Caleb agreed. "From what I understand, it's not easy to know when someone's having a problem with their appendix."

A look of doubt flashed onto Leona's face, and Lydia felt relief when her daughter finally nodded and said, "I'll have the class make John some get-well cards tomorrow. After school's out for the day, I'll see about getting a ride to Lancaster so I can visit him at the hospital."

Jacob folded his arms and shook his head. "Not me. I ain't goin' to no hospital. Never again!"

Chapter 34

The following afternoon, shortly after Leona's students went home, Jimmy showed up at the schoolhouse to drive her to the hospital. He promised to take her by Abby's quilt shop afterward so she could deliver Abner's valentine to Mary Ann.

"I appreciate you doing this for me," Leona said as Jimmy opened the door on the passenger's side of his pickup.

"I'm willing to drive you wherever you need to go, so don't hesitate to ask." Jimmy smiled. "That goes for anyone else in your family who might ever need a ride."

"Danki." She said, sliding into her seat.

He closed the door and came around to the driver's side. "Have you been ice-skating lately?" he asked, once he was seated and had shut his own door.

Leona shook her head.

"Maybe we could go again this Saturday and then have lunch somewhere afterward."

"You—you mean, just the two of us?"

He nodded. "If that's all right with you."

Leona knew it wouldn't look good if she went skating alone with Jimmy. If anyone saw them together, they might assume she and Jimmy were on a date.

She studied his handsome face. Was a date what he had in mind?

"You're awfully quiet," he said. "Are you afraid I might fall on the ice again?"

Leona's fingers trembled as she snapped her seat belt into place. "I'm concerned that someone might get the wrong idea if they see us alone together."

"We're alone now."

"This is different. You're driving me somewhere. Ice-skating by ourselves would be more like a—"

"Date?"

She nodded. "Some young Amish women do date English fellows when they're going through *rumschpringe*, but once a woman has been baptized and joined the church, she's expected to date only Amish men."

"Have you found a special Amish man yet?" he asked.

"No, and I'm not looking."

"If I were Amish or you were English, would you go out with me?"

Tears pricked the back of her eyes. "You're not Amish, and if we started courting, I would be shunned."

"Eli has explained some things about your way of life, and I realize how serious a shunning can be." He started to reach across the seat, but pulled his hand back. "Can we still be friends?"

She nodded slowly. A friendship with Jimmy was all she could ever have, even if he was Amish or she was English.

❧

"What a surprise seeing you today," Mary Ann said when Leona walked into the quilt shop shortly before closing time. "I'll be leaving soon, and Abby's already gone for the day."

"I've been to the hospital to see John, and I asked Jimmy—he's my driver today—if he'd bring me here before taking me home."

"How's my nephew doing? Is he gonna be okay?"

"The doctor said it will take awhile for John to feel like his old self again, but he will live, and for that I'm very grateful."

"Me, too." Mary Ann took a seat on the stool behind the counter. "Whew, I'm tired, and my feet are hurtin' something awful. It's been a long day."

"I know how you feel." Leona opened her purse and reached inside. "I came by to give you this," she said, handing Abner's envelope to Mary Ann.

"What is it?"

"Why don't you open it and see?"

Mary Ann grabbed a pair of scissors and sliced the envelope open. When she pulled out the card, she smiled and said, "This is a surprise. We haven't exchanged valentines since we were kinner."

"Oh, it's not from me."

"Who then?"

"Take a look inside."

Mary Ann's brows puckered as she read aloud what had been written inside the card. "A rainbow in the sky reminds us that God keeps His promises. A honeysuckle vine reminds me of you—pretty and sweet. Happy Valentine's Day—Abner Lapp."

"Well, what do you think?"

Mary Ann let the card slip from her fingers as she stared at Leona with obvious disbelief. "You're playing matchmaker?"

"Not really. I'm more the message deliverer."

"Are you trying to set me up with Abner?"

"It wasn't my idea. Abner asked me to give you the valentine, and he wants to know if you'd be willing to let him court you."

Mary Ann's mouth dropped open. "Why didn't he ask me himself?"

Leona leaned on the edge of the counter, wondering if she'd made a mistake by agreeing to act as Abner's go-between. "He's worried you might say no."

Mary Ann stared at the card for several seconds. Finally, she turned it over and reached for a pen.

"What are you doing?"

"Writing him a note in return. Since you're so good

at playing messenger, I figured you'd be more than happy to deliver my response to him."

"What are you going to say?"

Mary Ann's lips slanted upward in a sly little smile. "Maybe I'll let him tell you that."

Leona clicked her tongue. It was typical of her good-natured friend to make her wait. Well, that was okay. She had made Abner wait when she'd promised to speak with Mary Ann on his behalf, so it was only fair that she'd have to wait to hear how Mary Ann responded to his question.

∞

"Did you hear about Mark Stauffer's barn catching fire?" Mom asked Leona when she returned home shortly before supper.

"No, I hadn't heard a thing. Of course, Mark and Nancy's daughter wasn't in school today because she's been out all week with a cold." Leona hung her heavy jacket and dark bonnet on a wall peg and moved over to the counter where her mother was making a salad. "How bad was the fire?"

"It burned clear to the ground. I'm sure they'll have a barn raising as soon as the weather improves."

"What was the cause of the fire? Do you know?"

Mom shrugged. "We haven't had any thunder or lightning lately, just a lot of snow. I heard from Fannie that the firemen found no sign of foul play, so they're thinkin' it was probably the gases from the hay that ignited the fire."

"I'm sorry to hear this. No one ever likes to lose a barn."

"At least they were able to get the livestock out in time." Mom picked up a tomato and sliced it into the bowl. "During the winter months, I sure do miss our fresh produce. These store-bought vegetables don't taste nearly as good as what we grow in our garden."

"What can I do to help with supper?"

"You can check on the biscuits baking in the oven."

Leona slipped into her choring apron, opened the oven door, and peered inside. "They're not done yet."

"So, how's little John doing?" Mom asked. "Since you were late getting home, I figured you'd gone to the hospital to see him again."

"I did go, and he's doing okay."

Mom smiled. "I'm sure John's folks are happy about that."

"Jah." Leona lifted the lid on the dutch oven near the back of their wood-burning stove and peeked at the fragrant, simmering stew.

"You seem kind of sullen this evening. Is there somethin' you're not telling me?"

Leona glanced at the door leading to the living room. "Where's Papa?"

"He's in the barn playing with your pup. Now that the goat's getting bigger, he seems to be losin' interest in it."

"I'm glad he's done with the goat, and it's good he's out in the barn."

"Why's that?"

"I don't want Papa to hear what I'm about to say. He might repeat it, and it would probably come out differently than the way I said it to you."

Mom nodded toward the table. "Let's have a seat, and you can tell me what's on your mind."

"What about supper?"

"The stew's done, and the salad's almost made, so we're just waiting on the biscuits." She ambled across the room and pulled out a chair. "I think we can rest our weary bones a few minutes, don't you?"

Leona took the seat opposite her mamm, grabbed

a handful of napkins, and started folding them in half. She wasn't sure she should be sharing the things that weighed heavily on her mind, yet the burden of keeping it to herself was too much to bear.

Mom leaned across the table, pulled the napkins from Leona's hands, and set them off to one side. "Are you feeling naerfich about something?"

Leona bit her bottom lip so hard she tasted blood. "Jah, I am a little nervous."

"What is it, daughter? Are you feeling sick?"

"Not physically."

"What are you saying?"

"I feel sick right here." Leona placed her hand against her chest.

Mom's eyebrows furrowed.

"I'm in love with someone, but it's an impossible situation."

"Is that all?" Mom waved her hand. "With love, there's always a way."

Leona blinked rapidly in an attempt to hold off the tears that stung the back of her eyes. "*Nee.* There's not a way—not for me and Jimmy."

"What was that?" Mom's mouth dropped open, and her eyes grew round.

"I–I'm not sure when it happened, but I–I've fallen in love with Jimmy."

Mom clasped her hands in front of her and placed them on the table. "Oh, Leona, this is a serious thing."

"It would be, if either of us chose to pursue it, but—"

"You've got to stop seeing him right away."

"That's going to be hard, considering that Jimmy often comes over here to see Papa and he's sometimes our taxi driver."

"It will have to end—all of it!"

"But, Mom, what reason would we give for shutting

Jimmy out of our lives? Papa's grown attached to him, and he'd be upset if Jimmy quit coming around."

Mom fiddled with the napkins she'd taken from Leona. "Does Jimmy know the way you feel?"

"I haven't told him, but I think he might suspect."

"Is he in love with you, as well?"

Leona drew in a shaky breath and released it slowly. "He hasn't actually said so, but I believe he might have feelings for me."

"Then we'll have to pray that he leaves Lancaster County—and the sooner the better."

"But Jimmy and I have agreed to be just friends, and even if we could be together, I would never open my heart up to another man and take the chance of losing him."

"That's *lecherich*, Leona," Mom said sharply. "We've had this discussion before, and you know how I feel about you closing off your heart to love because you're afraid of what the future might hold." She pursed her lips. "I want you to fall in love and get married someday—just not to an Englisher."

"You might think it's ridiculous for me to feel the way I do, but the man you love didn't die." Leona cringed, wishing she could take back her words and feeling awfully guilty for having said them. "I'm sorry, Mom. I didn't mean that." She sniffed. "I know how close Papa came to dying; truth be told, you really did lose him, because most of the time, he doesn't know who you are."

Mom dropped her gaze to the table and breathed slowly in and out. Finally, she lifted her head. "Would you mind going out to the barn to tell your daed that supper's almost ready?"

"Sure, Mom." Leona pushed her chair aside, grabbed her heavy shawl from a wall peg, and opened the back door. *It was a mistake to tell Mom how I feel about Jimmy.*

I thought she and I had been drawing closer, but she doesn't understand how I feel about anything. I wish I had never confided in her!

Chapter 35

Jimmy was pleased that he'd been invited to help raise Mark Stauffer's new barn. It meant the Amish he'd been living near these last nine months had accepted him.

Have I really been here that long? he mused as he pulled into the open field where dozens of Amish buggies and several cars were parked. *I still don't know who my real family is or even if I could give up my modern way of life to join the Amish faith. Since I now know the Amish won't prosecute Jim for his crime, maybe I need to search harder for my family and start asking more questions. I could even run an ad in the paper or hang some signs around the county announcing that a man who had been kidnapped when he was a baby twenty years ago has returned to the area looking for his Amish family.*

His thoughts drifted back to the day he'd finally believed Jim's story about the kidnapping, and he moaned. *What a mess I'm in, all because of one man's sinful deed. I don't know who my real family is or even where I belong. I'm in love with an Amish woman, but I grew up English, so I don't know if I could ever leave that way of life. Even if I did join the Amish faith, there would be no guarantees that Leona and I could be together. She's been through a lot and is hiding from love to guard her heart from further pain.*

As Jimmy opened his truck door, the truth slammed into him with such force he nearly fell out of his truck. As he stood and regained his balance, a blast of chilly March air took his breath away.

I've been hiding, too, he thought. *By refusing to talk to Jim and being unwilling to let go of my anger, I have pulled away from God.*

Jimmy gulped in some air. *Jim is the only dad I've ever known, and no matter how hard I try to forget him or how many times I call him Jim, he will always be Dad to me.*

He reached inside the truck for his cell phone, which he'd left lying on the seat. *I'd better call Dad right now and tell him I forgive him.*

"I'm glad you finally got here, Jimmy," Eli called as he bounded across the open field where several other cars had parked. Eli had ridden over to the Stauffers' place with his folks this morning, and they had left an hour sooner than Jimmy had.

"I'm glad I was invited," Jimmy responded as his friend drew near. He placed the phone back on the seat. *I've waited this long to call Dad; I guess a few more hours won't matter.*

Eli clasped Jimmy's shoulder. "Of course you'd be invited. After all, you work for our bishop's son, and you've shown yourself to be a good friend to many who are here today."

"Any idea what I can do to help?" Jimmy asked as he and Eli headed toward a group of men who stood near the foundation where the new barn would be.

Eli nodded toward the tall Amish man with a long, flowing beard who stood on the other side of the yard talking to some of the men. "That's Yost Zimmerman, and he's the one to ask. Yost has built more barns and been in charge of more barn raisings than anyone I know."

Jimmy hurried off to speak with Yost, but he'd only made it halfway there when he spotted Abraham Fisher and his two youngest boys. The twins were joking around, grabbing each other's hats and throwing them in the air, and Abraham had even gotten in on the act.

Jimmy felt a pang of jealousy as he thought about

how he'd always wanted a brother or sister. *I wish my dad had paid me a little more attention instead of being too busy with his work so much of the time.* Jimmy thought about his mother and how she had been the one to see that he'd been able to do some fun things. She had taken him to the park when he was little, seen that he'd gone to church activities, and had been there to listen whenever he needed to talk. *If I ever have the opportunity to be a father, I'm going to be there for my kids, and I'll make sure they have good memories from their childhoods.*

Jimmy's thoughts went to Leona. She was the kind of woman he would like to marry, but she was out of his reach—unless he decided to join the Amish faith, and he didn't know if he could do that. *Give me some sense of direction, Lord,* he prayed. *Show me what I should do about this, and when I talk to Dad, give me the right words.*

∞

"Where's your mamm today?" Naomi asked Leona as they entered Nancy Stauffer's kitchen to prepare the noon meal."

"She stayed home with Papa."

"Is your daed sick?"

"He's fine. Mom decided it wasn't a good idea for him to come here today."

"How come?"

"He'd have probably wanted to climb onto the roof with the others who are building your brother-in-law's barn." Leona shook her head. "The last thing we need is for Papa to fall again."

"I should say so. And we must pray that none of the men gets hurt today."

"That's for sure." Leona moved across the room to see where her help was needed, and Naomi did the same.

A short time later, Leona stood at the kitchen sink

peeling carrots and watching the progress on the barn out the window. She spotted Jimmy among those on the ground handing pieces of wood up to the men on the roof. Since the day he'd driven her to the hospital to see John, he hadn't spoken more than a few words to her.

It's probably best that he's kept his distance, she thought with regret. *Every time we've been close, I've found myself wanting more than either of us can give.* She squeezed the carrot in her hand so hard she feared it might break, so she relaxed her grip. *It's best that Mom decided not to come with me today. Since she's so afraid Jimmy might lead me astray, she'd probably have watched my every move.*

Leona's thoughts wandered back to a conversation she'd overheard a few weeks ago between her mamm and Arthur. She'd gone to the barn to feed her puppy and had spotted the two of them standing inside one of the horse's stalls, speaking in hushed tones. . . .

∽

"I tell you, son, that Englisher is getting too close to your sister," Mom said. "I fear if something's not done about it soon, Leona will get hurt. I think you should let Jimmy go."

"You mean fire him?"

"Jah."

"Aw, Mom, you can't ask me to do that. Jimmy's a good worker, and he has a lot of knowledge when it comes to painting. Besides, since Richard's on vacation right now and a couple of the fellows are down with the flu, I need Jimmy more than ever."

"What if he talks Leona into leaving the Amish faith?" Mom persisted. "Can't you see what that would do to our family?"

"Leona's strong in her beliefs. I'm sure she ain't goin' nowhere."

"If she does up and leave, then you'll be to blame." Mom turned on her heel and rushed out of the barn. Arthur just stood there, scratching his head.

~~~

"Leona, did you hear what I said?"

Leona whirled around as her thoughts returned to the present. "Huh?"

"I wanted you to know that we've got everything ready, so when you're done with the vegetable platter, you can bring it outside to the serving table," Nancy said.

"Okay."

Nancy moved to Leona's side. "Are you all right? You seem kind of distracted today."

"I'm fine. Just caught up in my thoughts." Leona grabbed a cucumber and started peeling it real fast.

"All right. See you outside in a few minutes," Nancy said before hurrying away.

When Leona stepped out the back door a short time later, she found herself scanning the yard, searching for Jimmy. She knew it was wrong to pine for something she couldn't have, but even though the voice in her head said no, her heart said something different.

She gripped the vegetable platter a little tighter. *I have to do something to fight this attraction, and I need to do it soon before I lose my heart to him and do something that would hurt my family.*

Forcing her thoughts to the job at hand, Leona joined the other women who were serving the men their noon meal. Plenty of food had been donated by the women in their community. While the men ate, they engaged in conversation, and some even told a few jokes.

"Did you hear the one about the Englisher who wasn't watching where he was going and ended up hitting the telephone pole?" Yost Zimmerman asked

Matthew Fisher as he elbowed him in the ribs.

"Can't say that I have."

Leona smiled and picked up a pitcher of water. Moving down the line, she refilled each of the men's glasses, and that's when she noticed Jimmy sitting at a table to the left.

"Looks like things are going pretty well today," Naomi said, stepping up to her. "The men have Mark's barn nearly half done already."

"It's good the weather's decided to cooperate."

"And it's nice to see so many of our English neighbors and friends here today." Naomi nodded toward the table on their left. "Jimmy Scott's a hard worker. I saw him hauling boards up to the roof earlier, and he seemed to be working every bit as hard as any of the Amish men."

Leona gave a slow nod.

"It amazes me the way he seems to fit in with our people. He's helped your daed in so many ways and has such a gentle spirit." Naomi continued to stare at Jimmy. "In some ways, he reminds me of my brother Samuel." She pointed to the table on their right. "See the way Samuel holds his head when he's talking?"

Leona craned her neck to get a better look.

"Jimmy does it the same way. I'll bet if he was dressed in Amish clothes and wore his hair like our men, he'd look Amish. Don't you think?"

Leona could only shrug, for if she'd said what was on her heart, she would have told Naomi that she wished Jimmy was Amish and she wished God would give her some guarantees that Jimmy wouldn't be taken from her the way Ezra had been.

"Guess I'll see if the coffeepot needs refilling," Naomi said as she moved away from the table.

Leona needed a few minutes alone, so she meandered around the side of the house and headed for the swing that hung from a huge maple tree. She seated herself and grasped the handles; then, digging the toes of her sneakers into the ground, she pumped her legs to gain momentum. She'd only been swinging a few minutes when she spotted Jimmy coming around the house. He headed to the table where several washbasins had been set out and seemed to be looking at something in the palm of his right hand.

Leona cringed when she saw him reach into his pocket and pull out a small knife. She hopped off the swing and hurried over to him. "Are you having a problem?"

He held out his hand. "This is what I get for not wearing gloves today."

She grimaced when she saw the ugly splinter embedded in the palm of his hand. "Let's go inside, and I'll see about getting a needle and some tweezers so I can take out the sliver."

He shook his head. "That's okay. I'm sure I can get it with the tip of my pocketknife."

Just thinking about what could happen if the knife slipped and cut into Jimmy's flesh caused Leona to flinch.

"It'll be all right. I've done this before."

"If you're determined to use the knife, then at least let me help you."

He smiled and placed his hand in hers. "You're an angel of mercy."

When Jimmy's skin came in contact with Leona's, she shivered.

"Are you cold?"

"I'm fine. Just a little nervous."

"I have complete faith in your surgical abilities," he said with a chuckle.

Leona held the knife as steady as her trembling fingers would allow, and it took her several tries before she was able to pry the tip of the splinter loose. When she saw blood oozing from his hand and heard Jimmy groan, her knees nearly buckled.

"Easy now. You've almost got it."

She exhaled a sigh of relief as she pulled the knife aside and saw the splinter attached to the end. "It's out."

"Danki." Jimmy leaned so close that she could feel his warm breath tickle her nose.

"You're welcome."

"What's goin' on here?"

Leona jumped back.

Jimmy did the same.

Abraham Fisher planted his hands on his hips and stared at them.

"I—I was taking a splinter out of Jimmy's hand," Leona stammered. She didn't know why she felt so flustered. They'd done nothing wrong.

Abraham glared at Jimmy. "I think you and me need to have a little talk—in private."

Leona didn't understand why Abraham wanted to speak with Jimmy alone, but she decided it would be best if she left. She gave Jimmy what she hoped was a reassuring smile and hurried away.

∞

Jimmy pulled a handkerchief from the pocket of his blue jeans and wrapped it around his throbbing hand. "What did you want to talk to me about, Abraham?"

The man grunted. "As if you don't know."

"If it's about—"

"Lydia Weaver had a talk with me the other day," Abraham said, cutting Jimmy off. "It seems that Leona informed her mamm that she's in love with you."

Jimmy's mouth fell open. "She. . .she said that?"

Abraham gave a curt nod. "Lydia's worried that

her daughter might do something foolish, like run away with you, and then she'd be shunned." He leveled Jimmy with a piercing gaze. "My daughter ran away from home once because she was influenced by a young English woman who didn't give a hoot about anyone but herself. I won't stand by now and watch the daughter of my good friend throw her life away on some English fellow who can't keep his hands to himself."

"Just a minute." Jimmy's voice raised a notch. "I've never touched Leona inappropriately. And you don't have to worry about her running off with me or being shunned."

Abraham opened his mouth as if to say more, but Jimmy sprinted off. "I'll never find what I'm looking for here, and staying in Lancaster County so long was a big mistake!"

Chapter 36

As Jim stepped onto the front porch of Holly's small, brick home, his heart began to pound and his hands grew sweaty. Today was Saturday, and she'd taken the day off, leaving her two employees in charge of the health food store. Jim wasn't working today, either, so he'd made plans for the two of them to tour the Museum of Glass as well as the Historical Museum in Tacoma. Holly had volunteered to fix Jim breakfast before they went, and even though he normally didn't eat much in the morning, he had accepted her invitation, wanting to have some time alone with her before their date.

He'd gotten to know her fairly well during the last few months as they had talked frequently on the phone, attended AA meetings, and had gone on several informal dates. She'd invited him to church a couple of times, but after his continued refusals, she had finally quit asking.

Jim knew that if he was going to move beyond friendship with Holly, he would need to open up and tell her the truth about Jimmy, which was what he planned to do this morning during breakfast. He had already lost two important people in his life, and he hoped his confession wouldn't end his and Holly's relationship, because he didn't think he could endure another loss.

With a trembling hand, Jim drew in a deep breath and rang the doorbell. A few seconds later, Holly greeted him with a cheery smile.

"Good morning, Jim. I hope you like blueberry pancakes and sausage links, because that's what I've fixed for breakfast."

The sight of her standing there in a pair of blue jeans and a pink T-shirt put a lump in his throat. He thought Holly was beautiful, no matter what she wore. Physically, she reminded him of Linda in that she had blond hair and blue eyes, but Holly's personality was a lot different from that of his late wife's. Holly was self-assured and outgoing; Linda had been introverted and afraid of many things. At least she had been in the earlier part of their marriage. After she started hanging around Beth Walters and attending church, she'd changed in many ways, although she'd never become as emotionally secure as Holly seemed to be.

Pulling his thoughts aside, Jim returned Holly's smile and stepped into the house, hoping she couldn't tell how nervous he was.

"Come out to the kitchen, and you can keep me company while I put breakfast on the table," she said, motioning him to follow.

When they entered the cozy room a few minutes later, Jim took a seat at the table, and she poured him a cup of coffee.

"Thanks. My nerves are on edge this morning, and this might help."

Holly chuckled. "I always thought coffee was supposed to make a person more jittery, not calm you down."

"Guess you're right about that."

Holly brought a platter of sausage over to the table and placed it near Jim. "There's no reason for you to be nervous. I'm not such a bad cook, and I promise you won't die from food poisoning."

"It's not your cooking that has me worried." He took a sip of coffee but set the cup down when he realized the drink was too hot.

Holly went back to the stove, and this time she returned with a stack of pancakes. When she set it on the table, she took a seat next to Jim. "Let's get started eating, and then you can tell me what's got you worried."

"Yeah, okay," he mumbled.

"It won't embarrass you if I offer a prayer of thanks for our food, will it?"

He shook his head. He was used to Jimmy praying at the table, and Linda had done it, too, after she'd gotten religious.

Holly reached for Jim's hand and bowed her head.

Jim did the same; only he kept his eyes open, staring at the floral design on the plate before him.

"Father in heaven," Holly prayed, "thank You for this food and bless it to the nourishment of our bodies. Thank You for good friends and good company. Amen."

When she let go of Jim's hand, he reached for his coffee cup again, this time blowing on it to make sure it was cool enough to drink. As he lifted it to his lips, his hand began to shake, and some of the coffee spilled out. He set the cup down quickly and grabbed a napkin.

"Are you okay?" Holly asked with obvious concern. "Did you burn your hand?"

He shook his head. "I'll be fine. Just spilled some on the tablecloth."

She leaned closer and took his hand. "You're shaking, Jim. What's wrong?"

He squeezed her fingers, hoping the strength he found there would give him the courage to say what was on his mind. "I—I need to tell you something. Something that's been eating at me for twenty years."

"What is it, Jim?"

He started by explaining how he and Linda couldn't have children, and how several attempts to adopt had failed. Then he told her about the excitement they had felt when they'd made contact with a lawyer from Maryland and how they'd gone there to adopt a one-year-old boy.

"But the adoption never happened," he said, shaking his head. "The birth mother changed her mind, and I left the lawyer's office that day empty-handed and wondering how I was going to face Linda when I returned to our hotel and told her we had no baby to take home."

"That must have been awful. How soon afterward did you get Jimmy?" The compassion in Holly's eyes let Jim know he had her sympathy, and it gave him the courage to go on.

"A few hours," he replied.

"Huh?" Her eyebrows lifted. "How could your lawyer set up another adoption in such a short time?"

"He didn't."

"Then how—"

Jim quickly related the story of how he'd gone to an Amish farm for some root beer and ended up leaving with a child.

Holly's mouth dropped open. "You—you kidnapped a baby?"

He nodded slowly.

"Does Jimmy know about this?"

"Yeah. He found out when he went to Bel Air, Maryland, thinking he could get some information about his birth mother. After talking to the lawyer, it came out that there had been no adoption." Jim paused and swiped the napkin he'd used for the spilled coffee across his sweaty forehead. "When Jimmy confronted me about the failed adoption, I felt I had no choice but to tell him about the kidnapping." He groaned. "At first he didn't believe me, but he did go to Pennsylvania in search of his real family. Now he's not speaking to me."

Holly sat staring at her hands now clasped in front of her.

"The last time we talked, he hadn't gotten any leads,

and I'm not much help because I can't remember where that Amish farm even was."

Holly lifted her gaze to meet his. "You're not the man I thought you were, Jim. You're not to be trusted, and I want you to leave—now." She pushed her chair back and dashed from the room.

❧

Leona's hand shook as she sank into the wicker chair on the front porch and read the letter Eli Raber had given her when he'd stopped by the house on his way to town a few minutes ago.

Dear Leona:

After my conversation with Abraham yesterday, I realized that I would be hurting you if I stayed here any longer. And it wouldn't be right for me to ask you to leave your Amish faith in order for us to be together. So I've decided to return to Washington and make peace with my dad and try to sort things out.

I came to Lancaster County in search of something from my past, but since I didn't find what I was looking for, I guess the Lord said no to my request. As much as I've come to love you, I don't see any way for us to be together.

I'm praying that God will heal your hurts and give you the desires of your heart. I'll never forget you or your family, and I'll continue to pray that your dad's memory will return. Even if that never happens, please remember these words from Romans 8:28: "And we know that all things work together for good to them that love God, to them who are the called according to his purpose."

You must learn to forgive and trust God

again, Leona. It's the only way you'll ever have
any real joy or peace.

Fondly,
Jimmy

Tears welled in Leona's eyes and blurred the words on
the page. Jimmy was gone, and he wasn't coming back.
He loved her, yet she knew that because he was English
and she was Amish they could never have a life together.

Despite the fact that, for so many months, Leona
had been afraid to fall in love again, it had happened,
anyway. She'd fallen in love with Jimmy, and now he
was gone.

She gripped the edge of the chair and squeezed her
eyes shut. *There's something in Lancaster County that is*
linked to Jimmy's past, but I have no idea what it is. If
Jimmy really loved me, why didn't he feel free to share it?

Suddenly, a thought popped into Leona's head, and
her eyes opened. "I need to speak with Abraham Fisher.
I need to find out exactly what he said to Jimmy that
made him decide to leave."

∞

Abraham was on his way to the barn when he spotted
a horse and buggy pulling into the yard. He waited to
see who it was, and when the horse stopped in front of
the hitching rail, Leona Weaver stepped down from her
buggy.

He lifted his hand and waved. "It's a nice, warm
Saturday morning, wouldn't ya say? A real pleasant
change in the weather, which means spring is just over
the hill."

"I need to speak with you," Leona said.

Leona's furrowed brows and puckered lips let
Abraham know something was amiss. "What is it? Are

you here about your daed? Is Jacob okay?"

"Papa's the same. I came to speak with you about Jimmy Scott. I'd like to know what you said that made him decide to go back to Washington."

"He went home, huh?" *Now that's a relief.*

She nodded.

Abraham kicked a small stone with the toe of his boot. "There ain't much to say. I told him how things were, and that's all."

"What exactly did you say to him?" she persisted.

"Said I'd talked to your mamm and that she was worried you might do something foolish and get yourself shunned."

Leona shook her head. "Mom ought to know me better than that."

"Jah, well, I thought I knew my oldest daughter, too, yet she ran off with Virginia Meyers all those years ago because she couldn't face what she'd done. That hurt our whole family."

"I'm sure it did, but Naomi did come back home."

He gave another stone a swift kick. "I also told that young fellow that I couldn't stand by and watch my good friend's daughter throw her life away on some Englisher who can't keep his hands to himself."

"Jimmy's a decent man. I was only helping him get a splinter out of his hand, and I—I don't feel you had the right to chase him off."

"The Englisher does not belong here, plain and simple." Abraham headed for the barn, and a sense of irritation welled up in his soul when he realized Leona had followed. He stopped inside the barn door and whirled around. "Your daed's been my best friend for a good many years, and there's no way I could watch some fancy, young know-it-all wreck the lives of everyone in your family."

Leona's chin trembled as she stared at the ground.

"Our lives were wrecked the day Papa fell from that ladder and lost his memory."

"That's not true. Jacob's learned to do many things since his accident. Arthur told me that your daed's painting skills are almost as good as they were before he fell."

"Who do you think taught Papa how to paint again?" Leona lifted her gaze, and Abraham saw tears shimmering in her eyes. "It was Jimmy, that's who."

He moved toward one of the mules' stalls, hoping she might take the hint and head for home. He felt sorry she was upset, but he couldn't deal with that right now.

Once more, she followed him. "I understand your concern for my daed, but Papa needs Jimmy's help. Can't you see that?"

"My concern isn't just for Jacob. I'm worried about you getting hurt or maybe shunned."

Leona sniffed and blotted the tears that had splattered onto her cheeks. "I would never do anything to bring shame to my family. There's no reason for you to be worried."

"Sorry I'm late, Papa," Jake said as he entered the barn. "I know you wanted to start plowin' the south field before noon, but Elsie's got the morning sickness real bad, and I didn't want to leave the house till her mamm showed up to help with the kinner."

Abraham shrugged. He was glad for the interruption. Maybe Leona would go home now and this discussion would end. "I haven't got the mules hitched up yet, anyhow," he said, looking at his son.

Jake glanced at Leona with a look of concern. "You okay?"

She gave a quick nod.

"What brings you over here this morning?"

"I needed to speak with your daed about something."

Jake looked at Abraham as if he expected him to say something, but Abraham just stood there.

"How are my girls doing in school these days?" Jake asked, turning back to Leona.

"Just fine. They're both eager to learn."

"Won't be but a few months, and the kinner will be out of school for summer break," Jake commented.

"That's true."

Abraham cleared his throat. "You ready to help with the mules, son?"

"Sure, Papa, but if you and Leona aren't done talkin', I can bring the mules out on my own."

"I think we've said all that needs sayin'." Abraham looked at Leona. "Isn't that right?"

She nodded, turned, and rushed out of the barn.

Chapter 37

*W*hat time is it? How long have I been here? Jim rolled over to the edge of the couch and shielded his eyes from the ray of sun streaming through the living room window. "Holly," he moaned. "I miss you, Holly. Why'd you have to turn your back on me when I needed your love and understanding?" He thumped the small pillow lying half under his head. *I wonder if she's sorry for leaving what we'd begun. I wonder if she regrets sending me away.*

A car door slammed somewhere outside. At least he thought it was a car door. It could have been coming from the TV. No doubt he had left it on last night when he'd passed out on the couch after downing too many beers. He'd been drinking pretty hard for the last several days. Or had it been weeks since he'd told Holly about the kidnapping?

Jim's head felt fuzzy, and his body felt like someone had used him as a punching bag. His mouth was dry and tasted like he'd been chewing on a dirty sock, but he didn't care. Jim didn't care about anything anymore. Two days after he'd made his confession to Holly, Ed had walked off the job, saying he was tired of covering for Jim.

Jim wasn't sure how long it had been since he'd gone to work, but that didn't matter, either. He had lost his wife, his son, and now his girlfriend, so what difference did it make if he lost his business?

Clump, clump, clump—he heard heavy footsteps on the porch. *Who'd be comin' here so early in the morning?* At least he thought it was morning. It could be afternoon for all he knew.

He heard the front door click open and tried to sit up, but a sharp pain sliced through his head, bringing him back to the couch. "Who—who's there?"

"It's me."

Jim squinted at the man who stood a few feet away holding a suitcase in one hand. "Jimmy?"

"Yeah, it's me."

Certain that he must be dreaming, Jim squeezed his eyes shut.

"I've wasted enough time in Amish country, and I've come home, Dad."

Dad? Jim opened his eyes and blinked a couple of times. Either he was in the middle of the best dream he'd ever had, or Jimmy really had returned home. He grabbed the edge of the couch and managed to pull himself to a sitting position, but his stomach rolled, and his head spun like a top. "Oh, I feel sick," he moaned, letting his head slip back to the pillow.

∞

Jimmy set his suitcase down and moved over to the couch. "Do you need me to get a bucket?"

"Beer. Get me a beer."

Anger boiled in Jimmy's chest like a raging sea. He'd given up on his mission to find his real family, said good-bye to the woman he loved, and driven over two thousand miles in four days to make things right with his dad. And for what? To find him like this?

"I'll get you some coffee, but no beer," he said, shaking his head in disgust.

"Beer. I need some beer."

"What you need is a swift kick in the pants."

His dad released a pathetic whimper. "You're right. I need to be punished. I'm a louse. The lowest of lows. The scum of the earth."

"You won't find any relief from your pain talking like that."

Dad turned his face toward the back of the couch.

Jimmy grimaced. *What made me think I'd be able to make peace with this man who can't even make peace with himself?* "I'm going to the kitchen to make a pot of coffee. I'll be back as soon as it's ready," he muttered.

No answer, just a muffled snort.

Give me the wisdom and strength to deal with this, Lord, Jimmy prayed as he left the room. *And show my dad what he needs to do to make things right.*

∞

As Leona helped her mamm hang their freshly washed clothes on the line, Ginger ran about nipping at the laundry basket and trying to steal the clothes that had yet to be hung.

"Get away now, you little rascal," she scolded, nudging the pup with the toe of her shoe.

One of the barn cats streaked past, and Ginger took off like a flash of lightning. Leona chuckled despite her dour mood, and her thoughts went immediately to Jimmy as they often did when she saw the puppy he had given her.

Ever since Leona had read Jimmy's note saying he was leaving Pennsylvania, she had grieved her losses and struggled with bitterness because of the things she and her family had been through in the last year. She'd thought she was coping better, but after Jimmy left, it seemed as though her wounds had been reopened and would never heal. She knew she couldn't continue to pine for a love she could never have, and she realized that she needed to get on with her life and try to strengthen her faith somehow. But that was easier said than done.

Leona also knew she had spoken out of turn

when she'd questioned Abraham about what he'd said to Jimmy. When she'd seen him at the general store a few days ago, she had apologized for her sharp words. Abraham had accepted her apology but said he felt they were all better off now that Jimmy had returned to Washington.

Maybe Abraham's right, Leona thought as she reached for a pair of her daed's trousers. *If Jimmy had stayed in Lancaster County and continued to work for Arthur, I would have suffered every time I saw him, knowing we couldn't be together.*

The same day Leona had spoken with Abraham, she'd also visited with Mary Ann in Abby's quilt shop. When she'd told her friend how she felt about Jimmy leaving and mentioned that her faith had weakened to a point where she could hardly pray anymore, Mary Ann had reminded her that it wasn't good to let disruptions and disappointments control your emotions or keep you from worshipping God. Leona hadn't argued. She knew Mary Ann was right.

One of the hardest parts about Jimmy being gone was that almost every day Leona's daed asked for Jimmy, wondering why he didn't come around and worried that Jimmy might be mad at him. Mom had explained several times that Jimmy had gone home to Washington, but Papa still kept asking and sulking around like he'd lost his best friend.

Leona glanced over at her mamm, who'd been busy hanging sheets while she did the clothes. "I'm wondering what God has in mind for our family," she said.

" 'And we know that all things work together for good to them that love God, to them who are the called according to his purpose,' " Mom quoted from the book of Romans. It was the same verse Jimmy had mentioned in the letter he'd written Leona.

Leona clipped a shirt to the line. "That verse really

confuses me, Mom. Everyone in our family loves God, and look how things have worked out for us. Papa still thinks he's a little boy, you've been having trouble with your blood sugar lately, and I'm en alt maedel schoolteacher pining for a love I can never have."

"You're not an old maid, and you shouldn't be pinin' for someone who doesn't share your faith," Mom said with a shake of her head.

"Jimmy may not be Amish, but he does have a strong faith in God."

"That may be, but since he's English and you're Amish, there can be no future for you together."

"I know. There's no future for me with any man."

Mom clicked her tongue. "I wish you wouldn't talk that way, Leona. Don't you think it's time you quit grieving for Ezra and get on with your life?"

Leona shook her head. "I'm just guarding my heart from getting hurt again."

"There are no guarantees in this life," her mamm said. "I think when the right man comes along you'll realize it's time to set your fears aside and trust God in all things."

"I'm finished with the clothes now," Leona said, feeling the need to change the subject. "So I'd better head out to the barn and get my buggy horse. I want to get to the schoolhouse before any of the scholars show up."

"You're right. You wouldn't want to be late, and I'm about done here myself." Mom drew Leona into her arms and gave her a hug. "I love you, and I've been praying that God will give you many good things in the days ahead."

Leona blinked to keep her tears from spilling over. "Danki. I want that for you, as well."

❧

"I—I've missed you, Jimmy." A tide of emotions welled up in Jim's chest as his son handed him a third cup of coffee.

"I've missed you, too, Dad."

"Why don't you have a seat and tell me why you've come home?"

Jimmy flopped into the rocking chair across from the couch with a groan. "I finally came to my senses."

"What's that supposed to mean?"

"It means I'm home where I belong. Going to Pennsylvania was a waste of time. I never should have left home in the first place, because I didn't find my Amish family and probably never would have even if I'd stayed and kept on searching." Jimmy looked around the room as though he was seeing it for the first time. "Guess I've been gone too long. Everything looks odd and almost surreal to me."

Jim could relate to that feeling. He'd spent most of his waking hours the last few days feeling as if he were in a dream. And when he hadn't been awake, he'd been in a drunken stupor. "I. . .I wish I could turn back the hands of time and put you back on the picnic table where I found you."

Jimmy stared at the unlit fireplace. "I came to the conclusion that I didn't belong there, yet a part of me wanted to stay."

"Why didn't you then?"

"I left to protect her."

"Who?"

"Leona."

"The bishop's daughter?"

Jimmy nodded slowly. "I'm in love with her, Dad."

"How does she feel about you?"

"According to Abraham Fisher, Leona loves me, too."

Jim frowned. "Then what's the problem?"

"I'm the problem." Jimmy touched his chest. "I'm English. She's Amish."

"You're not really English. You were born Amish, and—"

"I know that, but I wasn't raised Amish; I don't know if I could ever convert." Jimmy released a deep sigh. "It wouldn't be right for Leona or me to give up the only way of life we've ever known in order to be together."

"Why wouldn't it be? I know plenty of people who've made huge sacrifices in the name of love." Jim didn't know why he was saying these things. He really didn't want Jimmy to live in Pennsylvania or join the Amish faith. He'd been hoping his son would come home, and now that he was here, he was saying things that might cause him to leave again. "I'm sorry things have turned out this way," he said. "If I just hadn't taken you from that Amish family when you were a baby, you would know where you belonged. You might even be married by now, or at least engaged to the woman you love."

"All the what-ifs won't change things between me and Leona." Jimmy leaned forward. "But there is one thing that can change, Dad."

"What's that?"

"Our relationship can change—and you can change if you want to."

"I tried that already." The taste of bile rose in Jim's throat. "I went to those stupid AA meetings, opened my heart to Holly, and look where it got me!" He squeezed his eyes shut in an effort to stop the pain. "She hates me now, Jimmy."

"I know Holly pretty well, Dad, and I doubt she's capable of hating you or anyone."

"You should have seen the look on her face when I told her I had kidnapped you. She said I wasn't the man she'd thought I was and that I couldn't be trusted. She was right, too, because I can't even trust myself." He grimaced. "I was so sure I could stay sober, but I'm weak and need a drink whenever things go sour."

"What you need is the Lord, Dad."

Jim waved his hand as though he were batting at a fly. "Don't give me any sermons."

Jimmy left his chair and knelt on the floor in front of the couch, then reached out and took Jim's hand. "The morning before I left Pennsylvania, I was going to call you and apologize for not returning any of your calls, and for speaking to you in such an unkind way after I finally realized you had kidnapped me."

"So why didn't you call me? Did you think it over, realize what a good-for-nothing I was, and then change your mind?"

Jimmy shook his head. "You're not a good-for-nothing, Dad. The reason I didn't call was because I got busy helping with a barn raising. And then, when I realized I needed to come home, I decided to surprise you by just showing up. Figured it would be better to apologize in person rather than on the phone." He paused. "And I wanted to let you know that I forgive you for what you did."

"I. . .I'm the one who needs to apologize," Jim blubbered. "And I don't deserve your forgiveness, either."

Jimmy looked like he was about to say something more, but the doorbell rang, interrupting their conversation. "Are you expecting company?"

Jim shook his head. "Didn't even expect you."

"I'll see who it is."

When Jimmy left the room, Jim sat up and reached for his coffee cup. He took a drink and was getting ready to swallow when Holly stepped into the room. He choked, sputtered, and spit the lukewarm coffee all over the front of his rumpled shirt. Holly was the last person he had expected to see today, and he didn't relish the idea of her seeing him like this.

Chapter 38

Leona had no more than taken a seat on the porch swing when Ginger jumped up, wagging her tail and whimpering as if she were starved for attention.

"You little *daagdieb*," she said, allowing the dog to flop across her knees. "That's right. You're nothing but a scamp. You're getting too big for this, you know that?"

Ginger responded with a grunt; then she wet Leona's hand with her sloppy tongue.

Leona sat there, petting the dog's head and listening to a chorus of birds from a nearby tree until she heard a horse and buggy plod up the driveway. She turned her attention to the yard.

Mary Ann waved from her open buggy, and as soon as she had it stopped near the barn and had hitched the horse to the rail, she headed for the house. "I was hoping I'd find you here," she said, stepping onto the porch.

Leona nodded. "I got home from school awhile ago and decided to sit out here before I help Mom with supper."

Mary Ann took a seat in the wicker chair near the swing. "Looks like you're in good company."

"I barely sat down, and she was up in my lap. Silly critter thinks she's still a little pup."

"She reminds me of Cinnamon," Mary Ann said, reaching over to stroke the dog behind one ear. "It was nice of Jimmy to give Ginger to you."

"Jah, but I still miss Cinnamon." Tears welled up in Leona's eyes and threatened to spill over. As much as she missed Cinnamon, she missed Jimmy even more.

"It's never easy to lose someone you love," Mary

Ann said. "But God is always there to help us through the pain, and He often gives us someone to replace the one we've lost." Her lips formed a little smile. "For whatever reason, God chose not to return our missing brother to us, but He gave Papa and Fannie twin boys. I know that even though Titus and Timothy haven't taken Zach's place in Papa's heart he's found comfort and joy in being able to raise them."

Leona thought about her own situation and wondered whom God had brought into her life to replace the ones she had lost. Cinnamon had been replaced with Ginger, and Jimmy had come along to make her laugh and enjoy some things after Papa had been taken from her because of his memory loss. She guessed God might have had His hand in all that. But what about Ezra? Who had taken his place in her heart? *Jimmy did,* a voice in her head taunted. *But you can't have him because he's English.*

"So what's the reason for your visit?" Leona asked her friend, needing to change the subject.

"I was on my way home from the quilt shop and decided to stop by and tell you thanks."

Leona tipped her head in question. "For what?"

"For paving the way for me and Abner."

"Oh, that. How are things going now that the two of you have begun courting?"

"Good. Real good." Mary Ann's face fairly glowed. "I'm thinkin' me and Fannie might need to plant a whole bunch of celery this year."

Leona's eyebrows lifted. "Has Abner asked you to marry him?" She couldn't imagine that the shy young fellow would move so quickly.

"Not yet, but I think it's only a matter of time. In fact, I wouldn't be surprised if we aren't one of the couples gettin' married this fall."

Leona clasped her friend's hand. "I'm glad things

are working out for you." *Sure wish something would work out for me.*

∞

"Wh–what are you doing here?" Jim sputtered as Holly took a seat on the couch beside him.

"I came to see you."

"I—I look a mess, and I'm sure I don't smell any better than I look," he said leaning away from her. "Besides, I've committed a terrible sin—I'm a kidnapper who deserves to be punished."

" 'He that is without sin among you, let him first cast a stone at her' " Holly said, reaching over to wipe the dribble of coffee from his chin.

"What's that supposed to mean?"

"It's from the book of John, Dad." Jimmy plunked into the rocker across from them. "Jesus was admonishing the Pharisees who wanted to stone an adulterous woman. He reminded those men that they weren't without sin, and if any of them thought they were, then they should be the first to stone the woman."

"Guess that never happened," Jim said, "because no man or woman who's ever been born has been perfect or without sin." He groaned. "Of course, some of us have committed a lot more sins than others."

"No one except Christ is perfect," Holly corrected.

"Right."

"Last night as I was reading my Bible, I came across John 8:7, and it caught me up short, reminding me that I had done many despicable things while I was struggling with my alcoholic addiction. It wasn't right for me to judge you, Jim." Holly placed her hand on his arm. "I hope you will accept my apology."

"Your apology?" Jim's nose burned, and his eyes stung as he struggled not to break down. "It's me who needs forgiving. I've always liked to be in control, and when I found out I couldn't father a child, I was so determined to give Linda a baby that I did something no decent man would even consider." He paused and looked over at Jimmy. "After I stole you from your real family, keeping you and hiding my secret became an obsession. With every lie I told, I fell deeper into my own self-made pit of misery. After a while, I'd told so many lies that I even began to believe them."

"That's how sin entraps us, Jim," Holly said quietly. "Each sinful thing we do, then try to cover up is compounded by the next sin and the next."

"Kind of like trying to cover up poor siding on a house by putting on multiple coats of paint without scraping and priming," he said. "Immediately, the paint job will start deteriorating because it wasn't prepped properly."

"Good illustration," Jimmy chimed in.

Jim sighed. "Any idea what this sin-sick man can do to free himself from the burden of sin and shame?"

"Yes!" Holly and Jimmy said in unison.

"I kind of figured you might."

Jimmy hurried across the room and pulled Linda's Bible off the bookshelf. "I'd like to read you something, Dad."

Holly slid over, and Jimmy took her place beside Jim. He opened the Bible, turned several pages, and pointed to a verse highlighted in yellow. "In Luke 5:31 and 32, Jesus said, " 'They that are whole need not a physician; but they are not sick. I came not to call the righteous, but sinners to repentance.' " He turned several pages. "And 1 John 1:9 says, 'If we confess our sins, he is faithful and just to forgive us our sins, and to cleanse us from all unrighteousness.' "

"All you need to do is call on God, Jim," Holly said, "Acknowledge that you're a sinner, ask His forgiveness, and accept Christ as your personal Savior."

"It's that simple?"

She nodded, and so did Jimmy.

"I. . .I don't how to pray—don't know the right words," Jim mumbled.

"There are no 'right' words." Jimmy reached for his dad's hand. "Just close your eyes and talk to God. Tell Him what's on your heart and confess your sins."

With a catch in his throat and tears blinding his vision, Jim released his burdens to God. By the end of his prayer, he knew with a certainty that he had found forgiveness for his sins through Jesus Christ.

∞

Jimmy yawned and stretched his arms over his head as he entered the kitchen the following morning. It was still dark outside, and it didn't feel right to be getting up so early to go to work. But he had agreed to act as his dad's foreman—at least until they could find someone to replace Ed. And since they had a paint job to do in Olympia, it meant they needed to get an early start. Jimmy had decided to make breakfast while his dad loaded their van with some supplies he kept in the garage.

He flicked on the light switch near the kitchen door and ambled across the room to turn on the coffeemaker. "Sure didn't have this little convenience in the trailer house I rented from the Rabers," he mumbled. "But then, I didn't miss having an electric coffeemaker so much, either."

During Jimmy's stay in Lancaster County, he'd become used to doing without a lot of modern conveniences. Living behind the Rabers' place had provided him with an opportunity to get better acquainted with Eli and his folks as well as learn many of the Amish ways.

While the coffee brewed, Jimmy went to the refrigerator and took out a carton of eggs. He removed six and cracked them into a bowl with the idea of making scrambled eggs. "These yolks are sure pale," he mumbled. "Nothing like the fresh ones Esther Raber used to fix for my breakfast."

The milk Jimmy added to the eggs was also store bought, and he knew it wouldn't be nearly as good as the fresh goat's milk he'd become accustomed to drinking. With the exception of his camera, there weren't too many modern conveniences he couldn't do without. He hadn't even missed watching TV while he was away, and he wondered if he would care to watch it now. Until he'd left Amish country, Jimmy hadn't realized how much he would miss the slower-paced, simple life.

"I told you not to bother with breakfast," Dad said as he entered the kitchen. "My stomach's not up for more than a cup of coffee and a doughnut this early in the morning."

Jimmy placed the frying pan on the stove and turned on the back burner. "You never have taken time to eat a healthy breakfast, Dad."

"Guess that's true."

"I figured after you and Holly started dating she might convert you into a health nut."

Dad removed two mugs from the cupboard and set them next to the coffeepot. "Holly has helped in many ways—getting me to go to AA meetings, listening to me gripe about complaining customers, and putting up with my sometimes gloomy moods." He grunted. "But I doubt she'll ever succeed in getting me to give up coffee and doughnuts."

Jimmy chuckled. "She has been good for you, and I'm glad she came by yesterday and had a part in leading you to the Lord."

"Yeah, me, too." Dad poured two cups of coffee,

hauled them over to the table, and took a seat. "I think the two of you saved my life yesterday."

Jimmy dumped the egg mixture into the pan and stirred it with a spatula. "Actually, it was God who saved your life, by sending His Son to die for your sins."

"I know, and I feel as if that five-gallon bucket of paint I've been carrying on my shoulders for many years is finally gone."

"Oftentimes, when someone confesses their sins and accepts God's gift of eternal life, they feel that way—like they're free from the burden that had been pulling them down."

Jimmy scooped the eggs onto two plates and joined his dad at the table. "Now that you've found forgiveness, in order to grow as a Christian, you'll need to get into God's Word and spend time in prayer. That will help you stay closer to Him."

Dad nodded. "I know that, too. I'm planning to go to church with you and Holly this coming Sunday."

"That's good news." Jimmy glanced at his dad. "Would you like me to ask the blessing?"

"I think I'd like to try my hand at that if you don't mind."

"Not at all." Jimmy closed his eyes, and his dad did the same.

"Dear God," Dad began in a hesitant voice. "I just want to say thanks for forgiving my sins—and for bringing my son home." There was a brief pause. "Oh, and thanks for this food I'm being forced to eat. Amen."

Jimmy chuckled and reached for the bottle of juice sitting in the middle of the table. "I'm glad things are back on track with you and Holly."

"Me, too," Dad said around a mouthful of egg.

"Are you getting serious about her?"

"Yeah. . .uh. . .well, sort of. Holly's a wonderful woman, but I'm not sure we could ever have a future together."

"Why not?"

Dad's eyebrows drew together. "As I'm sure you know, your mother and I had a lot of problems during our marriage."

Jimmy nodded. He remembered hearing his folks disagree about many things during his childhood. He had found Mom in tears more times than he cared to admit.

"Most of our problems were my fault because I frequently lost my temper and didn't treat your mother with the respect and love she deserved." Dad moaned. "I'm afraid if I were to get married again, I'd mess things up."

Jimmy touched his dad's arm. "Of course you would have your share of problems, but you're a Christian now; with the Lord as your guide, you will not only be able to deal better with your dependence on alcohol, but I think that marrying Holly, or any Christian woman, would be different for you this time around."

His dad stared at him a few seconds, and then his lips curved into a smile. "How'd you get to be so wise for one so young?"

"I'm not sure how wise I am, but I did learn a lot about love and marriage from Eli's folks. I've never met a more devoted couple than Philip and Esther Raber."

"You miss those people, don't you? I can see the look of longing on your face."

Jimmy nodded. He missed everyone he'd come to care about in Lancaster County—Leona Weaver, most of all.

"Do you miss the Amish way of life, too?"

"Yeah, I guess I do. Somewhere along the line, I learned to appreciate the simpler things. In fact, I was reading my Bible before I went to bed last night, and I came across a verse of scripture that made me stop and think."

"What'd it say?"

"It was from the book of Psalms, chapter 27, verse 11. 'Teach me thy way, O Lord, and lead me in a plain path.' "

Dad stared at him with a wrinkled forehead. "Do you think you belong here?"

"I'm not sure where I belong anymore."

"As much as I would hate to lose you, I want you to be happy, Jimmy."

"I want you to be happy, too." Jimmy's throat clogged with emotion. Feeling the need to change the subject, he said, "We'd better eat so we can get on the road, don't you think?"

"Yeah," his dad said with a nod. "This is the first day of my new life, and I want to start it off on the right foot."

Chapter 39

You seem kind of distracted today. Is everything all right?" Holly asked Jim as they walked hand in hand along Owen Beach.

"I've had a lot on my mind lately," he admitted.

"Have you scheduled too many paint jobs?"

"Not really. Since we've had so much rain this spring, we haven't been able to do many outside jobs, but I'm sure the weather will cooperate soon."

As they continued down the rocky beach, Jim prayed for God's direction and the courage to say what was on his mind. Finally, he halted and dropped to one knee.

Holly squinted at the stones in front of him. "What's down there? Did you find another agate?"

Jim shook his head and stared up at her. His mouth felt dry, and he could barely breathe. He couldn't remember being this nervous since he was a teenager preparing to ask one of the high school cheerleaders for a date. "I'm. . .uh. . .in love with you, Holly, and I'm hoping that we can—well. . .uh. . .when the time is right, would you consider marrying me?"

Nothing. No response. Holly just stood there with her lips pursed and her forehead wrinkled.

"If you don't say something soon, my knee's going to give out."

Holly's face relaxed, and she placed both hands against his cheeks. "I think we both need more time to get to know each other and allow our relationship to mature." She smiled. "But yes, when the time is right, I will consider becoming your wife."

Jim stood, and drawing Holly into his arms, he

kissed her gently on the mouth. When the kiss ended, he pulled back slightly. "How about the two of us going somewhere nice for lunch to celebrate my six-week sobriety and our future possible engagement?"

She nestled against his chest and murmured, "That sounds good to me."

∞

When Leona stepped out of her buggy and headed for the schoolhouse early one morning in May, she was surprised to see Abner standing on the front porch. She glanced around thinking he might have brought his brother to school, but she saw no sign of Emanuel. "Guder mariye, Abner," she said as she reached the porch. "What brings you by here this morning?"

"Good mornin' to you, too." He stared down at his boots. "I. . .I wanted to tell ya something."

"Oh? What's that?"

Abner shifted his weight from one foot to the other and slowly raised his head to meet her gaze. "I. . . uh. . .wanted you to know how grateful I am that you put in a good word for me with Mary Ann."

Leona smiled. "I heard the two of you have been courting."

He nodded and leaned against the porch railing. "I've asked her to marry me in the fall, and she said she would."

Leona's smiled widened. "Congratulations! I'm happy for both of you."

"I'm glad you approve."

"Of course. Why wouldn't I? You're a nice man, and you'll be getting a *wunderbaar* woman."

"Jah, I agree." Abner turned to go, but he'd only taken a few steps when he turned back around. "Mary Ann's prayin' you'll fall in love with someone soon."

Before Leona could offer any kind of sensible reply, Abner sprinted across the lawn and hopped into his buggy.

" 'Mary Ann's prayin' you'll fall in love with someone soon,' " she mumbled. "Mary Ann must believe in miracles."

∞

"What can we do to help?" Leona asked as she and her mother stepped into Naomi's kitchen two weeks later. Their entire family, including Arthur and his brood, had been invited to the Hoffmeirs' for a picnic supper. Abraham and all of his family had also been included, and most of the men were in the backyard setting up tables.

"Ruth, Elsie, and Darlene are getting the meat ready to barbecue," Naomi said, nodding toward the counter where three of her sisters-in-law stood. She motioned to the table. "Abby, Mary Ann, and Nancy are making up the salads."

"My daughter and I can carry the plates and silverware outside if you'd like," Leona's mamm volunteered.

"Danki." Naomi smiled. "Many hands make light work."

"That's so true," Abby agreed.

"Lydia, if you don't mind taking over the job of flattening ground beef into patties, I'd like to help Leona set the table," Mary Ann spoke up. "It will give us a chance to visit before the meal is served."

"Don't mind a bit." Mom went over to the sink and washed her hands, and Leona opened the silverware drawer to take out what they would need.

"You're awful quiet this evening," Mary Ann said once she and Leona were outside on the porch. "Did you have a rough week at school?"

"Nothing out of the ordinary. I'm just feeling kind of down."

"Sorry to hear that. Maybe some time spent with family will cheer you up."

"Jah, maybe so." Leona draped her arm across Mary Ann's shoulder. "Abner dropped by the schoolhouse a few weeks ago and told me your good news. I'm real happy for you."

"Danki."

Leona sighed and stared at the porch.

"Are you sure you're okay? You look so down in the mouth."

"I'm feeling kind of frustrated over Papa."

"How come?"

"He hasn't been the same since Jimmy left, and he even seems to have regressed some."

"In what way?"

"He blabs everything he hears, teases my dog unmercifully, and bothers Mom to no end whenever she's trying to get things done. He won't even go on any paint jobs with Arthur now."

"I didn't realize that, and I'm sorry to hear it." Mary Ann placed a stack of paper plates on one of the picnic tables and turned to face Leona. "I hope I'm not speakin' out of turn here, but I don't think you've been the same since Jimmy left, either."

Leona sank to the wooden bench with a sigh. "I do miss him. The two of us had become friends, and—"

"And I have a hunch that you're in love with him." Mary Ann took a seat beside her. "Don't try to deny it, because it's written all over your face."

Leona stared at her hands, folded in her lap. "I know it was wrong to allow myself to have feelings for him, but it happened before I realized it."

"Then it's good that he left. If he'd stayed, you might have gone English and been shunned."

"Now you sound like your daed and my mamm." Leona bristled. "Don't you think I'm strong enough in the faith not to run off?"

"Others have done it," Mary Ann reminded. "And some families in our community have been torn apart because of the shunning that's followed."

"I would never do anything to hurt my family. They've been through enough already." Leona folded her arms. "Besides, even if Jimmy were Amish, I would never marry him."

"I read a verse of scripture in my Bible the other day," Mary Ann said, "and I'm thinkin' it's one you ought to hear."

"What was it?"

"First John 4:18, and it goes like this: " 'There is no fear in love; but perfect love casteth out fear: because fear hath torment. He that feareth is not made perfect in love.' You need to let go of your fears and open your heart to love again." Mary Ann squeezed Leona's fingers. "Just make sure it's with a nice Amish fella."

"I think we should get the table set like we came out here to do," Leona said. She'd heard enough talk about love and marriage and needed to think about something else. She quickly placed the silverware around the table. When she was done, she moved on to the next group of tables.

A few minutes later, a car rumbled into the yard and parked near the barn. When the driver stepped out, Leona's mouth fell open and she sank to the nearest bench. "*Was in der welt*—what in all the world?"

❦

"Now what's that fellow doin' here?" Abraham grumbled to Fannie as he motioned to the car that had pulled into the Hoffmeirs' yard. "I thought Jimmy Scott had gone home for good."

"Guess you were wrong about that." Fannie gave Abraham a gentle nudge with her elbow. "Be nice, Husband. Enough unkind words have already come from your mouth concerning that boy, and it's not your place to be judging him."

"I've only been trying to protect Jacob and his family."

"Jah, well, don't you think you ought to leave that job up to God?"

Abraham knew his wife was right. The Bible taught that only God had justification to judge. Even so, it gave him cause for concern when Jimmy walked up to Arthur and said, "After a lot of thought and prayer, I decided to return to Lancaster County to take care of some unfinished business. I'm hoping you might hire me again."

"Jah, sure, I'd be happy to." Arthur grinned at Jimmy and shook his hand. "You're a hard worker, and I've missed your helpful suggestions."

"Thanks. I appreciate that." Jimmy looked like he might be about to say something more, but before he could get a word out, Jacob sauntered up to him wearing a smile that stretched from ear to ear.

"Where have ya been?" the man asked, giving Jimmy a thump on the back. "I've sure missed ya."

"I've missed you, too." Jimmy shook Jacob's hand. Then he glanced over at Arthur. "I stopped by your place first but soon realized you weren't at home. Then when I arrived at Eli's house, he said you and your family were over here."

Leona stepped forward then, and Abraham held his breath, afraid of what she might say.

"It's nice to see you," she said, smiling at Jimmy in a way that made Abraham's stomach clench.

"It's good to see you, too, Leona." Jimmy's face

turned as red as a tomato, and he glanced around the yard. "I didn't realize you were having a big gathering here. Sorry for interrupting."

"You ain't interruptin'." Jacob pointed to the barbecue that had recently been lit. "Why don't ya stay and eat supper with us?"

"That's a fine idea. We'd like you to join us," Arthur said with a nod.

"Are you sure you wouldn't mind?"

"Not a bit." Jacob thumped Jimmy on the back once more. "You can sit by me."

Abraham groaned and shook his head. *I think it would have been better if I'd stayed home today.*

Fannie reached for his hand and gave it a gentle squeeze.

❧

When the meal was over, Leona took a seat in a chair she'd placed under a maple tree. She needed some time alone to sort out her feelings for Jimmy. She caught a glimpse of him playing a game of horseshoes with Jake, Norman, and Samuel Fisher. She was happy to see Jimmy but knew that having him living and working among her people again would be difficult. Still, it was wonderful to observe how happy her daed seemed to be. She hadn't seen him smile so much since Jimmy left Lancaster County a few months ago. *I'll simply have to deal with this. It wouldn't be fair to Papa for me to ask Jimmy to leave again.*

"Those four playing *hufeise* seem to be having fun, don't they?" Fannie said to Abby as the two women walked past Leona.

"Jah," Abby replied. "If I didn't know better, I'd think Jimmy could be one of their brothers."

"What would make you say something like that?"

Fannie asked her daughter.

"Jimmy's hair is almost the same shade of brown as Samuel's, and he has the same color eyes."

Leona squinted to get a better look. Abby was right. Jimmy did look similar to Samuel. If he'd been wearing Amish clothes, the two of them could have been mistaken for brothers. She leaned back in her chair and tried to relax. *It's just wishful thinking because I'd like for Jimmy to be Amish. Just because he's come back to Lancaster County doesn't give me the right to start hoping, wishing he were one of us.*

Leona's thoughts were halted when she heard a strange popping noise. She tipped her head and listened. There it was again. *Must be some birds or squirrels playing in the tree.* She glanced into the branches but didn't see anything out of the ordinary.

"Leona, get up! *Kumme! Schnell!*" Papa hollered from across the yard.

Why was her father calling for her to come quickly? Leona figured her daed had one of his silly jokes he wanted to share or had found some critter he thought she might like to see, so she was tempted to ignore his call. But out of respect, she stood and hurried over to the porch where he sat in a wicker chair. "What did you want, Papa?"

Before he could reply, an ear-piercing crack rent through the air. Leona whirled around in time to see a huge limb from the maple tree crash to the ground. It landed on the chair she had occupied moments ago, smashing it to bits.

She gasped and covered her mouth with the palm of her hand. "Oh, Papa, how did you know?"

Her daed looked bewildered at first, but then a slow smile spread across his face. "God put a voice in my head that told me to holler for you."

A feeling of gratitude swelled in Leona's soul, and

she dropped to her knees beside her daed. All these months, she'd been sure God could no longer use Papa because he'd lost his memory and couldn't fulfill his role as their bishop, but now she realized that wasn't the case. She reflected on the last half of Luke 18:16, which she'd read the other day: "Suffer little children to come unto me, and forbid them not: for of such is the kingdom of God." Even though her daed thought and acted like a child, God had used him to warn her, which had saved her life.

At that moment, Leona also realized that, even though God had allowed some terrible things to happen in her life, He'd always been there offering His love and tender mercies. *God doesn't want me to be afraid of living or loving. He wants me to put my trust in Him.*

"I'm sorry, Papa," she sobbed. "Please forgive me for ignoring you so many times, and for—for doubting your love."

He patted the top of her covering. "I forgive you, Ona."

∞

When Jimmy heard Jacob's cry for Leona to get up, followed by a loud *crack*, he froze. The last time he had looked in Leona's direction, she'd been sitting in a chair under the maple tree. She was gone now, and her chair was lying flat on the ground with a huge limb covering it.

He glanced quickly across the yard, and when he spotted Leona kneeling in front of her father, he dropped his horseshoe on the ground and raced through the grass. "Leona, are you okay?" he panted, kneeling down beside her.

Her face was flushed, and her eyes shimmered with tears. "Thanks to Papa's warning, I'm fine."

Jimmy reached for Leona's hand, not even caring what the people who were watching might think about the gesture. "I haven't had the chance to tell you this yet, but the reason I came back to Pennsylvania wasn't just to work for Arthur."

"It wasn't?"

He shook his head. "You see, the truth is, I'm really—"

"Zach Fisher!" Jacob leaned forward and touched the back of Jimmy's right ear. "You've been gone such a long time. How old are you now, Zach?"

Chapter 40

Jimmy sat next to Leona, trying to process what Jacob had said. *He must have me confused with someone else—someone from his childhood, maybe.*

Leona looked at Jimmy as though she were seeing him for the first time; then she looked back at her father and said, "Papa, what are you talking about? This is Jimmy Scott, not Zach Fisher."

"Jah, that's right," echoed several others who had gathered around Leona soon after her near mishap with the tree.

With a shake of his head, Jacob reached over and pulled Jimmy's ear partway back. "Abraham, you'd best take a good look at this."

Abraham, who had been standing behind Matthew, stepped forward. "What's wrong with you, Jacob? You're acting so *fremm*."

"Strange as it may seem, look here; he has a red, heart-shaped birthmark, just like Zach's."

Abraham hesitated but finally moved in for a closer look. Before he had a chance to say anything, Naomi pushed through the crowd and rushed over to Jimmy. "What birthmark? Let me see."

"My Zach did have a red blotch behind his ear that looked sort of like this," Abraham said as he leaned his head closer to Jimmy, squinted, then stepped back. "But you don't expect us to believe this is the same boy."

Naomi groaned. "Oh but, Papa, what if it's true?"

It seemed as though everyone was staring at the mark behind Jimmy's ear, and it made him feel like a bug under a microscope. Who was this Zach they were talking about, and what did it have to do with him?

Pushing himself to his feet, Jimmy turned to face Jacob. "When you were a boy, did one of your friends have a birthmark like mine?"

Jacob shook his head. "You're Zach." He pointed to Abraham. "He's your daed."

A murmur went through the crowd; then everyone began talking at once. Jimmy felt as if his head might burst wide open, and he held up his hands to quiet them. "Would someone please tell me who Zach is, and what's all the fuss about my birthmark?"

"It's nothing." Abraham compressed his lips and folded his arms across his chest. "Jacob has you confused with my son who was kidnapped."

The shock of Abraham's words left Jimmy's mouth feeling so dry he could barely speak. Could the Fishers be the Amish family he had been searching for? Was it possible that Abraham, a man who obviously didn't care for him, was actually his father? Could he have been living and working among his own people all those months and not have known it? Jimmy swayed unsteadily as the possibility sank in.

"Are you all right? Maybe you'd better sit down." Leona reached up and took hold of Jimmy's arm, and he dropped to the ground beside her again.

"I have a story to tell—one I think you all need to hear," he rasped.

"We don't need any stories," Abraham grumbled. "We've already heard enough ridiculous talk."

Naomi took a seat on the other side of Leona. "What story, Jimmy? I'd like to hear what you have to say."

"Well, I don't want to hear it." Abraham folded his arms and scowled at Jimmy as if he'd done something horribly wrong.

Feeling more nervous by the minute, Jimmy moistened his lips with the tip of his tongue. He was determined to tell his story, even if Abraham didn't want to hear it. "The thing is, I grew up in Washington State, but I. . .uh. . .wasn't born there."

"What's this got to do with anything?" Abraham's tone was one of impatience, and he turned away with a huff.

He'd only taken a few steps when his son Samuel spoke up. "I think we should listen to what Jimmy's got to say, Papa. He might know something about my missing bruder."

"I agree with Samuel," Matthew put in. "We need to hear Jimmy out."

Abraham shook his head, but Fannie took hold of his arm. "Your boys are right about this, Abraham. We all need to listen to Jimmy's story."

Abraham shrugged, but he also stopped walking.

"I didn't know any of this until last spring, when Jim, my English dad, informed me that I wasn't born in Washington. He said I was born here, in Lancaster County." Jimmy paused and drew in a quick breath. "When I was a year old, my sister left me sitting on a picnic table while she went in the house to get some cold root beer for an English man."

"Oh!" Naomi covered her mouth with the palm of her hand and stared hard at Jimmy.

"*Puh!* That don't prove nothin'." Abraham grunted. "Lots of folks knew that story."

"I thought we were going to hear Jimmy out," Fannie said.

Abraham squinted at Jimmy again. "Tell us what else you know about that day."

"The name of the man who went there to buy root beer is Jim Scott. I grew up thinking he was my father. It wasn't until shortly after my twenty-first birthday that I learned I had been adopted and that my folks had gotten me through a lawyer in Bel Air, Maryland."

Jimmy gulped in another breath of air. "So I went there to speak with the lawyer, but I was in for a big surprise."

"What surprise was that?" Matthew asked.

"I was told that there had been no adoption for Jim and Linda Scott through that office. The lawyer said my dad—Jim—never left his office with a baby because the birth mother had changed her mind and decided to keep the child."

Abraham gave Jimmy another one of his irritating scowls. "What's this got to do with my missing son?"

"I'm getting to that." Jimmy glanced at Leona, hoping she might say something that would give him a little encouragement, but she just sat there.

"Uh. . .anyway," he continued, "after I left the lawyer's office, I called Jim and demanded to know what had happened at the lawyer's office. He admitted that the adoption had fallen through, and then he told me some wild story, which I was sure he had made up, about him driving onto an Amish farm and asking for root beer, and my Amish sister going into the house to get the root beer and leaving me on the table. He said I was wiggling around, and he was afraid I might fall off, so he picked me up."

Jimmy paused again and swallowed a couple of times. "Then, with no thought of the consequences, Dad—I mean, Jim—dashed to his van and drove off."

Everyone who had gathered around Jimmy gaped at him without uttering a word. Jimmy wasn't sure if they thought he was some kind of a nut, or if they believed his wild story. He decided he'd better get the rest told while he still had a captive audience.

"So then, when we got to the hotel where Jim's wife was waiting, he told her that I was the child they'd come to adopt."

Naomi's sister Nancy let out a yelp. "Ach, my! You really are my little bruder!"

"I told you," Jacob said with a nod.

Abraham stood with a stony face, but Naomi reached across Leona and grabbed hold of Jimmy's arm. "If what you've told us is true, then why haven't you said something to one of us before now?"

"And why'd you return to Washington and then come back again?" Jake asked.

Jimmy looked at Leona to gauge her reaction. Tears shimmered in her green eyes, but she was smiling. It bolstered his courage enough to say more. "I came here last summer with the hope of finding my real family, but every lead I had turned out to be a dead end. No one I spoke with knew anything about a kidnapping that had happened twenty years ago. And then I started working for Jacob and knew I needed to stick around to see what the Amish were all about."

"That doesn't explain why you never asked any of us if we knew anything about a kidnapped baby," Norman spoke up.

"I wanted to, but I was afraid if I blurted something like that out and nobody believed me I might be asked to leave." Jimmy groaned. "I was also concerned that if the truth came to light and I did actually find my family that my dad—Jim—might end up in jail."

"The Amish don't prosecute," Samuel said.

Jimmy nodded. "So I've been told."

"So what was your excuse for not saying anything then?" Norman asked.

"Jah," Jake agreed. "If you really had been kidnapped and wanted to find your real family, I would think you would have left no stone unturned."

"I did ask a couple of people, but they didn't know what I was talking about."

Abraham's frown deepened. "Who'd you ask?"

"I mentioned it to Jacob, but he didn't seem to understand much of what I had said. I also asked Eli, and he said he'd never heard anyone around here speak of losing a baby that way." Jimmy shrugged. "So I figured no one else in the area would know anything or believe my story."

"Eli's not been around long enough to know what happened back then," Jacob put in. "He and his folks moved here from Indiana four years ago. You should have asked someone who's been livin' here longer."

All eyes turned from Jimmy and focused on Jacob, and his wife grabbed him in a hug. "Oh, Husband, you remember who you are!"

" 'Course I do. I'm Bishop Jacob Weaver, and you're my wife, Lydia."

Leona stood and leaned close to her daed. "Do you know me, Papa?"

"Said I did when I called you over here a few minutes ago, didn't I?"

She nodded and wrapped her arms around his neck. "We've had two miracles today. Your memory has returned, and Abraham's son has come home!"

Abraham stood slowly shaking his head as though in a daze. Jimmy, feeling much the same, struggled to his feet and moved over to stand beside Abraham. "Soon after I went back to Washington, I realized that while I'd been living and working here, I had discovered a side of myself I didn't know existed." He paused and waited to see how Abraham would react.

"Go on."

"Then I read a verse of scripture found in Psalm 27:11 that made me stop and think about my life."

" 'Teach me thy way, O Lord, and lead me in a plain path,' " Abraham quoted.

Jimmy nodded. "I believe the Lord showed me through that verse that deep down inside I really am Amish, and I have decided that I want to follow the Plain path."

Abraham shifted from one foot to the other. Then he took one step forward.

Jimmy swallowed hard in an attempt to push down the lump that had lodged in his throat.

"I can't believe that after all these years God would finally answer my prayers." Abraham paused. "But I believe He has, and—" His voice broke, and he rocked back and forth on his heels. "And after I've treated you so badly, thinking you were out to destroy Leona's life—"

"It doesn't matter now. Nothing matters except trying to make up for the years we've lost." Jimmy opened his arms, and giving no thought as to whether he would be accepted, he embraced his father.

Abraham held his body rigid at first. Then he hugged Jimmy so hard he could barely catch his breath. "There's so much I want to tell you, son. So very much."

"And I want to hear it all."

Everyone shed a few tears as they took turns hugging Jimmy and welcoming him home.

"There are many things that each of us wants to hear." Naomi smiled at Jimmy. "We want to know the details of your life out there in Washington, too."

Jimmy nodded and reached for Leona's hand, pulling her gently to his side. "If there's no objections, I'd like to do whatever is required of me in order to join the Amish church." He looked over at Jacob, who winked at him, and then he smiled at Leona and said, "If this special woman will have me, I hope to make her my wife some day."

Leona looked a bit hesitant at first, but then her face relaxed and she looked at her father. "Well, Papa, what do you have to say about that?"

Jacob nodded and thumped Jimmy on the back. "I always knew I liked you—even when you weren't Zach Fisher."

After everyone's laughter died down, Jimmy sent up a silent prayer. *Thank You, God—for bringing me home.*

Epilogue

Eighteen months later

"Congratulations on your marriage." Jim hugged the newlyweds as they all stood in the Weavers' front yard, following the wedding ceremony. "Thanks for inviting Holly and me to witness your vows. I'm so proud of you, Jimmy—I mean, Zach." He swallowed hard. "I know Linda would be proud, too."

"Mom. She was my mom," Zach corrected. "And it's okay if you keep calling me Jimmy, because until I found my Amish family, it was the only name I'd ever known. To tell you the truth, even after living here over a year as Zach Fisher, I'm still trying to get used to my real name." He smiled at his bride, and the tender look she gave him spoke volumes. Jim was pleased with his son's choice for a wife. He knew from all he'd heard about the bishop's daughter that she was a special woman.

"Are you ready to meet Abraham now?" Zach asked.

Jim nodded, but he didn't move from the spot where he and his own new bride stood on the Weavers' front lawn.

"It's going to be all right, honey," Holly whispered in his ear. "The Lord will help you through this and give you the right words." She stepped away from Jim and took hold of Leona's arm. "Why don't we let our men tend to business while the two of us get better acquainted?"

"I think that's a fine idea." Leona gave her husband a hug. "I'll see you inside for the wedding supper."

Zach led the way, and Jim followed him across the yard to where a tall, bearded man stood talking with Bishop Weaver near the barn. When they approached, the bishop nodded and said, "I'd best go inside and see how things are going."

Zach stepped up to the other man and touched his shoulder. "Abraham, this is my dad—I mean, Jim Scott."

As Jim reached his hand out to Abraham Fisher, his throat felt so clogged he wasn't sure he could speak. "For many years, I dreaded the thought of meeting you, but now I'm thankful God has given me this opportunity to tell you how sorry I am for taking your child."

Abraham nodded. "You already apologized in that letter you sent soon after Zach returned to Pennsylvania."

"Yes, but I. . .I needed to say it in person." Jim paused to regain his composure. "What I did was unthinkable, and I wouldn't blame you if you never forgave me for kidnapping Jimmy—I mean, Zach."

"In Matthew 6:14, Jesus said, 'For if ye forgive men their trespasses, your heavenly Father will also forgive you.' " Tears gathered in the corners of Abraham's eyes. "Many years ago, I forgave the one who had taken my son away, even though I didn't know if I'd ever see my boy again."

Zach squeezed Jim's arm, and he found comfort in the reassuring gesture. "I want you to know that, even though what I did was wrong, God used my horrible deed to bring about something good," Jim continued.

"What was that?" Abraham asked.

"If it hadn't been for your son's influence and the Christian example he set, I never would have come to know the Lord as my Savior."

Abraham gave his beard a couple of quick pulls. "I remember one time, soon after Zach's disappearance, my friend Jacob Weaver told me that God could take something bad like Zach being kidnapped and use it for good." He clasped Zach's shoulder with one hand and Jim's with the other. "I believe He has done just that."

⟨∞⟩

Leona stood on the front porch talking to Holly and Fannie. Her gaze traveled across the yard to where her husband stood with the two men who both called him son. Leona marveled at the way God had brought Zach Fisher home to his real family, yet she couldn't help but feel some concern. She wanted to feel hopeful over the prospect of Abraham and Jim having this discussion, but a thread of caution wove its way into her soul. Would Abraham even speak to the man who had taken his son away? She knew Abraham had told Zach he'd forgiven Jim Scott, but now that the two of them stood face-to-face, would he still feel that way?

"My husband's done a lot of growing," Fannie said as though she could read Leona's thoughts.

Holly put her arm around Leona's waist and gave her a gentle squeeze. "Mine has, as well."

Leona nodded as tears clouded her vision. She had done a lot of growing in the last eighteen months, too. No longer was she bound by fear or consumed with bitterness. The day God saved her life through her daed's urgent call was the day she'd come to realize that, while there are no guarantees in life, God wanted her to trust Him completely. So, setting her fear of losing Zach aside, she had agreed that he could court her.

Zach joined the women a short time later. "I left my two daeds to talk things out. I think everything's going to be fine."

The screen door opened, and Naomi stepped onto the porch carrying a gift in her hands. "This is for you and Leona," she said, handing the package to Zach.

He balanced the box on the porch railing, and he and Leona opened it together. Inside was a small patchwork quilt. Zach stared at it several seconds; then a light dawned. "I think I've seen this before—or at least a quilt just like it. I found it in a bag of paint rags in my dad's garage when I was a kid."

Naomi nodded. "Abby Fisher gave it to me after she returned from a trip to Montana several years ago. She said an Amish woman she knew had found it at a thrift shop somewhere in the state of Washington." She smiled, and tears sprang to her eyes. "I recognized it right away and knew it had been your quilt when you were a baby. It was with you the day you were kidnapped."

"So that's why Jim seemed so upset when I showed it to him. He'd obviously been hiding it from my mom, afraid she might ask where he'd gotten it." Zach clutched the quilt tightly. "He must have gotten rid of it soon after that, because I never saw it again."

" 'And we know that all things work together for good to them that love God, to them who are the called according to his purpose.' " Holly quoted Romans 8:28 as she touched Jimmy's shoulder.

He nodded. "I have to agree with that."

A gentle wind lapped the hem of Leona's blue wedding dress as the sun slipped from behind the clouds. At that moment, she knew for certain that God controlled everything in the universe. Her hand trailed along the edges of the narrow white ties of her kapp as she gazed at the pink, puffy clouds. "Thank You, Lord," she whispered. "You have given us all so much to be thankful for on this special day."

Jimmy took hold of her hand. "And I thank You for the love You've given me through all my family." He gently squeezed her fingers. "I especially thank You for allowing me to know, love, and finally marry the bishop's sweet daughter."

About the Author

New York Times, award-winning author, Wanda E. Brunstetter is one of the founders of the Amish fiction genre. Wanda's ancestors were part of the Anabaptist faith, and her novels are based on personal research intended to accurately portray the Amish way of life. Her books are well-read and trusted by many Amish, who credit her for giving readers a deeper understanding of the people and their customs. When Wanda visits her Amish friends, she finds herself drawn to their peaceful lifestyle, sincerity, and close family ties. Wanda enjoys photography, ventriloquism, gardening, bird-watching, beachcombing, and spending time with her family. She and her husband Richard have been blessed with two grown children, six grandchildren, and two great-grandchildren. To learn more about Wanda, visit her website at www.wandabrunstetter.com.

OTHER BOOKS BY WANDA E. BRUNSTETTER

Adult Fiction

THE PRAIRIE STATE FRIENDS SERIES
The Decision
The Gift

The Half-Stitched Amish Quilting Club
The Tattered Quilt
The Healing Quilt

THE DISCOVERY SAGA
Goodbye to Yesterday
The Silence of Winter
The Hope of Spring
The Pieces of Summer
A Revelation in Autumn
A Vow for Always

KENTUCKY BROTHERS SERIES
The Journey
The Healing
The Struggle

BRIDES OF LEHIGH CANAL SERIES
Kelly's Chance
Betsy's Return
Sarah's Choice

INDIANA COUSINS SERIES
A Cousin's Promise
A Cousin's Prayer
A Cousin's Challenge

SISTERS OF HOLMES COUNTY SERIES
A Sister's Secret
A Sister's Test
A Sister's Hope

BRIDES OF WEBSTER COUNTY SERIES
Going Home
Dear to Me
On Her Own
Allison's Journey

Let's Keep In Touch!

Want to know what Wanda's up to and be the first to hear about new releases, specials, the latest news, and more? Like Wanda on Facebook!

 Visit facebook.com/WandaBrunstetterFans